BREAKNECK

ERICA SPINDLER

SPHERE

First published in the United States in 2009 by St Martin's Press
First published in Great Britain in 2009 by Sphere
This paperback edition published in 2009 by Sphere

A CIP catalogue record for this book
is available from the British Library.

ISBN 978-0-7515-4093-2

Typeset in Sabon by Palimpsest Book Production Limited,
Grangemouth, Stirlingshire

Printed and bound in Great Britain by
Clays Ltd, St Ives plc

Papers used by Sphere are natural, renewable and recyclable
products sourced from well-managed forests and certified in
accordance with the rules of the Forest Stewardship Council.

Mixed Sources
Product group from well-managed
forests and other controlled sources
www.fsc.org Cert no. SGS-COC-004081
© 1996 Forest Stewardship Council

Sphere
An imprint of
Little, Brown Book Group
100 Victoria Embankment
London EC4Y 0DY

An Hachette UK Company
www.hachette.co.uk

www.littlebrown.co.uk

To Nathan, with love

ACKNOWLEDGEMENTS

One of the many fun (and challenging) things about writing fiction is wading into unknown territories, then writing convincingly about them. *Breakneck* explored territory that was well outside my comfort zone. Luckily, there were folks out there willing to share their knowledge – and share it in a manner that a '404' like me could understand. Any mistakes are mine, not theirs.

Thanks to the following:

Guy Williams, President/CEO, Gulf Coast Bank & Trust.

Joe Mariano and Michael D. Perry, computer geniuses.

Chief of police Stephen Dickson, Police Department, Rockton, Illinois. (Thanks, Sue, for the introduction!)

In addition, big thanks to Jennifer Weis for her insight in making *Breakneck* all it could be. Also to the entire St Martin's crew for their enthusiasm and creativity.

And finally, to the people who make my writing life run smoothly, day in, day out: my agent, Evan Marshall; assistants, Beth Jackson and Evelyn Marshall; my family – the most supportive ever – and my God for the many blessings.

1

Rockford, Illinois
Sunday, January 11, 2009
3:05 A.M.

The kid's eyes snapped open. *Matt Martin. Twenty-one-year-old computer-hacking loser.* It took only a moment for his expression to shift from sleepy confusion to horrified realization: there was a stranger in his bedroom. That stranger held a gun to his head, to the tender place between his eyes, just above the bridge of his nose.

The one called Breakneck smiled grimly. 'Hello, son.'

The kid went limp with terror. His mouth worked but no sound emerged.

'The gun I'm holding to your head is nothing fancy. An old-fashioned .38 caliber, semiautomatic. Serviceable at best.'

He kept his voice low, tone soothing. 'What's unique about this situation, of course, is the weapon's proximity to its target, your brain. When I pull the trigger, the bullet will rocket from the chamber and explode out of the barrel and into your head. In response, your brains will explode out the back of your skull.'

Breakneck firmed his grip on the weapon. 'The sound will be muffled by the fact that the barrel is pressed to its target, the mess contained by the pillow, bedding and mattress.'

The bony young man began to shake. The smell of urine stung the air. Unmoved by the kid's fear, he went on, 'I'm going to ask you a few questions. Your life depends on your answers.'

The kid's eyes welled with tears.

'I know who you are and what you do. I want what you stole from me.'

'I don't know what you're—'

'Where is it?'

'What? I don't . . . who are y—'

'I'm the guy you shouldn't have fucked with. I want my information. And I want my money.' He increased pressure on the gun; the kid whimpered. 'What do you think, son? Do we do this the easy way? Or the messy way?'

'Easy,' he whispered.

'You jacked some information. And some money. Five hundred grand.'

Recognition flickered in his horrified gaze.

Of course it did. One didn't forget stumbling onto that kind of money.

Especially a small-time little shit like this one.

'I see we're on the same page now. Good.'

'I didn't take your money.'

'Who did?'

'I don't know!' His voice rose. 'No one!'

His eyes darted back and forth. A clear sign he was lying. Breakneck could almost hear him thinking. Mentally scrambling for a way out, weighing his options: *Give him the information? How much – or how little – would keep him alive? Did he dare lie? Struggle? Beg? What were the consequences of each?*

All animals responded to predators in the same way, Breakneck knew. They fought for survival. Using whatever means at their disposal. Over the years, he had seen them all.

Some predators, however, were so smart, so skilled, the fight was as pathetic as it was futile.

'I don't want to hurt you, Matt. But I will. I'm going to

2

count to three and then I'm going to pull the trigger. One,' he said softly. 'Two . . . thr—'

'Okay, I found it, but I didn't move it!'

'Who did? A name.'

'I don't know . . . an e-mail address and screen name, that's all I have. It's marioman. At Yahoo. Check for yourself . . . on my laptop. I'm Gunner35. My password's 121288. You can get it all with that. I promise . . . go see. It's all there.'

The kid's voice rose as he spoke. Breakneck laid a gloved hand over his mouth to quiet him. 'You did good, Matt. Real good. Thank you.'

He moved quickly, snapping the young man's neck before he had a clue what was happening. With little more than a gurgle, Matt Martin died.

2

Moonlight bathed the room in icy blue. Detective Mary Catherine Riggio slipped out of bed and into her robe, then crossed to the window. The full moon had transformed the winter night into a sort of twilight zone, a surreal landscape caught between daylight and dark.

'You okay?'

She looked over her shoulder to the bed. The man in it. She smiled, liking the way he looked there. The way he was looking at her.

'I'm fine. I couldn't sleep, that's all. Sorry I woke you.'

'You didn't.'

'Liar.' She turned back to the window. 'It's beautiful.'

'You're beautiful.'

She didn't think of herself that way, she never had. The proverbial tomboy, always scrambling to keep up with her five macho brothers. But he made her feel beautiful. Womanly.

Dan Gallo had come into her life and made her believe in things she never had before.

'Marry me.'

She glanced back at him. 'Very funny.'

'Do I look like I'm joking?'

4

M.C. searched his serious expression. She voiced the first thought that came into her head. 'You're out of your mind.'

'Why?'

'We hardly know each other.'

'Six months.'

'Not long enough.'

'When it's right, you know it. It feels right to me, M.C.'

He held her gaze. She pressed her lips together, panic licking at her. The past six months had been the happiest of her life. Her cousin Sam had introduced her to the handsome psychologist, then goaded her into accepting the man's invitation to dinner.

She could hear her younger cousin's argument even now: 'What's the problem, M.C.? He's good-looking, single *and* Italian. What more could you want?'

Not a cop. Check. *Not a psychotic criminal.* Check.

Almost too good to be true. So, she had gone on a date. That one had led to others and within weeks, to their spending all their free time together.

Still, the idea of committing terrified her. The thought of losing him terrified her more.

'What about you, Mary Catherine?' Dan asked softly. 'Does it feel right to you?'

She squeezed her eyes shut. *Dear God, it did.* He sat up and the blanket slipped, revealing his naked shoulders and chest. 'I bought a ring.'

'You did not.'

His mouth curved into the crooked little grin she loved. 'I did. But I'm not going to let you see it until you say yes.'

She wanted to. But she was a cop. She'd been badly burned before. Reckless wasn't in her nature.

She opened her mouth to ask for more time; 'Yes' slipped out instead. It felt so good, she said it again, on a laugh. 'Yes, I'll marry you!'

He let out a whoop and jumped out of the bed. She met him halfway; he caught her in his arms and spun her around. They fell onto the bed, alternately laughing and kissing, whispering like kids sharing the best secret ever.

'Want your ring?' he asked. 'It'll make it official.'

'Damn right,' she teased. 'Otherwise I'm still available.'

'Brat.' He kissed her again, then climbed out of bed. Moments later he returned with a small leather box.

With trembling fingers, she opened it. A no-fuss, no-muss, emerald-cut solitaire. He slipped it on her finger; it fit perfectly. It fit *her* perfectly. Tears flooded her eyes.

'If you don't like it, the jeweler said you could exchan—'

'I love it,' she said, lifting her gaze to his.

'Are you certain? I want you to have a ring you lov—'

'I love you,' she whispered, then brought his mouth to hers and drew him with her to the mattress. There, she showed him how utterly happy he had made her.

3

The call had dragged M.C. out of the warmth of Dan's arms before the sun had even cracked the horizon.

Homicide. Downtown, Rock River Towers.

So much for the cocoon of love, she thought, thirty minutes later as she drew to a stop in front of the apartment complex. Rock River Towers had long been considered one of the city's premier addresses. Fourteen floors. Amenities. River views. Some of its shine had faded as this part of town had lost its luster, but certainly not all.

Bracing herself for the blast of frigid air, M.C. killed the engine and swung out of her SUV. She supposed she should be used to the cold, having lived in northern Illinois her entire life, but on mornings like this she fantasized about moving to Florida.

Hunching deeper into her coat, M.C. glanced around. Four cruisers, her partner Kitt's Taurus, the Identification Bureau guys. She crossed to the first officer. 'Grazzio,' she greeted the rotund, veteran patrolman, 'how's it goin'?'

'I'm cold,' he said. 'And hungry. I'm getting too old for this crap.'

'Tell me about it,' she said. 'What've we got?'

7

'According to his driver's license, one Matt Martin. Lived in unit 510. Corroborated by the name on number 510's mailbox.'

'Anything else?'

'Part-time student at Rock Valley. Studying computer science. Got that from a neighbor.'

The junior college, affectionately called 'Rock Bottom' by the locals. 'Who found him?'

'A neighbor called. Because of the smell.'

'You have contact info?'

'Got it. Vic's been dead awhile.'

M.C. didn't bother asking him how long, that'd be up to the forensic pathologist and ID guys to establish.

The elevator took her to the fifth floor. She stepped off and the smell hit her hard. M.C. dug a small jar of mentholated ointment from her pocket, applied a smear under her nose, then started down the hall.

The smell would have been subtle until the apartment door was opened. It reminded her of the time the family deep freeze in the basement had gone kaput. Nobody'd had a clue until her brother Max opened it. The house stank for months after.

Martin would have some damn unhappy neighbors for a while.

M.C. reached 510 and greeted the officer standing duty. He handed her the scene log. She signed in, then handed it back. 'Coroner's office been contacted?'

He grunted an affirmation and she stepped into the stifling hot apartment – and immediately began to itch in her wool sweater.

Her partner, Detective Kitt Lundgren, poked her head out the bedroom doorway. Early fifties, a veteran of the Violent Crimes Bureau, Kitt had endured some of the worst life had to offer – and come out stronger. When they'd been paired to work the notorious Sleeping Angel Killer case, M.C. had considered Kitt a burned-out head case and fought the partnership.

Now, M.C. couldn't imagine the job without her.

'Body's in here,' Kitt said.

M.C. nodded and headed that way, picking her way around debris. 'What's the thermostat set on? Eighty?'

'Could help establish TOD. Maybe he was killed before the outside temp rose. What was it this past weekend?'

'Single digits. Could be the perp wanted to speed up the decomposition process?'

'Last to the party again,' ID Bureau Detective Rich Miller called as she entered the room.

The Identification Bureau served as the department's crime scene techs. They did it all: collected and processed evidence, dusted for prints, photographed the scene, even gathered insect life from corpses.

Bobby Jackson, the newest member of the ID team, snapped her picture and grinned. 'Poor Mary Catherine, dragged out of her nice, warm bed.'

He didn't know the half of it. She smiled at the thought, wondering how long it would take Kitt to notice the ring. A part of her wanted to shout out her happiness, but the other wanted to hold it close for just awhile longer.

'If you two don't mind,' M.C. said, 'Mr Martin here is needing some attention.' Without waiting for a response, she turned her attention to the victim. He rested on his back in the bed, covers up to his chest, head at an unnatural angle. The arm under the bedding lay over his chest, the other on top of the covers, at his side. It didn't look as if he had struggled against his attacker, though looks could be deceiving.

He'd been tall and skinny with a shock of bleached blond hair. Here, as in the living room, junk food and fast-food wrappers were scattered about. A half-dozen empty energy drink cans littered both nightstands. His favorite appeared to have been Red Bull.

She gazed at them. Energy drinks had become popular with young people. Too popular. The media had been buzzing with stories of their use – and abuse.

Had he used the caffeine-loaded drinks to stay awake? M.C. wondered. To study? Or do something else?

'No blood,' Kitt said.

M.C. inspected the hand on top of the blanket. 'Nails appear clean.'

'Check this out,' Kitt said, indicating an angry-looking bruise on his forehead, between his eyes.

Perfectly round. Like the ring on a bull's-eye.

M.C. drew her eyebrows together. 'What the hell made that?'

'Our victim found himself in a tenuous position, Detectives.'

They turned. The statement had come from Francis Xavier Roselli, the coroner's lead pathologist. Small, precise and a devout Catholic, the first thing Francis did at every scene was cross himself, whisper a prayer for the departed's immortal soul and ask for the guidance of St Luke.

'Excuse me?' Kitt said.

'Our vic had the business end of a gun pressed to his head.' The pathologist worked his fingers into snug-fitting latex gloves. 'Pressed quite firmly, judging by the color of the bruise.'

It's why he hadn't struggled.

'The outline's crisp. Your perp never wavered. His hands were not shaking.'

M.C. indicated the circular, yellow stain on the light-colored covers. 'Scared the piss out of the poor kid.'

'Then he killed him,' Kitt murmured. 'That's cold.'

'But he didn't shoot him,' M.C. added. 'Interesting.'

Francis joined them. 'It looks to me like the perpetrator broke his neck. I'll know the full story after autopsy.'

'When?'

'Tomorrow, midday.'

The pathologist didn't expect a comment, nor did he wait for one. While he examined the victim, M.C. and Kitt took in the rest of the apartment.

Not the typical college kid's bachelor pad. M.C. moved her gaze over the apartment's spacious interior. Nice place, though the kid had pitted it out. Drink cans and food wrappers littered every table. Dirty clothes strewn on the floor, furniture. She stepped over an open bag of corn chips. If Matt Martin had owned a vacuum, he'd never used it.

10

Stylistically, the furniture was a mixed bag. But it was all of good quality. Leather couch and armchair. Tall, ornate armoire. Marble-top dining table.

'Imagine what the bathroom's going to look like,' Kitt said.

'I'd rather not, thanks.' She picked up a cup containing a nasty-looking black liquid. She sniffed it and made a face. 'What the hell?'

Kitt peeked over her shoulder. 'Chewing tobacco.'

She set the cup back down. 'What do you think the rent on this place is?'

'Dunno. Seven bills, maybe more.'

'Probably more.'

'He lived well for a twenty-one-year-old, part-time student.'

'No joke.' M.C. checked the front closet. She thumbed through the several coats that hung there, including a leather bomber jacket and a topcoat. A *cashmere* topcoat, judging by the feel of it.

They made their way into the kitchen. The refrigerator and freezer were well stocked. A wine rack sported a couple of bottles of red wine. Nice bottles. Ones that went for twenty bucks apiece.

Better than she could afford.

M.C. glanced over her shoulder at Kitt, who was leafing through a stack of mail on the counter. 'This kid have a job other than being a student?'

'Could be his parents have money.'

'Could be. Or he has a job that pays well.'

'Like dealing.'

'That'd be my guess.'

'Which would explain how he ended up dead.'

'Exactly.'

M.C. brought her left hand to her head. 'So, we begin with his fam—'

'What the hell is that?'

'What?'

'That.' Kitt grabbed her hand. 'It's a ring!'

M.C. laughed and held her hand out.

'My God, when did that happen?'

'Last night. I thought maybe he'd talked to you?'

'Not a word.' Kitt lifted her gaze from the ring. 'And you said yes?'

'Obviously.' M.C. frowned. 'You sound surprised.'

'You two hardly know each other.'

'Six months.' It was weird hearing her own protest being offered to her and defending it with Dan's. 'Long enough to know he makes me happy.'

Kitt opened her mouth as if to say more, then shut it and shook her head. 'Congratulations.'

'You were going to say something else, what was it?'

'I just want to make sure you're doing this for the right reasons. And not because of Lance and how that—'

'I'm not.'

'Or because you're turning thirty and you think you have to be—'

'Married? Because that's what my mother's drummed into my head?' She sent Kitt an exasperated look. 'I've never done what my mother thought I should before. Why would I start now?'

Kitt laughed. 'She's going to be ecstatic.'

'We'll see. After all, Dan's only *half* Italian.'

'Detectives?' They turned toward Francis, standing in the bedroom doorway. 'I'm finished here,' he said, removing his gloves.

'Any surprises?' Kitt asked.

'None. No outward evidence of drug use, though toxicology will give us the full picture.'

'What're you thinking about time of death?'

'It's hot in here, which would have accelerated the process . . . Best guess is late Saturday night, early Sunday morning.'

M.C. had come to learn that Francis's 'best guess' was always damn close. Ever humble, Francis Xavier Roselli described himself as 'competent.' As far as M.C. was concerned, the man was brilliant.

'I see congratulations are in order, Detective.'

Brilliant and observant, obviously. 'Yes, thank you.'

12

'Who's the lucky guy?'

She told him, feeling herself flush. Moments later, as they left the apartment, Kitt leaned toward her. 'I never thought I'd see hard-as-nails M.C. Riggio beaming like a teenager in love.'

M.C. swallowed a laugh and scowled at her partner. 'Put a sock in it, Lundgren.'

4

Notifying a victim's next of kin was a wrenching, thankless task. M.C. wished she could pass the job off to somebody else. She couldn't. The great majority of murders were committed by those closest to the victims. Being the one who delivered the bad news also meant being the first to see the reaction to that news.

She and Kitt climbed out of Kitt's Taurus. Judging by this West Side house, the family was solidly middle class. A silver minivan was parked in the drive, under a well-worn basketball hoop.

'You or me?' Kitt asked as they approached the front door.

A Christmas wreath still hung there, a sad-looking Santa surrounded by worn silver bells. 'You.'

Kitt nodded and they crossed the porch. Mothers responded better to Kitt. She supposed that was because Kitt had been a mother – and had lost a child.

They rang the bell. A dog began to bark. A minute later a woman in a pink velour jogging suit came to the door.

She peered suspiciously out the sidelight at them.

M.C. held up her badge. Beside her, Kitt did the same. 'Police,' she said.

The woman stared hard at their IDs, then unlocked the dead bolt. Cracking open the door, she gazed out at them.

'Mrs Martin?' Kitt asked.

'Yes?'

'Detectives Riggio and Lundgren, RPD.'

'Justin really is sick, Officers. I know he's missed a lot of school and believe me, I'm not happy about it, either.'

She thought they were truancy officers. 'We're Rockford Police, Mrs Martin. We're not here about Justin.'

'Then why . . . who . . .'

There was no kind way to deliver such news. The best way, M.C. had learned over the years, was to simply say it – as gently but firmly as possible.

'Do you have a son named Matt?' Kitt asked.

'Matthew, yes.' Fear raced into her eyes. 'What's happened?'

'I'm afraid we have some bad news. Your son's dead, Mrs Martin. I'm so sorry.'

The woman simply stared at her, as if unable to fully grasp what Kitt was saying. 'Dead? I don't understand.'

'He was murdered.'

'I just talked to him. He was fine.'

'When was that, Mrs Martin?'

'Yester— no, Saturday. You have the wrong Martin.'

'I'm so sorry,' Kitt said gently.

'Mom? Is everything okay?'

Another son. The previously mentioned, absent from school Justin, she would bet. Judging by his size, he was close in age to Matt.

He crossed to the door and laid his arm across his mother's shoulders. The picture of the man of the house, even with a bright red nose and fever-glazed eyes.

'They say your brother's . . . that Matt's—' The woman choked back the rest.

Kitt helped her out. 'Your brother's dead. I'm so sorry.'

Again, the dumbfounded, disbelieving gaze. The gradual realization, denial, then horror.

The young man blinked. 'I don't . . . no, that can't be.'

15

'Are you certain?' the woman asked, tone pleading. 'Maybe you made a mistake?'

'Perhaps we should sit down?'

The woman nodded and led them to a small, neat living room. Without speaking, they all sat.

'It happened at his apartment. Although how he died hasn't been substantiated yet, it was obviously a homicide. I hate to have to do this now, but it's imperative we move the investigation forward as quickly as possible. I need to ask you a few questions. Are you able to answer?'

Justin spoke first. 'I am.'

'How old are you, Justin?'

'Eighteen.'

'And Matt was twenty-one?'

'Yes.'

'Were you close?'

He nodded, throat working. 'I was going to live with him when I . . . when I graduated this spring.'

'He had a nice place,' Kitt said softly. 'How long had he lived there?'

'Six months, I guess.' He looked at his mother in question; she concurred.

'He was in school?'

The young man nodded. 'Rock Valley. He was a computer major.'

'He have a girlfriend?'

'No. He was a total geek.'

'How about friends? He have many?'

'Yeah, he had friends. They were mostly like him. Liked computers. Computer games, the Internet.'

'We'd like to talk to them. They might be able to help.'

Justin stood. 'I'll write down their names. The ones I know, anyway.'

He left the room and Kitt turned her attention back to the woman. 'Did Matt have a job?'

'He repaired computers. Freelance. Out of his apartment.'

She reached for a tissue and immediately began to shred it. 'I was so proud of him. He never asked me for a penny.'

16

M.C. noted the fact. Interesting, considering his lifestyle. The computer repair business would have had to have been extremely lucrative.

Or Matt Martin had had another source of income.

'Was your son ever in any trouble?' Kitt went on.

'Never. He was a good boy. Quiet.'

'No problems with drugs?'

'No. Absolutely not.'

Justin returned and handed M.C. a piece of loose-leaf paper. He had written a half-dozen names on it. Besides two of them he'd included a phone number. 'Matt was clean. Totally. Didn't smoke, either.'

'We noticed a lot of empty energy drink cans in the apartment.'

'He used them to stay awake. To study. Play on the Internet.'

'He didn't like to sleep,' the woman added. 'Even as a child.'

'Can you think of any reason someone would want him dead?'

Justin suddenly looked stricken. His eyes filled with tears; his throat worked. He shook his head.

'Mrs Martin?'

'No,' she whispered. 'I can't believe this is happening.'

Moments later, M.C. and Kitt were on the street, standing beside Kitt's sedan.

M.C. frowned. 'I didn't see a computer at Martin's apartment. Did you?'

'Odd, a computer geek with no computer.'

While Kitt dialed Jackson and Miller, M.C. trotted back up to the Martins' front door. Justin opened it before she knocked. 'I have one more question,' she said. 'What kind of computer did your brother have?'

'A Dell laptop.'

'He ever lend it out or—'

'No way. He wouldn't even let me use it.'

M.C. returned to Kitt, who was ending her call. 'Jackson and Miller?' she asked.

'Still at the scene. No computer in the apartment or his vehicle.'

5

'Good morning, Detectives,' the VCB secretary called in a chipper voice as M.C. and Kitt entered the office. 'It's been a busy one, I hear.'

M.C. cocked an eyebrow. The secretary, always chipper, seemed particularly buoyant today. 'Are you feeling all right, Nan?'

'Excellent, thank you.' She turned to Kitt. 'You have three messages, Detective.'

She handed them to Kitt, then beamed at M.C. 'Two for you, Detective Riggio.' She held out the two message slips. 'And one waiting at your desk. Oh, and after you retrieve your messages, Sal wants an update.'

As they left the office, the woman called out, 'All your messages, Detective Riggio. There's one waiting on your desk.'

'I think she wants you to check your cubicle,' Kitt said.

'And I think she's slipping some happy juice into that Big Gulp she's always sipping . . .'

The words died on her lips. A vase of roses sat on her desk. White and red. Fully opened. Fragrant.

From Dan, they had to be.

18

She crossed to them, bent and breathed in their perfume, then plucked the card from its holder.

You've made me the happiest man in the world. Love, Dan.

M.C.'s eyes flooded with tears. Kitt peeked over her shoulder and read the card. 'This is a quality man you've landed, partner. I'd definitely keep him. But I'm afraid it shoots the happy juice theory to hell; Nan read the card.'

M.C. wanted to come back with something light and funny; instead, she opened her phone and dialed his number.

'I got the flowers,' she said when he answered. 'They're beautiful.'

'Not as beautiful as you are. I can't stop thinking about you. I can't stop smiling.'

If this conversation had been someone else's and she had been eavesdropping, she would have thought it corny. Depending on her mood, maybe even nauseating. But it wasn't someone else's and she felt as breathless as she sounded.

'Me either,' she said.

'Did you tell your family?' he asked.

'I haven't had time. How about you?'

'I talked to Erik.'

Erik Sundstrand, his best friend and former colleague. 'What did he say?'

'Nothing I didn't already know. That I was one lucky SOB. And that he thought you had better sense than this.'

She laughed. Kitt tapped her watch and pointed toward their deputy chief's office. 'I've got to run. Tonight's pasta night, let's break the news there.'

'That's so perfect, you'd think I planned it. Call me later.'

He ended the call and she held the phone to her ear a moment before letting go. She found Kitt grinning at her.

'What?'

'You know what. Just promise me you won't turn into Bridezilla and that you'll keep the ooey-gooey crap to a minimum.'

On a laugh, M.C. promised. They started for Sal's office. Their superior officer's door was open; Kitt tapped on the casing and he waved them in.

'I don't have much time,' he said. 'Fill me in.'

Salvador Minelli, Deputy Chief of Detectives, was a no-nonsense, by-the-books kind of guy. Tough but fair, he would give his detectives some rope – but not enough to hang themselves or the department. Especially the department.

M.C. liked working under him because she always knew where she stood.

'Victim's name is Matt Martin,' Kitt began. 'Twenty-one years old, part-time RVC student. Killed sometime over the weekend. No sign of a struggle or robbery.'

'Neck was broken,' M.C. said. 'No defense wounds. Just a bull's-eye bruise between his eyes.'

'From?'

'The barrel of a gun.'

'Yet the perp didn't shoot him. Interesting.'

'Mom and brother claim he was clean, but this was no random act,' Kitt said. 'The kid was involved with someone or something—'

'Our guess is something.'

'—that got him killed.'

'Drugs?'

'It would be the natural choice. I had a couple officers canvass his neighbors. Nobody had any problems with him.' M.C. checked the notes the officers had given her. 'Really quiet. Rarely had guests. No parties. And nobody saw or heard anything unusual in the past few days.'

Kitt took over. 'I notified the college, got a list of Martin's teachers. Thought we'd question as many as possible this afternoon and see if we can reconstruct his last twenty-four hours.'

'You want me to hand this to Baker and Canataldi?'

'Hell, no,' M.C. said. 'Why would we?'

'Speak for yourself, partner.'

'Seems you both have situations. You, Detective Lundgren, are off to Mexico in a couple weeks.'

'Fourteen days until paradise,' she said, grinning. 'Just me, Joe and the beach. No cell phone.'

Kitt and her ex had been cautiously working at a

reconciliation. Their marriage had fallen apart after the death of their only child and Kitt's spiral into despair and alcoholism. Over the past six months they'd taken it one day at a time, both afraid of being hurt again.

They had decided the next step was a vacation together – no work, all play. Just the two of them.

'And you' – he turned to M.C. – 'may be too distracted by a recent development to fully focus right now.'

'Blinded by love,' Kitt agreed. 'In full Bridezilla metamorphosis.'

M.C. ignored their teasing. 'How did you know?' she asked.

'The flowers. Nan read the card. Besides' – he grinned – 'that's a sizable rock. It's hard to miss.'

By the end of the day, M.C. and Kitt had spoken to all but one of Matt Martin's teachers. They'd learned that Martin had been quiet to the point of antisocial and that he'd been a barely average student. He hadn't had any friends, as far as any of them had known; likewise, no enemies.

'The last professor,' Kitt said, reading the list, 'one Doug Deadman, computer science.'

'Deadman?' M.C. raised her eyebrows. 'You're kidding, right?'

'Nope. Bet you a grande latte, Deadman means "deadly boring" in Latin?'

'You're on.'

They caught the professor locking his office, presumably leaving for the day. He proved to be nothing like they expected. Young – probably in his early thirties – good-looking and buff. His light tan screamed outdoorsman and vitality; his clothing, urban cool.

Kitt owed her a latte.

'Professor Deadman,' M.C. said, displaying her shield. 'Detective Riggio. My partner, Detective Lundgren. We were hoping for a few minutes of your time.'

He frowned slightly. 'May I ask what this is about?'

'Matt Martin.'

His expression cleared. 'Of course, I'm sorry. Come in.'

He unlocked his office door and waved them in. 'I should have made the connection right away,' he said as they sat, 'but I didn't expect anyone to need to contact me.'

'We're attempting to question everyone who knew Matt and recently spent time with him.'

He nodded. 'Anything I can do to help.'

'Martin was a student of yours?'

'Last semester, yes.' He rubbed his temple, expression turning grim. 'We're pretty upset around here. The college arranged counseling for anyone who needed it. The dean asked us to take it easy on our students, academically speaking, for a couple weeks.'

He moved his gaze between the two of them. He sat back in his chair and waited. As he did, his jacket opened, revealing a T-shirt that asked the question: Does Fuzzy Logic Tickle?

'What can you tell me about Matt?' M.C. asked.

'Nice kid. *Really* into computers.'

'What does "really into computers" mean?'

'They rocked his world. No, let me amend that – they were his world.'

'Girlfriend?'

'Nope. Not that I know of anyway.'

'Good student?'

'In my classes. He wasn't a whiz in his others.'

'Can you hazard a guess why?'

'I can offer more than a guess. He talked to me about it. Came to me before he dropped a couple of his classes. They bored him.'

'What did you advise him to do?'

'Tough it out. Stick with the classes.' He leaned forward, expression earnest. 'I told him he needed a degree to compete out in the marketplace. But you know how these computer geeks are.'

'Actually, we don't. Profile them for us.'

'Sure. But remember, this is all generalizations.'

'That's what a profile is, Doug. Generalizations based on fact.'

'Geeks are bright but socially inept. They eschew sleep,

powering up on energy drinks to stay connected all night. The lifestyle is tough to fit into a nine-to-five world.

'They tend to socialize online and steer clear of flesh-and-blood relationships. They're not athletic. Mouse potatoes, they're called.'

'Funny.'

'I've got lots of 'em. They're not teenagers, they're "screenagers." The most knowledgeable, technically proficient person in a group is the "alpha geek." The printed word is "treeware." You, Detective Riggio, could be called a "four-oh-four."'

'Really? And what's that?'

'Clueless, technologically speaking.'

She was, indeed, a 404. 'And how do you know that?'

'You look like you spend more time outside than in – no tube tan.' At her expression, he explained that a tube tan was being pasty-faced from spending all your time in front of a monitor. 'Plus, your profession is very ungeek.'

'I'll take that as a compliment.'

'It was.'

Kitt cleared her throat. 'Was Martin the alpha geek?'

'Not in our group.'

'Then who—'

'I was.' He grinned. 'That's why I get the big bucks.'

Kitt stepped in again. 'Actually, Professor, *you* don't fit that profile.'

'I hear that all the time. My mom always told me I was her rebel.'

'Could Martin have been dealing drugs?'

His eyebrows shot up. 'Matt? That wouldn't be my guess, no.'

Kitt stepped in. 'What would be your guess, Professor?'

'I'm not saying he was into anything illegal. But if a kid like Matt Martin chose a crime, he'd be a cracker.'

'A what?'

'Criminal hacker.' He leaned forward. 'Hacker refers to programming-intense geeks, but the media's erroneously made it synonymous with cracking.'

A smile tugged at M.C.'s mouth. He sounded not only sincere, but indignant as well. He was a geek, after all. 'Criminal hacking,' she repeated. 'You mean like identity theft.'

'Information theft. We're a computerized world, Detective. Everything we have and are is out there, begging to be stolen. All it takes to do it is the will and the skill.'

'Thank you, Professor.' They stood, crossed to the door and stopped. 'By the way, where were you this weekend?'

'Skiing. I just arrived back in town this morning.'

Which explained the tan. And depending on Francis's determination of TOD, provided him an alibi. 'Didn't classes start today?'

He frowned slightly. 'I was due back Saturday. All flights in and out of Denver were canceled.'

They thanked him again, gave him their cards, urging him to call if he thought of anything else.

'Criminal hacking,' Kitt said as they crossed RVC's parking lot. 'It sounds right and would explain the missing computer.'

'It works for me. I'll get a subpoena for Martin's financial records.'

'And I'll check Professor Deadman's alibi. Then, while you're eating pasta and sharing good news, I'll see what I can find out about criminal hackers.'

6

Dan pulled up in front of the home M.C. had grown up in, an old farmhouse that had been swallowed by the suburbs. By the vehicles parked in the drive and on the street, she saw her brothers had already arrived.

M.C. smiled thinking of her five brothers. She adored them, and had bestowed pet names on each: Michael had earned 'The Overachiever' by becoming a chiropractor and fulfilling their mother's wish for a child she could brag was a doctor. Neil was 'The Suck-up,' for giving Mama a grandchild and Tony, Max and Frank were 'The Three Ass-kissers' for naming the restaurant they'd opened after her.

M.C. alone had been left to carry the banner of 'Black Sheep' and major disappointment. Until tonight. This was a first for her, she realized. The first time she walked into her mother's house knowing she wasn't going to be the focus of her mother's disappointment.

M.C. felt Dan's gaze and looked at him.

'Ready?' he asked.

'Completely. What about you?' she teased. 'Nervous? There's no backing out now.'

25

'Like I'd want to.' One corner of his mouth lifted. 'Although, your mother's always a bit of a wild card.'

'A bit?' M.C. laughed softly and leaned across and kissed him. 'Not to worry. Tonight, you'll be a hero. Trust me.'

They climbed out of his sedan and started up the walk. The old house, with its wide front porch, rambled. A good thing it did, too. It had housed five rough-and-tumble boys and one girl who'd done her best to outdo them all.

Tonight, the porch was empty. Even Michael and Neil, famous porch flies that they were, had been chased in by the bitter cold. Typically, no matter the weather, someone would have been on the porch to call out to her as she arrived. The banter and playful ribbing would begin, then spill into the house with them.

They reached the front door and let themselves in. The smell of her mother's traditional cooking – of roasted meats and vegetables, Italian spices and red sauce – assailed her. Home, she thought, breathing it in.

Michael caught sight of her first. 'Little sister!' he boomed, wrapping her in a bear hug, 'late as usual.'

'Give her a break,' her sister-in-law Melody said, pushing past him to give her a hug, 'she was keeping the streets safe.'

They turned their attention to greeting Dan just as Max, Frank and Tony emerged from the living room, arguing over something, as was typical for them. How they'd managed to create a successful, growing business without killing one another was a mystery to her.

More hellos and hugs. Neil appeared next, but before he could utter a word, his five-year-old son caught sight of her. 'Auntie Crackers!' he cried, barreling across the room and launching himself into her arms.

'You're getting too big to do this, you know that? What if I drop you?'

She pretended to be losing her grip on him and he let out a high-pitched squeal of delight, clutching her neck tightly.

He had named her Crackers because of the pack of animal crackers, or other goody, she always brought him.

Her brothers had loved the name and encouraged its use – always with a correction: 'No, Ben, Auntie *is* crackers.'

They did so now, and then burst out laughing, Dan with them. 'Very funny,' she said, playfully glaring at him. 'I expected at least *you* to side with—'

Her mother poked her head out of the kitchen. 'Mary Catherine, thank God you're here. I need to speak with you.' She shifted her gaze to Dan. 'Alone.'

'Lots of drama today,' Melody said softly. 'But she wouldn't talk to me about it. Sorry, I didn't have time to warn you.'

M.C. smiled at her sister-in-law, unperturbed. Tonight, not even her mother could pop her happy bubble.

Dan bent close to her ear and whispered, 'Go get her, baby.'

A moment later, the kitchen door swung shut behind her and she greeted her mother. 'Hi, Mama, what's—'

'I dreamed you died last night.' Her mother crossed to her and caught her hands, gripping them tightly. 'And you know my dreams have been psychic. The night before your father fell over dead of a heart attack, I dreamed we lost him.'

'At a Cubs game.'

'It was symbolic.'

'When I died, was I at a Cubs game?'

'This isn't funny, Mary Catherine. You were home in bed. Alone and dead.'

And here she worried a bad guy would get her. 'You're certain I wasn't just sleeping?'

'You were dead,' she repeated. '*D-e-a-d*. A mother knows these things.'

They also knew how to drive their grown children out of their freaking skulls. M.C. decided it might be best to keep that observation to herself.

Instead, she eased her hands from her mother's. 'Mama, I have news. Look.'

Her mother stopped, stared, then let out a shriek. 'The Blessed Mother has answered my prayers!'

At the commotion, the entire family descended upon them. Her mother announced the news, which was followed by hugs, backslapping and laughter. Benjamin got in on the act, even though he didn't have a clue what was going on.

Later, at the dinner table, after the platters had been passed and plates filled, her mother said, 'We must start planning immediately. When's the date?'

M.C. glanced at Dan. 'We haven't even discussed it.'

He caught her hand. 'The sooner the better, as far as I'm concerned. Though we're in no hurry.'

Her mother crossed herself, no doubt in thanks that her only daughter wasn't pregnant.

'The ceremony must be at St Bernadette's.' She looked at Dan, her eyes narrowed. 'A good Italian boy like you, you're Catholic?' He nodded and she beamed. 'Of course you are.'

Her mother was strictly old-school in her beliefs. She had pitched a fit when Neil became engaged to Protestant Melody, but had forgiven her when she'd agreed to convert. M.C. decided not to spoil the moment by sharing that Dan hadn't practiced his faith in years or by reminding her he was only half Italian.

Tonight she would allow herself to bask in the warm glow of approval.

'You're planning on a big wedding, of course.'

'We haven't talked about tha—'

'We should reserve the Italian-American club tomorrow.'

From the corners of her eyes, she saw Michael choking back a laugh. 'Mama, I don't think—'

'I'm anxious to meet your family,' she said to Dan.

'Mom and Dad moved to Florida last year. But of course they'll come for the wedding.'

'What about your brothers and sisters?'

'I'm an only.'

The table went dead silent. M.C. could almost hear her mother's thoughts: *What kind of self-respecting Catholic family has only one child? And Italians no less.*

'I had a sister,' Dan said. 'She died as a baby and my parents weren't able to have any more kids.'

Understanding and sympathy crossed her features. 'The Lord's ways are mysterious,' she said. 'I'm certain you and Mary Catherine will fill their home with grandbabies.'

M.C. choked on a sip of water. Michael lost his battle and laughed and Max, Frank and Tony snickered in unison.

'Mama, you're getting a little ahead of things. We haven't even discussed children.'

Dan squeezed her hand. 'But I'm sure we'll want a dozen.'

By the time the last cannoli had been consumed and the table cleared, her mother had planned an engagement party for the weekend. Family and close friends only, at her brothers' old town Mama Riggio's location.

Much later, as M.C. lay in Dan's arms sleepy and satisfied, she smiled. 'Thank you for being so patient with my mother.'

He threaded his fingers through her hair. 'Your mother's great.'

'She's a human steamroller.'

He laughed. 'She approves. That's a good thing.'

M.C. tilted her face toward his. 'It wouldn't matter if she didn't. You're my choice.'

He kissed her again. 'Then it looks like we have it all.'

7

'Morning, partner,' Kitt said, setting a grande latte on M.C.'s desk. 'Debt fulfilled.'

M.C. took the cup and grinned. 'You're a lifesaver, you know that?'

She said she did and parked herself on the corner of M.C.'s desk. 'How'd it go last night?'

'As expected. Mama's already planning a gigantic wedding and filling our house with babies. By the way, if you and Joe don't have plans for Saturday night, Mama's throwing an engagement party.'

'We'll be there.' Kitt rummaged in her tote. A moment later, she popped the top on a can of V8.

M.C. sipped her latte, frowning. 'Vegetable juice? What's the deal?'

'It's called desperation. I've got thirteen days before I have to wear a bathing suit in public. A bathing suit which I shopped for on Saturday.'

M.C. made a face. Every woman's nightmare, no matter her shape or size. A trip to the gynecologist, followed by a spin in a dentist's chair was less traumatic than shopping for a new bathing suit.

'Don't bother offering encouragement or empty platitudes. I know Joe loves me just the way I am and that I'm in damn good shape for being fifty-one. But it's hard not to compare myself to all those blasted magazine ads.'

'Empty platitudes?' M.C. said around a swallow of coffee. 'I was going to commiserate with you. I feel your pain.'

Kitt rubbed the bridge of her nose. 'Tell me why I allowed Joe to talk me into Mexico? What's wrong with New York in January? Or Boston?'

'Why? Because we're freezing our asses off here. Because lying on a beach with the man you love, warmed by the sun and light-headed from one too many virgin margaritas sounded like heaven on earth.'

'Then reality set in.' She looked at the can of vegetable juice then lifted her gaze mournfully to M.C.'s. 'I'm not a supermodel, M.C.'

She said it with such seriousness that M.C. laughed. 'Get over it, partner. None of us are. Let's talk about Martin.'

Kitt seemed only too happy to forget about bathing suits for a while and launched into what she'd learned. 'Last year cybercrime cost businesses fifty billion, and consumers five billion. And those numbers are going up all the time. Not only does it seem like easy money to kids who get sucked in, it's hard for law enforcement to track and feels like a victimless crime.'

'Pretty tempting trio.'

'And one more thing, it's federal. And you know what that means. FBI.'

M.C. leaned back in her chair and let out a long breath. 'I figured that, but was hoping to ignore it as long as possible. Those guys get involved, we're out. Or playing second fiddle to a group of people who flunked kindergarten because of their inability to play nice with others.'

Kitt grinned. 'Personally, I'd be happy to hand this one over. One less thing to clear off my plate before Joe and I head to Mexico.' She finished her juice and tossed the can in the trash. 'There you have it, the unvarnished truth.'

'That doesn't sound like the Kitt Lundgren I know and love.'

'Get used to her. That old Kitt, the one with workaholic, OCD issues? She's gone. The new Kitt is relaxed. She takes vacations. A quiet day comes along, she doesn't fight it. She doesn't trump up things to do.'

M.C. laughed. 'That I'll have to see to believe. Let's go chat with Sal.'

Sal advised them to immediately contact the FBI cybercrimes unit. If Martin was involved in criminal hacking, they would come aboard eventually anyway, might as well take advantage of their ability to quickly access information.

Although M.C. wasn't happy about it, she didn't have a choice.

The special agent in charge of the Rockford cybercrimes unit was Jonathan Smith. He offered to save them a trip, if they could wait until midday to meet. He was coming their way.

He arrived just after two. He was tall, with a pleasant face, nice smile and a firm handshake. His dark hair had the beginnings of gray and his navy suit needed a good press. Not quite the intense, buttoned-down agent M.C. was used to.

They shook hands, then led him to one of the interview rooms.

'What do you have?' he asked after they had taken their seats.

'So far, little.' M.C. slid the case file across the table. He flipped it open, scanning the information while she spoke.

'Matt Martin. Twenty-one-year-old computer geek. Murdered over the weekend. Pathologist estimates his TOD as somewhere between late Saturday night and early Sunday morning.'

The agent studied the crime-scene photos. 'Go on.'

'Computer is the only thing missing. He lived very well for an unemployed student.'

'His family—'

'No financial help there,' Kitt said. 'They believed he repaired computers out of his apartment. So far we've found nothing to substantiate that.'

'We interviewed his professors. One of them suggested cybercrime as an explanation for his lifestyle.'

Jonathan Smith was quiet a moment, continuing to study the photos, then looked up, moving his gaze between them. 'What about the last twenty-four hours of his life?'

'A neighbor saw him retrieving his mail Friday afternoon, about four. He was carrying a Wendy's bag. She remembered because he ate some fries in the elevator and she's on a diet. Said she couldn't stop thinking of those fries all weekend. Ended up blowing her diet on a supersize Sunday afternoon.'

Kitt took over. 'He made a couple calls from his apartment. Ordered pizza on Saturday, using his credit card to pay. Upshot is, he never left his apartment.'

Agent Smith nodded, eyebrows drawn slightly together. 'He fits the profile, no doubt. Right age. Married to his computer, no visible means of support.' He tapped one of the photos. 'Even the energy drinks and junk food. Is toxicology back yet?'

M.C. shook her head. 'Though we found no drug paraphernalia or needle tracks, nothing like that.'

The agent stood. 'I'll start digging, get ahold of Martin's financials. Anything I find out, I'll pass along. Cybercrimes might be our baby, but this was a murder on your turf. I understand that and will keep you in the loop.'

'We appreciate that,' M.C. said as she and Kitt followed him to his feet. She indicated the paperwork. 'You can keep that information, it's a copy.'

'Thanks.'

They walked him to the elevator. When the door closed behind him, Kitt looked at M.C. 'He seemed way too agreeable to be FBI.'

'I'm with you. No wonder he's stuck working the Rockford satellite office.'

8

Thursday, January 15
5:47 P.M.

M.C. arrived home to find her twenty-two-year-old cousin Tommy Mariano waiting for her. His silver Honda Element sat idling in her drive, a steady plume of exhaust spiraling up from the tailpipe.

When she pulled into the drive beside him, he cut the engine and popped out. 'Hey, cuz,' he called. ''Bout time you got home.'

'Shouldn't let your car idle that way,' she said. 'It's bad for the environment.'

'I was freezing.'

'Then call first.' She hugged him. 'All that said, it's nice to see you. What brings you by?'

'I hear we're celebrating this weekend.'

'Good news travels fast.'

'The communication networks in the greater metro area have been on fire.'

She laughed. 'C'mon in.'

He followed her into the house. 'I can't believe my favorite cousin's getting hitched.'

'Because you listened to all the "hopeless spinster" talk.'

'Nah, because you're way too cool.'

'Good answer. Want a beer?'

'Beer's always good.'

She got them both a can and they settled on the couch. Her mother had two sisters, Bella and Catherine. Her aunt Catherine – who also happened to be M.C.'s godmother – had two sons, ten months apart. Tommy was the older of the two, Sam the younger.

For a moment, the only sound in the room was the pop and hiss of the cans being opened. M.C. took a swallow. 'It occurs to me, this stuff tasted better when I was twenty-two.'

'Yup, you're definitely getting old. It still pretty much rocks my world.'

That comment would have bothered her a few weeks ago, with her thirtieth birthday looming. Not anymore, even though thirty had arrived. 'What's new with you?'

'School's back in session. My final semester before I cram for the CPA exam. It sort of blows my mind.'

Hers, too. She used to babysit him and his brother. 'How's Sam?'

He hesitated, his expression stiffening slightly. 'You know Sam. Sometimes he can be such a dick.'

Besides being brothers, he and Sam were best buds *and* polar opposites. 'Try having five brothers,' she countered. 'Five sometime dicks. No pun intended.'

Tommy said nothing, just looked at her. Something in his expression made her frown. 'Is something going on? Are you and Sam fighting?'

He held her gaze. He opened his mouth, then shut it. Opened it again, then shook his head, smiling stiffly. 'Nah. Sam and I are cool. Other than him trashing my place and cleaning out the fridge.'

She wasn't convinced. 'You know you can always come to me, right? Talk to me about anything? Just like when we were kids.'

He nodded and rolled the can between his palms.

'Does it get any easier?' he asked, turning serious. 'Life, that is.'

'Wish I could help you out there.' She took another swallow of the beer. 'Some days are good. Some are great. And a bunch of 'em suck. But it beats the alternative.'

He drained his beer, his normally easygoing expression turning sulky. 'Yeah, I guess.'

'You guess? You're twenty-two, how many problems could you have?'

'You'd be surprised.'

'Give it your best shot.' Her cell went off; she saw it was Dan. 'Hold just a second, Tommy. Hey, hon.'

'Hey to you. I'm pulling in the drive. You up for some dinner?'

'I'm starving.' She smiled at her cousin. 'Tommy's here. Come in and say hello.'

'Ask him to join us. See you in a sec.'

She ended the call and turned her attention to Tommy. 'So spill it. What's the issue?'

'Sorry, cuz.' He stood. 'There is no issue.'

M.C. followed him to his feet. 'If there was, you'd tell me. Right?'

'You used to babysit us, M.C. Who was the biggest tattletale ever? Who couldn't keep a secret if his life depended on it?'

'You.' She laughed. 'You told Sam there was no Santa Claus and turned over on me that time I sneaked out to go to a party. Little shit.'

He grinned and started for the door just as Dan arrived. 'For the record, Sam spilled the beans about Santa, not me. And you had it coming. You were *supposed* to be baby-sitting us.'

'You were supposed to be sleeping, and the party was right next door.'

'What am I interrupting?' Dan asked. 'Family feud?'

'Just some friendly reminiscing.' She stood on tiptoe and kissed him, then turned back to Tommy. 'Want to join us for dinner?'

'Thanks, but all this true love crap gives me indigestion. Besides, I've got homework.'

He headed to his car. 'If you change your mind about talking,' she called after him, 'let me know.' He promised he would, climbed into his car and drove away.

9

Saturday, January 17
7:30 P.M.

The phone had been ringing off the hook all day. Family and friends, calling to congratulate her. Word had spread and the number attending the engagement party had ballooned.

In the midst of all that, M.C. had gotten a serious case of cold feet.

She had pushed past it, donning the red dress she had raced to Cherryvale Mall to buy just a few hours ago, after she'd decided the black one she had planned to wear made her look like she was in mourning. It was a celebration, after all. She had fussed with her hair and makeup – something she rarely did – and met Dan at the door with a confident smile.

What a faker. Her feet had gone from cold to icy.

'We're here,' Dan said, putting the car into park. She drew in a ragged breath and he looked at her. 'Are you all right?'

'Yes . . . no . . .' She swore. 'I don't know.'

He angled toward her. 'Talk to me.'

She opened her mouth, shut it, then tried again. 'I feel like we're moving too fast.'

'It's just a party.'

'No.' She shook her head, blinking against tears. 'It's a

38

ring, too. A picture in the newspaper. A promise in front of everyone I care about.'

For a long moment, he was silent. She knew her words hurt him, but she had to be honest. He deserved it. Their relationship deserved it.

'Do you want out?' he asked quietly.

She didn't have to think about it. 'No.'

'Good. So take a deep breath and get your sexy ass in there.'

She laughed. 'No wonder I love you, you always know just what to say.'

'I am a shrink, you know.' He threw open his car door.

'Wait.' She caught his arm. 'Do you love me?'

'Madly.'

'It's okay that I'm a cop? I sleep with a gun, Dan. I keep crazy hours. I spend time at the morgue.' He opened his mouth to answer, she stopped him. 'My family's big and loud and my mother's a major pain in the ass. We'll never be alone. Someone's always going to be sticking their nose in our business. Holidays will be insane.'

The corner of his mouth lifted. 'Finished?'

'No.' She took a deep breath. 'I'm not a traditional woman, and I'll never be a traditional wife. I don't have it in me, Dan.'

'I fell in love with you,' he said. 'A bad-ass with a family that's certifiable. If I'd wanted a traditional "little woman," I would have found one. You just have to trust.'

'I'm a cop. Cops don't trust very wel—'

He caught the last with a kiss and calm flowed over, just like that. He drew away. 'Ready to go to a party?'

She nodded and they climbed out of the car, crossed the full parking lot. This old town location Mama Riggio's had been her brothers' first. It remained M.C.'s favorite. The block of funky here-and-gone businesses in rehabbed storefronts was just so . . . Rockford. At least, the Rockford she had grown up in, before the east side of town had exploded with upscale residential developments and the proliferation of shiny new strip malls and national chain restaurants to go in them.

They stepped inside. The restaurant and bar was packed, the fun Italian soundtrack cranked up to compete with the din of conversation. The hostess saw her, waved and called out congratulations. 'They're all in the party room,' she added.

On their way back, Dan caught sight of Erik in the bar. At the same moment, Erik saw them and motioned them over. Holding her hand, Dan led her through the sea of people. M.C. had to admit she found Dan and Erik's friendship surprising. They were so different. Ten years apart in age, worlds apart in upbringing. Even physically, they were opposites. Erik was movie star good-looking: fair hair, threaded with silver, and just enough of a scruffy beard to give him a sexy, lived-in look.

Dan was younger, tougher. Dark-haired and good-looking in a bad boy, west Rockford sort of way. The guys from west Rockford had street smarts and swagger. Notorious hellraisers, they prided themselves on not backing down from a fight – and usually had the scars to prove it. She should know, all five of her brothers fit that description to varying degrees.

But the two men had much in common, as well. Both were psychologists and advocates for young people. They'd met when Dan went to work for Kids in Crisis, the mental health facility Erik founded to provide counseling and psychiatric care for kids whose families couldn't afford a hundred bucks an hour for therapy.

'My God,' Erik said to her, 'you're gorgeous.' He kissed her cheek, then turned to Dan. 'Lucky bastard. You always were.'

It was ironic, that comment coming from a card-carrying member of the Lucky Sperm Club. Like only a very small percentage of the world population, Erik had gotten it all with one shot – looks, smarts and money.

Erik turned back to her. 'Congratulations. Have you set a date?'

She laughed. 'No. And I'm sure by the end of the evening I'll have been asked that question by fifteen different aunts.'

'You could elope?'

'Not a bad idea.' Dan laid an arm across her shoulder. 'What do you say, babe?'

'My mother would kill herself. Or kill you.'

'Good point. Extravaganza it is.'

Erik paid for his drink and they made their way to the party room. As they entered and people caught sight of them, they turned and clapped. The scene felt bizarre to M.C. What had she done to earn applause? Fall in love? Be loved in return?

She hadn't done anything to deserve applause. Instead, she'd been given a wonderful gift.

They made the rounds, together and separately. Tommy and Sam were there. Both of them gave her bear hugs, complete with beer breath and slurred greetings.

'I hope neither one of you are driving.'

'Chill, M.C. We're cool.'

Cool wasn't the term she would have chosen. *Inebriated* would be. 'I see that,' she said. 'Should I take it you've resolved your issues?'

Sam frowned. 'I never have issues with my big bro. He's my hero.'

They fell out laughing, the way young men sometimes did when they've had too many beers for their own good. M.C. decided to switch to mineral water. She didn't care to be the designated driver at her own party – but someone had to.

She caught sight of Dan and saw he already had switched to Coke. He looked her way and blew her a kiss. Her cousins snickered and she scowled at them. 'Someday you'll be getting married and I'll remind you how awful you were.'

'We're happy for you,' Tommy said. 'We're glad you're getting married.'

'Yeah,' Sam jumped in. 'We love weddings. Well, wedding receptions. All those ladies, sipping champagne and feeling romantic.'

'You two are pigs, you know that?'

Obviously they did. And were proud of the fact. As she left them to their carrying-on, Dan rejoined her. 'What was that all about?'

She filled him in, finishing just as the toasts started. The toasts led to more drinking, which led to more mingling. The night was perfect until they ran smack into her cousin Gina DeLuca, the back-stabbing Italian Barbie doll and M.C.'s lifelong nemesis.

'Hello, Mary Catherine.' She then turned to Dan, greeting him in a husky purr. 'Dan, it's so good to see you.'

He looked annoyed. M.C. frowned. 'You two know each other?'

'We worked together,' he said, 'at Kids in Crisis.'

'I'm Erik's office manager. I'm with him tonight.'

M.C. saw Dan frown and made a mental note to ask him about it later. She hadn't seen Erik with Gina, but she had been a little busy.

'It's been lovely, Dan. Congratulations.'

They watched her walk away, then M.C. looked at him. 'Not my favorite relative. Lots of history.'

'I gathered.' He paused. 'Anything you want to share?'

'Not tonight. I'm too happy.' She squeezed his hand. 'But I'm surprised Erik brought her tonight. She doesn't seem his type.'

'All women are Erik's type. That said, I'm surprised, too.'

Moments later, she was snagged by her mother and aunts. Dan extricated himself to go have a chat with his best man.

Within moments, her aunts and mother had launched into a sermon extolling the virtues of a huge wedding. 'You don't have to worry,' her mother said. 'I'm paying for everything.'

That got M.C.'s attention. 'That's crazy, Mama. Dan and I have our own money.'

'Your father – God rest his soul – and I planned for this.'

'You planned for this?'

'Put away a little money every month.'

For a wedding? Some parents saved for an education, hers had saved for a wedding. 'I don't know what to say, Mama.'

'The bride's parents give her away, that's the way it's done.'

'Since she had so long to save,' her aunt Bella said, 'you can have a big wedding.'

'A spectacular wedding,' Aunt Catherine added.

'Dan and I haven't discussed the size of the—' She glanced past her mother and saw Dan talking to Gina, head bent to hers. As she watched, Gina laid a hand on his arm.

Aunt Catherine dragged her attention back. 'I'm your godmother, listen to me. Your mother has been waiting thirty years for this, it wouldn't be right not to let her enjoy herself.'

M.C. frowned. She supposed the old 'but it's my wedding' argument would seem ungrateful. Her first official step in her metamorphosis into Bridezilla. As her aunt extolled the many benefits of a big wedding, M.C.'s gaze drifted back to where Dan and Gina had been standing. They were gone.

She scanned the thinning crowd, but didn't see either of them. The hair at the back of her neck prickled, and she scolded herself for it. Just because she didn't see either of them didn't mean they were together. Dan's dislike of her cousin had been obvious. With a small sense of relief she realized she didn't see Erik either.

'Mary Catherine? Are you listening?'

'Of course.' She smiled at her aunt. 'Whatever you think's best. I see some of my guests are leaving. Excuse me.'

That hadn't been a lie, though it had been an excuse. She found Dan in the bar with Kitt and Joe, Gina nowhere to be seen. M.C. had to admit she felt more than a little paranoid.

'Hey, babe,' Dan said, putting his arm around her and drawing her against him. 'There you are. Forgive me?'

Again the prickle. Again she shook it off. 'For what?'

'Leaving you alone with your mother and aunts. Was it too horrible?'

'Excruciating. You owe me, big time.'

Kitt and Joe used that opportunity to call it a night. Within thirty minutes most of the family had made their exit as well. Arm in arm, M.C. and Dan made their way to the parking lot, only to find Tommy, Sam and Aunt Catherine in a scuffle over Tommy's car keys.

'I can drive,' Tommy insisted, slurring his words. 'I'm not leavin' my baby here.' He patted the hood of his Element. 'N't doin' it.'

43

'You're drunk,' his mother said. She glared at him, then his brother. 'You're both drunk.'

'He's drunker than I am,' Sam said proudly, then smiled stupidly at Tommy. 'I can hold my liquor better than you can.'

'Stuff it, twirp.'

M.C. stepped in. 'Sorry, boys, neither one of you is driving anywhere. And I've got the badge to back that up. Keys, please.'

She held out her hand. Tommy looked like he wanted to argue, but decided to throw up instead. Luckily, he managed to dart to the back of the vehicle before he did.

Her aunt looked worried. 'He's really sick. This isn't like him. Sam, yes. But not my Tommy.'

M.C. sent an apologetic look Dan's way; he grinned and stepped in. 'Just to be on the safe side, take Tommy with you, Catherine. I'll drive his car to his apartment. M.C. can follow in mine. It's on our way.'

M.C. retrieved Tommy's keys, then watched while Sam and Dan got Tommy into their mother's car. Safely on their way, Dan handed her his car keys. 'What was that you said earlier about your family?'

'Welcome to my world. Gonna change your mind?'

'Not on your life.'

She stood on tiptoe and kissed him good-bye. 'See you at Tommy's.'

She watched him pull out of the lot, then hurried to Dan's sedan. A minute later she was buckled in and on the road.

Traffic was light. She made it to Tommy's in good time. Dan was there, waiting. She pulled into a spot close to his and waited, but he didn't emerge from the Element.

She climbed out and started toward him. He'd fallen asleep, she realized. He sat with his head against the rest, eyes closed. She tapped on the glass. 'Dan?'

He didn't move. She heard the shriek of police sirens, it mixed with the heavy thud of her heart against her chest wall. Suddenly panicked, she yanked open the car door and grabbed his shoulder. He fell forward, face hitting the steering wheel.

The lingering scent of gunpowder stung her nose. She drew her hand away; it was wet, sticky. Blood, she realized. She stared at her hand, a scream rising in her throat. The cruisers arrived. Three of them, blue lights flashing crazily. An officer pushed her out of the way and went for Dan.

As if in slow motion, she sank to her knees, one hand to her stomach, the other to her mouth. She watched in horror as the officers scrambled to help him, listened as they swore in defeat.

'Cancel the EMTs,' one said into his radio. 'Contact the VCB and coroner's office. We're securing the scene now.'

10

Sunday, January 18
2:15 A.M.

Kitt launched herself out of her Taurus. 'Where's Detective Riggio?' she shouted to the nearest uniformed officer.

'Cruiser,' he answered, indicating which one.

Kitt headed that way, heart pounding, thoughts racing. The call had awakened her from a deep sleep. She hadn't been able to grasp what the communications officer was saying and had asked her to repeat it twice.

M.C.'s fiancé was dead. Shot in the head. M.C. was at the scene.

She found her partner. She sat huddled in the front passenger side of the cruiser. The door was open, she was wrapped in a blanket.

She stared blankly ahead, not moving except to twist her engagement ring.

'Hey, partner,' Kitt said softly, squatting in front of her. 'I came as soon as I heard.'

M.C. lifted her gaze to Kitt's, but didn't speak. The anguish she saw in her friend's expression broke her heart. Words were inadequate, but they were all she had. 'I'm so sorry, M.C.'

Tears rolled slowly down her cheeks. 'I don't understand how this happened.'

'I know.' She gathered M.C.'s hands in hers. They were ice-cold and she rubbed them.

'We were just together. He left a minute before me . . . I don't understand . . . why . . . Dan? Why him?'

Kitt's own eyes filled. How many times over the years had she been asked that by a victim's loved ones? How much easier it had been to offer them glib reassurances than it was to face her friend now with nothing but those same words.

'I don't know,' she said softly. 'But we'll find who did this, M.C. We'll find out why. I promise.'

They'd called Michael to come care for M.C.; Kitt saw that he had arrived. He looked devastated. She motioned him over.

'Michael's here,' she said, squeezing M.C.'s hand reassuringly. 'I've got to do my job, but I'll keep you posted. I'll be back.'

She met Michael's concerned gaze. He nodded and she stood; he took her place. M.C. fell into his arms, clinging to him as she sobbed.

Kitt walked away, fighting the knot of tears in her throat. She would keep her promise to M.C. Whatever it took, she would find who had done this and make certain they paid.

11

Kitt parked in front of M.C.'s small, brick home, a grande latte clutched in her gloved hand. Sighing, she climbed out of her vehicle. Dan's murder was looking like a random act of violence, a case of Dan being in the wrong place at the wrong time. One of the building's tenants had seen a stranger in the building. She had shouted through her door that she was calling the police. Then she had.

Dan had parked in a spot that faced a side fire exit. The bullet had entered through the windshield, hitting Dan nearly between the eyes. He had been killed instantly.

The detectives assigned to the case speculated that the perp fled the building by that exit, emerging to find Dan looking right at him. He'd killed him and run.

None of the apartments had been broken into, thanks to the quick action of the eagle-eyed citizen. Her action had also, most probably, led to Dan's murder.

How did she tell her best friend that the man she loved had simply been in the wrong place at the wrong time? How did she tell her that 'these terrible things sometimes happen' or that 'God works in mysterious ways'?

Kitt drew a deep breath and climbed the stairs to M.C.'s

front porch. Propped against the front door was an envelope and a small bouquet of flowers, the kind that could be purchased at any grocery store. No doubt left by someone whose heart was in the right place but couldn't face M.C.'s grief.

Kitt collected them, then rang the bell. Family was staying with M.C., rotating every few hours. Sal had granted her an open-ended leave, though Kitt knew her friend well enough to suspect neither of those would last long before they began to grate.

Today it was Melody. She had been crying. Kitt handed her the bouquet and card. 'These were out front.'

Melody nodded. 'Go ahead and take her the card. I'll get the flowers in a vase.'

'How is she today?' Kitt asked.

'About the same. Not talking much. Not eating.'

'It's going to take time,' Kitt said softly. 'I've been in a similar spot.'

She nodded. 'She'll be glad to see you.'

Melody went to attend to the flowers; Kitt crossed to M.C.'s bedroom door and tapped on it. 'It's me. You awake and up for a visitor?'

She was and Kitt entered. The room smelled of flowers. M.C. was fully dressed, in soft pants and a battered, oversized sweatshirt, sitting cross-legged on the bed. Kitt saw the sweatshirt was from Notre Dame, Dan's alma mater. M.C. looked lost.

'I brought you a latte.'

'Thanks.' She stretched out her hand and Kitt gave it to her. She took a sip, then set it aside.

'I have news as well.' Kitt told her then, delivering the information the way she would to any victim's family – without fanfare or inflection, just the facts.

For a full minute after she finished, M.C. simply looked at her. Then she shook her head. 'I can't believe . . . you're saying I lost him because of . . . bad luck? You're telling me, if he'd selected a different parking spot, he'd be alive. Or if I'd given him one last kiss or he'd missed one more stoplight,

49

he'd be alive. You want me to believe that and do what with it? Take comfort?'

'I'm sorry, M.C. I'm just relaying what we've pieced together so far.'

'It sucks.'

Yes, it did. Kitt cleared her throat. 'Martin's funeral's today. The feds are handling the video surveillance, giving us complete access to recordings. I'll be there with a half-dozen other RPD officers.'

M.C. didn't comment, and Kitt wondered if she had even been listening. Her gaze landed on a bottle of pills on the nightstand. She picked it up. 'What are these?'

'Sleeping pills.'

'Are they helping?'

'I took one. I won't again.' She tipped up her chin, as if daring Kitt to argue. 'I don't want to sleep. Not that way. They make me forget. And remembering is all I have left.'

Tears flooded Kitt's eyes. She knew how her friend felt, exactly. That's the way she had been after Sadie passed. She'd wanted to cling to the memory of her daughter every moment, no matter how painful it was.

'It'll get better. I know it doesn't feel like that now, but—'

'Life goes on,' she said bitterly.

'Yes.' Kitt cleared her throat. 'You want to talk about him?'

M.C.'s throat worked. She shook her head, looked away.

Seconds ticked past. Kitt remembered the card. 'I almost forgot. This was propped against your front door. There were flowers, too.'

'I don't want it. You read it.'

'It's a condolence card, I'm sure.' M.C. didn't respond and Kitt carefully loosened the flap, eased out the card. The image of a magnificent sunset; a line of Scripture about God's love.

Kitt held it out. 'You're sure you want me to read it? Whoever left it cares about you. It might make you feel better.'

M.C. took it from her hand, read the front, then opened it.

Her expression changed to one of shocked disbelief. 'My God.'

'What?' Kitt plucked the card from M.C.'s nerveless fingers. It read: *Maybe you're better off. He wasn't that nice a guy.*

12

Kitt drew to a stop in front of Joe's California cottage–style house, the home they had shared during their marriage. She gazed at the soft, welcoming light spilling from the windows.

Although she and Joe hadn't moved back in together, they had settled into a nightly routine. He prepared their evening meal; she cleaned up after. When she stepped inside, the smell of home cooking would surround her; she would call out a greeting and head for the kitchen. He would have a mineral water with lime waiting. They'd embrace, kiss, sip their drinks as they shared tidbits of their day.

There were times she didn't want to discuss the events of her day. She wanted this time with him to be her sanctuary. Not tonight. Tonight she needed to talk, to share her sadness over what had happened to M.C. and how it had dredged up her own feelings of loss.

Kitt killed the engine, collected her things and climbed out of the car. Moments later, she dropped her keys on the entryway table and breathed in the smell of something spicy, like a mixture of beef, tomatoes, chili peppers and onions.

'Joe,' she called. 'I'm here.'

'In the kitchen,' he called back.

Once upon a time, before the leukemia had taken Sadie from them, her arrival would have been greeted by both her daughter and husband emerging from the kitchen, all smiles. She missed that – along with about a million other things about being a family.

But they were forging a new 'normal,' she reminded herself. Attempting to create new traditions, a comfortable, loving 'now.' One begun with a giant spray of flowers and a card vowing to try if she would.

That's what the trip to Mexico was all about. Finding their way, working to establish their post-Sadie, post-breakdown, post-divorce relationship. Working to be okay with missing what they had lost – and enjoying what they still had.

M.C. was just at the beginning of that journey, and Kitt ached for her.

She made her way to the other room. Joe stood near the sink, leaning against the counter, reading the sports section of the *Register Star*. The waning light filtered through the window above the sink, softening the lines etched around his eyes and mouth, lines that had changed his face from youthful to weathered. But in an attractive way, one that revealed character.

'Something smells wonderful,' she said.

He looked up and smiled. Her heart did a funny little flip. After all these years, still all the man had to do was smile and she turned to mush. Having that much power over another person ought to be illegal.

'Carne asada. In honor of our trip.' He tossed aside the paper, crossed to her and kissed her. 'Nine days and counting.'

She tipped her head back and gazed at him. His eyes seemed even bluer than the day they'd met. She'd been fifteen, he seventeen. Babies themselves, for heaven's sake.

She threaded her fingers through his light-colored hair. 'It's getting so gray.'

'Beats the alternative.'

'I'm not complaining.' She smiled. 'My silver fox.'

He grinned at her. 'Funny, you're as blond as ever.'

53

'It's a miracle.'

He laughed and released her. 'How was your day? Any progress in nailing Dan's killer?' He handed her a mineral water.

'No, unfortunately. It's looking more and more like a wrong place, wrong time sort of thing.' She sipped the water, then set it down.

She crossed to Joe and slipped her arms around his waist. 'It's always senseless but . . . M.C. took it hard.'

He rested his chin on her head. 'I know how difficult that must have been for you. How it must be . . . thinking of losing Sadie. The way that hurt.'

Still hurt. She squeezed her eyes shut and concentrated on his warmth, the sound of his breathing. On the thankfulness she felt at having him to hold again.

After a moment, she loosened her hold and met his eyes. 'She got this nasty, anonymous card today. The sender suggested Dan wasn't such a nice guy. That M.C. was better off without him.'

'My God.'

'It was sick. Cruel. Who would do that to her?'

He didn't have an answer, of course, and she went on. 'I didn't know what to do or say. It was just so awful.'

He rubbed her back lightly. 'How did she respond?'

'She got angry and ripped it up.' A knot of tears settled in Kitt's throat, she cleared it. 'Then she asked me to leave. She wanted to be alone.'

He pulled away, searching her gaze. 'Let's sit down, I think we need to talk about something.'

He turned off the stove and got himself a beer. They sat at the kitchen table, across from each other.

He began hesitantly. 'I know how close you and M.C. are. How much you've been through together. And I . . . know how you are.'

She waited. He cleared his throat. 'Our trip, leaving M.C. so soon after this, is it going to be a problem for you?'

Kitt had wondered that herself. Had turned the question over in her mind. She told him so. 'A part of me thinks we

54

should cancel. But another part says we should go. This isn't something that's going to go away any time soon. Certainly not in the week we're away. And M.C. has a big family, lots of people who care about her.'

'But only one partner.'

'She'll still need me when I get back,' Kitt said softly, comfortable with her decision. 'Maybe more.'

He searched her gaze. 'You're certain? Because if you feel differently, just tell me now.' A rueful smile touched his mouth. 'So I can adjust to my disappointment.'

'I'm positive.' She smiled and reached across the table and caught his hands. 'In nine days, you and I are leaving for Mexico.'

13

The day of Dan's funeral dawned bright and cold. His parents had flown in from Florida. They were lovely people, and M.C. thought she would have liked having them for in-laws. Although they had never met before, their shared bond of loving Dan had connected them. Every time M.C. looked at the couple, she couldn't help remembering her mother's comment that she and Dan would fill his parents' home with grandchildren.

M.C. held herself stiffly through the service, surrounded by her mother and brothers. She feared if she gave in to tears, she might never be able to stop them.

Dan's wish had been for cremation, so there would be no interment at the cemetery, no bite of cold wind against her cheeks, no smell of freshly turned earth.

His parents had brought photos and lovingly arranged them. Dan as a baby, a toddler, a schoolboy. Dan graduating from high school, then college. The day he had received his doctorate, his arm slung around his mother's shoulders, beaming at the camera. M.C. had supplied their engagement photo for the grouping, encased in the lovely frame her mother had given her at the party.

Looking at them was almost more than she could bear.

56

Erik came up to her after the service. He kissed her cheek and expressed his sympathy. 'If there's anything I can do,' he said. 'Please, call me.'

She didn't know why that simple offer – one many people had spoken in the past days – from Erik affected her so deeply. Her eyes had filled, tears choking her. She'd managed a nod and to squeeze his hand.

Hours later she sat in her dark bedroom, holding the framed photo of her and Dan, wearing the sweatshirt that had been his and still carried his scent, though it seemed to grow fainter by the day.

Exhausted, she couldn't sleep. Her thoughts raced with snippets of conversations from the past days, playing and replaying in her head:

Wrong place, wrong time . . . If there's anything I can do . . . Maybe you're better off without him . . . Who could be so mean, so cruel . . . I'm so sorry for your loss . . . for your loss . . . so sorry . . .

M.C. brought the heels of her hands to her eyes. She couldn't go on this way. If she did, she'd go mad.

Photo clutched to her chest, she sprang out of bed and began to pace. The house was completely quiet. She had sent everyone home, refused all offers of company. She didn't want or need babysitters.

She strode to the living room, then the kitchen. The refrigerator was packed with things to eat, food didn't appeal. She could knock herself out with alcohol, or the pills Erik had prescribed.

M.C. flipped on the overhead light and stared at the wine rack. Is that how it had started for Kitt? she wondered. When she lost Sadie, did she turn to drink to stop the pain? To slow her mind from or quell the tormenting 'what-ifs'?

She turned her back to the wine and strode to the living room. There she snapped on another lamp, hoping the artificial light would somehow chase her dark thoughts away.

From out front came the rumble of a car engine, then the squeal of tires.

Right out front, she realized, and darted for the door. She yanked it open and stepped out onto the porch, but she was too late to catch more than taillights disappearing into the night.

It'd been nothing, she thought. Kids parking, spooked when she flipped on her light. She turned to go back inside, then stopped, heart in her throat.

A paper, fastened to her door. A folded piece of loose-leaf. She freed it from the tack, then unfolded it.

The simple message had been created on a word processor using various fonts and font sizes, the finished product an odd-looking imitation of the clichéd kidnapper's note. It read: *How well did you really know Daniel Gallo?*

Bile rose in her throat; her hands began to shake. Who was doing this? Who could hate her so much? The urge to tear it up, the way she had the first one, surged through her.

Instead, she stared at the pieced-together sentence. And grew angry. Anger became fury. And from that fury sprang steely resolve. Sudden, complete calm.

She was going to find the son of a bitch who was doing this. And when she'd finished with them, they'd be damn sorry they had decided to play this game.

14

M.C. decided to start with Erik. Not only had he known Dan well, he was a shrink. Maybe he could offer insight into the kind of person who would do this. When she called, she learned he was working from home. He invited her to come by anytime.

She pulled into his drive and killed the engine. The Sundstrand family home was a local landmark and an architectural award-winner. Located on the Rock River, the home cantilevered out over the river, all glass and hard angles.

Erik himself answered the door. He looked tired and she wondered if he was having as much trouble sleeping as she was. 'Thanks for taking the time out to talk to me.'

'Anything I can do to help. Come in.'

The interior of the home was spectacular. Any other time, she would have been craning her neck to take it all in. Not today.

He ushered her into a large living room that jutted out over the river. 'When the house was built in the early fifties, it was considered avant-garde,' he said. 'Now it's called a contemporary classic. Go figure.'

'Can we sit down, Erik? There's something I have to show you.'

'Sure.' He led her to the couch. A laptop computer sat open on the coffee table; he closed it, then collected the surrounding papers and stuffed them into his briefcase.

She handed him the message. 'Someone left me this. It's the second one.'

She watched as he unfolded the sheet, then read the single sentence. His eyebrows shot up. 'This is disturbing. I'm sorry someone subjected you to this, especially now.'

'That's why I'm here.' She leaned slightly forward. 'Who would do something like this?'

'I take it that's not a rhetorical question?'

'No.'

'Tell me about the first note.'

'It came in the form of a condolence card, two days after Dan's murder. It said, exactly: "Maybe you're better off. He wasn't that nice a guy."'

'So the first came before the funeral—'

'And this one after. Two A.M. last night, to be specific.'

He nodded and rubbed his stubbled jaw. 'The question is, what's motivating this person? Jealousy? Hatred? A need for revenge? Or is it simply the sick joke of a twisted mind?'

'I assume those are all possibilities?'

'I would think so, yes. How were these delivered?'

'Tacked to my front door.'

'So, in addition to knowing about you and Dan's engagement and his murder, they know where you live.'

'It's someone close to me,' she said.

'Within your personal sphere.'

'You're thinking like a cop.'

'The work's similar. The psychiatrist attempts to uncover the truth, the same as a cop. To understand the "why." The difference is, we're looking for emotional truth, and our goal is to help the individual once that truth – or motivation – is revealed.'

She had never thought of it that way, but it made sense. 'And the cop aims to help *society* by getting the individual off the street and behind bars.'

He picked up the note again, studying it. 'The person who

did this is taking a big chance. By leaving them on your doorstep, he risks not only capture in the act, but forensic capture as well. You're a cop, after all. In addition, a good bit of thought was put into this second letter. It wasn't done on a whim.'

'You're saying this is a highly motivated individual.'

He nodded. 'And it's not an intellectual motivation. It's emotional. And highly personal.'

Which opened some doors and closed others. 'Thank you, Erik.' She stood. 'I won't take up any more of your time.'

'It's not a problem. Ever.' He walked her to the door. When they reached it, he met her eyes. 'There's something you didn't ask me,' he said. 'And I'm surprised by it.'

'What's that?'

'You haven't asked if there's any truth in these messages.'

She hesitated only a heartbeat. 'I loved Dan,' she said softly, holding his gaze. 'I trusted him. So you see, I didn't ask the question because I already know the answer.'

15

M.C. climbed into her SUV. She clenched her shaking hands in her lap. Why had Erik said that? Had he been testing her? Attempting to plant a seed of doubt? Or had it simply been one of those shrink comments?

You haven't asked if there's any truth in these messages.

Damn him. If she went back now and asked him why, he would know she wasn't nearly as confident as she acted.

She drew in a deep, steadying breath and cranked the engine. She backed out of Erik's drive, forcing her thoughts to what she had learned from him. Erik had confirmed some things for her. Things she had known but been afraid to rely on in her frayed emotional state.

The person sending the notes was someone within her personal sphere. And they were highly motivated.

Time to fill Kitt in. M.C. grabbed her phone from the console and flipped it open. She saw that she'd missed a call from Tommy and that he'd left a message. She accessed the voice mail: 'It's Tommy. I know you probably hate me now . . . I'm so, so sorry . . . if I hadn't gotten so drunk . . . Dan wouldn't, he—'

He choked on the words, then went silent. A moment

later, he began again. 'I don't have classes today . . . I'm home. If you can bear to speak to me, call me. Okay?'

Tears stung her eyes. Tommy blamed himself for Dan dying. And the truth was, she had been blaming Tommy, too. In the pit of her gut and a secret corner of her heart, she had been shaking with rage and pointing her finger at him. Hating him, just the way he'd said in his message.

She pulled to the side of the road and stopped. Tommy was just a kid. Kids did stupid things – even steady, dependable ones like Tommy. The person she should be angry with was the SOB who pointed his gun at Dan and pulled the trigger.

She dialed Tommy back; the call went directly to voice mail. She started to leave a message, decided against it and dialed Kitt instead.

Her partner picked up right away. 'M.C.? Are you all right?'

'I'm fine, just wanted to fill you in.'

Her words were met with silence. M.C. realized why: she sounded like her old self. As if none of this had happened and it was just another day on the job.

'I got another one of those oh-so-fun anonymous notes last night. At two A.M. Bastard tacked it to my front door. This one asked how well I knew my fiancé.'

Kitt made a sound of sympathy. 'Bring it in, I'll take care of it. Pass it on to the ID guys, see what they—'

'Thanks, partner, but I'm taking care of it myself. Already paid a visit to Erik. He confirmed what I was thinking, that the person who sent me these is acting out of a strong emotion like hatred or envy and is in my extended circle of family and friends.'

'It makes a sick sort of sense,' Kitt said, 'though it's still hard to believe.'

'Tell me about it. I'm heading over to Tommy's place now. The kid's blaming himself for Dan's—' She couldn't bring herself to say the word. 'Anyway, I don't want him doing that.'

'I know I already asked, but are you sure you're all right?'

M.C. thought for a moment. 'Depends on the definition of all right, partner. If it includes brokenhearted and mad as hell, then yeah, I'm okay. If it includes refusing to sit back and let the wheels of justice turn without me while I turn into a sniveling victim, I'm doing good there, too.'

Again Kitt was silent. When she finally spoke, M.C. heard what she thought was relief in her friend's voice. 'Welcome back, partner.'

16

M.C. had underestimated how being in the place where Dan had been shot would feel. Her palms began to sweat, her heart to race. Every fiber of her being urged her to turn and run.

Through sheer force of will she kept on, turning into the parking lot, finding a spot, stopping. Cutting the engine.

But as hard as she tried, she couldn't keep her eyes from going to the spot where he'd died. Another vehicle sat there, as if nothing had ever happened. Life went on.

Don't fall apart, Riggio. You can do this.

She took a deep breath and climbed out of her SUV. Eyes fixed on the building's entrance, she crossed the parking lot, reached the door and stepped into the common foyer. It was an older building that had been rehabbed, so it had the best of both worlds: character and modern comforts.

An apartment lay to her right and left, dead ahead a staircase and an elevator. Tommy lived on the second floor; she took the stairs. She reached his door and knocked, then when he didn't respond, rang the bell.

'Tommy,' she called, 'it's M.C.' Still he didn't answer, and she knocked again. The door creaked open.

A prickling sensation at the back of her neck, she eased her Glock from her shoulder holster. Weapon out, she nudged the door farther open with the toe of her boot, then stepped inside.

She heard running water. The shower, she realized. The idiot kid had left his door open and gotten in the tub. She closed the door behind her and went around the corner to the bathroom.

She tapped on the door. 'Hey, kiddo, it's M.C. Ever occur to you to make sure your front door is secure before you take off all your clothes and get in the bath?'

He didn't respond and she rapped on the door, then cracked it open. 'Tommy, are you okay?'

When he still didn't answer, her heart jumped to her throat. 'I'm coming in!'

She heard the panic in her voice and attempted to check it, tried in the fraction of a minute it took to cross to the shower to convince herself everything was fine. That she was about to embarrass the hell out of them both. Twenty years from now he would be telling people how his cop-cousin burst in on him while he was taking a shower.

She reached the tub, and pushed aside the curtain. All the comforting little scenarios in her head evaporated like a last warm breath on a frigid night. Tommy lay in a crumpled heap, the now-cold water streaming down on him, lips blue.

Above the shower's reach, a spray of red. Blood. Brain matter.

With a cry, she stumbled backward. Tommy wouldn't be sharing any stories ever again.

17

M.C. dropped to her knees. Curving her arms around her middle, she rocked back and forth, small guttural whimpers spilling from her lips.

No . . . this couldn't be . . . Blessed Mary, Mother of God . . . a dream . . . pray for us sinners now . . . Wake up, Mary Catherine, make it go away . . . and at the hour of our death . . .

But she wasn't asleep. It wasn't a nightmare. She lifted her head. Dear Jesus, how could this be happening? Two people she loved, gone. First Dan. Now Tommy.

Both taken from her. Both shot in the head.

Dan. Tommy. She straightened, realization washing over her. Both dead. Killed, essentially, in the same location. In the same manner.

Not a random act. Not a case of wrong time, wrong place.

Could what she was thinking be true? Could Dan have been mistaken for Tommy? Her thoughts hurtled crazily forward. Someone had spotted an intruder in the building. They'd called the police. Dan had been in Tommy's car. Waiting for her. The shooter had emerged from the building and believed he had stumbled onto his target. When he had realized his mistake, he'd come back to finish the job.

One big problem, she acknowledged. Why would anyone have targeted Tommy?

Something had been troubling him. He had tried to talk to her about it. Had acted out of character by getting drunk.

Could that something have gotten him killed?

She pulled herself together and inched back to the tub. Bile rose in the back of her throat. Not her Tommy, she thought, light-headed. Not quick with a smile and helping hand Tommy. It hurt almost more than she could bear.

Divorce yourself, Riggio. Figure it out. Do the job.

M.C. turned off the water and squatted beside the tub. Careful not to touch anything else, she moved her gaze carefully over the body, stopping at the wound site. It looked like a single shot had killed him. The bullet had entered his left temple and exploded out the right.

She moved her gaze to his forearms and hands. No defense wounds that she could see. If there'd been any trace evidence on his person or matter under his nails, the shower had most probably destroyed it.

She needed to call Kitt. Get the ID team over—

From the other room came the creak of the front door opening, footfalls. M.C. crept to the doorway, then waited, listening. The footfalls came closer, then stopped.

Heart pounding, she waited, counting silently down from three. *Two . . . one—*

'Tommy? You here, bud?'

Sam. She lowered her weapon, moved into the doorway. She worked to slow her racing heart, her breathing. 'Hello, Sam.'

'M.C.?' His gaze dropped to her gun, then darted back up to hers. 'What're you doing?'

His brother was dead. Murdered. How was she going to tell him?

18

Kitt found M.C. and Sam sitting in the common area outside Tommy's apartment. Sam's face was ashen, his eyes glazed and red-rimmed from crying.

M.C. had her arm around him. She looked calm. Almost fiercely determined.

Two cruisers had arrived with Kitt. A uniformed officer tromped up the stairs to begin securing the inner perimeter. The other officer, at street level, the exterior.

'Sam, this is Officer Thomas,' Kitt said. 'If you need anything, let him know.'

M.C. stood. 'I've got to go inside with Kitt. You'll be okay?' He nodded and lowered his head to his drawn-up knees.

Kitt touched her arm. 'You're sure you're up to this?' she asked softly. 'I can take it from here.'

'I've got it. Absolutely.'

She sounded completely confident, the old M.C., not daunted by anything. Kitt searched her gaze, then indicated the door.

M.C. led her inside. 'This morning,' she said, 'Tommy left me a message on my cell phone. Said he wanted to talk and that he didn't have classes today and was home. I called him back, it went straight to voice mail, but I came over anyway, thinking he was here.'

'What time did he call?'

She opened the phone, checked her call history. 'Eight thirty-six. I knocked and rang the bell. When I got no answer, I knocked harder. The door opened.'

They reached the bathroom. 'I heard the shower. I figured he'd—' She cleared her throat. 'He was forgetful like that sometimes. Trusting, too. Not so worried about things like locks and alarms.'

'What happened then?'

'I called out. When he didn't respond, I got that feeling. You know what I'm talking about.'

Kitt did know. That sense that something was terribly wrong.

'I knocked on the bathroom door, called out. When he didn't respond, I poked my head inside. I noticed that although the shower was on, there was no steam. I found him there.'

Kitt inched closer to the tub. Her chest tightened at the sight. She could only imagine what it must have been like for M.C. She looked over her shoulder at her friend. 'I'm so sorry.'

For a split second, M.C.'s expression went soft with pain, then it hardened. 'I turned off the water. Pathologist will have to confirm, but it looks like just the one shot.'

It did look that way. 'Anything missing?' Kitt asked.

'Haven't checked.' She took a deep breath. 'You know what this means, right? Dan wasn't random. Whoever killed him thought he was Tommy.'

Kitt frowned, turning over the pieces of the puzzle in her head. 'It's possible, no doubt about it. But I think it's premature to call that a certainty.'

'I know this is right. I feel it.'

'So why'd somebody want Tommy dead?'

'I don't know. That's what we've got to find out.'

Kitt heard Sorenstein and Miller in the other room. 'ID's here,' she said softly. 'While they do their thing, let's take a look around.'

The two detectives entered the room and crossed to M.C. 'Riggio,' Sorenstein said, not quite meeting her eyes, 'I heard. This really sucks.'

'Geez, M.C.,' Miller added awkwardly, 'if there's anything, you know, that I can do, let me know.'

The situation made them uncomfortable. They understood M.C.'s pain, but couldn't allow themselves to fully empathize. Opening that door was too scary. Because once open, who knew if they could get it locked down again?

'There is something,' M.C. said. 'Help me nail the bastard who did this.'

That they could deal with, Kitt acknowledged. Action. Retribution. Justice.

'You've got it.' Sorenstein looked at Miller, as if for confirmation. 'We'll nail this son of a bitch, don't you worry.'

She and M.C. started their search in the living room. Kitt moved her gaze over the orderly room. Tommy hadn't lived like a self-supporting college student. No milk-crate book-shelves or thirdhand sofas.

Instead, the furnishings looked new. Pottery Barn, she thought. Or Rooms To Go. Clean, contemporary, comfortable.

'How long's Tommy been in this apartment?' she asked.

'Six or eight months.'

'Nice place.'

She saw her partner frown slightly as if she read her thoughts: *Where'd he get the money to outfit the place?*

'Tommy worked,' M.C. offered. 'Did freelance book-keeping and taxes. For family and friends. Home businesses and small outfits that couldn't afford to hire a dedicated employee or an accounting firm.'

They made their way from the living room to the kitchen and dining area. A few dishes sat in the sink, Kitt saw. She moved her gaze over the space. Several of the cabinet doors stood slightly ajar. She did a quick, visual search of them.

'Nothing out of order here,' she said.

'Here either,' M.C. said, shutting the pantry.

Kitt crossed to the refrigerator. Several photos adorned its front. In one, Sam and Tommy stood smiling at the camera, a pretty girl standing between them. Shoulder-length brown hair.

She took down the photo and turned it over. Tommy hadn't labeled it, though it was date stamped November of this past year, just two months ago.

Kitt secured the photo under the magnet and opened the refrigerator. The contents were spare, only the necessities: beer, a carton of milk, leftover pizza, fried chicken and take-out cartons of something that had been Asian but was now fuzzy and green.

She moved on to the freezer. Nothing but ice cream and sugar-free Popsicles. A container of what looked like leftover lasagna.

'Bedroom?' M.C. asked.

Kitt agreed and they headed for it. Again, they found an orderly room. Bed made. Clothes neatly hung in the closet. Not even a dust bunny under the bed.

On the dresser lay Tommy's wallet and a smattering of change. Kitt opened it. 'Forty bucks inside. A credit card. Robbery wasn't a motive.'

Kitt frowned, suddenly realizing what they hadn't seen. 'You said Tommy called you?'

'From his cell. He didn't have a landline.'

'So, where is it? I haven't seen it.'

'He used the second bedroom for an office,' M.C. offered. 'Maybe it's in there.'

'Let's check his coat and pants pockets, then hit the office.'

The phone wasn't in any of his pockets, it proved not to be in his office either. But that wasn't the only thing that appeared to be missing.

'Where's his computer?' Kitt asked. She motioned toward the desk. 'He has everything but, including a printer.'

'Detective Lundgren?' Officer Thomas poked his head into the bedroom. 'Mariano's neighbor's out front. She says she saw a girl running out of Tommy's apartment, about an hour ago.'

72

19

The neighbor, Mrs Roselyn Newhaus, occupied the apartment across the hall from Tommy's. Kitt introduced herself and M.C. and asked the woman if they could have a few moments of her time. The woman's gaze drifted toward Sam, still huddling outside Tommy's front door, head on drawn-up knees.

'Come on in,' she said.

When she had closed the door behind them, she narrowed her eyes on M.C. 'I've seen you around before.'

'Detective Riggio knew Tommy Mariano,' Kitt said.

'Knew? What's going . . . is Tommy—' She motioned to Officer Thomas. 'He wouldn't tell me anything.'

'Tommy Mariano's dead,' Kitt said softly.

The neighbor brought a hand to her throat. 'Oh, my God. What – I mean, just a few days ago that young man . . . in the parking lot—'

Kitt cut her off. 'Officer Thomas told us you saw someone running from Mr Mariano's apartment.'

'I was bringing up the groceries,' she said, bobbing her head. 'A girl came running down, nearly knocking me over. She didn't even say she was sorry, just kept going.'

'Can you describe her?'

'Twenty-something, I'd guess. She was thin, with shoulder-length brown hair. Wearing a bright pink jacket. She didn't even apologize,' she said again. 'I thought that was rude, but now I . . .'

She let her words trail off. Kitt stepped in. 'You saw her come out of Mr Mariano's apartment?'

The woman frowned, as if in thought. 'Yes . . . no. I guess I assumed she'd been visiting Tommy. Because of her age.'

'But she could have been visiting someone on the upper floors?'

'Yes.'

'Would you recognize her if you saw her again?'

'I didn't get a good look at her face. She had her head down. And like I said, I had my arms full and she was running.'

Damn it. Kitt handed the woman her card. 'If you think of anything else, don't hesitate to call. It could be important.'

She said she would and they exited the apartment. Sam looked up, expression shattered. 'What'd she say?'

'Are you able to answer some questions?' Kitt asked instead.

'I guess.'

'Tommy have a girlfriend?' she asked.

'No, not really.' He turned his lost gaze on M.C. 'Why Tommy? How could this have . . . how could it have . . . how?'

Kitt felt sorry for him. He didn't understand that in this screwed-up world, bad things happened to good people. That sometimes life sucked. That it could be unfair, ugly and very cruel.

He hadn't known that. Not really. Not until now.

M.C., Kitt could hear, struggled to steady her voice. 'I don't know why,' she said quietly. 'And I don't know who. But I intend to find out. We intend to.' She covered his hands with hers. 'Can you help us?'

'I'll try,' he whispered, 'I don't know if I can, but . . .'

74

His words trailed off. She tightened her grip on his. 'You were closer to Tommy than anybody. Something you know, something that may seem totally inconsequential to you, could be the key to why this happened. And to who did it. Do you understand?'

He nodded and she went on. 'Had you noticed anything unusual about Tommy lately?'

He shook his head. 'No.'

'Any new friends?'

He answered in the negative again.

'He seem on edge? Nervous or agitated?'

He clasped his hands together. 'Same old Tommy.'

'Any change in his habits?'

'What do you mean?'

'Eating, sleeping? His study or social habits?'

When he said no, she pressed him. 'You're sure? Think carefully.'

He paused before answering, as if searching his thoughts. 'Same old Tommy,' he said again. 'I crashed here Tuesday night and other than—'

His voice wobbled, and he looked quickly away, fighting tears. She gave him a moment. When he had collected himself, she pushed on. 'Other than what, Sam?'

'Nothing. I got here about five. He was studying. I ordered some pizza. We ate. Had a couple a beers. After that he had some work to do. Not schoolwork, his bookkeeping stuff.'

'While he was doing that, what did you do?'

'Cruised the Net. Played 360.'

'And no one called or stopped by?' He shook his head and she went on. 'What time did he finish working?'

'Eleven or so. We had another beer, talked for a while, then crashed.' His voice shook. 'We always talked.'

'Nothing different about Tuesday?'

He hesitated a moment. 'We talked about . . . Dan. What happened. He felt really bad about . . . he felt like it was his fault.'

M.C. flinched, but when she spoke, her voice was steady. 'The Thursday before the party, he stopped by my place, wanting to talk about something. Then he changed his mind. You have any idea what might have been bothering him?'

He frowned, then shook his head, eyes welling with tears. 'I wish I could help.'

Kitt gentled her voice. 'Just a couple more questions, Sam. Do you think you can handle that?' He nodded; she continued. 'Tommy's computer isn't in his apartment. Any idea where it might be?'

He blinked. 'Not in the apartment?'

'No. Could he have lent it out or sent it to the shop?'

'No way would he have lent it out. That'd be like letting someone borrow your toothbrush or pillow. He didn't even like me on it, mostly because of all his client stuff.'

'What about a repair shop?'

Sam drew a shaky breath. 'He had a friend who was a tech guy. Made house calls. I think he was a client of Tommy's, too. I met him a couple times.'

'Can you think of any reason someone would want him dead?'

'God, no! Tommy was—' He choked on the words and cleared his throat. 'He was the . . . greatest.'

He broke down then, sobbing inconsolably. Kitt watched as M.C. folded him into her arms, then slipped back into the apartment.

20

After a time, Sam stopped crying, his body ceased to shudder and his breathing steadied. He eased away from M.C., met her eyes, the expression in his brokenhearted. 'How am I going to tell Mom? How can I—'

He choked the words back; she caught his hands and squeezed them. 'You're not,' she said softly. 'I am.'

His eyes welled again. 'What do I do now? I don't know what to do.'

He meant now, this moment. But also, she knew, from this moment forward. The rest of his life. He had lost his brother and best friend.

'We'll take it one day at a time, both of us.' She released his hands. 'I need to talk to Kitt, then I'll take you home. Okay?'

He said it was and she reentered the apartment. Kitt and Francis stood outside the bathroom, deep in discussion. M.C. struggled to compose herself. To clear her features of even the smallest hint of her true feelings.

She was not going to be sidelined from this case. She was not going to be forced to take an extended leave of absence. Somehow, she would convince Sal to allow her to work this case.

Francis caught sight of her and his expression softened with sympathy. He crossed to her and laid a hand on her arm. 'I'm sorry for your loss, Detective.'

Two losses, she silently corrected. First Dan. Now Tommy. 'Thank you, Francis,' she said instead, voice surprisingly steady. 'I appreciate that. What are you thinking so far?'

He hesitated a moment, as if startled by her demeanor. 'In terms of cause of death,' he said, 'what you see is what you get here. One shot to the occipital lobe. He didn't die instantly, but it was quick.'

For that, at least, she was grateful.

'As I told your partner, you'll have my report first thing in the morning.'

Kitt joined them. 'Take a look at this.'

She held out a photograph. It pictured Sam, Tommy and a pretty brown-haired girl wearing a *pink* jacket.

The girl the neighbor saw fleeing the scene?

'It was on the refrigerator,' Kitt said. 'Thought I'd mosey next door and see if Mrs Newhaus can ID this as the girl fleeing the scene.'

'Sam's still here. Let's see what he can tell us about her.'

Kitt frowned slightly. 'I appreciate you wanting to help out, but—'

'I'm not "helping out." I plan to work the case.'

'M.C., I don't think—'

'I've got it together,' she said firmly to Kitt. 'I promise you I do.'

'You might think you do, but you're still dealing with Dan's murder. And now Tommy—'

'I have to do this.'

'Your family needs you,' Kitt said gently. 'Go to them.'

M.C. squeezed her eyes shut. She needed them, too. She wanted to weep. To hold tightly to a loved one and grieve. Then to take a pill or drink a bottle of wine, crawl under the covers and hide from it.

But she had tried that course. And had felt lost.

She thought of her aunt Catherine. Devastated. Confused. Of her mother. The rest of the family.

Counting on her. To answer their questions, to reassure them that everything that could be done would be done.

As a cop, only she could do that. And as family, only she cared enough not to let go or give up. Not to settle for the easy answers.

Determination surged through her, energizing her. Giving her a sense of purpose. The purpose offering a way out of grief. Offering a lopsided sort of calm.

'You're right, Kitt. My family needs me. That's why I have to do this.'

Kitt sighed. 'What about Sal?'

'What about him?'

'Even if I humor you, do you really think he's going to go along with this?'

'How about this,' M.C. said, 'you humor me and I'll worry about Sal later.'

For a long moment Kitt was silent, then she looked at M.C. 'This isn't healthy. I've been here, chosen the path you're contemplating. It didn't take me anywhere good, M.C.'

'I know what I need to get me through this.' When her partner still hesitated, M.C. looked her in the eyes. 'This is the only way I can help. The only thing *I* can do. Don't take it away from me. Please.'

They gazed at each other for a long moment, then Kitt relented. 'At the first sign you're losing it, you're out of here.'

'That's not going to happen. I can promise you that.'

Even as M.C. confidently said the words, she acknowledged to herself that she was a liar. As of this moment, she was in uncharted waters. She didn't really have a clue what she was – or wasn't – capable of.

21

When they exited the apartment, Officer Thomas informed them that Sam had gone outside to smoke, making their decision of whom to show the photo to first.

The neighbor stared hard at the photo, then shook her head. 'It could be her. The jacket looks right, the hair . . . But I can't say for sure.' She handed the photo back, expression apologetic. 'I wish I'd gotten a better look at her face. I'm so sorry.'

They thanked the woman and went in search of Sam. They caught him on his way back upstairs, the cold and smell of smoke still clinging to him.

M.C. handed him the photo. 'Who's the girl, Sam?'

His expression changed subtly. 'Just a girl.'

M.C. arched her eyebrows in disbelief. 'She's in a photo of you and Tommy, a photo posted on Tommy's fridge. One dated back in November. What's the deal?'

'Her name's Zoe,' he said, jamming his hands into his pockets. 'She liked Tommy.'

'Liked,' Kitt repeated. 'What does that mean?'

'She was sort of chasing him.'

'And how did he feel about her?'

He shifted his gaze to M.C. 'I don't think Tommy would like me talking about this to you.'

'Tommy's dead,' Kitt said bluntly. 'I'm sure he'd want you to tell us anything that could lead to his killer.'

'But she didn't kill him.'

'Really? You're so certain?'

'She's a . . . girl. And she was head over heels for him.'

Kitt leaned slightly forward. 'Bizarre as it may seem to you, Sam, but many a murder is committed in the name of love.' She shifted her attention to her partner.

'How did Tommy feel about her?' M.C. asked.

'He wasn't in love with her.'

'But they were sleeping together?'

He shifted from one foot to the other, ears turning pink. 'Not routinely.'

'But they had? Slept together?'

'Yes.'

Promising. Kitt glanced at M.C. and saw by her expression that she was thinking the same thing. Girl fleeing the scene, same general description as a rejected lover. It didn't take a genius to put two and two together. Or to see that this scenario blew her theory that Tommy's killer had shot Dan in a case of mistaken identity.

'How many times did they sleep together?'

'A couple. More than a couple, three or four times.' Sam looked from one to the other of them. 'He was trying to break it off.'

Better and better.

'How would you characterize the relationship? For Tommy?'

'Fun. About the . . . you know.'

'The sex?' Kitt asked.

'Yes. Then she started getting kind of freaky.'

'Freaky?'

'Possessive. Calling all the time. Following him. Crying. Tommy hated that.'

'Did this Zoe go to school with Tommy?'

'No.'

81

'Where did he meet her?'

'Spanky's.'

A club popular with twenty-somethings. 'What about her last name?'

He spread his fingers. 'I never asked. He never said.'

Not so surprising. 'Was she a student? Did she work? Anything you can tell us might help.'

'Student, I think. Don't know what she was studying or where. That's all I know. Do you think . . . that she might . . . be the one?'

'It's possible, Sam. Although at this stage many things are possible.'

'But she . . . she seemed okay. Certainly not like a wacko who'd get a gun and—'

'Shoot somebody in the head?' Kitt filled in. 'That's the thing about the real world, Sam. The bad guys don't always look like the bad guys.'

22

Kitt sat in the quiet office. The majority of the VCB had called it a day. Sal was in his office, on the phone. When he finished his conversation, she would update him on the day's events.

Her hands trembled. She curled them into fists. She and M.C. had taken Sam to his mother's. M.C. had been determined that she share the horrible news, that it would be better coming from her, family.

But nothing could make such news better, Kitt acknowledged, and she wished she could expel the memory of those minutes from her head. The woman's keening cries. The way she had flailed at M.C., blaming her, cursing her – until she had finally collapsed, weeping.

How much pain could one family bear? Kitt wondered. How much could M.C. bear?

Kitt was frightened for her partner. Although M.C. had maintained calm, it had been robotic. A coping mechanism, Kitt recognized. She had been there once herself.

And she understood how much M.C. needed to work this case. She wished to God she didn't.

The Sleeping Angel Killer. Her desire to nail him had nearly destroyed her.

83

She knew from personal experience that right now, for M.C., the line between right and wrong, logical and irrational had blurred. And that in her longing for justice, she would act in ways she never would otherwise.

Another road she'd been down. Another dead end.

Kitt passed a hand over her face, remembering. She hadn't had anyone watching out for her. Her partner had been a good guy, a good friend and cop. But he hadn't had a clue what she was going through. Or what lengths she would go to get what she wanted.

Sadie dying. A madman killing girls Sadie's age. Blond and blue-eyed like her daughter.

Kitt rubbed the bridge of her nose, remembering how her race to save Sadie and stop the SAK had become tangled in her mind. Reliving the desperation she had felt. The relentless sense of urgency that had held her in its grip, day and night – if she could do nothing to save her own child, at least she could save someone else's.

But, like Sadie, the SAK had slipped through her fingers. And the obsession had destroyed her marriage and nearly ended her career. Before it was all over, it had almost cost her her life.

Kitt lowered her gaze to the desk, to the Mariano file. She flipped it open. Photographs. Of Tommy, lying in the bathtub. One side of his head partially blown away. Horrible to look at.

And she hadn't loved him.

M.C. had.

Sal would not allow M.C. to work the case. The victim was family. M.C. was already traumatized by the loss of her fiancé, also to a gunman's bullet.

But Sal's resistance wouldn't deter M.C. All those years ago, it hadn't stopped Kitt. If anything, it had fueled her determination. Emboldened her.

Kitt glanced at the photo once more, firming her resolve. She knew what she had to do. But it would cost her. Big time.

Cancel her trip. Take the lead. Convince Sal to allow M.C. into the loop.

Her throat tightened. Damn it, it wasn't fair! She and Joe deserved this trip. They deserved a second chance.

But M.C. had been there for Kitt when she most needed her. M.C. had put her beliefs, her ambitions, on hold to help Kitt.

But this wasn't about putting career ambitions on hold. This was about her and Joe's relationship. This was her life.

But it was also about friendship. Trust. A partnership.

How was she going to explain this to Joe?

Taking a deep breath, Kitt stood and headed for Sal's office. She needed to do this now, before she changed her mind.

The deputy chief's door stood slightly ajar; when she saw he had ended his phone conversation, she knocked.

He motioned her in. 'How's Riggio?'

'Hanging in there. Maintaining.'

He gazed at her a minute, then nodded. 'Where do we stand?'

'The good news first,' she said. 'We have a suspect. A rejected lover. According to Tommy's brother, she'd been following him. In addition, a neighbor saw a young woman of the same general description fleeing the scene.'

'Pick her up.'

'That's the bad news. At this point, all we have is a first name. Zoe. But it shouldn't take us long to find her.'

He nodded. 'Go on.'

'Mariano's cell phone is missing. She may have been the last person to call him, or perhaps had sent telling text messages. We suspect she snatched it in an attempt to conceal her identity.'

'No landline at his apartment?'

'Nope. Which isn't all that unusual. Living by cell phone alone is becoming a common occurrence, especially among young people. In addition, Mariano's laptop computer's missing.'

He frowned. 'What about that other recent case? Wasn't a computer missing from that scene as well?'

'The Martin homicide, yes. I explored the possibility of

85

the two cases being related, but think the rejected girlfriend's a stronger lead. Especially in light of the neighbor's report of a young woman fleeing the scene.'

'I agree. What next?'

'We have a photo of the girl. We plan to talk to Tommy's professors and classmates, see if anybody recognizes her.'

He cocked an eyebrow. 'We?'

'Requesting permission to have Riggio assist.'

'This victim was family,' he said. 'And she's already reeling from her fiancé's death. Not happening.'

'Not immediate family.' Kitt went on. 'And it's feeling like a quick close. We pick up the girlfriend, she's got the phone, she's got the computer and it's over.'

'If you think I'm going to let Riggio work this, you're out of your mind.'

Undeterred, she pressed. 'Not work. Assist only. Slightly more than tagging along.'

'What about Mexico? You're off in—'

'My plans have changed.'

His eyebrows shot up. 'Excuse me?'

'The trip's been canceled.'

'Since when?'

'A few minutes ago.'

He frowned. 'I know what you're trying to do, and it's a mistake.'

'I don't think so.'

'I appreciate your dedication to your partner, but I can't let you do this.'

'It's already done.' Kitt leaned forward. 'M.C. needs this, Sal. She needs to work. She needs to feel like she's *doing* something.'

'I'll put her on a desk. Or pair her up with White.'

'You know that's not good enough. I'll monitor her. If she shows any signs of cracking, she's out.' She held up a hand to keep him from responding. 'You have my word on that.'

'What about Joe?'

The question was too personal, none of his business. But she and Sal went back a long way. He had been a good friend to her. Such a good friend that without him she might not have a badge.

'He'll understand,' she said, praying it would be true. 'Mexico was just a vacation. This is—'

'Just another case,' he finished for her.

'Not to M.C. She needs me.'

'You're certain about this?'

'Absolutely.'

'If I agree, Sergeant Haas and I will be on you like white on rice.'

'Bring it on. The first sign Riggio's on shaky ground, I pull her.'

Sal studied her for a long moment. 'I don't know. I don't like it. Last thing I want is one of my detectives crashing and burning on the job.'

'You owe me,' she said, heart thundering. 'For the Sleeping Angel. I'm collecting.'

He narrowed his eyes. Kitt held her breath. Deputy Chief of Detectives Salvador Minelli was a powerful man. Liked and well-connected. And she had a sketchy record and history of instability. This could blow up in her face.

'That sounded like a threat,' he said softly.

'No sir. Just an observation.'

'One screwup and you'll wish to God you'd gone to Mexico.'

She already did. 'Yes, sir.'

'Close the door behind you.'

'Yes, sir. Thank you, sir.'

When she reached the door, he stopped her. 'And, Detective?'

She looked back at him. 'Don't ever do that to me again. You won't like what happens.'

23

Kitt waited for Joe. They had decided to meet for a quick dinner at Mary's Market Café and Bakery, one of their favorite places. They served house-made soups, sandwiches on their freshly baked breads, salads and all manner of bakery goodies and desserts.

Located near Joe's home, Mary's had started as a meeting point, a nonthreatening place to reconnect, to hesitantly test their chance of a reconciliation. As that reconciliation had started to become a reality, instead of meeting there, they went together – sometimes just rolling out of bed, throwing on jeans and baseball caps; other times, making a morning of it by hopping on their bikes and cycling to the café.

It was here, over a light supper, that the idea of the Mexico trip had been born. Ironic because here it was going to die.

Only postponed, she told herself. Joe would be disappointed, but he would deal with it. They both would.

He arrived, caught sight of her and started her way. A moment later, he bent and kissed her. 'Did you order?'

She said she had and he slipped into the chair across from hers. He reached across the table and caught her hands. 'How's M.C.?'

She had called earlier in the day, told him about Tommy. 'In my opinion, not good. She has her armor in place, acting all extreme Robocop. I'm worried about her.'

'Justifiably so.' He rhythmically trailed his thumb across her knuckles. 'I can't believe Sal won't insist on a leave of absence.'

'She needs to be involved. I understand her, Joe. What she's going through. Because I've been there. I've been to the place where all I could think of was solving a case.'

He tightened his fingers on hers. 'It was a screwed-up place to be, Kitt. It cost us our marriage, jeopardized your career. Your life.'

'I know that, though when I was in the middle of it, I had no objectivity. I'm afraid that's where M.C. is.'

'I'm sorry for her. I wish there was something I could do.'

'There is.' He didn't respond and she went on. 'If I work the case, Sal's agreed she can tag along.'

'So work the case. When we leave for Mexico, you hand it to another detective.'

'It doesn't work that way.' She drew a deep breath, then released it slowly. 'We have to cancel, Joe. I can't go. I want to, but—'

'If you wanted to go, you would.'

'M.C. needs me. Without me, she'll be shut out.'

'And maybe that's for the best. For her and the investigation.'

The server delivered their chicken potpies. She seemed to sense the tension between them and disappeared without her usual greeting. Joe pushed his aside. 'With the Sleeping Angel Killer, you *were* where M.C. is now. You know how dangerous it is when a cop loses objectivity—'

'That's why she needs me. I know her. I can be objective for her.'

'Ten days, Kitt. You can't be away from the badge for ten lousy days? This is such bullshit!'

'Timing is everything in a homicide investigation, you know that. Sal agreed to let her assist under the condition I watch her like a hawk.'

Comprehension crossed his face, angry color followed. 'You're not asking me about this, are you? You've already made a decision.'

'Try to understand—'

'This trip was about *us*. You and me. Yet you made the decision to cancel without even consulting me. Nice, Kitt.'

'We won't lose all our money, the trip insur—'

'I don't care about the money!' The words exploded from him. People at the next table turned to stare. He lowered his voice. 'I care about us. You promised.'

'How could I imagine this would happen? First Dan's killed, then Tommy. Joe, this isn't any stranger whose life's been upended. This happened to M.C. My friend. My partner.'

'I thought you wanted me to be your partner, Kitt? Your life partner.'

'I did. I do.'

'Three days ago, I asked you if you wanted to cancel. You said, "No." You were positive.'

'Things have changed.' She held a hand out. 'Please, try to understand—'

He shook his head. 'That's the problem, I do understand. You're putting the job before our relationship.'

'This is a special situation.'

'They all are, Kitt. This time M.C. needs you. Last time it was the little girls. Next time it'll be Sal. Or someone else.'

Her face flushed. 'It's so easy for you. Your work isn't life and death. Did the walls go up on schedule? Did the roofer order the right color shingles? Is the tile laid correctly?'

'Sadie was the only one who could keep you grounded. And she's gone.'

'Don't use her that way.'

'I'd never use Sadie as a tool to hurt you. It's just true, Kitt. It's a fact.'

'You're not being fair,' she said softly. 'You're not even trying to understand. We can take a trip together anytime.'

'But we won't, will we?' He let out a long, weary-sounding breath. 'It's you, Kitt, who haven't been fair to me. You who seems unwilling to understand.'

They stared at each other, both angry and hurt, neither willing to budge. How could they feel the same when they stood on opposite sides of the issue?

Because in the end, she acknowledged, they wanted the same thing. She had to find a way to convince him of that.

'Joe, I—'

Her cell vibrated. She checked the display, saw it was HQ. She hesitated and he laughed, the sound tight. 'Answer it.'

She opened the device. 'What?'

It was Miller, from ID. 'Compared the bullet retrieved from Dan Gallo to the one from Mariano. They were fired from different guns.'

That pretty much killed M.C.'s same shooter theory.

'Thought you'd want to know.'

'Thanks, Miller. I appreciate it.'

'Did it for Riggio.' It sounded like his mouth was full. 'She asked me if I could expedite.'

So much for her partner being safely cradled in the bosom of her grieving family. And just as Kitt had expected: M.C. was stepping up, making unauthorized decisions. 'When did you last speak with her?'

'A couple hours ago.'

'I'll pass along the information.'

A moment later she reholstered the phone. She looked at Joe. 'I've got to go.'

'Of course you do.'

His sarcasm stung. 'Joe, please—'

'Don't say anything else, Kitt. Just go.'

She collected her things, then stood. 'I love you.'

He stared at her for a moment, his expression bleak. 'I love you, too.'

24

Thursday, January 22
8:55 P.M.

M.C. paced her living room, too agitated to be still. The blood thrummed in her head; her thoughts raced. First Dan. Now Tommy.

The memory of her aunt's sobs and flailing fists filled her head. Gradually, the entire family had filled her aunt's small home. She'd had to face her brothers' endless questions, her mother's despair, other family members' angry disbelief. All directed at her.

How could this have happened? Why did it happen? What do we do now, M.C.?

She stopped pacing and rubbed her arms, suddenly cold. They were all counting on her. Looking to her for answers. And she had promised to bring them those answers. To take care of everything.

She fought tears. But how? At this moment, she felt nothing but broken.

Broken. Her gaze drifted to her bedroom doorway. She imagined walking through that doorway, crossing to the nightstand, to the bottle of pills that sat there. Would anyone blame her for grabbing a few hours of oblivion? A few hours without the agony of having lost both the man she loved and a young man who had been like another brother?

She stiffened, turned her eyes away. Being weak wasn't an option. Succumbing to oblivion wasn't an option. Not now.

Her cell phone vibrated and she grabbed for it, hoping it was Sorenstein with news that would link Tommy's and Dan's murders.

'Riggio.'

'Are you awake?'

Kitt. 'Are you kidding. I may never sleep again.'

'Watch what you say, partner. You're under the microscope.'

'What do you mean?'

'I'm out front. We need to talk.'

Moments later, M.C. and Kitt faced each other over M.C.'s kitchen table. 'Do you still want to work this case?' Kitt asked.

'Hell, yes, I want to work it.'

'Good. I made arrangements with Sal. He's allowing you to assist. Although tag along is a better description of what he agreed to.'

M.C. searched Kitt's expression, noticing for the first time that her eyes were red and puffy, her face blotchy.

She'd been crying. M.C. frowned. 'What did you do to make this happen?'

'Canceled my trip to Mexico. Agreed to watch you like a hawk.'

For several seconds, M.C. simply stared at her. Then she shook her head. 'But you and Joe . . . that trip was so important . . .'

Her words trailed off as she realized what Kitt had done for her. What she had sacrificed. 'I don't know what to say. I can't believe you did this for me.'

'Hear me out before you say anything. The deal I made with Sal, I'm dead serious about it.' Kitt leaned toward her partner; M.C. saw that she trembled. 'I've been where you are, M.C. Brokenhearted, looking for the job – or even

93

vengeance – as a way to escape. That road leads no place good. I lost five years of my life on that road. I lost my husband and the respect of my fellow officers. I'm not going to sit back and let you make the same mistakes I did.'

'I won't. I promise.'

'I'm not going to tiptoe around the truth. I'm going to play it like I always do, brutal or not. You might not like what I have to say, but I'm going to say it.'

'I'd be insulted by less.'

'You say that now, but—'

She held up a hand to stop Kitt. 'I can handle it. You're the boss. I'm allowed to tag along. Period.'

Her partner silently studied her, then nodded. 'Okay. We're in this together.'

Tears stung her eyes and she reached across the table and touched Kitt's hand. 'Are you certain you want to do this? I know how important this trip was to you and Joe. And if you want to change your mind—'

'It's done. I'm not going to change my mind.'

'What can I do?'

'Stay cool. Follow directions. Be honest. If you're losing it, tell me.'

'In other words, don't give Sal an opportunity to chew on your ass.'

'With that in mind, no more special requests of ID. Everything comes through me. Everything.'

'The ballistics results are in,' M.C. said.

'They didn't match. I'm sorry.'

M.C. felt as if the wind had been knocked out of her. She had been so certain they would. She let out a long breath. 'Okay. Dealing with it. What now?'

'Tommy's murder, what are our possibilities?'

'Robbery's improbable, considering. Ditto for a random act of violence.'

'A drug or gang-related murder?'

'Possible but unlikely.'

'That leaves us the rejected lover. Hell has no fury, and all that.'

94

'Zoe,' M.C. agreed. 'She shoots him, grabs the cell phone and computer and runs.'

'Why?'

'She's hoping to protect her identity. My guess is there were a shitload of incriminating e-mails on the computer. She may have even threatened him. Ditto for the phone log and text messages.'

'We have one other angle to consider. Matt Martin. Also a twenty-something student, killed in his apartment. His computer also missing.'

M.C. turned that over in her mind. 'That would mean Tommy was involved in something that got him killed.'

'Like criminal hacking.'

She pressed her fingertips to her temples, struggling for detachment. To reconcile the possibility that her cousin might have been a thief with the young man she had known and loved.

'If this is too difficult for you—'

'No, it's . . . that's just so not Tommy. He was a great kid. Always. Hard worker. Honest. Quick to offer help.'

'He lived well for a student.'

Same as Martin had.

'He worked hard. Did freelance accounting.'

'ID collected the files from his office,' Kitt offered. 'On my way over here, I stopped by the PSB and took a peek. Made a list.'

Kitt retrieved it from her bag and handed it to M.C.

'Your cousin had twenty-five business clients. All small, one-or two-person outfits. With the exception of Mama Riggio's. Frankly, that seems like a leap of faith for your brothers.'

'Tommy started as a busboy for them when they first opened. Besides, if you can't trust family, whom can you trust?'

'Bella's Biscotti,' Kitt read.

'Aunt Bella and Aunt Catherine's company.'

'Match Point?'

'Tennis shop.'

'Rent-a-Geek?'

'The tech guy Sam told us about, I'll bet.'

Kitt rattled off the others. They included two catering businesses, an in-home child care center, a couple of cleaning services and her cousin's beauty shop, among others.

'In addition,' Kitt said, 'he did taxes for about three dozen individuals, including you and your mother.'

M.C. gazed at the list, frowning. Could Tommy have been involved in criminal hacking? She just didn't think so.

'Personally, I like the girlfriend for this. It's nice and neat.'

'Personally, I do too. I say we subpoena Tommy's financial records anyway, just in case the girlfriend angle peters out.'

'You're in charge.'

'Tommy on MySpace? Or Facebook? Zoe may be on his list of friends and have left him messages.'

'I'd be surprised if he wasn't on at least one of them. I'll check it out tonight.'

Kitt stood and grabbed her coat from the back of the chair. 'I have a list of Tommy's professors. Let's start there bright and early tomorrow. I'll pick you up at eight.'

She started for the door. M.C. followed her. 'Wow, a driver and a babysitter.'

'I said I was going to keep my eye on you.' Kitt stepped out into the cold, black night, then glanced back at her. 'I just want you to be prepared, M.C. You might learn some things about your cousin . . . and Dan for that matter, you'd rather not have known.'

25

M.C. had been ready and waiting when Kitt tooted the horn for her at seven fifty A.M. She looked like she hadn't slept, though Kitt couldn't say much about that – she hadn't either.

She'd tossed and turned, thinking of Joe, their relationship, remembering his bleak good-bye. Praying she hadn't killed whatever shot they'd had of getting back together.

'I didn't have any luck accessing Tommy's MySpace or Facebook pages,' M.C. said. 'They were private, which means you have to be a "friend" to see his page. I figured Sam could help, but he didn't answer my calls so I left him a message.'

Kitt nodded and turned onto Easton Parkway, the entrance to Rockford College, a small liberal arts school known for its rigorous academics. 'I called ahead. The dean of students is expecting us. She suggested we see Tommy's adviser first.'

'Professor Rick Taylor,' M.C. said, reading from the list Kitt had assembled, then pointed. 'Visitor parking.'

'That's us.' Kitt followed the signs, parked and they climbed out.

They started across the parking lot, heading toward Scarborough Hall, where Tommy's adviser's office was located. Students streamed around and past them, a few sending curious glances their way. She supposed that she and M.C. didn't look the part of either student or teacher.

They reached the building. Inside, after consulting the building directory, they made their way to the professor's office. M.C. tapped on the closed door. A small, nearly bald man with big eyes and a well-trimmed beard appeared at the sidelight window.

'Professor Taylor?' M.C. held up her shield. 'Detectives Riggio and Lundgren.'

He reminded her of a cross between a hobbit and an elf and as he opened the door, she had to keep herself from glancing down to see if he had feet to match.

'Hello, Detectives.'

'Thank you for taking the time to meet with us this morning.'

'Unfortunately, I don't have too long. I have a nine o'clock lecture to finish preparing. I've been out of town the last couple of days.' He moved his gaze between them. 'How can I help you?'

'We're investigating the death of—'

'Tommy Mariano, I know. But how can *I* help you?'

'I understand you were his academic adviser.'

He nodded. 'He was a good student. Serious about his studies and future. I work with too many kids who hardly give a shit. Mommy and Daddy expect them to get a degree and the kids expect to be given one.'

Kitt hid her surprise at his language. She would have expected a professor to sound more . . . scholarly. And certainly be more discreet.

'Tommy didn't have that entitlement thing going on. He was working his way through and had his eyes fixed firmly on his goal. Refreshing change of pace for me.'

'And what, in your opinion, was his goal?'

'Get his degree. Be hired by one of the big Chicago accounting firms. Make buckets of money. Not my opinion, by the way. That's a fact. He told me.'

Kitt saw M.C. frown slightly. 'When's the last time you spoke with Tommy?'

'Thursday last week.'

'What did you discuss?'

'Nothing much. We're a small college. We make a point of checking in with our students regularly. I saw Tommy at least once a week.'

He paused, eyebrows lowered in thought. 'Recently, something was troubling him. He was distracted. Remote.'

'When did that start?'

'A week or two ago.' He paused, as if for a mental review. 'Yes, two weeks.'

'You know your students awfully well.'

'What's that supposed to mean?'

The man possessed an arrogant air that set Kitt's teeth on edge. 'Nothing at all. Just stating what seems to be a fact. What alerted you something was wrong? Had his grades fallen? Had one of his teachers come to you or—'

'His behavior, Detective. I work closely with my advisees and I know immediately when something's not right.'

'Did you try to talk to him?'

'Yes. He said he was fine. Just "a little tired."'

'But you didn't buy that?'

'No.'

'Do you recognize the girl in this picture?'

Kitt handed it to him. He studied it a moment, then handed it back. 'Sure. I saw her around a couple times.'

'With Tommy?'

'Yes. And the one they're pictured with. His brother, right? Sam.' When she nodded, he added, 'Like I said, I make it a point to know my advisees. Tommy was a good guy.'

'You know her name?'

'Sorry. Seems to me the brother would know. Try asking him.'

Kitt stepped in again. 'Who were Tommy's close friends?'

'He didn't have many close friends. I'd classify him as a loner.'

'Excuse me?' M.C. said, an edge in her voice. 'Everyone we spoke with said—'

'He was likable. Extremely. But not that social.'

99

'Could he have been doing drugs?' Kitt felt M.C.'s glance and ignored it. 'Could that account for the change in his demeanor?'

'You're looking for a reason he was killed.' The man stroked his beard, expression thoughtful. 'Anything's possible. Believe me, teaching young people, I've seen it all. Truth is though, I don't think so. Not Tommy Mariano. I'd go for the fatal attraction girlfriend first.'

'The fatal attraction girlfriend,' M.C. repeated. 'Did we say anything about that?'

He cocked an eyebrow. 'I'm not stupid, Detective. A nice kid's shot dead. You show me a picture of a girl you're looking for. It's not rocket science.'

Kitt stepped in before M.C. had a chance to retort. 'You're a smart guy, Professor Taylor.'

'I am, indeed.'

Arrogant bastard. 'You said you were out of town the last couple days?'

'Yes. An academic seminar at the University of Chicago. About the politics of economics.'

'Sounds fascinating.'

'It is, actually.'

'It was a two-day seminar so you stayed overnight?'

'Yes.'

'What hotel?'

He frowned. 'Hotel? No, I stayed with a friend. He teaches at the university. European literature.'

'What's his name? Your friend's?'

'Pardon me?'

'Your friend's name. You do know it?'

He bristled. 'Of course. But why do you need it? That makes no sense.'

When she didn't respond, he looked at Kitt. She simply gazed back at him.

He made a sound of annoyance. 'I don't want him involved in this.'

'In what?'

He flushed. 'This. The investigation.'

'Why would he be? I don't understand.'

Playing dumb – an investigative tactic as old as time. And irritating as hell to someone like Taylor.

'My friend had nothing to do with this.'

'Are you saying you did? Or is there some other reason you don't want to give us your friend's name?'

'Danny Stephanopolis.'

'European history?'

'Literature,' he corrected. 'University of Chicago. Happy?'

'Happy?' Kitt repeated. 'We're investigating the murder of a bright young man with his entire life before him. What do you think?'

Moments later they exited the building, following the professor's directions to Nelson Hall. The dean of students was next on their hit parade.

'What did you think of Taylor?' M.C. asked.

'Pompous ass.'

'We struck a nerve by asking his friend's name. What's your theory?'

'Could be a number of things. One of them being he's lying about his whereabouts these past two days.'

'Easy enough to verify.'

'The question is, why would he lie?'

M.C. frowned. 'What he said about Tommy's goal being to make buckets of money working for a big Chicago firm wasn't right. Tommy was all about home and family. Always had been.'

'The good news is he recognized our girl.'

They crossed the tree-lined walkway to Nelson Hall. 'Dean Johnsen claims to be able to put a name to every face on campus. Maybe we'll have more luck with her.'

The dean's office was located on the second floor; Kitt opened the door for M.C. They were greeted by the dean's secretary, a grandmotherly type with a warm smile.

'You must be the detectives. I'm Connie. Dean Johnsen's secretary.'

'Hi, Connie,' M.C. responded, returning her smile. 'We appreciate the dean taking time out to speak with us.'

'Of course she would! What a horrible thing . . . Tommy was such a sweet boy.' Her eyes filled with tears. 'I cried when I heard.'

'Did you know him well?'

'I know all the boys and girls. And they're all special to me.' She cleared her throat. 'I've been here thirty years. I'm retiring in May.'

'Congratulations.'

'Not my choice, actually. But thank you anyway. I plan to make the best of it.'

'Tell me, Connie, do you know any reason someone would have wanted to harm Tommy Mariano?'

'Oh, my gosh, no! Like I said, he was a sweet boy.'

'When was the last time you saw him?'

'This week. In the Lion's Den. That's our student center. He was eating French fries.'

'Was he alone?'

'No. He was with a girl.'

Kitt's heart beat a bit faster. 'A girlfriend?'

'Maybe. They definitely knew each other well.' She leaned slightly forward. 'I could tell by their body language.'

'What do you mean?'

'They weren't holding hands or kissing, but their heads were close together.'

'Was she a student here?'

'No.'

'What day was that?' Kitt asked.

She drew her eyebrows together in thought. 'This Wednesday. They were deep in conversation. Something real personal.'

The day before he died. 'Did you speak to him? Or over-hear them?' She shook her head. 'Then how did you know their conversation was "real personal"?'

'Again, body language. She had her hand on his arm and it seemed as if she was pleading with him.'

Pleading. And twenty-four hours later he's dead.

'Was this the girl?' Kitt asked, holding out the photo.

'I think so. Yes.'

'Absolutely, yes?'

She bit her lower lip, looking hesitant for the first time. 'I didn't get a good look at her face, but I'm 90 percent certain.'

'Had you ever seen her before?'

'No. Like I said, she's not a student here.' Her expression went soft with distress. 'Things like this don't happen in Rockford. And they don't happen to our students.'

'She's right, Detectives. This is a safe campus. Very much a family atmosphere.'

They shifted their attention to the stately brunette crossing the room, hand extended. 'You must be Dean Johnsen?'

'Yes. Madeline Johnsen.'

M.C. reached her first. 'Detective Riggio. My partner, Detective Lundgren.'

'Come into my office.' She motioned to the inner doorway, then looked at her secretary. 'Connie, hold all calls.'

Kitt moved her gaze over the room. Clean lines. Functional and no-nonsense, like the woman who sat behind the desk and faced them now.

'We're all devastated. This is so horrible . . . such a tragedy. Anything we can do to help, anything at all.'

'Thank you, Dean. Is this girl a student here?'

Kitt handed her the photo. The woman studied it a moment, then handed it back. 'No, I don't recognize her.'

'You're certain she's not enrolled?'

'Absolutely. We have less than seven hundred full-time students and pride ourselves in being the choice for those who want to be more than a face in the crowd.'

'Ever see her on campus?'

'Again, no.' She looked genuinely regretful. 'Did you try Rock Valley? She might be a student there.'

'Thank you. We will.' Kitt slid the photograph back into her coat pocket. 'We'll need Tommy's class schedule, student rosters for those classes.'

'Class rosters?' she repeated.

'We'd like to question his classmates.'

When she hesitated, Kitt added, 'A minute ago you assured us you'd help in any way possible.'

'And I will. However, privacy issues don't allow me to simply hand over the names of our students.'

'We could subpoena them. But that takes time. Time we can't afford. What if another one of your students dies?'

The woman paled. 'Certainly you don't think . . . that's not a possibility?'

'We can't rule it out. Another student death would be terrible publicity for the college.'

M.C. stepped in. 'All it takes is one tragedy and your every decision is criticized. Virginia Tech is a prime example.'

Kitt agreed. 'And I'd hate to see that sort of thing aimed your way.'

'Let me consult with the college president. Ultimately, it's his call.'

Kitt understood the game. Pass the hot potato, a time-honored tradition. If something bad happened, the next guy's neck would be the one on the chopping block.

'Can you call him now?'

'He's in a meeting this morning.'

She said it quickly, so quickly M.C. was certain it was a lie. She let it pass.

'I'll e-mail him immediately, then follow up with a call to his secretary.'

Another time-honored tradition, pass the buck in writing. And cc the hell out of it.

She stood. M.C. followed her to her feet. 'When will you have a chance to speak with him?'

'By noon.'

'I look forward to hearing from you. Thank you for your time.'

26

Friday, January 23
9:00 P.M.

M.C. turned onto her street, rolling slowly past the darkened homes of her neighbors. Twelve hours had passed and they were no closer to identifying the girl in the picture. M.C. acknowledged fatigue. Frustration. She and Kitt had spent the entire day tracking down people who had known Tommy; all but a few had heard about the murder already and had been shocked, devastated or a combination of the two.

And not one had recognized the girl in the photo by name, though like Connie in the dean's office, a number had 'seen her around.'

She and Kitt had also passed Martin's photo by Tommy's friends, neighbors and Aunt Catherine. They'd cross-checked schools, clubs and organizations, going back to their elementary school years, looking for a connection point between the two young men – and had come up empty.

Tomorrow we bury Tommy. M.C. involuntarily tightened her fingers on the steering wheel.

Another funeral. The second time in two weeks she had to say good-bye to someone she loved. Dan's image filled her head and for a moment, the longing that filled her was so great she couldn't breathe.

She struggled past it, tears burning her eyes. *Focus on tomorrow, Riggio. The job at hand. Catch the son of a bitch.*

M.C. had reviewed the plans. Cameras would be positioned at all the funeral home's entrances and exits; the committal at the cemetery would be monitored by detectives. Photos of Zoe had been distributed to all the officers working the funeral.

A murderer attending his victim's funeral wasn't an unusual occurrence. The reasons they did were as varied as those of murder itself. Some went out of grief or to pay their respects, twisted as that sounded. Some came to relive the thrill of the kill. And still others out of simple, if morbid, curiosity.

Would Zoe be there? And if she wasn't, what did *that* say about her innocence?

As she neared her house, M.C. saw a bright yellow Jeep Cherokee parked in her drive. Sam's car.

He'd surfaced. Finally. She had tried him three times during the course of the day without a response. Even Aunt Catherine hadn't been able to reach him.

She pulled into the drive, parked beside the Jeep and climbed out. Sam sat on her front steps, his head in his hands. He looked up at her when she reached him. He'd been crying. A bottle in a paper bag rested on the porch beside him.

'You're drunk,' she said.

'I didn't know where else to go.'

He'd always gone to Tommy, she realized, a catch in her chest.

With a terrible sense of déjà vu, she held out her hand. 'Car keys, please.' He dug them out of his pocket and handed them to her. She dropped them into her purse and sat down beside him. 'How long have you been here?'

He shrugged. 'Does it matter?'

'Maybe. It's pretty damn cold.'

'I'm okay.'

'Lucky you. But I don't have a bellyful of booze keeping me warm.' She stood. 'Come on in. You hungry? I'll get us something to eat.'

'I guess.' His words slurred slightly.

They entered the house and he followed her to the kitchen. She peeked in the refrigerator, then looked over her shoulder at him. 'I have some leftover cheese cannelloni. Or I could make you a peanut butter sandwich.'

'I'll take the sandwich.'

'Good choice. Glass of milk?'

'Beer.'

'I don't think so. Coffee?'

'You got this all wrong, cuz. I'm not looking to sober up.'

'Then you came to the wrong place. And now you're stuck with me.'

He groaned. 'You're such a bossy bitch.'

She smiled. 'I'll take that as a compliment.'

'You would.'

She chuckled and got busy. He sat slumped at the kitchen table while she made the sandwiches. She'd babysat for both him and Tommy when she was a teen and they were annoying-as-hell grade-schoolers. She knew how he liked his peanut butter sandwich: chunky peanut butter, slathered on thick, topped with banana slices. Or miniature marshmallows. She opted for banana tonight; he had enough sugar in his system for one night.

She set the food on the table in front of him.

'I'll take a milk,' he said, tone grudging.

'Good thinking.' She nudged her glass across the table and went to pour herself another. By the time she'd returned to the table, he'd already finished one of his two sandwiches.

'Want to talk about it?' she asked, then took a bite.

'Not really.'

'Then why're you here?'

'I told you, I had nowhere else to—'

'Go? Please, we both know that's not true. You have a home, a bed. Friends to drink with.'

'Screwups like me.'

Now they were getting somewhere. 'You think you're a screwup?'

'Everybody does. Don't pretend otherwise.'

'Look, Sam' – she washed down a bite of sandwich with

107

a swig of milk – 'you're twenty-one. You're a guy. And you're Italian. Being a screwup is practically a requirement.'

'Tommy was all those things and he wasn't.'

True. Aunt Catherine used to joke that Tommy had been thoughtful even in the womb: she'd had no morning sickness, a quick, nearly painless birth and he'd slept through the night starting at two weeks old.

With Sam, on the other hand, she'd had morning sickness for damn near the entire pregnancy, a difficult birth and, to add insult to injury, he'd been colicky. If she remembered right, he'd still not been sleeping all night at two years old.

'Tommy was a . . . special case.'

'Of course he was,' he said, tone bitter. 'I should be the one who's dead.'

'Don't say that. It's not true.'

'You're the one who said it, he was the special one.'

'Special as in "not the norm." It's okay to be a normal kid, Sam.'

'I'm twenty-one. Hardly a kid.'

M.C. didn't smile. She knew it would either infuriate or insult him. 'A normal young man then. We all make mistakes. We all struggle to find our place in the world.'

His eyes welled with tears. 'Why'd this happen? Why didn't I stay over that night? Maybe then . . . maybe I could have saved him.'

Her bite of sandwich caught in her throat. She fought to swallow it, overcome with her own guilt. Eyes burning, she reached across the table and covered his hand with hers. 'Do you think I haven't thought the same thing? That I haven't wished I'd answered his call? Stopped by his place instead of Erik Sundstrand's?'

'You can't understand.'

'No?' Her voice cracked. 'What about Dan? I ask myself why? I think, if only I'd driven Tommy's car. If only I'd been right behind him. Or delayed his departure. Five minutes, Sam. And Dan would be alive.'

Sam's face screwed up with pain. 'He was my brother, my best friend. I miss him so much. I can't believe he's gone—'

He broke down, sobbing. She went around the table, drew him up and into her arms. She held him while he cried, unable to hold back her own tears.

She would find the person who did this to them, she silently vowed. She had to. For closure. Without it, she didn't know if they would be able to go on.

'I'm okay,' he muttered, pulling awkwardly away from her, turning his head.

'Don't be embarrassed,' she said softly, her own voice thick. 'It's okay to cry.'

'Doesn't mean I have to like it. And I'm *not* embarrassed.'

She didn't press the issue. 'You need to get some sleep. Tomorrow's going to be a hard day.'

'I'm not going to the funeral,' he said. 'I can't.'

'You're his brother, you have to.'

'No, I don't. Tommy would understand.'

'Time to grow up, buddy. Your mother needs you there.'

'She has lots of people to take care of her.'

'But she only has one son.'

He wanted to argue, she could tell. To his credit, he held back. 'C'mon,' she said. 'Help me make up the couch.'

Making up the couch consisted of throwing down a pillow and a blanket. She found him a spare toothbrush and advised he use it. 'I'm leaving early tomorrow. You want me to wake you up?'

'Yeah. Though I can be a little scary in the morning.'

She laughed. 'I'm a Riggio. You can't scare me.' She crossed to the light switch. 'Get some sleep.'

He stopped her before she flipped off the light. 'M.C.?' She met his eyes. 'Thanks.'

She realized that it was she who was thankful. She had arrived home wired, sleep a million miles away. Now her bed beckoned and sleepiness tugged strongly at her, so strongly she could barely keep her eyes open.

Sam's pain had taken her outside her own.

'I'm glad you came to me, Sam. Sleep well.'

27

To M.C.'s surprise, Sam was already up when she made it to the kitchen the next morning. He had figured out how to operate the coffeepot and was watching it brew. His hair was wet. His laptop computer sat open on the kitchen table.

'Hey,' she said. 'You already showered?'

'I hope you don't mind?'

'Mind? I hate to tell you this, but you stank.'

'That wasn't my bod you were smelling, it was my breath.'

She laughed. 'Took care of that too, I hope.'

'I did. You want me to breathe on you?'

The coffee burbled its last and she crossed to the pot. 'I'll take your word for it.'

'I got your message about Tommy's MySpace page.' He motioned toward the laptop. 'I meant to do this last night, but frankly—'

'Were too drunk to remember your password?' She poured them both a cup of the coffee and handed him his.

He took it, one corner of his mouth lifting in a sheepish grin. 'Pretty much.'

'You want some cereal?' She took a box from the pantry and shook it. 'Clusters and twigs.'

'That stuff tastes like cardboard.'

'But it's really, really good for you.'

'No Cocoa Puffs?'

'Not a one. There's sugar in the bowl in the cupboard above the coffeepot.'

While she poured both of them a bowl of the cereal, he retrieved the sugar. Amused, she watched as he spooned an inch-thick layer on the contents of his bowl, then took a bite and murmured his approval.

'By the way, does your mother know where you are?'

'I called her last night, before you got home. Told her I was staying with you. Good thing you invited me, huh?'

She rolled her eyes. 'Yeah, good thing.'

He sat at the table in front of the computer, keeping his cereal bowl a safe distance away. Smart move, she thought. Within family circles, Sam Mariano had long been called Pigpen.

He took a bite, typed in what M.C. presumed was a username and password, navigated a bit, then turned the computer toward her. 'Voilà.'

Tommy's MySpace page.

She stared at the screen, dominated by two photos of Tommy. In one, he was hamming for the camera – acting like a big, stupid guy. In the other, he and Sam stood, shirtless, an arm looped over the other's shoulder, grinning from ear to ear.

A lump formed in her throat. Brothers. Best buds. Not a care in the world.

She glanced at Sam, then wished she hadn't. He looked shattered.

She dragged her attention from the two photos to the page format. A bio section called About Me. Another devoted to interests: Favorite music. Books. Movies. Then another called Details. Here he'd posted things like body type, zodiac sign and sexual orientation.

She scrolled down to an area devoted to his friends. It consisted of a collage of snapshots, each labeled with a name.

'There she is,' Sam said. 'Zoe. Click on her name.'

M.C. did. It took them to Zoe's page. She called herself 'the "Z" girl.' About Me was empty and information in the other areas was useless. She was an Aquarian. Single. But occupation was blank. As was residence, schools and so on.

'Damn it,' she muttered. 'No last name, no address. Nothing.'

'Last names are actually against the rules. So are addresses. You can get kicked off for posting that stuff, though a lot of people do it anyway.'

'This has been wiped.'

'Wiped?' Sam repeated. 'What does that mean?'

'Sanitized. Cleaned of anything we might have been able to track her by. Look, her bio's blank. Is there a back door?' she asked.

'To her information?'

'Yeah, somewhere else personal data is found.'

'You have to provide all that stuff when you register.' *And she'd need a subpoena to get it.*

'I've been thinking, M.C.,' he said. 'I want to help you catch the guy who did this. I think I can.'

Without giving her a chance to react, he went on. 'I'll hit the clubs. Zoe's bound to show. When she does, I call you and keep her in sight until you get there.'

'Sam—'

He cut her off. 'Before you say no, keep in mind that if I question someone they'll be a lot more willing to be real with me, since I'm not a cop.'

She pushed her bowl of soggy cereal away. How did she explain to him that not being a cop was exactly why he shouldn't do it? 'Sam,' she said gently, 'I appreciate you wanting to help. I know Tommy would, too. But you need to leave it to me and Kitt.'

'I know I can do this!'

'I know you can, too. But that doesn't mean you should. Have you considered that what you're proposing could put you in harm's way?'

'Harm's way? C'mon, M.C. That's just drama.'

112

'Drama? Somebody out there, perhaps this Zoe you want to lay in wait for, shot Tommy in cold blood. What's to say they wouldn't do it again?'

'What do you mean?'

'Kill again,' she said. 'Kill you. To protect themselves.'

His expression lost its puppy dog earnestness. Obviously, he hadn't thought of that.

Damn, he was young.

'Besides, this might not be just about Tommy.' She retrieved the photograph of Matt Martin and handed it to him. 'You ever see this guy before?'

He frowned. 'Why?'

'Just answer the question. Do you recognize him?'

For long moments, he stared silently at the picture, then shook his head. 'Who is he?'

'Name's Matt Martin. Matthew. You ever hear the name before?'

He scrunched up his face in thought. 'It sort of sounds familiar but not really. It's kind of an ordinary name.'

'Ever hear Tommy mention it?'

'No.'

'You're absolutely certain?'

'Yeah, I guess. I mean, absolutely sounds so final.'

'Think carefully. It's important.'

He was quiet for a moment, then met her eyes. 'I never heard Tommy say that name. Absolutely. Why?'

'He was murdered. About a week before Tommy.'

'Murdered,' he repeated. 'Oh, my God.' She saw a half-dozen emotions skip across his features, the last being understanding. 'You think the same person who killed Tommy killed this guy?'

'Not necessarily, but there are some similarities between the two deaths so we have to pursue it.'

'So you're looking for a connection between them. Like, if they were friends or classmates.'

'Yes. And if we find one, it blows the jilted girlfriend theory to hell. And presents other issues.'

At his blank expression she explained. 'That Tommy was

involved with something that got him killed. Or that we have a serial killer out there. One who's targeting young men.'

Like Tommy. And like Sam.

He stared at the photo. 'Who was he?' he asked, voice shaking. 'Not his name, but who—'

'A computer science student at RVC. I can't tell you more than that. Sorry.'

They parted a short time later. M.C. took one last glance back at him as she pulled away from the curb.

He looked like a lost little boy.

28

Cold and damp. The sun hidden by low-hanging, gunmetal-gray clouds. A day to bury a murdered son. A young man who'd had his entire life before him.

M.C. stood graveside, shoulder to shoulder with her brothers, holding one another up. She looked out at the crowd that had gathered, the sea of blacks and browns, punctuated by the white of tissues, the sound of weeping, the priest's strong voice.

'. . . *we fell from grace and death entered our world . . .*'

Her gaze touched on Aunt Catherine. Looking at the pain etched on her features was almost more than she could bear. Beside her stood Sam. His hand on her arm, expression stoic. Almost frozen.

'. . . *we ask you to look upon this grave and bless it . . .*'

The church had been filled to overflowing. Family. Childhood friends and ones from the college. Teachers past and present. Acquaintances and the curious. Tommy had been universally liked.

'. . . *we commit to the earth the body of your servant, Thomas Anthony Mariano . . .*'

The service had been draining. She had been torn between

115

personal grief and the job. She had found herself anxiously keeping tabs on her fellow detectives, their progress. If something happened, she wanted to be ready.

'*We ask all this through Christ our Lord.*'

'Amen,' M.C. responded.

They began to lower the casket into the ground. Aunt Catherine sagged against Sam, her high, anguished cry catching on the breeze, carrying. Sam steadied his mother, his own face contorting with grief.

'*. . . we commit Tommy's body to the earth, for we are dust and unto dust we shall return . . .*'

On her right, Michael caught her hand and held it tightly. She saw that he was crying. On her left, her brother Neil held on to Melody, eyes bright with tears. She had wept so many tears in the past two weeks, but now her eyes were dry.

Why? M.C. wondered. She wanted the release tears would bring. The comfort of falling apart. Instead, bottled-up grief fueled her determination, her longing to punish. Dan had been snatched from her. Now Tommy.

Both investigations nowhere yet. Dan's at a standstill. Not for long. She would find their killers, she would bring them to justice.

Seeking vengeance was a sin. Even more so here, in front of God. She knew it, but it raged inside her anyway.

Was Tommy's killer here? she wondered. Be it Zoe or another? If so, what was he or she thinking? Secretly smiling? The thought made her angry. Her cheeks grew hot with it.

Beside her, Michael stirred. She sensed him looking at her, concerned.

'It's over,' he said softly.

It was. The tight clusters of loved ones had begun to disperse. Sam was leading Aunt Catherine to the limo. Mama had offered her home for family and friends to gather; she and several other relatives had been cooking nonstop since yesterday.

They could have had Mama Riggio's cater it; her brothers had offered. But food, the act of lovingly preparing with hands and heart then sharing with family, was an integral part of their lives. A way to celebrate, to grieve, to show respect and express love.

'Are you okay?' Michael asked.

'Yes.' She responded automatically, her voice robotic to her own ears. 'I'm fine.'

He searched her expression. 'You don't look fine. You don't sound fine.'

'I can't believe he's gone. Either of them.'

'I'm here for you, you know that. Right?'

She stood on tiptoe and kissed his cheek. 'I do know that, Michael. Thank you.'

'Detective Riggio?'

She turned. Agent Jonathan Smith stood behind her. 'I'm sorry for your loss,' he said.

'Thank you.' She waited. The agent's gaze slid momentarily to Michael before returning to hers. 'Could I have a moment?'

She squeezed her brother's hand. 'I'll be there as soon as I can. Tell Mama and Aunt Catherine.'

He nodded, bent and kissed her cheek. 'See you in a little bit.'

She watched him walk away, then faced the agent. 'How can I help you?'

'Your brother?' he asked.

'One of them. I have five.'

'A big family. That's nice. I'm an only.'

'I find it hard to believe you've sought me out for small talk, Agent Smith. Especially here.'

'I have information. About your cousin.'

Her eyebrows shot up. 'My cousin Tommy?'

'Yes. About his murder. It might shed some light.'

'Let me get my partner.'

M.C. scanned the group, looking for Kitt. When she found her, she saw her partner had already spotted the agent, and nodded at M.C.'s motion to join them.

A moment later Kitt reached their side. 'Agent Smith,' she said. 'This is a surprise.'

'He says he has information about Tommy's murder.'

'Information that might shed light on his murder,' the man corrected.

M.C. motioned them to follow her out of earshot of the others. There, she turned to Smith. 'I'm listening.'

'Your cousin contacted me three days ago.'

M.C. wasn't certain what she had expected him to say, but it wasn't that. 'Tommy contacted you?'

'Our office. The cybercrimes unit.'

M.C. frowned. 'Go on.'

'Tommy claimed a "friend" of his had become involved with a group of cyberthieves. This "friend" wanted out. But the ring's leader refused to let him go and had threatened him.'

'Threatened him how?'

'Bodily harm.' Smith cleared his throat. 'So he turned to the bureau for help.'

He'd needed help, that's why he'd come to see her that Thursday before the party, she realized. But he'd chickened out. Then, after Dan was killed, he wouldn't have come to her. Because he blamed himself for Dan.

Kitt stepped in. 'Specifically, what kind of help?'

'He wanted to know whether, if this "friend" provided evidence against the ring and its leader, he could avoid prosecution.'

'What did this ring of crackers steal?'

'Credit card numbers. Bank account numbers and passwords. Other personal information. Though I don't know what kind of information they specialized in. Or their method of acquiring it. Different groups, different methods.'

The agent cleared his throat again. 'Some of the groups are strictly small time,' he continued. 'Others are international cartels as intricate and sophisticated as the mafia.'

'But harder to catch,' Kitt said.

'Yes. Because of the nature of the crime. Information is jacked, then electronically transferred from one account to another. It's not until goods are purchased with the stolen numbers that we have a physical lead to trace. And then all we get is the reshipper or money mules. Because the crimes are electronic, the folks up and down the line are untraceable. Sometimes, they don't even exist.'

'Don't exist?' M.C. repeated. 'How so?'

Smith rubbed his hands together. As cold as it was, M.C. wondered why he didn't wear gloves. 'Jacked computers used as "bots" that receive and send information. I believe the group Tommy, or his "friend," was involved in was local, made up of young people. The leader is most probably older and has some sort of influence over them.'

'How do these kids hack into your computer?' Kitt asked.

'Lots of ways. By driving through neighborhoods armed with nothing but a laptop, searching for an open, unsecured wireless network. When they find one, they log on, then using specialized software, begin downloading your secrets.'

'What if you don't have any secrets for these crackers to steal?' M.C. asked.

'We all have secrets, Detective Riggio. The keys to our kingdoms, whether large or small. Usernames and passwords. Credit card numbers, socials, birth dates.

'It's so easy,' he continued. 'A keystroke logger delivered through e-mail attachments, by way of "free" software and cookies. Phishing scams that trick you into handing over the keys. And now the Evil Twin Attack.'

Kitt arched her eyebrows. 'Evil Twin?'

'The cracker sits in a public hot spot, like a coffee shop or airport. His computer is fitted with Hotspotter software, which allows his computer to overpower the legitimate access provider, basically taking its place. When the unsuspecting customer logs on to the free wireless, he's logging on to the Evil Twin, basically handing over all his personal information.'

'I use hot spot Wi-Fi all the time,' Kitt said. 'So does Joe.'

'The keys to the kingdom,' Smith said again. 'These crooks can even read your e-mail.'

M.C. frowned, thinking of the family gathering at her mother's, aware of the minutes ticking by. 'When did Tommy call you?'

'The day before his murder. Wednesday afternoon, the twenty-first. He refused a meeting. Said he wanted my assurance, then would confer with his friend and call me back. Next thing I know, he's dead.'

M.C. glanced at Kitt. She saw that she was also thinking about Matt Martin.

'Tommy's computer was missing,' Kitt said. 'Also his cell phone. We were focusing in another direction, but this changes things.'

'Martin could be the friend Tommy referred to,' M.C. offered.

'He could be,' the agent agreed, 'but consider this as well, Detective Riggio. There was no friend. Tommy had involved himself with this group of crackers. They killed him because he wanted out. Or because they learned he had contacted the bureau.'

M.C. had told herself she was prepared for this possibility, but she stiffened anyway. Offended. 'If Tommy said he was calling about a friend, he was.'

Smith's expression turned pitying. 'I understand, Detective. It's hard to see flaws in the ones we love.'

'I knew Tommy. You didn't.'

He held her gaze for a long moment. 'You may be right. It doesn't change the fact that he contacted me about a group of cyberthieves. Or that he very well may have been killed because of it.'

Smith paused. 'I want this group. You want Tommy's killer. I suggest we work together. We bust this thing open, we both get what we want.'

'Mutual cooperation?' Kitt said.

'Absolutely.' He smiled, a lopsided curving of his lips. 'Think about it. You have my card, call me when you've had time to process.'

29

Saturday, January 24
3:00 P.M.

Kitt sat at her computer. After the funeral, she'd returned here to study the surveillance tapes and wait for M.C. to return. Agent Smith's bombshell had come at the perfect time. It gave them a motivation for both Tommy's and Martin's murders. Linking the two crimes opened up the investigations.

So what part did the fleeing girl play in the scenario? Was she the friend Tommy had been trying to help? Had there been any friend, or as Agent Smith suspected, had Tommy himself been involved with the cyberthieves?

She liked the latter. It was cleaner. More true to life, as cynical as that was. In real life the one who looked guilty almost always was, and few people were eager to extend a helping hand to a friend in trouble – especially trouble with the law.

M.C. would resist the suggestion that her cousin was involved in anything illegal. She was too damn close to look at it objectively.

Which was where Kitt came in.

She glanced at the clock, thoughts turning to Joe. He'd come to the funeral. She'd been working; they hadn't spoken.

She had planned to catch him after the committal, but he'd slipped away without a word to her.

Her chest tightened. The silence had hurt. It still did. She felt as if a part of her had been ripped away.

Maybe the best part.

'Hey.'

Kitt looked up at her partner. She had changed out of her black suit and into a pair of comfortable-looking chinos.

'Hey back. You okay?'

'Yeah.'

'How'd it go?'

'As well as can be expected. A young man with his whole life before him is dead.'

'You could've taken the rest of the day.'

'That wasn't happening. Especially now.'

After Agent Smith's bomb.

'What are you thinking?' Kitt asked.

'Tommy wasn't involved. He was helping a friend, just like he said.'

'You're certain?'

'I knew Tommy. What he was – and wasn't – capable of.'

'And he wasn't a thief?'

'Absolutely not. Period.'

'But this makes sense,' she said softly. 'You can see that, right? You can see this is a huge step forward in the investigation?'

'Yeah, I see that. I'm not totally blinded by my affection for Tommy.' She leaned toward Kitt, expression fierce. 'Tommy was telling the truth. Trying to help a friend who was in trouble. He was like that. A good guy with a big heart. That's what he was trying to tell me on my birthday.'

Kitt couldn't help but think of Tommy's nice apartment, of Matt Martin's place. Of the kind of income needed to support that. She kept her thoughts to herself. For now.

'Okay,' Kitt murmured, 'we have a motivation for the killings. A friend confided in Tommy. He was in trouble. Big trouble. He'd done something stupid. Illegal. Now he wanted out. But others were refusing to let him go.'

122

'Tommy steps in. Calls the bureau. The ring's leader finds out about his involvement, that he called the feds, and kills him. Or has him killed. Which would explain the seemingly random, execution-style shooting.

'Execution-style,' M.C. went on, 'the same way Dan was killed. This reopens the possibility that Dan's death was a case of mistaken identity. It makes sense.'

Kitt agreed. 'Have you spoken to White about this?'

Detective White was the lead in Dan's murder investigation. 'Last we spoke, he'd hit a wall. I'll fill him in, see where this takes him.'

'So, who's Martin?'

'The friend. Obviously.' M.C. tucked her hair behind her ear. 'Think about it, the missing computers make sense now. There's information on the computers that'll lead to the cyberthieves.'

'But if Tommy was only helping Martin, why take Tommy's computer?'

M.C. frowned slightly. 'The friend shared information. Or they worried that he had. He knew too much. It was a precaution.'

Kitt sat back in her chair, running through the possibilities, deciding their next step. 'The money changing hands is all electronic. We subpoena both Martin's and Tommy's financial records.'

'Absolutely. Next we establish a physical connection between Martin and Tommy. So far, no one I questioned recognized Matt Martin as being a friend of his.'

'That doesn't mean he wasn't. We keep digging.' Kitt paused in thought. 'We still have a young woman fleeing the scene. And the mysterious, jilted girlfriend Zoe.'

'Who may be one and the same person.'

'And Agent Smith? We cooperate with him?'

M.C. nodded. 'I say yes. I'll call.'

Kitt tossed the agent's card on the desk. M.C. flipped open her cell phone and punched in the number. The man answered on the first ring. 'Special Agent Smith.'

'It's Detective Riggio.'

'Yes, Detective?'

'I've processed. Mutual cooperation and full reciprocity?'

'You bet. In that vein, I've just obtained Martin's financial records and am in the process of acquiring Mariano's.'

'I'll expect to hear from you soon then.'

A moment later, she flipped the phone shut and looked at Kitt. 'He's got Martin's financials already and is working on Tommy's.'

'I say we move forward on our own subpoenas as well. Agent Smith's definition of mutual cooperation and full reciprocity may not be the same as ours.'

'I'll bet it's not. We've both worked with the bureau before. Damn I hate those guys.'

'We stay one step ahead of him,' Kitt said. 'The minute we don't, he'll dump our butts.'

M.C. nodded. 'The truth is, this time I don't care how it gets solved or who gets the credit. I just want to get it done.'

'You want to tell Sal about this?'

'Sorry, partner,' M.C. said, clearly not sorry at all. 'This is your case. You get to deliver the good, the bad and the—'

'Ugly,' Kitt finished. 'Lucky me.'

30

M.C. readily admitted there were disadvantages to having a large extended family. The biggest: everyone always being involved in your personal life, like it or not. The concept of actually having – or keeping – a secret was laughable. But there were advantages also.

When you were in trouble, you always had someone to call. And someone who would not only listen, but solve the problem. M.C. had a plumber and an electrician in the family; Michael was a chiropractor; she had a cousin who was a hairdresser, one who was a dental hygienist and another who did bikini waxing – not that she had actually availed herself of that particular helping hand. Between aunts, uncles and legions of cousins, there was almost no aspect of life in which M.C. had to fly solo.

And it just so happened that her aunt Bella's oldest daughter, Carla, was a City Bank loan officer.

The same institution where Tommy had banked.

M.C. parked in front of the West State and Wyman streets branch of City Bank. She climbed out of her vehicle, flipping down the driver's side visor to display her Rockford Police Department ID.

125

The bank receptionist contacted Carla, who told her to send M.C. back.

'Mary Catherine!' she exclaimed when she saw her. 'What a surprise.' She came around her desk and hugged her. 'You don't bank with us, do you?'

Carla was one of those unfortunate women who had hit the five-foot mark and stopped growing. In height, anyway. Her top-heavy apple shape – so popular in high school – now teetered on the edge of melondom.

It didn't help that Carla came from a family who loved food. She was Italian, after all. To cook, eat and share the dining experience ranked right up there with birth and baptism.

M.C. shook her head. 'I came to see you.'

'That's so sweet.' She motioned to one of the chairs, shut the office door, then went around to her own. 'I didn't have a chance to talk to you at Tommy's service. I still can't believe . . .' She made the sign of the cross. 'Poor Aunt Catherine. And Sam.'

She lowered her voice. 'And how about you? I'm so sorry . . . it's all been so awful.'

'I'm hanging in there. Concentrating on finding Tommy's and Dan's killer.'

'If there's anything I can do—'

'There is,' she said softly. 'I need your help, Carla.'

'You've got it.' She leaned forward in her seat, waiting.

'Tommy banked here, am I right?'

'I believe so, yes.'

'Good. I need a favor.'

As she said the words, M.C. felt a bit like Don Vito Corleone in *The Godfather*. And by her cousin's expression, Carla was feeling the same way.

'I can't imagine how I can help, but I'll do what I'm able, of course.'

'We're working on a subpoena for Tommy's bank records. I have no doubt we'll get it. This is a murder investigation and we have just cause.'

'So what's the problem?'

126

'It could take two weeks. The grand jury has to convene, then approve the subpoena – then it goes through channels here at the bank. I don't have that kind of time.'

Carla nodded. 'I can attempt to speed up the process here at the bank, no problem.'

'I was hoping for something more immediate.'

Her cousin frowned. 'That's the best I can do, M.C. I'm sorry, but—'

M.C. cut her off. 'Here's the deal. You owe me, Carla.'

Her cousin glanced at her office door, as if to make certain it was closed, then leaned toward M.C. 'You're not seriously calling in a ten-year-old marker?'

'Afraid so. Sorry.'

While she'd still been a uniformed officer, she had helped Carla out. A guy had been bothering her; M.C. had paid him a little visit – in uniform – and basically scared the crap out of him.

Carla lowered her voice. 'I could lose my job.'

'You won't.'

'You don't know that.'

'Ten years ago, I could have lost mine.'

Her cousin groaned and dropped her face into her hands.

'It's for Tommy. And Aunt Catherine.'

She groaned again. 'I woke up this morning and thought "What a wonderful day. What could possibly go wrong?"'

'Look, you're just getting me information I'm going to get anyway. Simply speeding up the process. No one will know – not even Kitt. And, you're doing it for altruistic reasons. It's not as if you just want to check his financials before you or a girlfriend dates him.' Before Google, there was Carla. 'I'm still amazed at the personal information available to financial institutions.'

Her cousin peeked at her through her fingers. 'That was a long time ago.'

'I have a very good memory.'

'You're evil, you know that?'

M.C. smiled, knowing she had her. 'Actually, I do.'

Carla swiveled her chair to face her computer. Her fingers

flew across the keyboard. 'Here we go,' she said. 'Thomas Anthony Mariano, 444 Gramercy Drive. One account, checking.'

They had found checking account statements in his apartment along with his accounting business records. Both were currently being reviewed by the department's number cruncher.

Carla's fingers went to work again.

'What now?'

She hit enter and looked at M.C. 'Cross-referencing by his social. He may have more than one account. The common denominator would be his social security number.'

She turned her attention back to her monitor. 'Here we go,' she said again, watching the computer screen, her eyebrows drawing together. 'This is going to take some time. He had six checking accounts.'

'Six? Are you certain?'

'Take a look for yourself.'

M.C. stood and went around the desk. Sure enough. She scanned the list: TAM Enterprises; Mariano Brothers; Mariano's, Inc.; Mariano's Client Services; Tommy's Total Fitness. And an account under his name, Thomas Anthony Mariano.

'Check the addresses,' she ordered.

Carla did. Only the last, under his own name, was listed to his Gramercy Street address. The others were linked to P.O. boxes. All different.

Carla looked over her shoulder at her. 'I don't want to alarm you, but this is unusual.'

M.C. scanned the list once more, a sick sensation settling in the pit of her stomach. 'Didn't all these different addresses attached to the same social raise a red flag?'

'There's nothing illegal about having your mail sent to different addresses. These are funded accounts. They're attached to Tommy's social security number so the IRS is happy.'

Tommy, what were you up to?

Not what Agent Smith claimed. That he was a cyberthief.

Part of a ring of thieves. No way. That wasn't the Tommy Mariano she'd known.

She shifted her gaze back to Carla's. 'As a financial institution do you have to submit deposit activity to the IRS?'

'Every bank has to comply with the Bank Secrecy Act. Basically, we monitor all transactions and report large transactions and suspicious activity.'

'What constitutes a large transaction?'

'Ten thousand dollars. A day, aggregate amount.'

M.C. frowned. 'That's a lot of money to me. But for someone like Donald Trump, I imagine that's pocket change.'

'Exactly. We use filtering software, smart programs that recognize transaction patterns. If you and the Donald both banked with us, Mary Catherine Riggio moving ten grand would generate a suspicious activity report but Donald Trump doing the same thing—'

'Wouldn't.'

'Yes.' Carla returned her attention to her computer. She scrolled through several pages, then looked at M.C. 'In terms of transactions, nothing here looks suspicious.'

'Except for the fact we knew Tommy and know he didn't own any of these businesses.'

'Yes.'

'I'll need account printouts.'

'M.C., this is more than—'

'It's really important, Carla. I wouldn't be here if it wasn't.'

She hesitated, then nodded. 'It'll take me a couple of hours. I'll call your cell when they're ready.'

31

Monday, January 26
Noon

M.C. sat at her desk, the account printouts spread before her. She couldn't believe what she was looking at, what it implied. That there had been no friend. Tommy himself had been involved in the illegal activities Agent Smith had detailed.

Tommy had had a half-dozen checking accounts. Even being math-challenged, she could see the money in and out was more than Tommy earned from his accounting business.

Most of the deposits were modest, a few hundred dollars. Amounts small enough to fly under the bank's filtering software. But when added up, the amount became significant.

Kitt's warning rang in her head: '*You might learn some things about your cousin you'd rather not have known.*'

No, she wasn't going there. Not yet. There *was* an explanation.

Stomach burning, M.C. reached for her roll of antacids, peeled off two and popped them into her mouth. Was this what Tommy had been trying to tell her? Is shame the reason he hadn't been able to? The reason he had gotten so drunk the night of her engagement party?

And ultimately why Dan had ended up dead?

130

Anger took her breath. No wonder Tommy had felt responsible. No wonder he had been afraid to talk to her. Stupid, shortsighted little shit.

She fisted her fingers, fighting the urge to scream out her anger and frustration. To flail at someone, to throw things. It was so unfair. Why Dan? He'd done nothing but love her.

She gazed at the printouts, vision blurring, fighting for control. Focus, she told herself. Solve this thing. Uncover the truth. Good or bad, the truth brought the comfort of closure.

Her vision cleared. After leaving Carla, she'd done a bit of research. What she was looking at was one way thieves got around the antimoney-laundering laws and safeguards. Bank accounts for fictitious businesses, attached to P.O. boxes or nonexistent addresses and oftentimes opened with stolen social security numbers.

As easy as online banking had made it for legitimate consumers, it had made it that much easier for crooks.

She flipped open her cell phone and dialed Sam. 'It's M.C.,' she said when he answered. 'I've got a question about Tommy.'

'Sure, M.C. What is it?'

'Did Tommy have another source of income, other than his accounting clients?'

For a moment, he said nothing. She sensed he was surprised. 'Not that I know of. Why?'

'Did it ever occur to you that Tommy lived pretty well for a student?'

'Not really. I mean, he had a good business. Besides, since I still lived at home and crashed at his place so much, I threw a little coin his way to help out. Mom did, too.'

'How much did you throw his way?'

'A few hundred a month. I don't know what Mom did.'

She made a note of the amount and to call Aunt Catherine. 'Nothing about Tommy's recent behavior or life seemed out of character to you?'

'Nothing. What's going on, M.C.?'

'I can't talk about it yet.' She slid the printouts into a file folder. 'Thanks, Sam. I'll talk to you later.'

She ended the call and looked up to find Kitt standing at her cubicle door. She was frowning slightly. 'What's up?'

'Checking out some facts with Sam.'

'What kind of facts?'

She hesitated, then slid the folder across the table. 'I pulled in a marker. Take a look.'

Kitt crossed to the desk and picked up the folder. M.C. watched while she read, seeing understanding move across her features.

After a moment, she lifted her gaze to M.C.'s. 'Who?'

'Promised I wouldn't tell.'

'You realize what this almost certainly means?'

'Of course.' Her desk phone rang. M.C. answered. 'Detective Riggio.'

'Mary Catherine Riggio?' a girl asked. 'Tommy Mariano's cousin?'

'That's right. How can I help you?'

'I was a friend of Tommy's. I was in his apartment that morning . . . but I didn't kill him.'

M.C. snapped her fingers to get Kitt's attention. 'Zoe? Right?'

She heard the girl suck in a sharp breath. 'How did you know my name?'

She was aware of Kitt contacting Communications, initiating the trace. 'You wouldn't believe what we already know. You're in some deep shit, Zoe.'

'I didn't do it!' she cried.

'Then why'd you run?'

'I was freaked out! I came to see him, to talk to him and then—' She bit the words back as if realizing they incriminated her. 'Yes. I let myself in . . . I had a key . . . I found him that way . . .'

'You took his phone to protect your identity?'

'No! It saw it . . . and I . . . just grabbed it.'

'I'm sure you'll understand why I find that hard to believe—'

'I've got to go.'

'No, wait! Come in, talk to me. Don't hang—' The dial tone sounded in her ear. 'Damn it!'

She swung toward Kitt. Her partner broke into a smile. 'Got her! Woodman's Food Market at 3155 Mcfarland. Between Spring Brook and Spring Creek roads. Cruisers are already en route.'

The Public Safety Building and Woodman's Market might as well have been located on opposite ends of the earth. A quick, easy way from one location to the other simply didn't exist, even with cherry lights and a siren.

When M.C. and Kitt arrived, five cruisers were lined up in front of the store's main entrance. Woodman's, a big box, employee-owned franchise based on a bulk-purchasing model, was four times bigger than an average grocery store. M.C. was familiar with it – not because she had ever shopped here, but because her mother was a huge fan of the prices.

She and Kitt climbed out of M.C.'s SUV and crossed to one of their officers. 'Status?' Kitt asked.

'Officers inside are doing a sweep, looking for the UNSUB. Seems only one employee even noticed her, and he didn't see her face.'

'If he didn't see her face, what did he get a look at?' M.C. asked, hearing the frustration in her own voice.

'A brown-haired young woman in a pink jacket using the pay phone.'

'What about surveillance cameras?'

'Unless she went deeper into the store, she's not going to be pictured. There aren't any cameras in this area.'

'Did you try the ladies' rooms?'

'Checked.'

'Stockrooms?'

'Ditto.'

'Damn it!'

Kitt glanced at M.C. 'On the phone, what did she say?'

'That she didn't kill Tommy.'

'Why was she in his apartment that morning?'

M.C. rubbed her temple, working to recall each word. 'She'd come to see Tommy, to talk to him. She had a key and let herself in. She found him in the shower.'

'What about the phone?'

'She has it. Just snatched it up when she ran.'

'You buying that?'

'Nope. But why call us?'

'Guilt. Curiosity.'

'Innocence. Fear.' She paused in thought. 'She was surprised I knew her name. Unsettled by it.'

The uniformed officer spoke up. 'You want me to stay put?'

M.C. looked at Kitt. 'Let's get someone from ID to dust the phone. It's a long shot, but we might get something.'

Her cell vibrated and while Kitt directed the patrolman, she took the call. 'Riggio.'

'It's Smith. I've got something you might be interested in.'

'Wow, full disclosure already.'

The man laughed. 'Surveillance tapes turned up a suspect. Strange-looking dude at both Martin's and Mariano's funerals. You get e-mail on your cell?'

'I do.'

'I'm sending now. See if you recognize this guy. Call me back.'

He hung up. A moment later, the e-mailed image came through.

M.C. gazed at the tiny, grainy image. She recognized him, all right. The man at both funerals was Tommy's academic adviser, Professor Rick Taylor.

32

Up until that point, checking Professor Taylor's alibi for the day of Tommy's murder hadn't been a priority. Now it was.

A couple of phone calls later, M.C. looked at Kitt. 'The son of a bitch lied to us. There isn't a European lit professor named Danny Stephanopolis at the University of Chicago. In fact, they checked the employee rolls, there's nobody by that name on staff.'

Kitt frowned. 'I didn't take him for a killer. A self-important blowhard, sure. But not a killer.'

'So why'd he lie?'

Kitt smiled. 'Let's go find out.'

Kitt drove and M.C. dialed Agent Smith. He picked up immediately. 'It's Riggio,' she said.

'What do you have?'

'The man's name is Rick Taylor. He's a professor at Rockford College and was Mariano's academic adviser. We made a couple of calls after receiving the photo. Turns out he lied about his whereabouts the day Tommy was killed. We're on our way to the college now.'

135

'Keep me posted. I'll dig a little deeper into Taylor's background. See if I find anything.'

He hung up and M.C. looked at her partner. 'I think we're making history here,' she said.

Kitt glanced her way. 'How so?'

'We've discovered a fed who's not a complete dick.'

Kitt laughed. 'Give him time. I have confidence.'

Within twenty minutes they were on the RC campus. As they made their way toward Scarborough Hall, they ran into Connie, the secretary to the dean of students.

'Hello, Detectives,' she called cheerily. 'How nice to see you again.'

'You, too, Connie,' M.C. responded.

'Who are you here to see today?'

No tap dancing around, no not-so-subtle inquiries. Balls out, Connie.

'Professor Taylor.'

'Oh, yes. He has afternoon classes.' She checked her watch. 'He very well may be in his office. If you need anything, you know where I am.'

They thanked her and within moments were tapping on Taylor's office door. He wasn't alone. A very good-looking male student was with him; they appeared to be in a deep, serious discussion.

The professor waved them in, expression annoyed. 'Detectives. What a surprise.'

M.C. ignored the sarcastic edge in his voice. 'Professor, we need to ask you a few more questions.'

'Now's really not a good ti—'

'Make it one.'

'I have a class in five min—'

'You're going to be late.'

He turned to the young man. 'Will, do you mind getting class started? I'll be there as soon as I can.'

'Sure,' the young man said, jumping up. He smiled at them. 'I better go, then.'

'I didn't catch your name,' M.C. said.

'Will Strong,' he replied. 'See you later.'

M.C. watched him walk away and turned to Taylor. 'One of your students?'

'A grad student.' He glanced at his watch, then met her eyes once more. 'Now, Detectives, what can I do for you?'

'One simple question. Why'd you lie to us?'

'Excuse me?' he said, bristling.

'There isn't a faculty member named Danny Stephanopolis at the University of Chicago.'

He stared at them. He opened his mouth, as if to argue, then shut it.

M.C. tried again. 'I repeat, why'd you lie to us?'

'Would you mind?' He motioned toward the open office door. When Kitt shut it, he cleared his throat. 'Do I need a lawyer?'

'Only you know that, Professor,' Kitt responded. 'Do you?'

He hesitated, then shook his head. 'I made up the story about a friend because I didn't want where I'd really stayed to leak out.'

'And where was that?' Kitt asked.

'Hotel Kalifornia.'

'So?'

'Chicago's a big city. People come in all colors and persuasions. Alternate lifestyles are accepted.'

Kitt took over again. 'Exactly what are you into, Professor Taylor?'

'Hotel Kalifornia is a rather well-known "gays only" establishment.'

'Hardly a crime.'

'This is a conservative community, Detectives. A conservative school. I have a reputation to protect.'

M.C. folded her arms across her chest, openly skeptical. 'Being gay is hardly the career-busting shocker of the fifties, Professor.'

'Look, I'm a full, tenured professor.'

'Good for you.'

'As such, I have a code of conduct to uphold. A higher standard.'

Kitt stepped in, shifting focus. 'How did you know Matthew Martin?'

His gaze swiveled to Kitt's. 'Who?'

'A young man found murdered in his apartment. Part-time RVC student.'

'Why should I have known him?'

'You tell us, Professor,' M.C. said. 'You were at his funeral.'

The blood drained from his face again. 'I didn't know him. But I did attend his funeral.'

Kitt jumped in. 'Why's that?'

He looked from one to the other, obviously unnerved by their tag team approach. 'I read about the murder and . . . I felt compelled to pay my respects.'

'*Compelled* is a strong word,' M.C. murmured.

He looked at her, frowning. 'What's that supposed to mean?'

'I'm not a full professor, but to me compelled implies being drawn by a strong force.'

'Is that what brought you there?' Kitt asked. 'A strong force?'

'Young people are my life. I've devoted myself to them. That boy's death was a horrible aberration. So was Tommy's. And I resent what you're implying.'

'And what's that, Professor?'

He flushed. 'That it's strange that I cared about this young man even though I didn't know him. Shame on you for that.'

'I'm sorry if you got that impression.'

'Bullshit. That's exactly the impression you wanted me to get.'

'Why are you upset, Professor Taylor?'

'Because two young men are dead. Perhaps you should be trying to locate their killer instead of wasting time hounding me?'

'Why do you believe these two boys were killed by the same person?'

The man looked startled. 'It seems logical.'

138

'In a twisted sort of way?'

M.C. changed tack again, acting on a hunch. 'Are you involved with a student?'

He was. She saw it in the way he reacted, the subtle altering of his expression and body language. The raw panic that raced into his eyes.

'You give yourself away, Professor. Were you two together that night in Chicago?'

He hesitated, then shifted uncomfortably. 'Yes.' He dragged a hand through his thinning hair. M.C. noticed it shook. 'He's older. Past the age of consent. A grad student.'

M.C. immediately recalled the handsome Will Strong. They had looked awfully cozy together. 'I'm not certain the administration would see it that way.'

'That's why I lied.'

'His name?' Kitt asked.

'I'm not giving you that.'

'Is there a problem?'

'I don't want him involved.'

She caught Kitt's glance. Her partner nodded in acknowledgment: it was the same thing he had originally said about his imaginary friend in Chicago. 'You've already "involved" him in this, Professor Taylor. And since you lied to us once, this time we won't wait to verify your story.'

'His name?' Kitt pressed.

He hesitated again. 'I really don't see why—'

'Will Strong, perhaps?'

Sweat beaded his upper lip. He opened his mouth as if to reply, then shut it.

M.C. gentled her voice. 'Everything you tell us is incredibly easy to verify, Professor. One call. A click on a computer keyboard.'

'Okay, yes. It's Will.'

M.C. felt ill. This was one of Tommy's teachers. His adviser. And he'd cared more about his skin – his reputation – than helping them catch Tommy's killer.

The saddest thing was, she wasn't all that surprised by it.

'If you'd told us the truth in the beginning, we wouldn't

be here now. We wouldn't have wasted valuable time cutting through your bullshit—'

'If this gets out, I'll lose everything. My tenure, my reputation. Will may lose his assistantship.'

'Ever heard the saying, "Don't shit where you eat," Professor Taylor?'

'Please, I'm begging you. Don't go to the administration with this. If the relationship comes out, I'll be ruined.'

Tommy was dead. Matt Martin was dead. She'd bet either one of them would take 'ruined' instead.

'I can't make that promise,' M.C. said. 'If shielding you compromises our investigation, you're flat out of luck.'

33

Her wedding day. Dan waiting at the altar for her. Smiling, handsome in his tux, holding out his hand. She tried to grasp it, but he was out of reach. She tried harder, stretching . . . she called his name. Cried out, but couldn't be heard above the roar of an engine.

Her eyes snapped open. Reality crashed in on her. Not an engine, her cell phone going off on the nightstand. The other side of the bed empty. No Dan waiting for her. Never again.

Pain speared through her. Her eyes flooded with tears. She grasped the phone, brought it to her ear. 'Riggio,' she managed, voice thick.

'Detective? This is Connie, from Dean Johnsen's office.'

M.C. worked to shake off the effects of the dream and the lingering fog of sleep. 'Connie? How can I help you?'

'I'm so sorry for calling you so early, but something was bothering me and I . . . I felt I needed to.'

M.C. dragged herself to a sitting position. The bedroom was cold. Shuddering, she climbed out of bed, grabbed her robe from the floor and slipped into it. 'I'm glad you did. What's going on?'

'It's probably nothing, but . . . yesterday, I saw Professor Taylor leaving, carrying a box.'

'A box?' M.C. repeated, arching an eyebrow.

'Yes, you know, like a moving box. I thought it quite odd. Will Strong was helping him,' she went on. 'He had a box, too. Have you met Will? A grad student. Especially fond of Professor Taylor.'

She knew about Taylor. His relationship with Strong.

'What time was that?' M.C. asked.

'Late. After five. I'd stayed to finish up a report for the dean.' She paused a moment, then continued. 'I'm certain Dean Johnsen wouldn't want me to say this but . . . Professor Taylor had some problems at his previous position. Something about involvement with students and an online group. Really messy.'

Bingo. M.C. kept her voice steady. 'What kind of group, Connie?'

'I haven't a clue. Truthfully, I'm not even supposed to know that. I happened to overhear . . . I'd prefer you didn't say where you learned that, by the way.'

'Do you know where I can find Professor Taylor this morning?'

'I happen to have his class schedule and personal contact information right here.'

The moment Connie had disconnected, M.C. rang Kitt. 'Looks like Taylor might've been cleaning out his office last night. Will Strong was helping him.'

'The bastard's bolting,' Kitt said.

'That's my thinking.' She rattled off the River Oaks Lane address Connie had given her. 'I'm leaving in five.'

'See you there.'

M.C. arrived first. The cluster of attractive town homes looked inviting, done in warm gray with deep red doors and shiny brass fittings. Window boxes adorned the windows, though now they were filled with snow instead of flowers.

She parked in front of Taylor's and cut the engine, noting the late-model Lexus parked in the drive. If Taylor had murdered Tommy, she would not let him get away. She would track him to the ends of the earth if she had to.

Kitt arrived and parked behind her. They both climbed out. 'The car being here's a good sign,' Kitt said, joining her at the base of the drive.

They crossed to the car; M.C. peeked inside. 'No boxes. No body.'

'Another good sign.'

They stepped up onto the small portico and rang the bell.

When he didn't answer, they rang again. Then knocked and called out. 'Professor Taylor? It's Detectives Riggio and Lundgren. We need to ask you a few questions.'

Nothing. M.C. looked at Kitt. 'Connie said his first class was at nine.'

'Could be sleeping in.'

'Let's give him a call.' M.C. dug in her coat pocket for the number. Kitt unclipped her phone and punched in the numbers as M.C. read them off.

'Ringing,' Kitt said. She held up a finger with each ring, then snapped her phone closed. 'Answering machine.'

'Try the cell number.'

Kitt did, then looked at her partner. 'Straight to voice mail.'

'A suspect preparing to flee.'

'Absolutely.'

M.C. tried the door and found it unlocked. She looked at Kitt. 'Just cause, partner. I'm going in.'

'If he's lying in bed, Sal will have our asses.'

Professor Taylor was, indeed, lying in the bed. But he sure as hell wasn't sleeping.

34

Tuesday, January 27
6:50 A.M.

'I didn't think we pushed that hard,' Kitt muttered.

'Me either.' M.C. crossed to the bed. It looked as if Taylor had shot himself. He lay on his back on the bed, legs dangling over the side. His right hand held a revolver, a Ruger SP101. Blood and brains splattered across the wall behind him as well as over the bedding and floor.

'What a mess.'

M.C. was aware of Kitt calling it in, of ordering the usual cast of characters to the scene: pathologist, ID team, a couple of cruisers to secure and control the area.

M.C. fitted on gloves, studying the victim. What did this mean? she wondered. Had he been that afraid of losing his position? Of being outed?

Or did he have darker secrets? Ones that involved cybertheft and murder?

At their original meeting, Agent Smith had said the ring of cyberthieves was made up of young people, but that the operation had likely been masterminded by someone older. Someone with access to youths. Someone they trusted.

Had Taylor been that person?

Kitt snapped her phone shut. 'Taylor had a Ruger registered in his name.'

'Let's have a cruiser pick up Will Strong. He very well may have been the last person to see Taylor alive.'

'I want to know what was in those boxes,' M.C. added, looking over her shoulder at Kitt. She found her staring at Taylor, expression odd. 'You okay?' she asked.

Kitt blinked and nodded. 'Yeah. Talked to Sal. He's on his way.'

The rest of the team began to arrive. The uniformed officers first, followed by ID.

They tromped in with Miller in front. He saw her and scowled. 'What the hell, Riggio? You couldn't let us have breakfast first?'

'You're right. What was I thinking? We should have let ourselves out so you could eat pancakes and sausage.'

Jackson reached the bed and put down his bag of equipment. 'Oh, man, the guy whacked himself? Who was he?'

'A suspect. We had reason to believe he was preparing to flee.'

'Looks like he did. He took the hard way, if you ask me.' Jackson smiled at her. 'Okay if I get my shots?'

'Go for it. We'll take a look around.'

The town house was beautifully furnished. Sort of classic marries modern. It shouldn't have worked, but it did. So neatly arranged, not an item out of place, it looked more magazine cover than lived-in home.

M.C. did a quick inventory of the layout. The town home appeared to be three bedrooms, two and a half baths on three levels. The second bedroom served as an office. The computer, she saw, was on. An Apple. Her brother Michael swore by the brand. Her brothers teased that he was a missionary, out to convert PC users everywhere.

She tapped the mouse and the screen sprang to life, filling with images of men in various forms of bondage. Some were performing sex acts on other men.

'Holy shit.' Sorenstein had come up behind her. 'That is so messed up. Miller, Jackson, come get a look at this.'

145

That brought not only his fellow ID detectives, but the rest of the crew as well. They gathered around her, gawking and commenting.

'Sick fuck.'

'No wonder he killed himself.'

'Oh, man, that's gotta hurt.'

'I didn't think a body could do that.'

'This guy was an *accounting professor*?'

The last came from Jackson. They all looked at him and a dull red flush crept up his cheeks. 'What? It's like a bunny rabbit being Jack the Ripper. You just don't expect it.'

'Party's over,' Kitt said tersely from the office doorway. 'I think everyone's had enough fun.'

They dispersed, though not without grumbling. 'What's going on?' M.C. asked. 'You look funny.'

'Come with me,' she said. 'Check out the third bedroom.'

Located on the uppermost level, it served as a sort of workout room.

Though not the kind of workout M.C. participated in.

The walls were mirrored. A single piece of equipment dominated the room, a sort of cross between a dentist's chair and a rack from the Middle Ages. Like a Pilates reformer from hell.

There were other goodies, too. Metal plates with heavy metal eye screws bolted into the wall. A large padded barrel on a wooden platform with leather straps anchored on both sides of the platform. For securing hands and feet, she guessed.

'It seems Professor Taylor still wasn't telling us the whole truth,' Kitt said.

'No wonder he was so desperate. He wasn't into your everyday reindeer games.'

They entered the room. The single window was covered with a darkening shade, a wooden blind hung over that. Even though his little fun factory was on the third floor, he'd taken care to discourage Peeping Toms.

The room had one closet, located to the left of the door. M.C. crossed to it. 'Room wasn't locked?' she asked Kitt.

'Nope.'

She tried the closet. It also proved unlocked. The contents were neatly organized. Whips. Shackles. What looked like a bridle. Digital camera. 'The guys will want to collect the camera, check the card.'

'No sign of a violent crime. He made no effort to hide his party favors.'

'I think that's all it was,' Kitt said. 'The photos will probably reveal whether he liked giving or receiving.'

Dominating. Or being dominated. M.C. just didn't get it. 'I hear Sal.'

They headed back to the main floor. She had, indeed, heard Sal's voice. Francis had also arrived and the two stood near the bed talking.

The pathologist caught sight of them first. 'You two are keeping me busy.'

'You sound like Miller,' M.C. said. 'Hate to burst everyone's bubble, but we're stuck in this workingman's nightmare, too.'

From the other side of the room Miller grunted. 'The difference is, you two are crazy.'

Francis cleared his throat. 'I was telling Sal, I'm guessing this is just what it looks like. Our friend here put the pistol in his mouth and pulled the trigger. Powder burns on his fingers and the bullet's entrance and exit location are consistent with that hypothesis. Additionally, there're no signs of a struggle. I've seen quite a few of these over the years, and this one looks exactly like 'em.'

M.C. turned to Sal. 'Gun's registered to him.'

'He leave a note?'

'Sort of,' Kitt said. She motioned to the home office. 'On the computer.'

Of course, M.C. realized. Not a traditional note – pictures of the whole truth. So they would know he killed himself so his darkest secrets wouldn't be revealed.

'Think he's your UNSUB?'

'No,' Kitt said. 'He was a sick SOB who got caught up in circumstances beyond his control.'

147

'If you had to guess,' M.C. added, looking at her partner in surprise. 'And don't hold back.'

Sal frowned. 'Can I speak with you two in private?'

They followed him to a quiet corner. 'How'd you being here go down?'

'The dean's secretary called me this morning. She'd seen him carrying out boxes the night before.'

'You assumed he meant to flee or was removing evidence.'

'Yes. In addition, she said Taylor had some trouble in a previous job, something about involvement with students and an online group.'

'Cyberthieves?'

'That's the conclusion we jumped to,' Kitt said. 'He didn't answer the door or phone; we found the home unlocked and came in to investigate. It was all by the book.'

'Good.' He moved his gaze between them. 'You seem to have differing opinions on whether he could be our guy.'

'There's a chance, sure.' Kitt looked at M.C. 'But my gut's telling me he knew his secret life was going to be exposed and he'd be ruined, so he offed himself. What would you do if you were a fortyish full professor stripped of your tenure? Exposed for being a sexual deviant, involved in an affair with a student? What school would hire you?'

From upstairs came Sorenstein's exclamation, 'Holy Mother of Christ!'

He'd found Taylor's playroom.

'Kitt may be right,' M.C. said. 'We certainly can't rule out his being our guy, but the evidence so far doesn't support it. And Kitt's theory rings true.'

Jackson called up the stairs. 'Two packing boxes are in the Lexus's trunk. Want to take a look?'

The three of them filed down to the first floor, then out to the vehicle. Jackson had carefully opened the first box, and she carefully thumbed through it: books, mementos, plaques. Framed photographs. Papers. The second contained more of the same.

'He'd cleaned out his office.'

'He'd left the boxes in his trunk, which suggests he meant to take off. The question is, what changed his mind?'

'I suggest you question the boyfriend,' Sal said.

'Next on our hit list, so to speak.'

35

Tuesday, January 27
9:20 A.M.

M.C. and Kitt found Will Strong pacing in interview room two. The moment they entered the room, he spun to face them. 'I had nothing to do with this!'

'With what?' M.C. asked.

'I helped him move his stuff, that's it. He was freaking out.'

'Again, Mr Strong, you didn't have anything to do with what?'

'His taking off! I told him to stay and fight! He didn't hurt either of those boys – he couldn't!'

'Professor Taylor planned to take off?'

'Yes, disappear.'

'Why?'

'You should know,' he said, tone bitter. 'He figured that with all your nosing around and pushing, our relationship would be uncovered and he'd be fired.'

'Professor Taylor's dead,' M.C. said bluntly. 'I'm sorry.'

He stared at her, face going slack with shock. After a moment, he shook his head. 'That can't be.'

'He killed himself, Will.'

'No.' He shook his head again. 'No, that isn't right.'

'What time did you and Taylor part company last night?'

'Seven or so.'

'You said he was freaking out?'

'He was extremely agitated.' The young man's hands fluttered; M.C. was reminded of caged birds. 'But I never thought he'd—'

He looked at them, expression turning guilty. 'Why didn't I? He was talking crazy.' He brought his hands to his face. 'I should have known. Should have considered this a possibility.'

M.C. felt half bad for the young man. If he was lying, he was doing a masterful job.

'Tell us about the problems he had at his previous teaching position.'

'At Hanover?'

Kitt didn't hesitate. 'Yes.'

'That was nothing. He was involved with a student. It was consensual. The administration found out and he lost his job.'

'What about the online group he was involved with?'

'The gay chat room? Big deal. What? We don't have a right to commune with friends?'

'Obviously, Hanover felt differently.'

He agreed. 'But Rick lucked out. The college wanted to keep it all hushed up. So they gave him a glowing recommendation.'

To quietly get rid of him. M.C. looked at Kitt, who nodded. 'We know about his sexual . . . preferences,' she said. 'We've seen his third-floor fun factory.'

Kitt jumped in. 'He liked to dominate, didn't he? And give pain?'

'You don't know anything about him,' he said, bitterness becoming anger.

'Then why don't you clue us in?'

'Rick couldn't hurt a flea. He liked being dominated, not the other way around.'

'And you were his partner?'

'I know what you're thinking. It wasn't that way.'

'What way is that, Mr Strong?'

151

'Sick. Ugly.'

'Then why don't you tell us how it was?'

'Fun. We played. Nobody got hurt.' He wrung his hands. 'He introduced me to the whole thing. At first, I thought it was fun. Exciting. Something different, you know.'

'He introduced you to bondage?' Kitt asked. When he nodded, she continued. 'You said, "At first." When did it stop being fun?'

'It started to get boring. Always the same thing. Sometimes I like straight sex, so to speak. I like to cuddle. But he never got tired of the other stuff.'

'Are you certain no one got hurt?'

'Yes. I was there.'

'Just the two of you?'

'Yes. I play it exclusive, Detective. So did Rick. You can't be too careful these days.'

Interesting comment, M.C. thought. Considering. Apparently, one person's careful was another's risky. 'Did he meet other young men over the Internet? Correspond with them? Do chat rooms?'

'No, absolutely not. The Hanover thing cured him of that.'

'Had he been found out by someone? Could he have been being blackmailed?'

'He would have told me. I'm sure of it.' He moved his gaze between them. 'He liked Tommy Mariano. Thought he was a real decent guy.'

'Was Tommy gay?' Kitt asked.

'No, unfortunately. We joked with him about it a couple times.'

'Tommy knew you were both gay?'

He lifted a shoulder. 'Sure. It's not a crime.'

'Did he know you were seeing each other?'

'Maybe he guessed. We didn't announce we were a couple or anything. Rick had his job to protect.'

'What about Matt Martin?'

'What about him?'

'Professor Taylor was at his funeral. He must have known him.'

'He didn't.' The young man's eyes filled with tears. 'What he said about that was true. He just wanted to pay his respects. And you turned it into something despicable.'

'We had reason to be suspicious. He lied to us, Will.'

He brought his hands to his head. 'If only he hadn't gone to that funeral, none of this would have happened. Everything would have been fine.'

And if only Dan hadn't offered to drive Tommy's car that night . . . or if Tommy hadn't gotten drunk or if he'd had the guts to come clean about what was going on . . .

She understood Strong's bitterness, his despair. If she allowed them to, her own 'if onlys' would eat her alive.

'I'm sorry for your loss,' Kitt said softly.

He dropped his hands and lifted his tear-streaked face to hers. 'Screw that. And you. Why couldn't you have left him alone? Why? He never hurt anyone!'

He broke down sobbing. Unmoved, M.C. slid him the box of tissues. As far as she was concerned, Taylor made his bed when he lied to them. If he had been truthful from the start, they would have verified his alibi and moved on.

When Strong had blown his nose, she asked, 'Did you know Rick owned a gun?'

He shook his head.

'I don't have any more questions, Will.' She looked at Kitt in question; her partner indicated she didn't either. 'We'll get an officer to give you a lift back to the college.'

'I'll call someone.'

She stood. 'If you change your mind, let us know.'

He nodded and followed her to her feet, looking dazed. M.C. led him to the elevator, punched the button for the first floor and said good-bye. The doors slid shut and she returned to the interview room.

Kitt sat where she had left her, staring blankly at the door.

'Partner? You okay?'

Kitt blinked. 'No, I don't think I am.' She stood and collected her things. 'I'm going home.'

M.C. didn't hide her surprise. She looked at her watch. 'Going home?'

'You heard me. I'm out of here.'

'But it's only—'

'I don't give a rat's ass what time it is. I've had enough. I'm spent. Tapped out. Going home.'

She slipped into her coat, movements jerky. 'If you do anything, get White to accompany you. Or somebody else, I don't care. Just document the crap out of it.'

M.C. stared at her partner, dumbfounded. She had never seen her this way before, even in the final throes of the Sleeping Angel case.

'Stop looking at me like that! Don't you get it? Don't you know what day this is? I should be packing for a trip! Looking forward to a vacation with the man I love. Instead I've been treated to some poor bastard's brains splattered all over a wall and photographs of people perverting the act of love.'

Her voice rose. 'I have no idea why I'm here. This whole thing is wrong. Totally fucked up.'

M.C. held out her hand. 'What can I do, Kitt? Tell me how I can help you?'

'Don't do anything, okay. Just let me go.'

M.C. did, hurting for her partner. For herself. For their losses. What they'd both sacrificed for the job, the things they suppressed day in and day out to do it. That she suppressed now.

Drawing a deep breath, she fitted the lid back on her boxed-up emotions and got back to work.

36

Joe had stayed home sick. Or so Kitt had been told by his secretary, Flo, when she'd stopped by Lundgren Homes looking for him.

The woman had been cool to her. Kitt had heard the condemnation in her tone.

Obviously, Flo blamed her for the trouble between Kitt and Joe. But whom else should she blame?

Her fault. All her fault.

It had begun to snow. One of those lovely snowfalls, all fat gentle flakes. The ones that dusted hats and eyelashes, and tingled on the tongue.

Sadie had loved snows like these.

Kitt parked in the drive beside Joe's truck. She climbed out and went to the door.

She was here to beg forgiveness. To plead for yet another chance. And to tell him the God's honest truth – she didn't think she could live without him.

Joe hadn't asked for his key back and she hadn't offered it. It was cheeky to be using it now, but she did anyway, letting herself in.

'Joe,' she called softly, unwinding her scarf and slipping out of her coat. 'It's me.'

She found him in the den, in his favorite chair – a battered leather recliner. A fire crackled in the hearth; the TV was off.

'Flo said you were sick.'

'I'm fine.'

She wished she was.

He turned his head, met her eyes. 'Can I help you?' he asked.

The way one would ask a stranger. Coldly. Shutting her out in a way he never had before. It hurt. It frightened her.

'I miss you.'

'I miss you, too.' He said it without emotion, as if any pain associated with the statement was a thing of the past. What if she had lost him for good?

'I made a mistake. I'm sorry.' He didn't comment and she clasped her hands together. 'I have this ridiculous sense of duty. This sense of responsibility to everyone and everything.'

'Everyone and everything except us. I don't know if I want to live that way.'

'I can change.'

'Can you?'

'Please, let me try.'

'Come here.' He held out a hand; she crossed to him and took it. He drew her down onto the chair. Kitt knew how to angle her body against his so that they snuggled comfortably together in the big old recliner. They had done it hundreds of times before.

She rested her head on his shoulder; he threaded his fingers through her hair – the gesture both absent and intimate.

'I was sitting here thinking of Sadie,' he said softly.

She smiled. 'So was I. Just before I got here.'

'I realized something that I hadn't before. She kept you centered, Kitt. She was what drew you home at night. Not me.'

'Not just Sadie. You, too, Joe.'

'Let me finish. What I realized was, she kept me grounded,

too. She filled up the spaces you couldn't. Does that make sense?'

Emotion choked her. She nodded in reply – she couldn't have spoken at that moment if her life had depended on it.

'Losing her changed everything.'

Tears stung her eyes. She wanted to shout that it wasn't true. But that would be a lie. Sadie's death *had* changed everything. The delicate balance that had been her and Joe, their life together; it had all been permanently upended.

She turned and tipped her face up to his. 'What are you trying to say, Joe?'

'We can't go back to the way we were. Because our Peanut's gone.'

The tears welled and rolled down her cheeks. 'Don't say that. We can try.'

'You still can't fill those spaces, Kitt. And it's not fair of me to ask you to try.'

'I'll give up police work. I've had enough. I'm ready to live like a normal person. A person whose bad turn at work doesn't include somebody's brains sprayed across a wall.'

'Thanks for sharing that.'

He said it lightly, but it was true. Normal people with normal lives wouldn't think to say such things.

'You'd be miserable. You'd hate me for it.'

'I wouldn't, I promise. I'll take up cake decorating.'

He laughed.

'I'm serious, Joe. I can't live without you.'

He held her gaze. 'I almost believe you.'

On her hip, her cell phone vibrated. Something akin to grief moved across his features. She felt him emotionally pulling away from her.

'Answer it,' he said. 'You know you want to.'

What she wanted to do was screw duty, let the device take a message. Whatever or whoever needed her attention would still need it a half an hour from now.

But she couldn't. She wasn't built that way.

'Lundgren.'

It was Nan. 'Hi, Detective. I thought you'd want to know. Your subpoenas are in.'

For Tommy's and Martin's financials.

Kitt thanked the woman and reholstered her phone.

'You have to go,' he said.

'I should.' She wasn't sure whether she felt him sigh or she just imagined it. It didn't matter; it didn't change what she had to do. 'I should,' she repeated, 'but I'm not.'

37

M.C. sat in the ten-car-deep drive-through line. Her stomach grumbled. She hadn't had anything but coffee since morning and if she didn't eat soon, she wasn't going to be any good to anyone.

The car in front of her inched forward; she followed. Kitt's leaving put her in a tight spot: Sal had agreed to her tagging along, not actively investigating. So she had set out to avoid him and HQ until Kitt got her shit together and back on the job.

It was the least she could do. She hated that her friend was hurting. Hated that the relationship she and Joe had worked so hard to repair had been redamaged because of her.

No, not because of her. Because of her and Kitt's friendship. Their loyalty to each other.

Kitt was the best friend she'd ever had. But what kind of friend had she been in return? She should have refused Kitt's help, should have insisted she go with Joe.

M.C. inched forward again, the move putting her next in line to order. Her cell vibrated. 'Riggio,' she answered.

'M.C., it's Sam. I found Zoe.' His voice shook. 'I met up with her at the A-list.'

159

A favorite lunch spot for college students. Suddenly food didn't seem so important. 'Is she still there?'

'She didn't kill Tommy,' he said instead. 'I asked her.'

She frowned. 'I thought I told you to leave the investigation to us.'

'She didn't, M.C. I believe her.'

'I'll be the judge of that. Is she still there?'

'No, but I know where she is.'

'Tell me. I'll go now.'

'I can't do that.'

'What?'

'I promised her I wouldn't.'

'You promised *her*?' The words exploded past her lips. 'Tommy's dead!'

'You think I don't know that?' he shouted back. 'He was my brother and my best friend!'

The blare of a horn came from behind her. She saw that the car in front had ordered and moved forward. 'I can make you tell me.'

'But you won't.'

'The hell I won't, you little brat.' She hadn't called him brat since he'd been in the sixth grade and had stolen one of her bras to show to his friends.

'She's scared.'

'If she's innocent, she has nothing to be scared of.'

'That's bullshit and you know it. You're the cops. You're looking for her.'

'She wasn't too scared to be bopping around town, did you think of that?'

'You're not going to change my mind, M.C.'

'Meet me at my place,' she said, checking over her right shoulder, then cutting out of line. 'I'm on my way.'

Sam was waiting for her when she got home. He looked at once hangdog and defiant. She lit into him the moment she was close enough for him to hear her. 'I can't believe you're siding with this girl. She may have killed your brother.'

'She didn't.'

'So she tells you. How do you know?'

'She's scared to death.'

M.C. took a deep breath, working to keep her cool. 'Do you trust me?'

'Of course I do.'

'Do you think I'm a good cop?'

He didn't hesitate. 'You're awesome.'

'Would I ever do anything to hurt you or—'

'I know where you're heading with this and—'

She stopped him. 'To hurt you. Or any innocent person?'

He rolled his eyes. 'No. Of course not.'

'Then trust me with this.'

'I can't. But she agreed to meet with you.'

M.C. narrowed her eyes. 'The catch?'

'You can't tell anybody.'

In an attempt to control her temper, she counted to ten before replying. She snapped anyway. 'Have you lost your freakin' mind? You're not Columbo, for God's sake.'

'Who's Columbo?'

'A character from an old TV show, a detect— It doesn't matter. You're not him, okay? You're just Sam. And you're way out of your league here.'

'Thanks a lot.'

'I didn't mean anything by that.'

'Right.' Color had crept into his cheeks. 'She gave me this. To give to you. As a sign of good faith.'

He held out a zip-style plastic bag. There was a cell phone inside.

'It's Tommy's,' he said.

M.C. stared at the plastic bag, the phone inside. A Razr, silver. Funny, she had seen Tommy talking on his cell dozens of times, but she'd never noticed what kind of phone he had.

'It's his,' Sam said, as if reading her thoughts. 'I called it.'

She took the bag and held it up to the light, inspecting it carefully. 'Why'd she take it?'

'Ask her.'

'Fine. I agree to her terms.'

'No one,' he said. 'Not even Kitt.'

'No. Absolutely not. We're a team.'

'Then she won't do it.'

M.C. turned and walked away, breathing deeply, working to control her anger. What could this girl have to gain by making this up? And if she was telling the truth, what could M.C. lose if she didn't go for it?

A lot. And if the girl turned out to be full of shit, the agreement would be off.

She searched his expression, weighing her options. 'Okay,' she said. 'But she'd better be on the up-and-up. Or you'll both regret it.'

Her full name was Zoe Elizabeth Petersen. She'd been in Sam's backseat the whole time, hiding under a blanket. And she looked legitimately terrified.

'I didn't kill Tommy,' she said when she was inside, seated on M.C.'s couch. 'He was my friend and I' – she glanced at Sam, her cheeks pink – 'I loved him.'

M.C. was unmoved by her wringing hands and teary eyes. 'How did you happen to be at his apartment that morning?'

'I knew his schedule,' she began, almost hesitantly, 'that he would be there. I wanted to see him. The day before he'd . . . broken it off. Said he didn't want to see me anymore.'

Her voice shook. 'I knew I could make him love me. I knew it. That's why I went to his place that morning. To tell him I'd do anything to make him love me.'

Her tone rang true. M.C. felt bad for the girl. She was too young to know you couldn't make someone love you. It never worked.

'You say you were prepared to do anything. What about killing him, Zoe? If he rejected you, were you prepared to do that?'

'No!' Her eyes filled with tears. 'How could I? I loved him.'

How? The line between love and hate was razor-thin – and just as sharp. M.C. had seen it cut many times. 'You arrived at his apartment, what happened then?'

'When he didn't answer, I let myself in.'

'The door wasn't locked?'

'I knew where he kept the spare key.'

'Then what?'

She opened her mouth to speak, but no sound came out. She squeezed her eyes shut – as if to block out the image in her head.

Sam slid an arm around her. 'I know it's horrible,' he murmured. 'But you've got to talk to M.C. She can help you.'

The girl nodded. M.C. noticed that her hands were balled into tight fists, her knuckles white from the pressure. 'I heard the shower running. I called out, when he didn't answer, I poked my head in and called again.'

She swallowed audibly. 'He still . . . didn't answer, so I crossed to the tub. Tommy was . . . there was blood . . . I—'

She turned and pressed her face into Sam's side.

'Why'd you take his phone?'

'I don't know.'

'That's bullshit.'

'I swear! It was there, on the bathroom counter. When I turned to go, I saw it and just . . . did.'

'Sorry, Zoe. This story's just not working for me.'

'It's true! I—' She trembled so violently she had to press her lips together a moment to gather the strength to speak.

'Why'd you run? You say you didn't kill him, that you were in love with him. So why run?'

'I was scared. I thought I heard someone in the apartment, I thought maybe it was whoever killed Tommy . . . I grabbed the phone and ran.'

'When you were entering the building, did you see anyone leaving in a rush? Anyone who could have been fleeing the scene?'

'I was lost in thought . . . I don't know . . . yes, maybe. There was someone . . . on the stairs.'

'Man or woman?'

'Man.'

'What did he look like?'

'I hardly glanced at him.'

'Tall? Short? Fair? Dark? Caucasian? African-American?'

'I don't know!' she cried, looking at Sam as if for support. 'Some guy, I was thinking about what I wanted to say to Tommy. I'm telling the truth!'

M.C. studied the girl. Her story didn't ring true. But the weird thing was, it didn't ring false either. 'How about when you were leaving?' she asked. 'See anyone then?'

'A woman. With groceries. I almost ran into her.'

She needed Kitt, M.C. realized. She needed her partner to help her sort through this. Separate the pieces and coolly analyze.

She had screwed up, M.C. acknowledged. By agreeing to this private meeting she had no videotape of the interview to review, no one to bounce her thoughts off. What had she been thinking?

She'd been offered an opportunity and had taken it. That was in the past. Now, she needed to focus on what to do next.

She returned her gaze to Zoe. 'Why are you here?'

'What do you mean?'

'Why'd you agree to talk to me?'

'Sam told me it was important. And that you'd believe me.'

'Would you be willing to put your version of the events in writing and sign it?'

She looked startled. 'I guess so.'

'Good. I'll bring you a paper and pen. And while you're doing that, I'll take a closer look at Tommy's phone.'

38

Tuesday, January 27
7:45 P.M.

M.C. sat at her kitchen table, staring at the small scrap of paper in front of her, at the one word neatly printed on it.
Breakneck.
When she'd opened Tommy's flip-style phone, it had fluttered to the floor. Zoe swore she hadn't put it there. That after pocketing the phone, she hadn't touched it except to put it in the Ziploc bag.

M.C. narrowed her eyes. Tommy's printing, she was almost positive. Except for his signature, he'd hardly ever written in cursive. Readability had been important to him, and he'd had the precise hand of an accountant.

What did it mean?

Sam and Zoe had left a couple hours ago. M.C. had spent the time since struggling to come to grips with what she had done – and where she went from here.

Zoe putting her statement into writing didn't change the fact that M.C. had compromised her badge and betrayed Kitt's trust. M.C. brought the heels of her hands to her eyes. Sal was right. So was Kitt. She was too close to this case. To the people involved.

But the truth was, she didn't care if she was too close.

She wanted Dan's killer. She wanted Tommy's. She would do whatever was necessary to make that happen.

She stood, crossed to the sink and gazed out the small window above it. Moonlight shone on the snow and she was reminded of the night Dan proposed. The memory brought a stab of longing – and grief.

She pushed it away, forcing her thoughts back to Zoe. What did the girl really want from M.C.? And where did she go from here?

She turned away from the window and the moonlit night beyond, her gaze returning to Tommy's phone. She should hand it over to ID so they could begin forensic analysis of the device.

How would she explain having it? To Sal? To Kitt?

Another lie. The truth to Sal would get her booted from the investigation, if not suspended from the force. The truth to Kitt would put her partner in the position of having to lie for M.C.

She wouldn't do that to Kitt. She'd screwed up her friend's life enough already.

At her hip, her own cell vibrated. She answered.

'Detective Riggio. It's Agent Smith.'

Turn the phone over to Smith, she realized. The bureau could have the information analyzed in half the time it would take her guys. And they would be satisfied with the agent's explanation of having gotten it from the local PD.

The thought left her feeling like a traitor.

'We need to talk,' Smith said.

'I'm all ears.'

'Face-to-face.'

'Apparently, today's my lucky day.'

'Excuse me?'

'Why not? I have news as well. Among other things, Professor Taylor killed himself.'

She heard the man's sharply indrawn breath. 'When?'

'Looks like sometime last evening. Put a gun in his mouth and pulled the trigger.'

'This complicates things.'

166

'Not necessarily. He may not have been involved. In fact, I don't think he was.'

'Then why eat a bullet?'

'I'll fill you in when we meet. When and where?'

Smith suggested a Loves Park diner. M.C. agreed and thirty minutes later she slid into the booth across from the agent. The place was quintessential Loves Park, from the orange vinyl booths to the big-haired waitresses in their matching orange uniforms.

'Ever been here before?' Smith asked.

'Never.'

'They have incredible homemade cookies. You can order them by the plate.'

Sure enough, you could. And as it turned out, Agent Smith had. Along with a big glass of milk.

Superagent Cookie Monster, M.C. thought as she watched him dunk one in the milk.

She settled on a cup of coffee. And his insistence that she try one of his cookies.

'You're not the typical agent,' she said.

He grinned. 'You mean all intense and hard-core?'

'Pretty much.'

'Don't let my cookies-and-milk image fool you. I get the job done. But the thing is, do I have to be a dick while I'm doing it?'

'As refreshing as I find it, it doesn't fit. Why the FBI?'

'Working for the government was in my blood. Dad was a scientist for the government, Mom a military linguist for the navy. They were both brilliant, by the way. And extremely well educated. They insisted I be as well. I speak Russian, Spanish, German, French and Italian. Not Arabic, however. Regrettably.

'I saw one of the bureau's recruitment pitches; it seemed like a good idea. What about your family?'

'Rockford working class through and through.' M.C. added cream to her coffee. 'Dad was a mailman, Mom a home-maker. She raised me and my five brothers and did a lot of ass-whooping and cooking in the process.'

'What was it like, growing up one of six children?'

'Imagine chaos. A battle of skills and wills, to snag the last pork chop, to get a shower while there was still hot water. Imagine constant sound and movement. What about you?'

He smiled. 'Stereotypical only child. Spoiled rotten.'

'As much as I'm enjoying the small talk, Smith, I'm wondering why you called me.'

He polished off a cookie, then retrieved a large envelope from the briefcase at his feet. 'I got your cousin's financial records.' He slid it across the table. 'Six accounts. One looked legitimate. Take a look.'

'I've already seen them.'

'That was quick for a local PD.'

'Even local PDs have connections. What about Martin's?'

'Same scenario. I'm sorry.'

'Why's that?'

'I know you wanted your cousin to be innocent. There was no "friend," Detective Riggio. We did the math, and your cousin made a hundred thousand dollars in unreported income last year. That doesn't include what he made from his accounting business and family gifts.'

You might learn some things about your cousin . . . and Dan for that matter, you'd rather not have known.

'The first of the questionable accounts was opened in July of last year. The others followed in quick succession. I'm sorry,' he said again.

She never would have figured Tommy for a thief. Never. 'I still want the bastard who killed him.'

'There's more,' he said. 'Something I didn't share with you.'

'Really? I'm shocked.'

Smith ignored the sarcasm. 'Tommy called me not once, but twice. The second time, he told me that his "friend" had hit the jackpot. An account with a half a million bucks in it, there for the taking.'

He leaned toward her. 'Let's just suppose Tommy or his

'friend' are using an Evil Twin. Some idiot logs on, goes to his bank to do his online banking or check his account balance.'

'But he hasn't logged on to the legitimate Wi-Fi.'

'Exactly. Our guy has just handed over his bank account numbers and passwords. But they can't shuffle on down to the bank to withdraw the cash. No ID. And too risky, even if they did.'

Smith drained the last of his milk. 'So they do online transfers, online bill pay and ACH credits. In amounts that fly under the bank's radar.'

'To different accounts.'

'And then they liquidate. Quickly.'

Username. Password. Keys to the kingdom.

'It's all electronic,' Smith said. 'No face-to-face at all.'

'What about the social security number on the bank accounts the money's transferred into?'

'Jacked information that leads to innocent civilians. Some don't even know their information's been compromised.'

'Problem,' M.C. said. 'The filtering software reports daily totals of ten grand and over. How do the crackers get around it?'

Smith lowered his voice. 'Online bill pay account. Our crackers use the information they hacked to access our guy's account and they start "paying bills." Eight grand to TAM Enterprises, six grand to Mariano Brothers. Tommy's accounts are perfect, they're all existing business accounts. It doesn't take long to move a lot of money.'

'You expected to see the half mil in Tommy's accounts?'

'I thought there was a good chance I'd see some of it. There or in Martin's.'

'Has anyone stepped forward and reported the money missing?'

'No.'

'Why not?' she asked. 'That's a lot of money.'

'You'd be surprised how little attention some people pay to their books. The idiot may not even have noticed yet.'

M.C. drew her eyebrows together in thought. 'Or maybe it's money that can't be reported missing?'

'I hadn't considered that,' Smith said.

'Maybe they didn't take it?'

'Somebody took it. The question is who?'

M.C. digested what he was saying, moving the pieces around, seeing where each fit best. Smith pressed forward. 'Here's what I think. Tommy was killed by someone in the group who wanted the money for themselves. Maybe even the "friend" who he was trying to protect. Five hundred grand can change a person from friend to foe damn fast.'

'Once Tommy contacted you, they figured killing him was the only way.'

He nodded. 'Yes.'

'So why kill Martin?'

'He knew about the money, too.'

'We made a deal,' M.C. said. 'Full disclosure. Yet, you're only sharing this now?'

'I'm disclosing. Take it or leave it.'

Typical FBI maneuver, expecting full cooperation and disclosure from the local police, but not willing to return the courtesy.

It pissed her off. But two could play that game.

She had planned to tell him about Zoe. About Breakneck. Had planned to hand him Tommy's phone. Screw that. From this moment on, she only revealed information when it would help her own cause.

'What about Taylor?' he asked.

'Not involved. We got too close to exposing his secret life, so he killed himself.'

'Secret life?'

'Bondage. He liked being dominated. Had his own little fun factory on the third floor.'

'You want me to follow up?'

'Go for it. Unless the pathologist delivers a shocker, it'll be classified as a suicide and we're out.'

'Anything else?'

'Not a thing,' M.C. said, taking perverse pleasure in the lie. She stood. 'Thanks for the coffee.'

As she walked away, M.C. smiled to herself. She was glad Smith had played it this way – it made her own choices so much more clear-cut.

39

M.C. paced. Her thoughts tumbled madly, one after the other. Five hundred thousand bucks. A lot of money. To a twenty-two-year-old it would seem like enough money to live on forever.

Enough to kill for.

It made more sense now, with 500K on the table. Someone wanted it. They were willing to kill for it.

Tommy hadn't had it. Neither had Matt Martin. It would have shown up in their accounts. They needed to subpoena Taylor's financial records as well. Never knew, he might surprise them all by being the bad guy.

Agent Smith had deliberately withheld key information. Big surprise. He had been certain the money would be in Tommy's or Martin's account. If it had been, he'd have had his case. He wouldn't have needed M.C. and Kitt.

But the money hadn't been there – so Smith had shared his big secret.

M.C. checked the clock. *Nearly 2:00* A.M. She couldn't sleep now if her life depended on it.

Go with it, Riggio. Use the energy.

She wouldn't turn to Agent Smith. Not until she had exhausted her own leads and sources.

What was her next step?

Get Sam to start analyzing the numbers on the phone. Assembling names and numbers for her. He had wanted to help; this was a way he could.

Her phone, clipped to her hip, vibrated and she jumped, startled.

'Riggio,' she answered.

'Rise and shine, Detective. Got a homicide.'

'Where?'

'Holly Grove. Female. Officers have secured the scene.'

'Did you contact Lundgren?'

'Called her first. She didn't pick up, home or cell.'

M.C. frowned. More bad news.

'Call Detective White in to assist me. Lundgren went home early yesterday with the flu.'

More like a meltdown, M.C. thought, praying the meltdown hadn't sent her partner running to the bottle.

'Nasty stuff,' the communications officer said. 'My husband had it. He wanted to die.'

So would Kitt if she'd fallen off the wagon. M.C. would personally kick her ass.

M.C. thanked the woman and hung up. Within five minutes she was dressed, her teeth and hair brushed, and walking out the door, a go mug of instant coffee clutched in her hand.

It'd snowed on and off since the previous afternoon and an inch-thick blanket of the stuff covered the ground. The plows were already out, she heard the rumble of one nearby and saw that the street in front of her house had already been cleared.

While her SUV warmed up, she dialed Kitt's cell. As expected, her partner didn't pick up.

'Yo, Kitt. On my way to a scene. Stuff to talk about. Get your sleepy butt out of bed and call me.'

Ten minutes later, she pulled up in front of the east side neighborhood home. Two-story, all brick, nice. Not grand, but comfortable. Welcoming front door, painted forest green, framed by gaslights.

Not so welcoming tonight, with crime-scene tape stretched

across the front lawn and the two RPD cruisers parked out front, cherry lights spinning.

The commotion had roused neighbors; up and down the block lights were popping on.

White pulled up behind her and she waited for him, despite the cold. 'Sorry to drag you out.'

'S'okay.' His smile was bright against his dark skin. 'Not that I'm unhappy to be here, but where the hell's your better half?'

'Under the weather. Maybe the flu.'

M.C. could tell he didn't wholly buy it, but knew better than to challenge her. 'What've we got?' he asked the scene officer.

'Dead girl. Jenny Lindeman. She lived in the basement apartment. Parents live upstairs.'

'They upstairs now?'

The young officer nodded. 'The mother found her. The apartment has a dedicated entrance, around back. Looks like the perp entered that way.'

'Anything else?' M.C. asked, signing the log.

'Just that yesterday was her birthday. She turned twenty-one.'

'Oh, man,' White said, 'that sucks.'

They followed the walkway around to the basement entrance. Another officer stood watch, stomping his feet to stay warm and looking miserable. The victim lay just inside the door. She wore drawstring pajama bottoms and a sweat-shirt that proclaimed:

24 hours in a day . . .
24 Diet Cokes in a case . . .
Coincidence?

No blood. No obvious body trauma. Her eyes were open, her mouth closed. Head twisted in an unnatural-looking angle. Like a doll who'd been manhandled by its spoiled owner.

Young person. What looked to be a broken neck. Shit.

M.C. turned to the officer standing duty. 'Do a sweep of the apartment. I'm looking for a computer. Any computer.'

'You remember your twenty-first?' White asked, squatting beside the body.

'Are you kidding? I have two older brothers. They took me out drinking, got me so loaded I puked all over their backseat.'

'That'll teach 'em.'

'That's what my dad thought. How about you?'

'Similar story.' He motioned to Jenny Lindeman. 'I wonder what she did to celebrate?'

'No computer,' the officer called. 'Lots of stuff that goes with a computer.'

That made three. M.C. glanced over at the officer. 'You're certain? It's important.'

'Yeah, I'm certain,' he answered, sounding annoyed.

White frowned. 'The Mariano and Martin murders, wasn't there something about a computer—'

'Being missing, yes.' She unclipped her phone, flipped it open. 'Check in the closets, under the beds, just to make sure. See if she's got a laptop.'

M.C. punched in Kitt's number. Sleeping Beauty needed to get her ass out of bed, meltdown or not.

And if Kitt needed help, she'd provide it – in the form of a cruiser and a couple of sleep-deprived colleagues.

40

Kitt groaned and cracked open her eyes. Her cell phone, parked on the bedside table, sounded like an airplane taking off.

She grabbed the vibrating device. 'Lundgren,' she mumbled. *'Buenos dias.'*

'It's M.C. What the hell are you saying?'

Kitt cleared her throat, peeked at the bedside clock and groaned. *It was 4:05 A.M. Damn.*

'Kitt, I hate to bother you, but—'

'*No comprende.* I'm on vacation.'

'Are you drunk?'

That made its way through Kitt's sleep-starved brain. 'I resent that question. No, I am not drunk.'

'I think it was fair, considering.'

She glanced at Joe, then brought the phone closer to her mouth. 'Put your mind at ease, partner. I haven't fallen.'

'Glad to hear that. There's been another murder. I need you here.'

'Don't you get it? There's always another murder. I'm taking the day off.'

'Kitt, listen. Another victim. Number three.'

176

'So it definitely wasn't Taylor.'

'No, it wasn't. And this bastard's active.'

Fighting the urge to clear the sheets, Kitt tightened her grip on the phone. She was spending the day with Joe. She'd given up ten days in Mexico, she wasn't giving up today. 'Call Detective White. I have the flu.'

'A girl this time. Yesterday was her twenty-first birthday.'

Shit. Shit.

No, it didn't matter. There'd always be another victim. She drew a line in the sand now. 'I'm not coming in.'

'Her neck was broken. Computer's missing.'

Kitt squeezed her eyes shut. 'Why today, M.C.?'

'I didn't do it. I'm sorry, Kitt. I need you with me when I question her family. Hell, I'm not even supposed to be here without you. Sal gets wind of this and he'll fry both our butts.'

Beside her, Joe stirred. She slid as quietly as she could out of bed. Not quietly enough. He opened his eyes. 'Hon?'

'It's M.C.,' she whispered.

He grinned sleepily. 'Tell her I said, "*Hola.*"'

On the other end, M.C. sucked in a sharp breath. 'Was that Joe? Did you spend the night with Joe?'

'None of your damn business. I'll be there as soon as I can.'

Kitt hung up, grabbed her clothes and slipped into the bathroom to dress. When she emerged, dressed, brushed and bladder emptied, she found Joe awake and waiting for her. He smiled sleepily. 'What's up?'

'I'm sorry. I've got to go. Just for a little bit. I promise.'

'Do what you've got to do, Kitt.'

'I want to spend the day with you. I do.'

'This is what I was talking about yesterday.'

'I don't want to go but I have to.'

'I'm not asking you to stay, damn it! Listen to me. We are who we are. We've got to come to grips with that, then see if we can make it work. There's no halfway.'

'We'll make it work,' she said. Crossing to him, she bent and kissed him. 'I'm going to do this as quickly as I can and come back. I'll check in, help process, then turn everything over to M.C. and White.'

'Kitt, it's okay if you can't—'

'I'm thinking banana pancakes for breakfast and nachos for lunch.'

Before he could respond, she kissed him again, then left.

Fifteen minutes later she made the scene. Typical scene, she thought. She knew all the players, anticipated their every move.

Every player except the victim. Every move but the killer's next.

She found M.C. with Francis, crouched beside the body.

'Broken neck,' he was saying. 'Quick and efficient.'

'No sign of a struggle,' M.C. said, glancing at her. 'Hands are clean.'

Kitt moved her gaze over the basement apartment's entrance, the positioning of the door in relation to the body. 'Looks to me like she opened the door, then stepped back so the person could enter. It was the last thing she did.'

'Killer came in, snapped her neck.'

'Anything besides the computer missing?'

'Nada. That we can tell, anyway.'

Francis cleared his throat. 'I'll run toxicology, see what shows up.'

Kitt nodded. Urine, blood, vitreous. The Holy Trinity of forensic toxicology.

'No drug paraphernalia that I saw,' M.C. said. 'My guess is she's clean.'

'I'll finish up,' Francis said. 'If anything unexpected pops up, I'll let you know.'

They thanked him and moved aside. 'Parents are upstairs?' Kitt asked.

M.C. said they were and they headed back out into the bitterly cold night.

As soon as they had moved out of earshot, M.C. stopped and turned to her.

'You slept with Joe, didn't you?'

'Again, none of your damn business.'

'You should be glowing.'

'I'm not?'

'Hell, no. You look like crap.'

'I didn't get much sleep. If you know what I mean.'

'That's just too much information.'

'You asked.'

M.C. started up the steps. 'Sounds like you guys are on the mend?'

'Maybe. Being here isn't helping the cause.'

'Sorry, partner. Unfortunately, I don't make the rules. Besides, you're the only one who knows the case as well as I do.'

'Let's do it then.' Kitt squinted at her watch, thinking of the pancakes. 'My flu's going to make a big reappearance in a couple of hours. I may even puke.'

'Give me a heads-up on that, okay? I'm pretty sure I won't want to be anywhere around when you do.'

They found the family huddled together in the large, homey family room. Someone had set a fire in the hearth and in addition to warming the room, it cast a friendly, flickering light.

The family didn't speak. They weren't crying. Weren't comforting one another. They simply sat, staring. Silent. As M.C. and Kitt entered the room, they looked at them. Their expressions ranged from angry to hopeful, devastated to blank.

A man and a woman. Kitt guessed them to be husband and wife, mother and father. Two middle-graders. One teen.

'I'm Detective Lundgren,' Kitt said softly. 'This is my partner, Detective Riggio. We're so sorry for your loss.'

Still no one spoke. The woman looked helplessly at them, throat working.

'We need to ask you a few questions.'

The woman nodded. 'Should the children . . . my sister, their aunt, is on the way. Should they stay or—'

'It'd be better if they waited in another room.'

'I'll take them,' the teenager offered, jumping to her feet. 'Come on, guys. Let's go play Nintendo.'

The two youngsters got to their feet and trailed their sister out of the room, both looking back at their parents in question. The woman smiled tremulously. 'It's all right, boys. We'll be right here.'

When they had disappeared from sight, she looked back at Kitt. 'They don't know what's happened, that Jenny's been—'

Murdered. An ugly word. Perhaps the ugliest.

The woman couldn't say it. The man hung his head.

The room was hot. Kitt unbuttoned her coat. From the corners of her eyes, she saw M.C. doing the same thing.

'When did you last see or speak with your daughter?'

'Earlier today. To wish . . . to wish her a happy . . . I guess that was yesterday now.' She glanced at her husband, then back at them. 'It was her birthday. Did you know that?'

'I heard that. I'm so sorry.'

'Look.' She pointed to a framed photo on the side table beside where she sat. 'Wasn't she cute? The cutest of my babies. My first.'

Kitt swallowed past the lump in her throat. It hurt. She understood this woman's pain. It didn't matter that the woman had three other children, Jenny had been her child, her baby. And now, that baby was no more, taken violently.

M.C. stepped in. 'You saw her?'

'Yes. We had cake and presents.'

'How did she celebrate her birthday?' M.C. asked.

'We had a family party. Like I said, cake and—'

'Did she go out with friends? Clubbing? I understand it was her twenty-first birthday.'

'She stayed in,' the man said suddenly, angrily. 'Same as she always did.'

'I'm sorry, did you say she stayed in?'

'She hardly ever left that machine.'

'What machine, Mr Lindeman?'

'That goddamned computer! I hate that machine. I wish they'd never been invented.'

'Honey, don't—'

'Like hell I won't!'

180

Kitt turned to him. 'Tell me about your daughter, Mr Lindeman.'

'I'll tell you this. I'm not all that surprised. How sad is that? My baby is dead and all I can feel is ang—' His throat closed over the words and he looked helplessly at his wife.

'It started when she was in the sixth grade,' she whispered, voice choked. 'She started failing at school. Withdrawing from her friends. Spending more and more time on the computer.'

'And before that?'

'A normal kid,' he barked out. 'Happy. Loved sports. Had a group of nice friends.'

'We tried taking the computer away,' the woman offered. 'Tried limiting her time on it. But she'd fly into rages.'

'Rages?' Kitt repeated. 'Describe them for me.'

'Screaming. Throwing things. Cursing at us, making threats.'

'Threats. Against you?'

'Yes. And herself. The other children. I was terrified.'

'What did you do?'

'We took her to a therapist. He told us she was depressed. Prescribed Zoloft.'

'Did things get better?'

'Somewhat. For a while. She seemed to function more normally.' The woman dragged in a broken-sounding breath. 'Then in eighth grade, she refused to go to school.'

'Refused?'

'Yes. Locked herself in the bathroom. No amount of threatening or pleading would help.'

'We had her hospitalized. Again, it helped for a short while.'

The man jumped in. 'Therapists, a bunch a high-priced quacks. Over the years, they diagnosed Jenny as bipolar, ADD, ODD, depressed. Always another diagnosis, another round of drugs. And short-lived results.'

'High school was a nightmare,' her mother went on. 'I quit my job to homeschool her, but that was worse.'

'So we let her quit school,' the man said defiantly, looking at them as if in challenge. 'She was sixteen.'

181

'How about friends?' M.C. asked. 'Have you met any of them?'

'Met her friends?' The man laughed, the sound harsh. 'Her friends don't have faces, just screen names.'

'How about a boyfriend?'

'Get real, Detectives. She hardly ever left her room.'

'So, she didn't work?'

'She did,' her mother said. 'A home-based computer job. She made enough to pay us rent and cover all her own expenses.'

And that fit the profile of a cyberthief. 'Tonight, did you hear anything? See anyone?'

'No.'

'A vehicle in front of the house?'

The woman broke down, sobbing. Kitt waited, giving her time to collect herself.

When she had, she asked gently, 'Did the other children spend much time with her?'

They simultaneously shook their heads. 'The boys hardly knew her, really. And Robin, our other daughter, tried to have a relationship with her but—'

'Nobody had a real relationship with Jenny.' The man sighed heavily, the fight seeming to have drained out of him. 'Even us, her parents.'

'Could we question Robin? Maybe she knows more than you think. Or maybe she saw something tonight.'

The man looked at his wife. She nodded, then asked, 'What about the young ones? What do I . . . we tell them?'

She didn't have a clue, Kitt acknowledged. How did one deliver that kind of news?

She took out one of her cards and wrote the name of the department's social worker on the back. 'Call her. She'll be able to help you.'

'That's what everyone always said,' Mr Lindeman murmured. 'But no one ever did. Not really.'

'I'm terribly sorry, Mr Lindeman,' Kitt replied softly. 'I truly am.'

'Was she still seeing a therapist?' M.C. asked.

The woman pressed the tissue to her eyes. 'He feels she's doing better. She seemed to be.'

'For God's sake!' the man exploded. 'She's not doing better now, is she?'

Mrs Lindeman began to cry again. Her husband slid an arm around her. 'I'm sorry, honey. I'm just so—' He cleared his throat and looked at them. Kitt saw tears in his eyes. Her heart broke for them both, for the whole family.

'Dr Erik Sundstrand,' he said. 'With Kids in Crisis.'

Beside her, M.C. caught her breath. Kitt worked to hide her own reaction. Within moments, they had wrapped up the interview and were outside, heading toward their vehicles. They reached M.C.'s first.

'Erik was Dan's best friend,' Kitt said. 'It's a connection between Tommy and Jenny.'

'We have one that's even stronger,' M.C. said. When Kitt looked at her, she added, 'My cousin Gina DeLuca. Erik Sundstrand's her boss.'

She unlocked the SUV and opened the door. 'Let's rendezvous at HQ, then decide—'

'Wait,' Kitt said, her gaze on M.C.'s door. She brushed away some snow clinging to it. Someone had keyed M.C.'s SUV. Not simple vandalism, however. The person who'd done it had left M.C. a specific message:

NOT A NICE GUY

41

Wednesday, January 28
6:35 A.M.

M.C. and Kitt followed each other back to the PSB and parked side by side in the garage. M.C. climbed out of her SUV, shaking with anger. She slammed the door and took in the message once more.

NOT A NICE GUY

She'd thought this asshole had decided to move on. Apparently not.

'You okay?' Kitt asked, slamming her own door.

'Pissed off. This makes three.'

'Any idea when it happened?'

M.C. shook her head. 'It could have been any time since it began to snow yesterday afternoon. I find it hard to believe it happened before. I wouldn't have missed it.'

'Think whoever is doing this might have a legitimate beef?'

M.C. managed to keep hold of her temper. 'I can't believe you just said that. There's nothing "legitimate" about this kind of hateful prank.'

'Then you think it's a prank? Someone's idea of fun? Or a way to get at you, under your skin?'

'What else? 'Cause I'm not buying "legitimate."'

'So blow it off, partner.' Kitt leaned toward her. 'Sal's waiting for us and unless you want an extended stay behind a desk, you've got to get a grip.'

M.C. nodded, knowing Kitt was right. As they headed into the building, then up the elevator to the VCB, she worked at getting her emotions in check.

Sal was, indeed, waiting for them. He didn't look happy. Their 'quick close' had burgeoned into three victims and a suicide – without a single suspect. No doubt the chief was breathing down his neck – not a position Salvador Minelli cared for.

'My office,' he barked. 'Now.'

They filed in. He snapped the door shut behind them. 'Sit.'

'If you don't mind, Sal,' M.C. said, 'I'd rather stan—'

'I do mind, goddamn it! Sit.'

He took his place behind the desk. 'Three victims now, is that what I'm to understand?'

'Yes, sir,' Kitt responded. 'The latest is Jenny Lindeman. Female. Twenty-one years old. Neck broken. Computer missing.'

M.C. jumped in. 'However, we have a motive now. Money.' She felt Kitt's surprised glance, but pushed on. 'And a solid connection between two of the victims.'

'Motive first,' he said.

'An account with a half-million dollars in it.'

'Explain.'

She quickly relayed what Agent Smith had told her. 'His theory, and Kitt and I agree, is that the kids have been killed by someone who either wanted to get their hands on the money or wanted to cover their tracks, should someone come looking for it. '

'Including us or the feds,' Kitt added.

Sal narrowed his gaze. 'And when did Smith drop this bomb?'

'Last night. Typical FBI.'

He moved his gaze between them. 'So, where's the money?'

'Smith already has financials on Mariano and Martin. Neither had it.'

'Maybe this Jenny Lindeman?'

'Maybe,' M.C. said. 'But I have the feeling that if she had the money, she wouldn't be dead.'

'The girl was seeing a therapist,' Kitt said. 'Otherwise, her world seemed limited to her family and her computer.'

'Not just any therapist. Dr Erik Sundstrand.' At Sal's expression, she nodded. 'Yes, *that* Sundstrand.'

Kitt jumped in. 'Which leads us to the connection between the victims. Connections, actually. Jenny was a patient of Erik Sundstrand's and took her appointments at the Kids in Crisis center. Gina DeLuca, who runs the center for Sundstrand, is also Mariano's cousin.'

Sal narrowed his eyes on M.C. 'And also *your* cousin. Is that right, Riggio?'

'Yes, sir.' She sat forward, hoping for the right balance of earnestness and solemnity. 'But DeLuca isn't really a cousin. Her mother married my dad's cousin, so she's a by marriage, no-blood-involved relation.'

'What the hell does that mean, exactly?'

'She's my dad's cousin's stepdaughter. Suffice to say, I'm most likely related in some fashion to, perhaps, 20 percent of the Italian-American population of Rockford.'

'Then as one of your "perhaps, by marriage, no-blood-involved" relations, peripheral involvement only. Watch your ass on this.'

'Yes, sir.'

He turned back to Kitt. 'And the other connection?'

'Weaker. Mariano also knew Sundstrand. Through M.C.'s fiancé, Dan Gallo. The two men were friends.'

Sal nodded, expression thoughtful. 'Could Gallo have been involved with the crackers?'

Kitt answered quickly. 'I'm thinking no. Considering the circumstances, it's looking like either a random killing or a case of mistaken identity.'

'I suggest you subpoena his financial information anyway. Just to keep it clean.'

'Already done,' Kitt said.

M.C. felt as if the wind had been knocked out of her. It took all her self-control not to defend Dan. Not to jump to her feet and shout out his innocence. She fought to keep it from showing and got stiffly to her feet. 'If that's all, Sal—'

'It's not. Sit back down, Detectives. I checked last night's scene log, Lundgren. You weren't there.'

'Actually, got there late. The flu, sir.'

'You seem to have made a speedy recovery.'

'Actually, I don't feel all that well.'

M.C. jumped in. 'She left early yesterday afternoon. Looked green around the gills. And feverish.'

He studied Kitt for a long moment, then turned his attention to M.C. 'So, you took it upon yourself to have the Communications Bureau call Detective White to the scene?'

'Yes, sir. I—'

He held up a hand, stopping her. 'Without consulting me?'

'Yes, sir. He's assisted me on this investigation and I—'

'I make those decisions. Understand?'

'Yes, sir.'

He turned to Kitt. 'We had an agreement, Detective Lundgren. You get the "flu" again and I'm pulling you both off. Is that clear?'

For a moment, Kitt sat unmoving, then she stood. 'I could puke on your shoes, Sal. Just say the word.'

'Puke on Riggio's shoes and bring me a picture. That's all.'

They filed out. As the door snapped shut behind them, M.C. looked at Kitt. 'I can't believe you went after Dan's financials. And behind my back, too.'

'Keeping it clean, just like Sal said.'

'Not influenced at all by my anonymous, car-carving friend?'

'It's called good investigation, M.C. You know that.' She lowered her voice. 'I know how hard this must be. I'm sorry.'

Sudden tears choked her. She struggled past them. 'Me, too.'

'Thanks, by the way. For backing me up.'

'Not your fault you got the flu.'

Kitt frowned slightly. 'When were you going to tell me about the money?'

'Been a little busy. You weren't exactly available.'

'Remember, partner, you get your ass in a sling, mine's in there with yours. Sal will be merciless.'

'Noted.'

'With that in mind, I'm thinking about quitting.'

'Quitting?' M.C. repeated. 'What—'

'This. The force.'

For a moment, M.C. couldn't speak. Then she realized what was going on. 'Joe's making you choose, isn't he?'

'It's me. I want a life.'

'You have a life. This is your life.'

'No, it's not. It's a job. Or should be.'

Day to day without Kitt. M.C. refused to even imagine it. 'What now?' she managed.

'Banana pancakes.'

'Kitt—'

'See you in two hours.'

M.C. watched her walk away, wondering what the hell she would do if Kitt actually did quit.

42

M.C. glanced at her watch. She needed to call Sam about Tommy's phone. She had, maybe, ten minutes before Kitt returned. Deciding that should be enough time, she dialed her cousin.

He answered, sounding sleepy. 'It's M.C.,' she said. Before he could respond, she asked, 'Do you still want to help me find Tommy's killer?'

'Hell, yeah.'

'Good. You know *the* phone?'

He was silent a moment, then made a sound of comprehension. 'Tommy's?'

'Yes, that one. I want you to perform an autopsy on it.'

'An autopsy? What the hell—'

'Every name and number in his contacts list. Every call sent and received. Put names with numbers. Addresses if you can get them. A transcript of all saved text messages.'

'When—'

'I want the information as soon as possible. Tonight would be good.'

'I don't know if I ca—'

She heard Kitt in the hallway. 'You can. I'll call you.'

189

She snapped the phone shut as Kitt entered the office. She glanced at her partner. 'How were the pancakes?'

'Great.' Kitt frowned. 'What's up?'

'Up?'

'The phone. Who were you— ?'

'Sam. He's still wanting to help us.' God help her, at least *that* wasn't a lie. M.C. cleared her throat, wondering if she looked as guilty as she felt. 'While you were enjoying home-made banana pancakes,' she teased, 'I ate a bag of sandwich cookies from the vending machine and wrote the Lindeman report. Thanks works for me.'

'See, that's what Joe and I are talking about.'

'Excuse me?'

'About balance. There's no balance there, M.C.'

'Balance where? What are you talking about?'

'Eating vending machine crap for breakfast. You didn't go home and shower. You probably just splashed cold water on your face and changed into the fresh shirt you keep in your locker.'

'What's wrong with that?'

'There's no balance, that's what's wrong with it. I want a job that doesn't consume me.'

'But—' The flutter of panic took her by surprise. The fear that Kitt really meant it. 'You can't quit, Kitt. You were lost without the force before. Remember?'

'That was different. That was forced leave. I was still reeling from Sadie's death. And I didn't have Joe. If I've got to choose between Joe and the badge, Joe wins, hands down.'

M.C. opened her mouth to argue more, then shut it. Wouldn't she feel the same, if she were in Kitt's place? She had lost Dan and would give up anything to have him back.

She didn't have that option. Kitt did.

'I understand,' M.C. said softly. 'But if you do decide to quit, I don't know what I'll do without you.'

The words, the naked honesty of them, hung in the air between them. After a moment, M.C. cleared her throat. 'Did a little research on Kids in Crisis while you were gone.'

She handed Kitt a sheaf of papers. 'Unlike his parents,

who dedicated their lives to building the family fortune, Erik's devoted his life to bettering the community by pouring that fortune – and his considerable energy and talent – into it. Kids in Crisis is one of his philanthropic endeavors – a mental health facility for kids whose families couldn't afford it. Their fees,' M.C. went on, 'are based on a sliding scale of the parents' income. Under a certain income, treatment is free. Over a certain income, the family pays the full rate – and everything in between. KIC, as it's called, has nonprofit status and subsists partly on grants – many of which are written by Erik himself.'

Kitt thumbed through the printouts. 'I met him at the party. He seemed like a nice guy. I didn't meet your cousin Gina.'

The image of Dan and Gina, that night at the party, filled M.C.'s head. Gina's hand on his arm. Dan's head bent close to hers.

'M.C.? Did you hear me?'

She blinked, refocusing on Kitt. 'Sorry, what?'

'Your cousin Gina was there, right?'

M.C. nodded. 'She was the Italian Barbie doll.'

Kitt cocked an eyebrow. 'Not your favorite person, I'm guessing. What's the story?'

'I'll tell you about it while we take a ride.'

Kitt nodded and they made their way from the VCB to the parking garage. They didn't speak until they had both climbed into M.C.'s Explorer and buckled up.

M.C. started the vehicle. 'As I told Sal, Gina's a cousin through marriage. My dad's cousin Mario married a woman who had two kids from a previous marriage, an eight-year-old boy and a ten-year-old girl.'

'Gina was the girl.'

'Right. We were the same age and started off being best friends. She proved to be a backstabbing, two-faced nightmare. One of those nasty kids who thinks it's fun to play mean tricks or find a way to get other kids in trouble.'

'But she played it all Miss Innocent for the adults, I'll bet.'

'Oh, yeah, little Miss Perfect. She turned on me when I

wouldn't go along with her schemes. I was her personal project all the way through high school. She even stole my first boyfriend, then dumped him.'

'Maybe she's the bad guy?' Kitt offered. 'Have you thought of that?'

M.C. imagined it and smiled. 'I've busted a lot of characters over the years, but never Barbie.'

'Italian Barbie,' Kitt corrected. 'That'd be so cool.'

'See, partner,' M.C. said, easing out of the parking spot, 'you can't quit. You'd miss all the fun.'

Kids in Crisis was located in a Riverside Drive strip mall, nestled between Walton's Hardware Supply and Dry Cleaning by Steve. The small waiting room was serviceable. Three young people sat waiting, two accompanied by a frazzled-looking parent.

They crossed to the receptionist's window and held up their shields. 'We need to speak with Gina DeLuca.'

The young woman stared at the badges, then nodded. 'Wait here.'

A moment later, Gina appeared, obviously unnerved. 'Mary Catherine?'

'Hello, Gina. This is my partner, Detective Lundgren.'

Kitt held up her shield. 'We need to ask you a few questions.'

Gina's gaze darted between them, a dull flush started on her neck and climbed to her cheeks. 'May I ask what this is about?'

'Of course,' Kitt said. 'A young woman named Jenny Lindeman. You do know her?'

'Yes . . . I – Let's talk in my office. I'll buzz you in.'

Moments later they were seated in Gina's cluttered office. M.C. began. 'How do you know Ms Lindeman?' M.C. asked.

'Jenny's a client of Kids in Crisis.'

'Was,' Kitt said. 'Jenny's dead. She was murdered last night.'

'Oh, my God.' Gina brought a hand to her throat. 'How . . . who . . . ?'

M.C. ignored the question. 'Which therapist did she see?'

'Erik.'

'Your boss.'

'Yes. And the center's founder.'

'How well did you know Ms Lindeman?'

'Not well.' Her gaze darted between the two of them. 'Like I said, she was a patient here.'

'Ever have a private conversation with her?'

'No.'

'You answered awfully fast, Gina.'

'Because I'm certain.' She shifted slightly. 'Decisiveness is one of the reasons Dr Sundstrand has placed so much trust in me.'

M.C. wanted to roll her eyes, but restrained herself. 'Did she have many friends?'

'I don't know. She came to the center alone.'

'Any enemies?'

'You'd have to ask Dr Sundstrand. I barely spoke to the girl. I could have him call you?'

Kitt ignored the offer. 'So you wouldn't know if she was involved in any illegal activities?'

'Of course not!' Color flooded her cheeks. 'Frankly, I'm a little surprised you'd even ask me that. It seems to me I made it clear I hardly knew the girl.'

'You did make that clear. However, hardly knowing someone means different things to different people, now doesn't it?'

'Perhaps you should speak to Dr Sundstra—'

'Yes, thank you. Could you see if he's available?'

He was in Chicago, they learned a moment later. 'If you'd like, I'll tell him you were here? Have him call you?'

'You do that.' Kitt handed the woman her card and stood. 'Thank you for your time, Ms DeLuca. We appreciate it.'

Gina led them to the door. 'Before you go, Mary Catherine, anything on Tommy's murder?'

'We're working on it. By the way, could Tommy have known Jenny?'

She blinked. 'Tommy know Jenny? I don't think so.'

193

'Why do you say that?'

'It just seems unlikely, that's all. I mean Jenny was a bit of a—' As if realizing her mistake, she bit back what she had been about to say. 'It just seems unlikely. But of course, it's possible.'

'You were about to say something about Jenny?'

She shook her head. 'More about Tommy. He was just so steady and . . . you know, well-adjusted.'

Moments later, they were buckled into M.C.'s Explorer and pulling away from the curb. 'She didn't ask about Dan, did you notice? And they knew each other.'

'I noticed,' Kitt said. 'I also noticed she didn't seem concerned about how you're doing.'

'But she asked about Tommy's murder. Interesting.'

'She seemed to be hiding something. Although her reaction to Jenny's death seemed genuine.'

'Maybe she's protecting somebody?'

'Maybe,' M.C. murmured, thinking once again of Dan and Gina, heads bent, deep in conversation. What, she wondered, had they been talking about?

43

Erik showed up unannounced at the PSB. M.C. met him at the elevators. 'Thanks for coming in, Erik. I appreciate it.'

'I just left Jenny's parents. This is devastating. Anything I can do to help, I will.'

'Kitt and I just need to ask you a few questions.'

'Like I said, whatever you need.'

She led him to one of the VCB interview rooms. Kitt met them there. 'Dr Sundstrand, it's good to see you again.'

She held out her hand; he took it. 'Please, call me Erik.'

Kitt motioned to the chairs. 'Can I get you coffee or a soft drink? Water?'

'I'm good, thanks.'

M.C. began. 'How long was Jenny a patient of yours?'

'I've treated her on and off since she was fifteen.'

'When was the last time you saw her?'

'This past Friday.'

'Was she having any problems?'

'As I'm sure you learned from her parents, Jenny had many problems.'

'Anything new? Problems with someone? A conflict?'

'No.' He shook his head. 'She seemed moodier lately.

195

Somewhat agitated. Not enough to sound any alarms. Just an observation.'

'Boyfriend problems, maybe?'

'She never mentioned a boyfriend.'

'What medications was she taking?'

'Zoloft.'

'Her parents said she worked from home. From her computer. Do you know what she did?'

'Sure. She conducted surveys for credit card offers. She talked about it, though not in-depth.'

'Was she involved in anything illegal?'

His eyebrows shot up. 'Pardon me, did you say illegal?'

'Yes. Were you aware of Jenny being involved in any criminal activities?'

'God, no. Jenny was extremely passive, Detective. She had constructed a life that required only a minimal interactive response from her. She was terrified of really living. Of real relationships. Of being hurt.'

Yet all her attempts to protect herself had led to her violent death.

M.C. jumped in. 'Do you know of any real-time friends she had?'

'No.'

'She never mentioned any friends at all?'

'People she knew from online activities.'

'Did she ever use their names?'

'I'm sure, though I can't recall them right now. She would often refer to them by their screen name, then when I queried, say something like, "My friend, Linda."'

'Would it be possible for you to get us those names?'

He ran a hand across his stubbled chin. 'That'd be a job. I'll need to go through my notes, maybe even my tapes.'

'It could be really important.'

He was quiet a moment, then nodded. 'I'll get Gina to retrieve my notes. It will take me a while to go through them.'

'How long has my cousin worked for you?' M.C. asked.

'A couple years.'

'Does the name Matt Martin mean anything to you?'

He thought a moment, then shook his head. 'No.'

'You're certain?' When he nodded, she continued. 'Could he have been a friend of Jenny's?'

'Maybe. Of course. But I don't know. She never mentioned him, at least that I can recall.'

'Are you aware if Gina and Jenny had a relationship outside Kids in Crisis?'

His expression altered slightly. 'What are you getting at, M.C.?'

'Are you aware of any relationship outside their contact at Kids in—'

'No, I'm not. Gina's a trusted employee.'

'Is that all she is?'

He moved his gaze between her and Kitt. 'I'm not sure what you're asking. Is she a friend as well as an employee?'

'At our engagement party, Gina told Dan she was your date that night. Are you and Gina having a relationship?'

He looked almost humorously surprised. 'No. And Gina wasn't my date. As far as I knew, she was an invited guest.'

'Why do you think she lied about that?'

He shifted in his seat. 'I have no idea and think it'd be wrong to speculate. I suggest you ask her.'

'We will.' Kitt stood. 'It's after-hours already, but the sooner we can get ahold of those names, the better.'

'I'll call Gina from the car. I'm sure she won't mind.'

That didn't sound like the Gina she knew, but M.C. kept that to herself. 'I'll walk you to the elevator, Erik.'

When they reached it, she punched the call button. He caught her hand. 'I've been thinking about you, M.C. Worried.'

'I'm okay.'

'It's a lot to deal with. First Dan. Then Tommy.'

'The case gives me something to focus on. Keeps my mind off missing him.'

He squeezed her fingers, then released them. 'If there's anything I can do. I miss him, too.'

The car arrived. He stepped in, but she held the door open.

'Can I ask you something, Erik? About Dan?'

'Sure, M.C.'

'He was the man I thought he was, right?'

He held her gaze, his unwavering. 'Absolutely.'

She released the door and it slid shut. He'd said it without hesitation, confidently. So why did she have this nagging feeling he was keeping something from her?

44

M.C. sat at the computer terminal, gazing at the illuminated screen. Three young victims. Three missing computers. A ring of cyberthieves. Five hundred thousand bucks.

The word *Breakneck*.

She had spent the last hour searching available law enforcement databases for references to the word – and had come up empty. She had hoped it might pop up as an alias. Or a reference to a known crime or group. Something that would open up an investigative door.

Any investigative door.

'Hey, Riggio.'

She looked over her shoulder. 'Jackson. This is a surprise. What brings you up from the tombs?'

The ID Bureau had earned a number of nicknames: dungeon, tomb, the box, hole and pit. The funny thing wasn't that the ID team had come up with most of the names themselves, but that they were terms of affection.

'Got the Lindeman photos.' He handed her a manila envelope. 'Figured you'd want them sooner than later.'

She smiled. 'Thanks, Jackson. I appreciate it.'

'You any closer to a suspect?'

'Some. Got a missing half mil on the table.'

'There's some motivation.' His gaze slid past her to the computer monitor. 'Breakneck. What's that all about?'

She glanced at the screen, then back at him. 'It's something that came out in an interview. I was doing a search, see if anything popped up.'

'Has it?'

'Not yet.'

'Breakneck,' he repeated, pursing his lips. 'Speed, maybe. Actual or chemical. Someone who breaks necks.'

Three victims. Two with broken necks. A no-brainer. Maybe. 'Tried both of those already.'

'I'll work on it,' he said as her cell phone went off. 'Let you know if I hit on something.'

She watched him walk away, then answered the call. 'Riggio.'

'I hear we have a third victim.'

Smith. 'Good news travels fast.'

'What can you tell me?'

'Jenny Lindeman. Twenty-one. Neck broken, computer AWOL.'

'And?'

Breakneck. 'We need to talk,' M.C. said.

'So talk.'

'Not here. Can we meet?'

'Where? When?'

'My place. Thirty minutes.'

45

Smith was waiting for M.C. when she arrived home. 'What's the big mystery?' he asked.

'Not out here. Inside.'

M.C. unlocked the door and let them in. 'I only have a few minutes,' she said as she closed the door. 'I've got something. Regarding the crackers.'

Smith arched his eyebrows in question. 'Something you haven't included your partner in on?'

She kept her voice even. 'Kitt doesn't need to know this.'

'I suggest you rethink that, Riggio. It's not going to take you anywhere good.'

'Let me worry about that.'

He shrugged. 'It's your partnership, your mistake to make.'

'Breakneck,' She said. A ripple of recognition crossed Smith's features. 'The word means something to you.'

'Yes. Where did you hear it?'

'I'm not going to say. What does it mean?'

He hesitated. 'It's a code name for a professional killer.'

'A hit man?'

'Yes.'

'Mafia?'

'Freelancer. Shit.' Smith turned and crossed to the window. 'This changes things.'

'That didn't come up in any of my searches.'

'It wouldn't.'

'Why?'

'Breakneck's been on the bureau's radar for quite some time. His name's been associated with several high-profile hits. An informant or suspect will call his name. Relay a story about him, his connections. But nobody's actually seen him.'

He turned and looked at M.C. 'Almost like a rumor. Or urban myth.'

'Until now.'

'Maybe. Been here before, I'm not getting excited yet.'

'Two of the victims' necks were broken. His trademark?'

'Yes.'

M.C. frowned. 'What does it mean? Why would this Breakneck be involved in Tommy's murder?'

'You're certain you heard right? You're certain Breakneck—'

'I've got it in writing, so to speak.'

'You located the girl.'

'I'd rather not say.' The evasion told the man everything he needed to know: that she had, indeed, located the girl.

'Again, you're on a slippery slope, Riggio.'

'I'm aware of that. I didn't have a choice.'

'Word of advice, there's always a choice.'

And she had made hers – keep information from her partner and out of proper channels. In essence, taking the law into her own hands.

A week and a half ago she would have sworn herself incapable of such a thing.

M.C. held Smith's gaze. 'I repeat, why would Breakneck be involved with Tommy's, Matt Martin's and now Jenny Lindeman's deaths?'

'I don't know.' He shrugged out of his topcoat and tossed it over the back of a chair. 'Let's look at what we have. A ring of cyberthieves, made up of young people. According to Tommy.'

'A source who's dead,' M.C. said. 'In addition, two other twenty-something kids are dead, their computers missing.'

'According to that same source, these thieves stumbled upon an account with a half a million in it.'

'Two of the victims had their necks very efficiently broken.' M.C. narrowed her eyes. 'Breakneck's trademark.'

Smith nodded. 'The cold, impersonal killing style fits. For Breakneck, it's just business.'

'Computers are missing,' M.C. said, thinking aloud. 'There's information on them Breakneck wants. The question is, what information?'

'Crackers hijack account numbers and passwords. Other personal information.'

'His personal information. Maybe.'

'The money,' Smith said. 'The five hundred K.'

'How did he find them?'

'Caught them in the act, maybe. Tracked them.'

M.C. looked at him. 'Wait. He's been hired to take them out.'

'Why?'

'The money, of course. Somebody wants it, free and clear. With no roads leading back to them.'

'And they have Breakneck take the computer to protect themselves from discovery.'

'Yes,' M.C. said, growing excited. 'This makes sense to me.'

'Maybe. Though does it make financial sense?'

M.C. saw where he was going with this. 'How much is a hit?'

'You're asking the wrong agent. Cybertheft's my area, not professional killers. I'm going to dig, see exactly what the bureau has on Breakneck, ask some questions. I'll get back to you.'

He grabbed his coat; M.C. walked to the door. She opened it to find Gina on her way up the front walk.

'You have company,' Smith said.

'One of my cousins.'

Gina reached them. M.C. introduced the two. Smith shook Gina's hand, then turned to M.C. 'I'll be in touch.'

M.C. watched him walk away, then turned to her cousin. 'This is a surprise.'

'Sorry to barge in this way, but I need to talk to you.'

'Come on in.'

They stepped inside. M.C. closed the door, but didn't offer the other woman a seat. 'What's up, Gina?'

She cleared her throat. 'It's about your visit this afternoon.'

Call her a cynic, but M.C. wasn't surprised. 'Do you have more information for me?'

'Earlier, I wasn't completely truthful with you. About Jenny.' She motioned toward the living room. 'Can we sit down?'

M.C. nodded and led her to the couch. Gina unbuttoned her coat, then sat, expression miserable.

'I knew more about her than I let on,' she said. 'More than I should have known.' Gina had removed her gloves and clutched them in her hands. 'I gave her a ride home once. Her car wouldn't start, it was quitting time . . . so I gave her a lift.'

Gina drew in a ragged breath. 'She didn't talk much. Was . . . unnaturally quiet. It made me curious. When I had the opportunity, I looked at her file.'

'A big no-no, I assume. Does Dr Sundstrand know about this?'

She shook her head. 'He'd be really angry. He might even fire me. Client files are confidential.' She leaned toward M.C., expression pleading. 'I feel just horrible about it. I'd never done anything like that before. Or since.'

M.C. might have been inclined to believe her if she didn't know her better. 'And that's it?'

'Not quite.' She lowered her eyes, when she looked back up they were bright with tears. 'I wanted to talk about us. Our relationship. How much it hurts that we're so distant.'

'Distant,' M.C. repeated. 'By that you mean we pretty much hate each other's guts.'

'I don't hate you, M.C. Far from it. But I know it's seemed like that over the years.' She cleared her throat. 'I'd like to put all that behind us. We're adults now. Professional women. We're *family*.'

She touched M.C.'s arm. 'We've just lived through a tragedy. Two, really. I'd like to think I've learned from it. That you have, too.'

M.C. wanted to suggest the only thing her cousin had learned was to cover her ass, but she let that go.

'Life's too short to harbor childish animosity,' she went on. 'And why? Because we're such different people? We were close once. Maybe we never will be again, but do we have to fling darts at each other?'

'I have no intention of throwing darts or anything else at you, Gina.'

Her cousin smiled tremulously. 'You're willing to let bygones be bygones?'

Gina, M.C. decided, was either an accomplished actress or sincere. M.C. voted for the former. 'Absolutely, Gina. That's all in the past.'

Gina's eyes filled with tears. 'I'm so glad. Thank you, Mary Catherine. This means so much to me.'

'Can I ask you a question, Gina?'

'Of course.'

'Are you and Erik seeing each other?'

She looked uncomfortable. 'Why? I mean surely you're not . . . I mean Dan hasn't been dead very lo . . .'

She let the words trail off. They hung unsaid in the air. *Dead very long.* Truthfully, she wasn't surprised Gina's mind had gone there first; that was the way she thought. No loyalty or real commitment.

'No,' M.C. said stiffly. 'That was an official question.'

'Oh, of course.' She cleared her throat. 'Workplace relationships are so sticky. Sleeping with coworkers . . . what a mess that can turn out to be. Let's just say, I've learned from my mistakes.'

'Is that a yes, Gina?'

'No, we're not currently seeing each other.'

'When did it end?'

'A while ago. Before you and Dan—'

She bit the words back and M.C. frowned. 'Before Dan and I what?'

She hesitated. 'Became a couple.'

Minutes later, M.C. watched her cousin ease her Mercedes out of the drive. She shut the door, then rubbed her cold hands together. How had Gina known when she and Dan became a couple? Gina had had a relationship with Erik. Could she have had one with Dan as well?

The thought left her feeling ill. She tried to push it away, but it crept back. If they had, why wouldn't Dan have told her? After all, they both had pasts, relationships they weren't proud of.

Maybe he hadn't told her because his thing with Gina hadn't ended.

'No,' she said aloud. 'You're not going to do this, Mary Catherine. He loved you.'

She flipped open her cell phone and punched in Kitt's number. 'Guess who just paid me a visit?' she said when her partner answered. 'My favorite cousin.'

'No kidding? Did she confess?'

'To having slept with the boss, yes. Past tense, according to her. And she admitted she lied to us about Jenny. Said she gave her a lift home from the center once. Also took an unauthorized peek at her files.'

'Charming. *If* we can believe her.'

'Exactly. Then she groveled, big time. Wanted to make amends with me. After all these years, because we're *family*.'

'Seems our Ms DeLuca's a bit nervous.'

'And looking awfully guilty. You might just get the chance to bust Barbie after all.'

46

Wednesday, January 28
10:20 P.M.

Two hours hadn't passed before Smith called with information. M.C. had agreed to meet him at this North Second Street McDonald's, a midway point between her west side and his east side homes.

They didn't go in. Instead, Smith climbed in the front passenger seat of her Explorer. 'Thanks for meeting me,' he said. 'I know it's late.'

'I don't sleep much these days anyway. What do you have?'

'The price of a professional hit depends on who's doing the hit and who the target is. The more experienced the hitter, the higher the price. The bigger the target, the higher the price.'

M.C. nodded. 'Makes sense. The bigger the target, the trickier the hit. Seems to me, if someone was trying to hit a celebrity or politician, they'd hire someone with experience.'

'Seems like a no-brainer. But there are a lot of stupid people out there.'

'And they're caught because they're stupid,' M.C. said.

'Breakneck's in a different category.'

'What's the range?'

'Ten grand up to the sky's the limit. Less for some dumb shit an even dumber shit picks up in a bar and recruits for the job.'

'From what you've told me, this Breakneck isn't the picked-up-at-the-bar type.'

'He's not. Our information indicates he's good. Very professional. Experienced.'

'These kids would be pretty low-profile targets.'

'I agree. Interesting, isn't it?'

'As in, it doesn't add up,' M.C. said. 'Let's look at our other option.'

'Our other option?'

'The kids jacked his information and got his money. It's personal, not a hired job.'

'Then it's not about the money.'

M.C. cocked an eyebrow. 'No?'

'According to my sources, option two takes us to an even scarier place.'

'Scarier for who? Us? Or the kids?'

'The kids. A professional is a killing machine. He – or she – doesn't think like us. He doesn't feel guilt or remorse. Everyone's a potential target and human life has no intrinsic value. He gets the job done, then moves on.'

Smith cleared his throat. 'If option two is his motive, the killings are about the information. His anonymity is everything to him. He lives – or dies – by it. He can't chance being found out. He can't chance his client list being compromised. He won't.'

M.C. was liking the sound of this. What it meant. 'He's tracking down everyone who had access to his information. Everyone who touched it, so to speak. And killing them.'

Smith nodded. 'Yes.'

'And he's finding them through their computers.'

'Maybe. Yes, maybe.'

M.C. suddenly felt cold. She rubbed her arms. 'There could be more of these kids. Sitting ducks.'

'We need to find them before he does.'

'How?'

'You may have already spoken to one of them.'

'Who?' But even as she uttered the question, she knew –
Zoe.

47

M.C. dialed Sam the moment Smith had driven off. 'Where are you?' she asked. She could hardly hear him for all the noise in the background.

'Spanky's.'

'We need to talk.'

'Shoot, cuz.'

His words slurred, ever so subtly. He'd been drinking.

'Not like this,' she said. 'Where's Zoe?'

'Don't know. I haven't seen her since—'

She cut him off, impatient. 'Can you reach her?'

'I can try. No promises.'

'If you do, arrange for us to meet.'

'Not unless you tell me why.'

'Excuse me?'

'You heard me. Tell me what's going on.'

M.C. admitted a grudging respect. It mixed with being royally pissed that he wasn't doing just what she'd told him to. 'Another person is dead. A girl this time.'

'My God. Who—'

'Name was Jenny Lindeman. We think Zoe may be in danger.'

210

'Zoe? But why?'

'Just trust me! I'll explain it all when you bring me Zoe.'

'What if she won't come?'

'If she resists, tell her about Jenny. If what I'm thinking is true, she'll come.'

'All right, I'll try.' He sounded rattled. 'But I can't—'

'Promise,' she finished for him. 'I know. You stay put. I'll meet you at Spanky's. And Sam?'

'Yeah?'

'No more alcohol.'

The club was hopping when M.C. arrived; she had to shimmy through the sea of mostly inebriated young people. She remembered when she had enjoyed this scene. Damn, that seemed ages ago.

She found Sam at the crowded bar. She pulled him away from his beer, leading him to what passed for a quiet corner, the hallway outside the johns.

'Did you reach Zoe?'

He nodded. 'On her cell phone. She said she would meet me here.'

'How long?'

'I didn't ask.'

'Where was she?'

He looked sheepish. 'I didn't ask.'

'Damn it, Sam. This isn't a game.'

He looked hurt. 'You didn't tell me to ask all that! You said to get her here, and that's what I did. Now you're going postal on me, what gives?'

A part of her wanted to lecture him. Tell him to use his head. Think for himself, take responsibility.

But the other part knew he was right.

'Sorry, kiddo. I can be a little intense.'

'S'okay, I should have thought of that myself. I'll text her.'

M.C. watched him as his thumbs quickly punched in the message, then sent it. There wasn't *that* much difference in their ages, but the difference in their technological immersion never ceased to amaze her.

211

Zoe replied nearly instantly. 'She's in the parking lot now,' he said.

'Tell her we'll meet her there.'

Sam replied, and they made their way to the front entrance. Zoe had ignored the last text and was showing her ID to the bouncer. She looked tipsy. Apparently, Spanky's wasn't her first stop of the night.

She saw Sam but not M.C. 'Hi, Sammy.'

'Hey, Zoe.' Sam slid his arm around her shoulders and turned her around. 'C'mon, baby. We need to talk.'

'But I want to dance.'

'We'll dance later.'

M.C. fell in step behind them. Obviously, Sam hadn't told her she would be here.

As they stepped fully out into the night, the cold air hit them, a welcome respite after the bar's humid interior.

'Hello, Zoe,' M.C. said.

The girl looked at M.C., then back at Sam. 'What's she doing here?'

'She needed to talk to us.'

'I told her everything I know!'

She sounded panicked. An interesting reaction from someone who had nothing to hide.

'A girl named Jenny Lindeman is dead,' M.C. said.

She froze. 'What?'

'She was killed in the same way as Matt Martin. And, like Martin and Tommy, her computer is missing.'

'That can't—' Zoe curved her arms around her middle. 'You're making this up.'

'I was at the scene. Yesterday was her twenty-first birthday.'

'I feel sick. I need to sit down.'

They led her to the curb. She sat and lowered her head to her knees. Several young people passed them, glancing sympathetically their way. No doubt they thought Zoe'd had too much to drink.

M.C. gave Zoe a minute to compose herself, then said, 'You knew her?'

'Why would I?'

M.C. didn't point out how unconvincing she was. 'We have reason to believe she, Martin and Tommy were part of a group of criminal hackers. They stole informa—'

'What the hell,' Sam burst out. 'No way Tommy was—'

She held up a hand, stopping him. 'They stole information, like credit card and bank account numbers, and sold it.'

'I wouldn't know anything about that,' Zoe whispered.

'Really? Then you wouldn't know anything about the half-million bucks Tommy came across in one of the accounts? The five hundred thousand dollars he had hoped to use as collateral to get himself – or a close friend – out of the group?'

The girl looked helplessly at Sam. He turned to M.C., expression disbelieving. 'This is messed up, M.C. You're calling my brother a thief?'

She went on as if he hadn't spoken. 'Because if you do know anything about it, you might be the next in line to die.'

Zoe looked stricken; she began to tremble. M.C. pressed her. 'I did a little research. Breakneck is the name of a professional killer. A hit man. He may have been hired to kill everyone who knows about the money. If you don't fall into that category, fine. But if you do, perhaps you'd like to change your story?'

The young woman brought her hands to her face and moaned.

'I don't have a lot of time,' M.C. said. 'And frankly, you may not either. What do you think, Zoe? Sticking with your original story? Or changing it?'

'I knew Jenny,' she whispered. 'She was one of the crackers.'

'Are you one of them?'

She nodded.

'Did you recruit Tommy?'

She lifted her gaze. 'He recruited me! I swear!'

The words reverberated through her. They hurt. She glanced at Sam; he looked sick.

'I needed the money. He told me it really didn't hurt anyone.

213

That the credit card companies didn't hold individuals liable for theft like that.'

A so-called victimless crime. Too bad the innocent always paid – in some form or fashion. M.C. forced herself to focus on the girl. 'And the five hundred thousand, do you have it?'

'No! I don't know anything about that!'

'That claim's getting old, Zoe.'

'We hacked and jacked. Turned around and sold the information. That's it. I never saw any money in any account. I swear!'

'You're lying.'

'I'm not! I—'

'Tommy called the FBI. He wanted out. He told the agent a "friend" was in trouble, he was helping them. This person had hit the jackpot.' She leaned toward her. 'I think you're that friend.'

'The FBI? Oh, my God!' She jumped to her feet. 'I don't want to go to jail!'

'I need names, Zoe. Anyone you know who was involved.'

'I have to think. I don't know . . . we mostly didn't meet one another. A few screen names—'

'Who first involved Tommy?'

She pressed the heels of her hands to her eyes. 'I don't know . . . I can't remember what he told me!'

She was sobbing now, hysterical. Sam put his arms around her. 'It's okay, Zoe. M.C. will take care of everything, you'll see.'

M.C. didn't know if her cousin believed that or was simply trying to comfort Zoe. If he believed it, he was mistaken. Now, however, was not the time to correct him.

'But we've got to help her,' he went on. 'If we do, it'll be all right.'

M.C. stepped in without confirming or denying. 'I'll need your computer, Zoe.'

'My computer?' she repeated, sniffling. 'Why?'

'If what we suspect is true, this Breakneck is finding the members of the group through the computers. Did you and Jenny Lindeman correspond?'

She went white. 'I don't understand.'

She didn't *want* to understand. 'Breakneck can use a reverse e-mail address search to get your name, address, map coordinates. It can all be had. Quickly. And cheaply.'

Zoe simply stared at her, expression horrified.

'The three of us are going to your apartment, Zoe. We're going to collect your computer and anything you might need for an overnight stay.'

'Overnight? Where am I—'

'If you corresponded with Jenny Lindeman, Breakneck either has your name already or will soon. I'm thinking staying at your own place would be an extraordinarily bad idea. Unless, of course, you want to die.'

48

Zoe lived in half a modest duplex on the city's east side, not far from Rock Valley College. The duplex was completely dark.

'You didn't leave a light on?' M.C. said.

'I forgot.'

'Don't be careless like that again. Anyone live on the other side?'

'Not right now.'

'Key.'

Zoe handed it to her and they made their way up the front walk. M.C. unlocked the door and entered the apartment first, weapon drawn.

'Light switch?' she asked.

'To the right of the door.'

M.C. found it. Light flooded the room. Relatively neat, M.C. saw. Pleasantly feminine.

Apparently empty.

'I'll check out the rest of the apartment. You two stay here.'

M.C. did a search, then returned to Sam and Zoe. 'Get your computer and overnight things.'

216

Zoe went to do as M.C. asked, but returned a moment later. 'It's gone. My laptop's gone.'

M.C. heard the blood rushing in her head. 'You're sure?'

'Yes.'

The killer had found Zoe already.

If she had been home, she would be dead.

'Pack a bag,' M.C. ordered. 'Take enough for several days. Everything you'll need. You're not safe here.'

49

After she had gotten Zoe calmed down and settled into the guest room, M.C. put on her warmest pajamas and made herself a cup of hot chocolate. She curled up on the couch, wishing she could get warm.

She hurt. She was disillusioned. Brokenhearted.

Would it have been easier learning the truth from outside the investigation? she wondered. She would have been angry. Outraged and disbelieving. She would have questioned her fellow detectives' every move.

And in the end, she would have been heartsick. Just as she was now. She rested her head against the sofa back. What had led Tommy to the place he ended up? Just old-fashioned, garden-variety greed? Or something bigger? Darker? Something none of them had had a clue about?

Her cell vibrated. It was Sam. 'I'm out front. I couldn't sleep.'

No big surprise there. 'Neither could I. I'm opening the door now.'

Moments later, she let him into the house. He made his way to the couch and flopped onto it. 'Where's Zoe?'

'Asleep.'

'Are you okay?'

M.C. picked up her cup, realized her hands were shaking, then set it back on the coffee table. 'Hanging in there.'

'He would have told me about this, M.C. I was his brother. I was thinking, if he recruited her, why didn't he try to recruit me?'

She thought a moment. 'Precisely why he didn't. He wanted to keep up the illusion of who he was, the kind of guy he wanted us to believe he was.'

It hurt to say the words; by the way he winced, it hurt him to hear them.

'I feel like crap.'

'So do I.'

Sam looked at her, tears in his eyes. 'I loved him. I looked up to him.'

'I know, buddy,' she said. 'I did, too.'

They fell into silence. Sam broke it first. 'I worked on Tommy's phone. Found something weird with twenty-five of the names in his contacts list.'

'Weird?' she repeated.

'You know, strange. About the numbers. Numbers that aren't numbers.'

M.C. shook her head. 'That doesn't make sense.'

'Sorry. I'm pretty tired. Numbers that aren't phone numbers.'

'Let me see.'

He retrieved a spiral-bound tablet from his backpack, opened it and slid it across to her. 'Look at that page. Do you recognize the names?'

She scanned the list. 'No.'

'Me, either. Now, check out the phone numbers.'

She did. 'Nine digits, not ten.'

'Right. A local number is seven. With an area code, ten.'

'So what are these?'

'Don't know. I did an online white pages search, just to be sure.'

'Maybe they're code,' she said. 'But for what?'

'And how do we decipher it?'

219

The information began to swim before her eyes. 'We don't, not tonight anyway. Let's work with the easy stuff first.'

He reached across, skipped back a few pages in the spiral. 'Confirmed names and numbers. Take a look.'

A hefty list, she saw. Broken down into the subheadings: contact list, calls sent, received, dialed and missed. Most were first names only. Some first name, last initial. Only a handful had full names. She would need to check those against Tommy's client list.

Many she recognized as family or Tommy's pals. She saw the FBI's number – twice.

'You say you confirmed these?'

'Either by phone or online.'

'Good work. What about his text messages?'

'Haven't looked at them yet.' He yawned. 'I'll start them now.'

'You need some sleep.' He looked like he wanted to argue; she cut him off. 'You work now, you'll make mistakes. Besides, I'm toast.'

'Can I stay here? The couch is fine.'

She thought of how he had often stayed at Tommy's. 'Sure, Sam. Hotel Riggio is open for business.'

50

After Sam had gone to bed, M.C. had tried to sleep. But her thoughts refused to allow it. She'd tossed and turned, picturing the strings of numbers in Tommy's contacts list.

Codes of some sort. Maybe. What other things were associated with strings of numbers? Zip codes. Bank accounts. Credit cards. Prisoner numbers. Addresses.

When the sun had finally begun to creep over the horizon, she'd given up on sleep and tiptoed out to the kitchen for coffee, closing the door between the kitchen and the living room so she wouldn't awaken Sam.

The only thing she knew for certain was, she needed Kitt's help. She needed her input. The time had come to confess her sins and beg forgiveness. She needed to do it in person. At HQ.

The thought scared the crap out of her.

She crossed to the coffeepot and refilled her cup, thoughts turning once again to the numbers in Tommy's phone. She worked to recall the names. Matt Martin had not been on the list. Nor had Jenny Lindeman. Zoe had.

Of course, those only represented the readily available lists. Once she came clean with Kitt and turned the device over to ID, they could retrieve *every* call ever made or sent.

Martin. Lindeman. Tommy. Zoe Petersen. She rubbed the bridge of her nose, running the names over in her mind. She wanted a direct connection between the victims. One stronger than—

The names, she realized. Matt Martin *and* Zoe Petersen. She unclipped her phone, called up Erik's number and punched SEND.

He answered, sounding sleepy. 'I have a question,' she said. 'Yesterday, you said you didn't recognize the name Matt Martin, but could he have been a patient at Kids in Crisis anyway?'

He was quiet. She wasn't certain if she had surprised him or if he was simply taking a moment to think.

'He could have. I'm certain he wasn't a patient of mine, but I have two other doctors on the team.'

'What about Zoe Petersen?'

'Again, not my patient. But that doesn't mean—'

She cut him off. 'How could we find out? It's important, Erik.'

'I'll call Gina. If she doesn't know offhand, she'll be happy to find out. Hold on.'

He put her on hold. A moment later, he returned. 'She's not answering, but she may be in the shower. Give me a few minutes, I'll call you back.'

Twenty minutes later, he called. 'She's still not picking up.'

'Damn it.'

'Look, I'm on my way in anyway.'

'How long?'

'Thirty minutes. Forty tops.'

Enough time to shower and dress. 'Talk to you then.'

The timing was perfect. When he called, she had finished bathing and had dried her hair.

'I'm here at the center, booting up the system. Okay, ready. What were those names?'

'Matt or Matthew Martin. And Zoe Petersen.'

'Let's look for Martin first.

'Sorry,' he said after a few seconds. 'No Matt Martin.'

'How about the other name? Zoe Petersen.'

'Hold on.' She heard the tapping of keys, a moment later, he said, 'Here she is. Zoe Elizabeth Petersen. She sees Dave Gilbert.'

They had it, a strong, physical connection between two of the crackers. 'You've helped more than you know, Erik. I'll explain later, but I've got to go.'

51

Jackson stood at the bank of vending machines, feeding one of them quarters. He looked fried.

Kitt shook her head. Another totally out-of-balance bastard.

'Hey, Jackson,' she called. 'What's your excuse, dude?'

He looked at her. 'Better stuff in these machines.'

She shook her head. 'Not that. For being here, looking like that, preparing to eat God knows what for breakfast.'

He grinned. 'Couldn't leave it alone.' A bag of bite-sized Oreo cookies dropped into the well and he retrieved them. 'You know what I mean?'

Unfortunately, she did. 'Take it from an old hand, ease up a little.'

She could see by his quizzical expression that her suggestion had made as much of an impression as being struck with a Nerf ball.

'Never mind, Jackson. Enjoy your cookies.'

'Thanks.' He ripped open the bag. 'Riggio around?'

'Not in yet.'

'I found something on that search she was doing. It's kind of obscure, probably nothing, but—'

'Which search?'

'Breakneck.' He popped several cookies into his mouth, then talked around them. 'I was going to catch up with her myself, but since you're here could I just pass it along?'

Breakneck? 'That'd be great,' she said, schooling her features. 'What do you have?'

'Popped up as a name in a suspect interview. A murder. Alexander Tandy. 'Bout ten years ago.'

Kitt searched her memory and came up empty. 'I don't recall a Tandy or Breakneck.'

'You wouldn't. It got turned over to the feds. Tandy was a federal witness, rumor was he was hit.'

'And Breakneck. The operation name or—'

'The hitter. Probably not related to your case, but you never know.'

Indeed. Sometimes not even about partners.

'You'll pass that along to Riggio?' he said.

'Count on it.' She forced a smile. 'Where'd the information come from?'

'Miller. The guy's memory blows me away.'

Blown away, now that was apt, Kitt thought as she headed down the hall. She couldn't believe M.C. would do this. Shut her out. Go solo. After what she'd sacrificed to keep M.C. on this case.

Could it be a mistake? Could M.C. simply have forgotten to mention the lead?

Riggio? Forget to mention a lead?

Kitt struggled to get a handle on her anger. And lost the battle. Dirty, rotten, two-timing little sneak. She'd jeopardized her relationship with Joe to help M.C. and this is how she repaid her?

So, where'd she get the information? And why was she keeping it from her?

Kitt returned to her desk and breathed deeply, working to regain control. To box up her anger and feeling of betrayal, and consider the situation analytically.

There were only a couple of reasons M.C. would have kept her out of the loop. To protect someone. Tommy, for

225

example. Keep details hidden until she had a clear idea of the whole picture. Or to protect herself. Because she had acted outside the law. To get information she otherwise couldn't. Or get it faster than she could playing by the rule book.

She didn't trust Kitt to play along.

Damn right, she wouldn't! She had assured Sal that she would keep M.C. in line. Protect the department.

Given *her* word. Sacrificed to do it.

Her cell vibrated; she checked the display. M.C., most probably to tell her she was on her way.

Kitt didn't pick up. She wanted to look her in the eyes when she confronted her. Wanted to be able to assess if she was telling the truth.

The thought rocked her. They had worked so hard to overcome their issues. Or so she had thought.

How would she ever be able to trust M.C. again?

52

Thursday, January 29
8:15 A.M.

M.C. fought to focus on the road. Her thoughts raced. Zoe had been a Kids in Crisis patient. Another link between the crackers. Another link that pointed toward Gina and KIC.

M.C. reached the PSB parking garage and swung in. Time to tell Kitt. Past time. Explain as best she could, beg her forgiveness.

She had screwed up, simple as that.

She had phoned Kitt and left a message; her partner still hadn't called her back. M.C. found a spot, parked and climbed out of her SUV. She hurried into the building and up to the Violent Crimes Bureau, blood thundering in her head.

She found Kitt at her desk, nose buried in her laptop. 'Big news, partner. We have to talk.'

'We do have to talk,' Kitt said, lifting her gaze. 'I have a message for you.'

'A messag—'

'From Jackson. About Breakneck. You want to talk about it here?'

M.C. caught her breath. Too late; she was too late. She pointed in the direction of the interview rooms. Kitt agreed and moments later, they faced each other in the closed room.

'Let me explain,' M.C. said.

'Explain what? Why you lied and kept facts from your partner? How you got those facts? That you have a second investigation going on behind my back?'

'I'm sorry.'

'I don't want or need your apologies. They don't mean anything to me. I backed you up. Gave a guarantee to Sal. Put my personal life on hold. For you. And this is how you repay me?'

'I had to do it. I didn't have a—'

Choice. She bit the word back, but it hung in the air between them. Mocking her.

'You promised me you'd be honest with me. That if you were losing it, I'd be the first to know. I'd call this losing it. How about you?'

'Sam found Zoe.'

She saw that it took a moment for Kitt to absorb what she was saying. When she figured she had given her enough time, M.C. added, 'She had Tommy's phone.'

Kitt sat down. 'Go on.'

'She didn't come forward because she was traumatized. Afraid of being arrested.'

'Of course she was!' Kitt burst out. 'She was there, she had the phone to prove it. She should have been officially interviewed!'

'True. I screwed up big time. But hear me out. She insists she found him after he was shot. She refused to come forward unless I met her alone.'

'And you agreed? Because of your personal involvement?' Expression disgusted, she got to her feet. 'You're no rookie, Riggio. You're a seasoned cop who should have known better. For God's sake, she could be anywhere now!'

'I know exactly where she is.'

Kitt brought her hands to her face; M.C. sensed she did so in an attempt to get a grip on her anger.

'She's in trouble, Kitt. She's on Breakneck's list.'

She dropped her hands and sat back down. 'Start at the beginning.'

228

M.C. did, beginning with Sam's surprise call that he'd found Zoe, the girl's offer of a conditional meeting, her decision to accept the conditions. 'The moment she handed me the phone, I knew how bad I'd messed up. But I was in it then and didn't know how to get out. I had her put her version of events on paper, then sign it.'

'Big deal. It'd be inadmissible.'

M.C. continued. 'Zoe claims she went to Tommy's that morning to convince him to love her. She let herself in and like me, found him in the shower.'

'And the phone?'

M.C. took a deep breath. 'She stuck with the story she told me the day she called me at the VCB. She saw it there on the bathroom counter, grabbed it and ran.'

'And this Breakneck, where did that come from?'

'A slip of paper, tucked between the keys and display screen of Tommy's cell phone.'

'It's falling apart for me.'

'I know, but I believe she didn't kill Tommy.'

'What about Jackson?'

'I was on the computer, he got a look at my search criteria. Asked me about it.'

Kitt looked thoughtful. 'He told me that Miller recalled Breakneck being associated with a murder. A hit. Feds took the case.'

M.C. nodded. 'That's what I learned from Agent Smith as well. Breakneck is thought to be a hit man. Very smart. Extremely dangerous. He's been on the bureau's radar for some time, but they've never come close.'

'You went to Agent Smith?' Kitt said, voice tight.

'I needed him. And I knew he wouldn't care how I got the information.'

'Where has all this subterfuge led you?'

'Breakneck is systematically killing the kids.'

'Why?'

'Two theories. First, he's been hired by someone to kill anyone who knew about the five hundred K.'

'Problem with the first theory?'

'This Breakneck is a pretty high-level hitter. And these kids seem like pretty low-level targets.'

'Second theory?'

'They jacked his information and money and he's taking them out, one by one.'

'Payback.'

'Maybe. Or maybe he's protecting his anonymity.'

'How did he find them?'

'The question of the hour.'

'And the problem with theory two.' She let out a frustrated-sounding breath. 'Where's the phone now?'

'I have it.'

'I want it, ASAP. The state crime lab's the only facility with the capabilities to retrieve complete forensic information from the device.'

'I had Sam do an autopsy on it.'

'Sam?'

She felt herself flush at Kitt's incredulous tone. 'A partial autopsy.'

'Anything?'

M.C. cleared her throat, feeling foolish. 'In Tommy's contact list, something, a code maybe, we haven't figured it out. Names with phone numbers that aren't phone numbers.'

'Where's the girl now?'

She hesitated a heartbeat, and Kitt made a sound of disgust. 'Still holding back, M.C.?'

'My place, for her own safety. Petersen and Lindeman communicated. I went with her to retrieve her computer . . . and it was gone.'

'She's one of the crackers.'

'Yes.'

'And Tommy, too?'

'Yes,' she said evenly. 'She says he recruited her.'

'And you believe her?'

'I don't want to. But yes, I do.'

Kitt gazed steadily at her. 'We need to bring Petersen in. Officially question her.'

'She's skittish, she might bolt.'

'We make certain she doesn't. It's for her own protection, as well as ours.'

'There's more. Zoe was a Kids in Crisis client. I found that out today.'

'Holy shit.'

'My sentiments exactly. If we're looking for a Svengali-type who sucks the kids in, who would bond better with a troubled kid than their therapist?'

'This puts everyone associated with KIC squarely in the suspect category, including Erik.'

'My thoughts exactly, though he was not her counselor.'

'And that's it, M.C.? Everything?'

'Yes.'

'How do I know you're telling me the truth?'

The question hurt. No doubt Kitt had meant it to.

And no doubt she deserved it.

'I guess you'll just have to trust me.'

'Right now, I'd call that laughable.'

Her cell phone vibrated. M.C. checked the display, but didn't recognize the number.

'Riggio.'

'M.C., it's Erik.' His voice shook. 'I didn't know what else to do, so I called you.'

'Take a deep breath, Erik. Tell me what's wrong.'

'It's Gina. I kept trying to reach her and couldn't so I swung by her house. She's . . . I found her and' – his voice rose – 'she's dead!'

The realization reverberated through her. For the space of a heartbeat, she couldn't breathe, let alone speak. 'Are you still at the scene?' she finally managed.

'Yes.'

'Call 911. Tell them what you told me. They'll send a cruiser. Stay put, but don't touch anything. Lundgren and I will be right there.'

231

53

Thursday, January 29
9:35 A.M.

Gina lived in the very nice east Rockford neighborhood, Willow Wood. With all new construction and large homes on acre lots, Willow Wood was a world away from the modest west side neighborhoods where M.C. and Gina had grown up.

M.C. pulled up in front of Gina's sprawling home. As she gazed at the structure, it occurred to M.C. that it didn't matter how lavishly you lived – when the party was over, it was over. You couldn't bring it with you.

The 911 cruisers had already arrived and the first officers were securing the scene. In the distance M.C. heard the wail of a siren – the EMTs, she thought.

Erik stood huddled on the lovely stone porch. He looked like he had aged ten years since she had seen him just the day before.

She and Kitt crossed to him. 'Erik?' she said.

He looked blankly at her. 'Thank you for coming.'

He said it as if he were hosting a dinner party. M.C. touched his hand. 'You're freezing.'

'I couldn't go back in there.'

'I understand. How about a blanket? We could talk in one of the cruisers?'

'I'm okay.'

He wasn't. But that wasn't for her to decide. 'I need you to tell us exactly what happened.'

He nodded, but didn't speak.

'Start at the beginning, Dr Sundstrand,' Kitt said. 'How did you come to be here?'

He shifted his gaze to Kitt. 'I couldn't reach her. Which was strange. I have an agreement with my assistants and managers, they're always accessible.'

Kind of like a cop. 'Go on,' M.C. said.

'I thought I'd better check on her. I worried she might be sick or . . . that something had happened to her.'

Kitt stepped in. 'Like what, Dr Sundstrand?'

'I don't know . . . an accident. Certainly not . . . this.'

Kitt drew her eyebrows together. 'That seems odd to me. Do you worry about all your employees that way?'

He looked startled by the question. 'What do you mean?'

'Checking on an employee's well-being at home.'

'You don't understand.'

'Clearly. Help me out here.'

'She was never out of touch. It was part of the job.' His expression tightened. 'I couldn't reach her. She lives alo— lived alone and I thought I should check on her.'

'Let's move on,' M.C. said. 'What happened next?'

'I rang the bell. When I didn't get an answer, I tried the door.'

'Front or back?' Kitt asked.

He hesitated a moment, looking confused. 'Front. It was unlocked.' He rubbed his hands together; M.C. noticed that he was trembling. 'I called out, then went looking for—'

He bit the words back, his gaze going to the EMTs who had arrived. He watched as they climbed out of the ambulance and hurried with their gear toward the house.

'You found Gina?' Kitt asked, drawing his attention back to their questions.

He squeezed his eyes shut. 'In her bedroom.'

That he had looked for her there, even in this situation, struck M.C. as too familiar for an employer-employee relationship

233

and seemed to confirm Gina's claim that they had been lovers. 'And she was dead?'

He nodded.

'You checked her pulse?'

'No. I didn't think . . . no.'

'Did you touch her in any way?'

He shook his head. 'I ran out here and called you.'

'Thank you, Erik,' she said gently. 'I need to go inside now, but I might have a few more questions. Would you mind waiting in one of the cruisers?'

Something moved across his expression. Realization that he may actually be under suspicion? Awareness of the precarious position finding Gina had put him in? Sudden, instinctive distrust?

Or maybe it was all her imagination?

She was aware of him watching her as she and Kitt signed the log and entered the house. M.C. glanced at her partner. 'Did Erik seem like he was being evasive to you?'

'I don't think he was telling us everything. The question is, what was he holding back?' Kitt looked at her. 'I want DeLuca's phones checked. Calls in and out.'

They followed the sound of voices to the victim. At the bedroom doorway, they met up with the EMTs, on their way out.

'Nothing we can do for her,' one of them said.

'Have a good day,' said the other.

M.C. and Kitt stepped into the large bedroom. Gina lay on her back on the floor, the once-lovely white carpeting around her blood-soaked. The blood made an irregular, menacing shadow around her head and shoulders.

She had been shot in the right eye. An ugly death; a gruesome scene. No wonder Erik seemed traumatized.

M.C. gazed at Gina, sadness washing over her. Her thoughts flooded with memories, most good, some bad. They had been family. Once upon a time, friends. A big part of each other's lives – even after Gina had turned against her. For wasn't that the nature of life? Equal parts joy and pain? The most memorable moments sometimes being the most painful?

234

'You okay?' Kitt asked, fitting on latex gloves.

'Hanging in there.' She followed Kitt's lead, then squatted beside the body. Gina wore wool slacks and a simple white sweater. The two whites, sweater against carpeting, played a strange visual peekaboo with her.

'No makeup on,' Kitt murmured. 'Looks like her hair was wet when it happened.'

M.C. shifted her gaze. 'Light in the bathroom's on.' She stood and crossed to the master bath doorway. Towels lay in a heap on the floor. She crossed to them, found them damp.

She turned to the vanity. Hair dryer out. Curling iron plugged in, its power light blinking frantically. Makeup, bottles and jars strewn across the vanity top. She pictured Gina as she had been not even twenty-four hours ago and a lump formed in her throat. What if Gina had been being real with her when she'd asked to make amends? What if she had sincerely been offering the olive branch?

'M.C.? Find something?'

She cleared her throat. 'Looks like a morning routine was under way in here. Helps establish TOD.'

She returned to her partner's side. Kitt looked at her. 'Maybe she had company?'

'Maybe.'

ID arrived. Miller, Sorenstein and Jackson.

'Yo, ladies,' Sorenstein said, 'we meet again.'

'Lucky us.'

Francis entered the room and their conversation. 'Looks to me like this one had no luck at all.' He slipped into his gloves. 'What've we got?'

'Gunshot,' Miller said. 'One Gina DeLuca. Dead as a door-nail.'

From the corners of her eyes, she saw Kitt open her mouth – no doubt to inform them of M.C.'s relationship to the victim. She laid a hand on her arm, stopping her. It would be out soon enough; for now she wanted this to be treated like any other scene.

'Thanks for that expert analysis, Detective Miller,' the pathologist said drily. 'But why don't I have a little look?'

M.C. and Kitt gave him space, using the time to inspect the rest of the house. It had four bedrooms, including the master. The other three were perfectly decorated and in perfect order. Their adjoining baths, also in perfect order. Each had a basket of sample-size personal care products on the counter.

'Your cousin did a lot of traveling,' Kitt said. 'It looks like these were plundered from hotels.'

She picked through a basket, reading the labels. 'The Phoenician, Phoenix; Ritz-Carlton, New Orleans; Grand Hyatt, New York. All that fun takes money.'

'Or a sugar daddy.'

'Let's check out the rest of the house.'

The kitchen was large and a real cook's wet dream. Somehow, M.C. didn't see Gina spending a lot of time cooking. 'One coffee mug in the sink,' she said. 'A bowl with the remnants of what looks like oatmeal.'

M.C. opened the dishwasher. It contained little – a half-dozen or so pieces of dinnerware. She moved on to the garbage bin. 'Not much here. Lean Cuisine box.'

'Looks like she stayed in last night. Alone.'

Kitt nodded. 'Interesting. What time was she at your place?'

'Around nine. Give or take.'

'After dinnertime. Question is, did she leave you and come straight here? Or stop somewhere on the way home. Think she had a regular guy?'

'Maybe Erik. I'll ask around.'

They moved on to the living room. The TV's remote lay on the comfy-looking couch, an afghan lay in a heap on the floor and on the table sat a plate decorated with crumbs.

'Cookie, I'm thinking,' Kitt mused.

'Could be cake. We Italians like our cake.'

'Whatever, all together it paints a picture of a woman who lived alone and who was home alone the night before she was killed.'

One room left. A home office, they saw.

M.C. moved her gaze around the overly accessorized office. 'No computer. Son of a bitch! The bastard beat us here.'

'It might not be what it looks like.'

236

'Do you really believe that?' M.C. crossed to the desk and randomly began opening drawers. Papers, pens and other supplies. A pack of sugar-free gum. Take-out menus. Photos.

She scooped them up and began thumbing through. 'Oh, my God,' she said. Pictures of Gina and Dan. Obviously a couple. Holding each other. Smiling for the camera, looking flushed and satisfied.

M.C. couldn't breathe. Couldn't take her eyes off the images. She was aware of Kitt coming up behind her, looking over her shoulder.

'This was before he met you, I'm sure of it.'

'Then why didn't he tell me?'

'When you met, he probably didn't even know she was your cousin. And when he found out, he knew it would upset you.'

'We were all there at the party. I saw them talking.' It hurt, M.C. acknowledged. God, it hurt. 'Why didn't he tell me?'

'He was going to tell you after. Or the next day. He didn't have the chance.'

'I'll never know,' she whispered.

'M.C.' – Kitt eased the photographs from her hands – 'don't do this to yourself. He loved you. He wanted to marry you. Whatever they had was nothing compared to that.'

'Detectives?' They turned toward the uniformed officer standing in the doorway. 'Pathologist is looking for you.'

'Got it,' Kitt said. 'Thanks.' She turned back to M.C. 'What do you want to do? Your call.'

'Go home, crawl into bed. Pull the covers over my head. And pretend I never saw those photographs.'

'Do it,' Kitt said. 'You have my permission.'

M.C. gazed at her partner, heart thundering. The urge to curl into a fetal position warred with one to come out swinging. Kitt wouldn't hold it against her if she retreated to lick her wounds. Wouldn't think less of her.

But she would think less of herself, M.C. acknowledged. Mary Catherine Riggio would not break. And she did not run.

'I'm not going anywhere. Not yet.'

'Good girl. Let's go.'

They returned to the master bedroom. 'Finished already, Francis?' Kitt asked.

'This one's pretty straightforward. Just like the others.'

'Certainly not "just like the others."'

'That's where you're wrong, Detective Lundgren. It's near exactly like the last one. And Tommy Mariano's. And Matt Martin's.'

'Explain.'

'Somebody knows what they're doing.'

'Yeah,' Kitt muttered, 'whacking people. Quite efficiently, too.'

'Actually, that's just it.' He removed his glasses and polished the lenses with his shirtsleeve. 'The human body is incredibly resilient. Delivering death is quite a bit more difficult than it seems. And it's almost never instantaneous.

'But,' he continued, 'there are places on the body when targeted that provide instantaneous death.'

'Instantaneous?' Kitt repeated.

'Death in about three seconds. In this case, a bullet to the eye. In your cousin's, a bullet to the temple. The two young people, expertly broken neck. All hit in "death targets."'

Death targets. The work of a professional.

Breakneck.

He slid his glasses back on. 'Additionally, no sign of a struggle. No defensive wounds. It doesn't appear there's any matter under her fingernails.'

'One shot,' M.C. murmured. 'Perfectly placed.'

Kitt looked at her. 'So, how'd it happen?'

'Sundstrand said the door was open. Did our perp let himself in, surprise her in the bedroom and *bam,* bullet to the brain?'

'Or, did she let our perp in, lead him to the bedroom where he offed her?'

'In other words, did she know her killer? Or not?'

'How long's she been dead?'

'Not that long. A few hours,' Francis answered.

'Was she waiting for someone? Perhaps Sundstrand? Maybe the door wasn't unlocked? Maybe he unlocked it?'

'Or someone else did?'

Kitt looked at her. 'We're going to need to bring Sundstrand in.'

'He'll lawyer up.'

Miller spoke up. 'Already has, if I'm right about the dude in the suit that pulled up. They're keeping warm in a monster Mercedes.'

54

M.C. and Kitt exited the house. Sure enough, a big, midnight blue Mercedes sedan sat idling in the drive. A distinguished-looking man sat behind the wheel, Erik sat in the passenger seat beside him.

Kitt looked at M.C. Her partner wore the glazed expression of someone who had reached maximum emotional load capacity. 'I've got to take this one.'

M.C. nodded. 'I'll give Smith a ring, let him know what's happening?'

'Go for it.'

They started toward the Mercedes. M.C. flipped open her cell phone and dialed the agent. She delivered her message, then turned to Kitt. 'He's on his way. Said it'd be twenty minutes.'

The Mercedes's doors opened and Erik and his lawyer emerged from the vehicle. Erik made the introductions. 'My lawyer, Rick Kolb.'

Erik Sundstrand was a wealthy man and a public figure. Guilty or innocent, he was smart enough to know to protect himself.

It pissed Kitt off anyway.

'Detectives,' the lawyer said. 'This is a terrible thing. Gruesome.'

'Murder always is.'

'Erik is committed to helping in whatever way necessary to see his employee's killer brought to justice.'

Sure he is. That's why he's paying you three hundred bucks an hour. 'I'm happy to hear that, Mr Kolb.'

'I'm concerned, however, about Detective Riggio's request for my client to wait here. Not only are the physical conditions intolerable' – all their gazes slid toward the Mercedes – 'but my client has experienced a horrible shock. To request he stay here at the scene is simply unacceptable.'

'Did Detective Riggio say you had to stay?' Kitt turned to Sundstrand, feigning surprise. 'I'm sorry, Dr Sundstrand. You're free to go, of course. But before you do, just a couple questions?'

'Sure,' he answered before his lawyer could warn him not to.

'How well did you know Ms DeLuca?'

'She was a valuable employee. Worked for me a couple of years.'

'Did you socialize with her?'

'No.'

If what the victim had told M.C. was true, then Sundstrand was lying. Kitt let it go. Better to catch him in the lie later than give him the opportunity to wiggle free now. 'Was she married?'

'Divorced.'

'Did you know her ex-husband?'

'Husbands,' he corrected. 'She was married twice. I never met either of them.'

Kitt glanced at M.C. for confirmation, got it and returned her gaze to Sundstrand. 'Did she tell you anything about her ex-husbands?'

He hesitated. 'Not much. Her first husband was her high school sweetheart. The second an orthodontist.'

'Any kids?'

He shook his head.

241

'She tell you anything about either divorce?'

'The first marriage was short-lived. They grew apart, she said. The second was acrimonious. There was infidelity involved.'

'On whose part?'

He looked surprised by the question. 'His.'

Kitt looked at her partner again, but this time she frowned slightly and shook her head. 'Name?' Kitt asked.

'His? DeLuca, I guess.'

'You guess? You don't know for sure?'

'No. We never discussed it.'

The attorney stepped in. 'Which is perfectly appropriate in this situation.'

Kitt pressed on. 'Did she have a computer?'

'Yes. She often e-mailed from home.'

'A laptop?'

'Yes. She brought it to the office occasionally.'

'Why?'

He looked surprised. 'So she could work from home.'

'You didn't worry she might steal sensitive information?'

'No, I did not.'

Kitt jotted his answer in her notebook. 'How much did you pay Ms DeLuca?'

The lawyer spoke up. 'I certainly can't imagine what that has to do with—'

'This is a beautiful home. There's a Mercedes in the garage. We're looking for a motive for her murder. Illegal activities would have provided for this lifestyle as well as for having gotten Ms DeLuca killed.'

'I'd have to check my files for the exact number, but around forty-five thousand.'

'What about alimony?'

'I don't know. I assume yes. Or some sort of settlement.'

Kolb spoke up. 'That's all for now, Detective Lundgren. As I said, Dr Sundstrand has been through a horrible experience and—'

'Surely not so horrible as the one Ms DeLuca's been through. Just one more quest—'

'I think you went over your quota, Detective. That's all.'

'Should we need more questions answered—'

'Contact my office.' He handed her a card. Kitt glanced at Erik; he looked apologetic.

'I wish I could tell you more,' he said to her, then turned his gaze to M.C., expression almost pleading, 'but I don't know anything else. She was just my employee.'

'You'll forgive us if we find that hard to believe.'

His gaze swung back to Kitt. 'What's that supposed to mean?'

The lawyer laid a hand on his arm. 'As I said, if you need anything further from Dr Sundstrand, I'll do my best to see that you get it.'

Erik moved his gaze between them. 'I'm so sorry, but I'd be a fool not to follow my lawyer's advice.'

'And he's no fool,' Kitt said softly as he and the lawyer climbed into their respective cars and drove away. 'But is he a murderer?'

M.C. didn't respond to the rhetorical question but said instead, 'He lied about his relationship with Gina.'

'Maybe. She may have lied to you.'

'That's right,' M.C. said, tone brittle. 'After all, it wasn't pictures of her and Erik we found.'

'M.C.—'

She cut her off, pressing on, 'Some of his facts were right, some wrong. Gina was married twice. But I'm certain her second husband wasn't an orthodontist, though I can't say what he did do. Infidelity was involved, though whether on his or her part is up for grabs. I've heard the story played both ways. DeLuca was her maiden name.'

'Big alimony or settlement?'

'No way. I would have heard.'

'Hey, Lundgren!' Sorenstein motioned to her from the porch. 'Got a minute?'

Kitt headed his way, while M.C. took a call. From the corners of her eyes, she saw Smith pull up.

She reached Sorenstein. 'What do you have?'

'Found this in the office trash.' He held up a crumpled

243

sheet of typing paper. She fitted on a pair of gloves, then took it from him.

A practice note, she saw. One that played with font faces and sizes. As if its creator had been trying out the various combinations for effect.

HOW MUCH DID YOU REALLY KNOW...HOW MUCH DID YOU REALLY...DAN Gallo...ABOUT DAN Gallo?

'That little bitch,' Kitt said. 'If she wasn't already dead, I'd kill her myself.'

'What do you want me to do with it?'

'Bag it. I'll tell Riggio.' Sorenstein headed back inside and Kitt turned to face Smith, who had joined her on the porch.

'You look pissed, Detective Lundgren.'

'I am royally. Gina DeLuca was one nasty piece of work.'

'M.C.'s cousin?'

Kitt frowned. 'Second cousin. By marriage. How did you know?'

'Met her last night. At M.C.'s.'

M.C. hadn't mentioned that Smith had been by. More of M.C.'s secrets and evasions? Kitt wondered. She didn't like the position they put her in. 'She worked for Dr Erik Sundstrand, managing Kids in Crisis.'

'Lindeman's shrink.'

'Yes. Turns out Zoe Petersen was also a patient of KIC.'

'That's three, then. Mariano had a familial connection to DeLuca, Lindeman and Petersen to KIC.'

'And Martin's the odd man out.' From the corners of her eyes, Kitt saw M.C. start toward them. 'There's more. The pathologist believes the placement of the bullet that killed DeLuca links her murder to Tommy's, Martin's and Lindeman's. In this case, the right eye.'

Smith didn't respond and she went on. 'All four victims were struck in a place that causes certain, near-immediate death.' She ticked off the previous deaths. 'Mariano, the temple. Martin and Lindeman, the neck. And now, the right eye.'

'Clever pathologist,' Smith said, rubbing his hands together.

M.C. reached them. 'That was Sam,' she said. 'Zoe's bored and wants to go out. She's driving him crazy. I told him to do whatever he had to, just keep her ass inside. That we'd be there ASAP.'

The agent looked at M.C., eyes narrowed. 'So, you *did* locate Petersen. What happened to mutual cooperation?'

'Playing it the same as you. Mutual cooperation with caveats.'

A smile tugged at his mouth. 'Where is she now?'

'Safe.'

'You hope.'

'I know.'

Smith sent M.C. a long, measured glance. 'I wouldn't get too cocky. Breakneck is brilliant. If he wants her, he'll get her.'

Kitt rolled her eyes at the comment. 'If DeLuca's death was related to the others, that means she was involved with the crackers.'

M.C. nodded. 'It makes some sense. Since she managed Kids in Crisis, she had access to young people. And ones who had already been in some sort of trouble.'

'A sort of prescreening process,' Smith agreed. 'She could read their files and basically cherry pick her candidates.'

Kitt went on. 'I'll make certain ID gets started on ballistics. If we're lucky, we'll get a match—'

Smith cut her off. 'We won't. A professional never uses the same weapon twice.'

Kitt stiffened, annoyed. 'Even professionals make mistakes.'

'Breakneck doesn't make mistakes.'

'You're assuming the killings are professional. This whole Breakneck thing may be an illusion.'

'It's not. I'd bet my reputation on it.'

'Ballsy.'

'I try.' Smith returned his gaze to M.C. 'If DeLuca was involved, it's a good bet Sundstrand is as well.'

Kitt had another horrible thought. One she wouldn't subject M.C. to, not yet: perhaps Dan had been involved with the crackers? It would be another explanation for the notes. One besides sheer meanness and jealousy.

245

'He found DeLuca,' she said. 'Called it in. We questioned him as much as we could.'

'He lawyered up.' It wasn't a question and Smith went on. 'You think he may be the orchestrator?'

'He certainly has the brains. The opportunity.'

'But what motive?' M.C. asked. 'He has more money than the Catholic church. He gives buckets of it to charity.'

True, Kitt acknowledged. But that hadn't applied to Dan. Or Gina. 'We're bringing Petersen in for formal questioning. There are some crater-sized holes in her story.'

'If she's underground,' Smith offered, 'I'd keep her that way.'

'But you're not in charge of this investigation,' Kitt said softly. 'I am. The RPD is. Unless that changes, we do it my way.'

M.C.'s phone went off and she excused herself. When she was out of earshot, Smith turned to Kitt. 'Look, Lundgren, you came on board late and you're not quite up to speed. I understand. But if you don't like the way we're playing, maybe you should get out of the game?'

Kitt sucked in a sharp breath. 'I don't think you have any say in it or how I do my job.'

'I have nothing against you. In fact, I warned Riggio she was heading down the wrong path by keeping you in the dark, but it was her call. Not mine. The truth is, I don't care about any of that, I just want these crackers. All of them. The entire ring.'

'And the murder investigation?'

'Your baby, have a ball with it.'

Kitt kept her anger in check, though with difficulty.

Smith went on. 'There are two kinds of law enforcement. Those who will do whatever it takes, and those who don't have what it takes.'

'The balls?'

'You said it earlier.'

'That's a rather dangerous position, Agent Smith. I don't play God.'

Smith shrugged. 'Maybe you should. Tell Riggio to

246

keep in touch. I'll work on getting DeLuca's financial information.'

M.C. strolled back to Kitt. She motioned to the agent. 'He had enough?'

'Apparently.'

'Are you okay?'

Kitt looked at her, her anger burgeoning into fury. 'I'm just dandy, thanks.'

M.C. frowned. 'Sam again. Wondering where we were.'

'I've got a question. True or false, Smith advised you that keeping me in the dark was a mistake.' When M.C. hesitated, she repeated her question. 'True or false?'

When M.C. still didn't reply, she swore. 'That's what I thought.'

'Kitt, wait. Let me—'

'Explain? No, thanks. You have an address for DeLuca's next of kin?'

'Her parents. They still live in the old neighborhood.'

'That's my next stop. You go get Zoe, bring her to HQ for questioning.'

M.C. frowned. 'What's going on here, Kitt?'

'I think it's time, partner. I'm officially sidelining you.'

55

Thursday, January 29
12:20 P.M.

Gina DeLuca's parents lived in a small, brick home in west Rockford. Kitt approached its front door, her steps heavy. Wishing she was anywhere but here, preparing to deliver the worst news a parent could get.

This had turned into one big, bad bitch of a day. Frankly, she'd had it. Stick a fork in her – she was done. With the job that continued to suck the life out of her. With her sense of duty to everyone but herself and Joe. Everything but her partnership with M.C.

She supposed she should still be angry. Over M.C.'s deceit. Hurt over the fact her partner had turned to Smith instead of her.

But how could she be? She felt too damn bad for her. And, despite the subterfuge, too proud. Not many could take the number of blows M.C. had and still be standing. Fighting back.

She sure as hell hadn't been able to. She had only pretended – with the help of the bottle.

She reached the door, drew a deep breath. Now it was time to face a mother and a father and tell them their daughter had been murdered.

Rita DeLuca answered her knock. 'Can I help you?'

Kitt held up her shield. 'Detective Lundgren, RPD. I'm afraid I have some bad news.'

'Rita, who is it?'

The woman turned toward the big man who stood in the doorway behind them. 'Police,' she said, voice trembling. 'A detective.'

He crossed to stand beside his wife. 'Mario DeLuca,' he said. 'How can I help you?'

'I have some bad news, Mr DeLuca. I'm so sorry.'

Rita shook her head. 'No,' she said. 'Not one of my babies. Please.'

'Has there been an accident?' he asked. 'Who? Which one?'

'Your daughter Gina was murdered. I'm so sorry for your loss.'

'Mary, Mother of God!' Rita DeLuca sank to her knees. 'Anything . . . take me . . . please, Lord, take me instead.'

Mario knelt beside her and gathered her against him. He looked up at Kitt. 'How did it happen?' he asked, tone fierce.

'She was shot,' she answered as gently as she could. 'In her home.'

'Who?' he asked. 'Who did this?'

'We don't know who. We hope you can help us.'

Rita visibly pulled herself together. They helped her to her feet and got her to the couch. Mario sat beside her, cradling her protectively against him, expression set as if in stone.

'This can't be possible.' He let out a great, shuddering breath. 'I have to call the boys. How will I tell them their sister is gone? How, Mama?'

'We need your help, Mr DeLuca,' Kitt said, taking a pocket-sized notebook from her jacket. 'I need to ask you both some questions. About your daughter's friends and lifestyle. About her boyfriend, if she had one. Something you know may lead us to her killer.'

Rita spoke suddenly, voice surprisingly strong. 'I hardly knew my Gina anymore. It started when she went to work for that man!'

'What man?'

'That rich man. Erik Sundstrand.' She all but spat his name. 'Suddenly, nothing was good enough for her. We weren't good enough for her. Stephen wasn't good enough for her.'

'Stephen?'

'Her second husband.'

'How long ago was this?'

'A couple years.'

'What about her first husband?'

'Chuck,' the woman said. 'They were so young. He had an ugly temper. She wanted to go to school and he wouldn't have it.'

'They divorced?'

'It was annulled, thanks to the Blessed Mother and Father McCormick.' She crossed herself. 'She went to Rock Valley and got her degree. That's where she met Stephen.'

'They'd been married about six months when she got the job with that Erik Sundstrand. Then the trouble began.'

Mario stepped in. 'She started putting on airs, raising her nose at everything she'd grown up with.'

Rita nodded. 'She stopped coming to Mass, didn't join us for family meals. Even her brothers didn't know her anymore.'

'Then' – Rita looked at her husband, then back at Kitt – 'she fell.'

'Fell?'

'Broke her marriage vows.' Her voice shook. 'With him. That devil.'

'Erik Sundstrand?'

'Yes,' Mario agreed. 'A devil all dressed up to look respectable.'

'What do you know about her finances?'

'We didn't speak anymore. But I saw that house she lived in. The fancy car she drove. How was she paying for those things?'

The very question Kitt wanted answered. 'Did she get a divorce settlement? Some sort of alimony?'

'From Chuck?' Mario asked, tone incredulous.

'Or Stephen. Isn't he an orthodontist?'

250

'An orthodontist?' he repeated. 'Stephen's a mechanic. A damn good one. He just opened his own shop. We're very proud of him.'

'We'll need to talk to him. Because of his past relationship with Gina.'

'I'll get you his number, his address.' Rita's eyes filled with tears. 'He has a new wife,' she said. 'A baby.'

New wife and baby, Kitt thought. New business. Didn't sound like a man who, overcome with rage or jealousy, had shot his ex-wife. Sounded to her like Stephen had moved on.

Rita DeLuca made a sudden, horrible sound. 'And now my girl's dead! My baby girl!'

Kitt stood. 'I'll be in touch, Mr and Mrs DeLuca.' She handed them each her card. 'If you need anything or have any questions, call me.'

The man walked her to the door. 'You'll catch the animal who did this, won't you?'

She wished she could guarantee that. Instead, after she promised to do her best and keep them posted of every development, she left them to mourn in private.

As Kitt stepped out into the bright, cold day she let out a shaky breath, opened her phone and dialed M.C. 'Things are not looking so good for Sundstrand,' she said when her partner answered.

She quickly filled her in on what she learned and how Gina's parents' version of the truth differed from Sundstrand's.

'He very well could be the one,' Kitt continued, crossing to her Taurus. She unlocked the door and slipped inside. 'His operation. He wants the money, he starts picking off everyone who knew about it.'

M.C. cleared her throat. Even so, when she spoke, her voice was thick. 'Erik Sundstrand is killing people over five hundred thousand? He was featured in a recent *Chicago* magazine as one of the wealthiest men in the Midwest. He's quite solvent.'

'Maybe the five hundred K wasn't the motive. Maybe protecting his reputation was. Maybe someone threatened to out him, and he's eliminating everyone involved.'

'It's hard to believe he was using Kids in Crisis as a way to recruit young people for criminal hacking. Maybe Gina's the one who lied. To him. To cover for her lifestyle.'

'And the affair?'

'Maybe a lie. Maybe not.'

'I find it strange he went looking for her like that, then let himself into her house—'

'The door was open.'

'He says.' Kitt pulled away from the curb. 'Then went looking for her in her bedroom. That's a pretty damn familiar way for a boss to act.'

'What about Breakneck?

'Maybe Sundstrand's Breakneck?'

'That's crazy.'

'Really? Think about it. He does it for the thrill. Because he's too rich, too bored, has too much. Who better? He's well connected. Brilliant and rich. Seems to me you're defending him pretty vociferously, partner. You having a hard time because he was Dan's friend?'

'I resent that.'

'Too damn bad. You know as well as I do that people do things you'd never imagine they could do, people who seem to have perfect lives, families or jobs. They steal, cheat and kill. Sometimes they even betray their friends.'

'Was that a shot, Kitt?'

'You decide.'

For a moment, M.C. was silent. 'If Erik's our guy, why hasn't he killed Zoe?'

'Because you have her safely squirreled away at your place. Speaking of, are you with Zoe now?'

'Almost home.'

'Almost . . . where the hell have you—'

'I had a personal stop to make. I'll meet you at my place.'

Before Kitt could respond, M.C. hung up.

56

M.C. beat Kitt there, but not by much. Her personal errand had been to pull onto a side street so she could be alone with her grief. She'd cried for Tommy and Gina. For the loss of Kitt's trust. For herself. For what she and Dan might have had – but mostly for what they'd lost.

She wished to God she had never seen those pictures.

She drew a deep breath, in control again. Ready to face whatever lay ahead. M.C. climbed out of her SUV and went to meet the other woman. They walked to the front door.

'Let's do this,' Kitt said.

M.C. nodded, unlocked the door. They entered the house and found Sam parked on the couch, watching TV. He looked over his shoulder at them.

'Where is she?' M.C. asked.

'In her bedroom. Sulking.'

She nodded and headed that way, Kitt with her. M.C. tapped on the closed door. 'Zoe, it's M.C. We need to talk.'

The girl didn't respond and M.C. tried again. 'It's important. We really need to speak with you.'

She still didn't respond and Sam wandered down the

253

hallway toward them, looking irritated. 'Cut the crap, Zoe,' he called. 'And get your butt out here.'

When that didn't produce the girl, Kitt tried the door. It was locked. She knocked loudly. 'Open up, Zoe. Now.'

M.C. frowned. 'I have a bad feeling about this.'

'Me, too.' Kitt looked at her. 'How about I kick it in?'

'Hell, no. This is my place, not some crackhouse.' M.C. rapped sharply on the door. 'Zoe,' she called, 'open the damn door!'

'I'll go outside,' Sam offered, 'and check the window.'

Moments later, he opened the bedroom door. He looked sheepish.

M.C. swore. 'She crawled out the window, didn't she? Damn it!'

Kitt flipped open her cell. 'I'll call it in.'

M.C. strode into the room. 'Her stuff's still here.'

'That's good news, right?' She glared at Sam, and he flushed. 'How was I supposed to know she'd sneak out? Last I saw her she stomped into the bedroom and slammed the door.'

'How long ago was that?'

'Twenty, thirty minutes. Not long.'

'Where did she want to go?'

'One of her friends called. Some party was happening.'

'What friend?'

'I didn't ask.' He jammed his hands into the pockets of his jeans, looking irritated. 'She's turning out to be a real pain in the ass.'

'Call her cell phone. Find out where she is.'

Not surprisingly, she didn't pick up. He left a message, then looked at her. 'What now?'

'Call her friends, find out if she's with them or if they've seen her.'

Kitt stepped in. 'I've notified HQ. They're putting out an all unit alert.'

'Let's try her apartment, then start hitting places she liked to hang out.'

'I'll go, too,' Sam said.

'No,' M.C. shot back, 'you stay. Somebody's got to be here in case she comes back.'

'I don't know what the big deal is,' he said. 'Her stuff's here, she'll be back.'

M.C. turned on him, furious. 'You still don't get it, do you? We're afraid she won't be able to come back.'

'Won't be able to—' He bit the words back, realization crossing his features.

Wouldn't be able to come back.

Because she would be dead.

57

Friday, January 30
6:40 A.M.

It had been a long, exhausting night without a sign of Zoe. They had checked and rechecked all of Zoe's favorite spots, her apartment, her friends. They had stationed a uniform at her apartment, just in case she showed up.

With the intention of grabbing a few hours of shut-eye, Kitt had called it quits around three A.M. She had crawled into bed with Joe – but had been unable to sleep.

Finally, about dawn, she had slipped out of bed and gone in search of coffee. Once brewed, she had sat at the kitchen table with it and Tommy's phone logs, which she had collected from Sam before heading home the night before.

She had studied the numbers until they swam before her eyes. She had made a list of the nonsensical ones, moving the numbers around, looking for a pattern or some sort of system.

Hoping something would jump out at her.

Nothing did.

'Hey, stranger.'

She looked up at Joe and smiled. 'You're a sight for sore eyes.'

'You, too.' He crossed to where she sat, bent and kissed her. 'Bad night?'

'Awful.'

'Want to talk about it?'

A part of her did. The part that had been deeply wounded by a friend's deception and betrayal. Confide her hurt to him. Let him be sympathetic and outraged.

But another part didn't want to speak of it – only of the resolution that had sprung from it.

'I've come to a decision, Joe. I'm leaving the force. As soon as I've closed this case.'

He searched her gaze. 'Are you sure?'

She nodded. 'Last night, no . . . the last few days sealed the deal. I'm not running. I'm not doing it to try to appease you. I'm tired. And I've just had enough.'

For a long moment, he simply gazed at her. 'What about M.C.? Have you told her?'

'Yes. But I don't know if she believes me.'

He reached across the table, curved his hand around hers. 'I'm not going to hold you to this. Give it some more time. Finish the case, then decide.'

'I'm not going to change my mind.'

'That may be. But it's your life. Your career. I don't want you to be unhappy or resentful. I don't want you to look back and blame me.'

'Thank you,' she said.

'Hungry?'

'Not especially. You go ahead.'

He did, scrambling a couple of eggs and popping bread into the toaster. When he had pulled it all together, he sat across the table from her. 'Phone numbers?' he asked, motioning to her list.

'Yes. Maybe. They're in some sort of code.'

'Where are they from?'

'Tommy's cell phone address book.'

'I used to be pretty good at that sort of thing, if you want me to take a crack at them. My brother and I used to make up secret codes, mostly to torment our sister and her friends.' He stood and crossed to the fridge. 'OJ?'

'Thanks.'

He poured them each a glass, then returned to the table. 'That's the interesting thing about cell phones. We carry our lives around in them. Who you call. Who calls you. How many times a day. Pictures of your friends, family, travels. They're technological snapshots of our lives. And not that many years ago, they didn't even exist.'

She looked up from the numbers. 'What did you say?'

He paused, a forkful of eggs halfway to his mouth. 'Not that many years ago they didn't even—'

'Not that. Before.'

'Who you call and who calls you. How many times—'

'—a day,' she finished for him. 'That's it.'

Son of a bitch. Zoe had been lying to them.

'What is it?' he asked.

'I've got to go.' She drained her glass of juice and got to her feet. 'I'll explain later.'

Her cell vibrated. She saw that it was M.C. 'Hey,' she answered. 'I've got news.'

'So do I. White called. They think they've found Zoe.'

'Where?'

'Floating facedown in the Rock River. I'm heading there now. Sinnissippi Gardens.'

'I'll meet you. Give me fifteen minutes.'

58

Friday, January 30
7:45 A.M.

White was waiting for M.C. when she arrived. 'Thanks for the heads-up,' she called, climbing out of her vehicle and crossing to him.

'Happy to help.'

'Who found her?'

'A motorist on the Whitman Street Bridge. Saw a swath of bright pink in the river and called it in.'

'Some eagle eyes.'

'No joke. And at this time of day, too. Personally, I have trouble seeing beyond my coffee cup until nine A.M.'

Kitt arrived, whipping into the parking area, tires screeching as she angled into a spot and hit the brakes. A moment later she joined them.

White filled her in, then held out a jar of Vicks as he finished. 'Water rescue just hauled her out. Have a smear?'

They both helped themselves, then headed down to the river's frozen edge. The Rock River had been known to freeze over completely, but not this year. It hadn't been consistently cold enough.

The dive team had deposited the corpse faceup on the

shore. Bright pink jacket and blue jeans. Long blond hair, now a tangled, stringy mess.

'She the girl you're looking for?' White asked.

M.C. gazed at the victim, relief flooding her. 'No. It's not Zoe.'

Kitt looked at her. 'The age is right. She could be one of our guy's victims.'

M.C. nodded, then lifted her gaze to White. 'She was floating?'

'Yup. Floating, but not a floater.'

'So she was most probably dead when she entered the water. Rules out suicide.'

Kitt agreed. 'She hits the cold water facedown, it prevents the air from escaping her lungs.'

White rubbed his hands together. 'The cold makes the water a bit more dense. That helps keep her up.'

Lungs were like sponges. Once they'd filled with water, down she would have gone. 'She wasn't hung up on something?' M.C. asked.

'Not when we got to her,' one of the water rescue team offered. 'She was like a bright pink bobber out there.'

Kitt cleared her throat. 'I want to know what killed her. I want to know when it happened.'

White nodded. 'I'll keep you posted.'

On their way back to their vehicles they passed ID. 'Don't blame us,' Kitt said as Miller opened his mouth. 'This one's White and Canataldi's.'

'Oh, sure, pass the buck.'

They reached the parking lot. Her cell phone went off. 'Riggio,' she answered.

'We've got Petersen, Detective. What do you want us to do with her?'

'Are you certain it's Zoe Petersen?'

'It's her, all right. Caught her going into her apartment. She showed me her ID just to prove she lived there.'

'Take her downtown and set her up in an interview room. Lundgren and I are on our way.'

59

Zoe stank of beer and cigarettes. Her mascara had run, making her look like a cross between a hair-band reject and a raccoon.

'Hello, Zoe,' M.C said. 'We were all really worried about you.'

'I'm sorry.' Her voice shook. 'I was bored. And Sam was being a jerk. So when my friend Alison called—'

'You sneaked out.'

She hung her head. 'Sam wouldn't let me go.'

'Because I asked him to make certain you stayed inside. For your own safety.'

Kitt spoke up. 'Your little rebellion could have cost you your life. You do get that, right?'

Zoe looked at Kitt then back at M.C. 'Who's she?'

'My partner, Detective Kitt Lundgren. We have to ask you some questions, Zoe.'

She clasped her hands together. M.C saw that they shook. 'I told you everything. You promised if I did you wouldn't—'

M.C. cut her off. 'I promised that if your story began to fall apart, I was going to haul your butt in for questioning. Your story's falling apart, Zoe.'

'Everything I told you was true. I swear!'

Kitt took over. 'Then you won't mind telling me the same story, right?'

'I guess. I—'

'Just so you know,' M.C. added, 'we're videotaping this interview.'

'Videotap—'

'Let's start at the beginning,' Kitt said, cutting her off. 'The first problem. You were not in love with Tommy Mariano.'

'I was!'

'Cell phones are snapshots of our lives, Zoe.' She thought of Joe, giving him silent props for the analogy. 'If you were so madly in love with Tommy, why didn't you call him more?'

'What do you mean?'

'In a month of calls, you only called Tommy twice.'

M.C. looked at Kitt in surprise. It seemed her partner could drop a few bombshells of her own.

'That can't be right.'

'I assure you it is. By any chance do you know how to use the text message feature on a cell phone?'

'Doesn't everybody?'

'Actually, I've never gotten the hang of it. But people tell me it's the most popular way young people communicate with one another. Is that true?'

'Sure. I guess.'

'How many times do you text during the day?'

'I don't know. I've never counted. A lot, though.'

'Then why wasn't there even one text message from you in Tommy's phone? I find that odd for a young woman who professed to be "madly in love."' She looked at M.C. 'Don't you think that's odd?'

'I do. Very.'

Zoe's already pale face went white. 'He didn't like me to contact him. So I didn't.'

'You weren't in love with him.'

'I was! I'd do anything for him. Anything!'

M.C. took over. 'The phone, remind me again why you took it.'

'Because it was there. I wasn't thinking . . . I just grabbed it.'

'Does the name Gina DeLuca mean anything to you?'

Her expression altered. Fear, M.C. thought. Was she afraid of DeLuca? Or of what they might have found out?

'She's a secretary or something. At KIC.'

'KIC?'

'Kids in Crisis. I hate that name.' She rubbed her arms, as if cold. 'I go to a doctor there. A shrink.'

'And that's the only way you know her?'

'Yeah. What's the big deal?'

'The big deal is, Gina DeLuca's dead. She was murdered. Yesterday morning.'

The girl just stared at her.

'Did you hear me?'

'How? I can't—' She brought a hand to her mouth, then dropped it. 'How?' she asked again.

'A gun. One shot to the head.'

She pressed her lips together, looking a hairsbreadth from falling apart.

'We believe the same person who killed her killed Tommy, Jenny and Matt Martin.'

She hugged herself. 'What should I do?'

'It's about what we're going to do,' Kitt said. 'We're going to have to hold you, Zoe.'

'Hold me?' she repeated, moving her gaze between the two of them. 'What do you mean?'

'Story's not adding up. I'm thinking maybe you killed Tommy. You were at the scene. You had his phone.'

'I didn't! I couldn't!'

'I want to believe you,' M.C. said softly, playing the good cop. 'Don't worry about her. Look at me. Talk to me.'

Zoe turned to M.C. Her lower lip trembled.

'Gina's the one who recruited you, wasn't she?'

'Yes.'

'Not Tommy.'

'No, not Tommy.'

'How did she approach you?'

'She gave me a ride home one day. My car was in the shop and my brother wouldn't come get me.'

'Go on.'

'She offered to buy me a drink. We had a couple margaritas and she asked me if I knew anything about the Internet.'

'And you said you did.'

She nodded. Kitt slid her the box of Kleenex. She took a tissue and blew her nose. 'Then she asked if I'd like to make some easy money. When I said sure, she told me how.'

'You knew what she was asking you to do was illegal?'

'Yeah. But she said it was barely a crime, that nobody got hurt. And I really needed the money.'

'Barely a crime,' M.C. said, glancing at Kitt. 'I've not heard that classification before. How about you?'

'Never.' She turned back to Zoe. 'You planted that piece of paper in Tommy's phone, didn't you? With the name Breakneck written on it. Why?'

'I was afraid. That Breakneck had something to do with Tommy's death. And Matt Martin's.' She drew in a shuddering breath. 'It was the username.'

'The username?' M.C. asked. 'For what?'

'The account with all the money in it.'

'The half million?' Zoe nodded. 'Where's the money now, Zoe?'

'I don't know. I really don't!'

'After everything,' Kitt said, voice steely, 'you understand why we don't believe you?'

'I'm not lying! Someone took it!'

'But not you?'

'Not me.'

'Who?'

She bit her lip and shook her head.

'Who took the money?'

'Tommy,' she said softly, then lifted her gaze. 'Tommy took it.'

'That's another lie,' M.C. said. 'We've accessed his accounts, the money's not there anymore.'

'It has to be! Tommy took it! Hid it somewhere. That's

why I went to his apartment that morning, to convince him to give it back.'

'Not to convince Tommy you loved him?'

She hung her head. 'I wish to God I'd never found that account. Everything was going so great until then.'

'You're the one who found it?'

'Me and Matt.'

'How?'

'Evil Twin.'

'You were together?'

Zoe balled the tissue in her fist. 'Yes, in Matt's car.'

'Where?'

'Rockford Bread Company.'

A sandwich shop near St Anthony's Hospital. 'Go on.'

'We used to go around lunchtime. They did a big business. A lot of drug reps stopped there for lunch and check their e-mail, pay bills. Whatever.'

'You'd go inside?'

She shook her head. 'Didn't have to. That day we found a spot right in front.'

'Anyone could have seen you.'

'So what? It's not against the law to sit in a parked car.'

'Who'd you tell?'

'Everyone.'

'What does that mean, everyone? Tommy?' Zoe nodded again. 'Gina and Jenny?'

'And the other crackers I communicated with.' She shredded the tissue. 'I'd never had anything like that happen before. We just took numbers. All that money . . . it was exciting.'

'Was Erik Sundstrand involved?' Kitt asked.

'I don't know.'

'Think, Zoe. Was he involved?'

'Gina talked about him all the time. I think they had something going on. I always thought maybe he was, you know, like the alpha geek or something.'

'The other therapists?'

She shook her head. 'Never mentioned them. Ever.'

'Did DeLuca recruit everybody?'

She shook her head. 'No. We told some of our friends. Introduced them to Gina. And there was this other guy.'

'Not Sundstrand?'

'No. She was sleeping with him, too. I caught them together once.' She wrung her hands. 'His name . . . what was . . . Dan!' she cried. 'That's right, Dan Gallo.'

60

M.C. sat alone in the ladies' locker room. She had excused herself from the interview and come here. She flexed her fingers, struggling to come to grips with what Zoe had said. To get a grip on her emotions.

She had it under control. She could handle this. Dan and Gina had been lovers. He had helped Gina recruit young people to become cyberthieves. He had been a liar and a chea—

Rage and betrayal swelled up inside her and she jumped to her feet. 'Damn it!' She kicked the metal locker. Pain shot up her leg. 'Asshole! Bastard!' She kicked the locker again and again, until exhausted and shaking, she sank to the bench.

She brought her hands to her face. Her cheeks were wet. Why was she crying? The bastard didn't deserve her tears. He'd broken her heart.

'You okay, partner?'

She looked up at Kitt, vision blurred with tears. 'I think I broke my toe.'

Kitt glanced at the battered locker door, then back at M.C. 'But you should see the other guy.'

M.C. wiped her nose with the back of her hand. 'What is it with me and men?'

267

'You don't even know for sure if this is true. Yes, Zoe knew Dan's name. But it could be just another one of Gina's lies.'

'Do you really think that?'

'Everything's still a possibility.' Kitt crossed to the bench and sat next to her. 'Gina was responsible for those notes about Dan. Sorenstein found evidence of it in her office.'

M.C. wasn't surprised. Truth was, she didn't think anything could surprise her, ever again.

'Why do you think she did that?' Kitt asked.

'Because she was rotten to her core and wanted to hurt me.'

'Maybe. Or because she was jealous. Angry that he'd refused to play along with her. Or laying the groundwork to shift the guilt his way. Look, this I am certain of, if he was involved, it was before he was with you.'

'You're certain of that?' M.C. challenged, tone brittle.

'Yeah, I am.' Kitt put her arm around her. 'People make mistakes. Bad choices. But they also can change. Love can change them.'

M.C. rested her head on her friend's shoulder. 'But I'll never know for sure about Dan, will I?'

Kitt let out a long breath. 'Maybe not. But you can believe the best.'

M.C. tried to laugh; it came out as a hiccup. 'What do I do now?'

'Help me solve this thing. Stop Breakneck. Bust his ass.'

She lifted her head, looked at her partner. 'I thought I was sidelined.'

'Like *that* works.' A hint of a smile curved Kitt's mouth. 'I need you, M.C. I need your help with this.'

M.C. searched her friend's expression, looking for pity. Insincerity. She found neither. Just a trusted friend who believed in her.

She wiped the tears from her cheeks, stood and held out her hand. 'It's you and me, partner. This asshole is toast.'

61

The way M.C. saw it, interviewing a suspect who had legal representation was a major pain in the ass. Attorneys were emotionless bastards, wise to police maneuvers and more often than not, aiding the guilty rather than the innocent. But this was America, and the guilty deserved every opportunity to wriggle off the hook.

M.C. narrowed her eyes, determined. If Erik had anything to do with this, she would see to it he was impaled on that damn hook. He could wriggle all he wanted, he was not going anywhere.

They reached interview room number three and glanced through the door's observation window. The two men looked completely relaxed, the attorney in a suit and Erik in jeans and a sweater that looked as if it cost as much as the suit. They'd both brought their Starbucks with them and were chatting.

It pissed M.C. off. She held the door open for Kitt, then followed her into the room.

'Hello, gentlemen,' Kitt said. 'Thanks for coming in.'

'Detectives,' the lawyer said, 'against my counsel, my client agreed to this meeting. Also against my counsel, he insisted on preparing a statement for you. Erik, you have the floor.'

'I presume you invited me down here because I was the one who found Gina,' he began. 'I was her boss and yet I was at her home and found her in her bedroom.'

Smart guy, M.C. thought. 'Go on.'

'If you think I had anything to do with her murder, you're barking up the wrong tree. If you suspect there was something more than an employer and employee relationship between me and Gina, you're right.'

The admission surprised her. She saw that it did Kitt as well.

'Gina and I had a brief affair. It's not something I'm proud of.'

'At the time of the affair, Ms DeLuca was married, was she not?'

'Separated. He had been unfaithful. She was vulnerable. Like I said, I'm not proud of it.'

'What happened to the relationship?'

'It burned out. We parted friends.'

'I find that hard to believe,' Kitt said. 'You parted *friends?* No hurt feelings. Just live and let live. Employer, employee?'

He looked uncomfortable. 'Yes.'

Kitt shook her head. 'You'll forgive me if I tell you I think your story is choreographed bullshit.'

The lawyer stepped in. 'Excuse me, Detective, my client is baring his soul in an effort to help—'

'Us catch the person who killed his employee and former lover? Or to save his own ass?'

'Both,' Erik answered. He leaned forward. 'I had nothing to do with her murder.'

Kitt snorted. 'We heard a different version of your relationship from Ms DeLuca's parents. According to them, you broke up their daughter's marriage.'

'That's not true.'

'According to them, their son-in-law was never unfaithful. Also, he was not an orthodontist, he's a mechanic.'

He shook his head. 'She told me—'

The attorney stopped him. 'I don't see what Ms DeLuca's ex-husband's occupation has to do with my client.'

'Give me two seconds and you will, Mr Kolb.' Kitt looked back at Erik. 'Gina DeLuca did not receive any kind of financial settlement from either of her marriages. Do you know how she afforded her lavish lifestyle on the salary you paid her?'

'No divorce settlement?'

'That's right.'

'Family mon—'

'Her father's a grocer; they live modestly.'

The lawyer huffed. 'Obviously, you have a theory, Detective. Stop playing games and tell us.'

'Gina DeLuca used her position at Kids in Crisis to recruit young people to be part of a ring of cyberthieves.'

'That's a lie!'

'These crackers, as they're called, stole information online, mostly credit card numbers, but also bank account and social security numbers, usernames and passwords.'

'That's enough, Detective Lundgren.' Rick Kolb got to his feet. 'I'm not going to allow you to make these kind of unfounded accusations—'

M.C. stepped in, her gaze on Erik. 'Kids in Crisis patient, *your* patient, Jenny Lindeman was recruited by Gina DeLuca. So was KIC client Zoe Petersen. I suspect as we dig, we'll find many others. Are you saying you knew nothing about these activities?'

'Yes, damn it!'

'This interview is over. Erik?'

Sundstrand nodded and stood. M.C. and Kitt followed them to their feet.

'Are you saying,' M.C. continued, 'that as owner of Kids in Crisis you had no part in these activities?'

'Erik, you don't have to answer that.'

He brushed his lawyer off. 'Not only did I have no part in them, you're going to have to show me solid proof to get me to believe what you're saying is true. I created Kids in

Crisis to help troubled kids, the thought that through the center they were exploited sickens me.'

Kitt took over. 'Here's something even more troubling, Dr Sundstrand. We believe Jenny Lindeman is dead because of her involvement with DeLuca's illegal activities.'

'The same reason Gina's dead,' Kitt added. 'And Tommy Mariano and Matt Martin. And maybe your friend Dan Gallo, too.'

He sat, looking stunned. He shifted his gaze to M.C. 'That can't be. None of it.'

Kitt went on. 'We fear that whoever's killing these people isn't done. Which means, anyone else Gina DeLuca might have recruited from Kids in Crisis is in danger.'

'What can I do?' he asked.

'First off, be completely honest with us.'

'I'm doing that.'

'Second, help us find any other Kids in Crisis patients who may be involved with the ring of cyberthieves.'

'How do I do that?'

'You tell us. You're the one who works with these kids. Seems to me, if anybody would have a handle on the psychological profile of the kid who'd get involved in cybertheft, it would be you, Dr Sundstrand.'

He nodded and stood once more. 'I don't know if I can make you understand how deeply I care about helping troubled teens. The thought that their relationship with Kids in Crisis could have hurt them in any way, let alone gotten them killed, is repugnant to me. If what you're telling me is true, and there are other young people involved, I'll find them. I promise you that.'

M.C. and Kitt escorted Sundstrand and his attorney out of the VCB and watched them walk away. 'Dr Sundstrand seemed a little too outraged for my comfort,' Kitt said. 'What do you think?'

'That I'm too fried right now to be much help.'

'Time to call in the reinforcements.'

'Smith?'

272

'He's all about the crackers. Let's give him something to chew on. No pun intended.'

M.C. agreed and dialed the agent. 'We've got major developments here with your cracker crew.'

'Where are you?'

'RPD headquarters.'

'On my way.'

62

Smith arrived with another agent. 'This is Special Agent Phelps. Detectives Riggio and Lundgren.'

They greeted the agent, who looked young. M.C. pegged him for a fresh-from-the-academy rookie.

'What've you got?' Smith asked.

M.C. began. 'Zoe Petersen. She admits to being one of the crackers. She was a patient at Kids in Crisis, DeLuca recruited her. She's the one who discovered the money.'

'Does she have it?'

'She says no.'

'In addition,' Kitt said, 'we pulled Sundstrand in for an interview. Considering how it's all coming down, he could be neck-deep in this thing. Claims he's innocent.'

The agent nodded. 'Naturally.'

'He lawyered up, big time. Rick Kolb.'

'To be expected. You taped the interviews?'

'Absolutely.'

'I'd like to review them.'

'I thought you would,' Kitt said. 'We're set up to roll.'

They started for the viewing room. 'You're still holding Petersen?' Smith asked.

'Got her. She's eating Fritos and drinking Coke in number two.'

'She hasn't requested representation?'

'Nope.'

'You offered it to her?'

'Of course. Here we are.'

They watched the videotaped interviews in silence. Both Smith and Phelps took notes.

When they'd reviewed both, M.C. shut off the machine. 'Well?' she asked. 'Thoughts?'

Smith steepled his fingers. 'Sundstrand's got the righteous indignation down pat. We're going to need rock-solid evidence to nail him down. But in my experience, the bigger they are, the harder they fall.'

'Or the more dramatic their escape,' Kitt muttered. 'Think O.J.'

'Petersen knows more than she's saying, in my opinion.' Smith looked at Kitt. 'I want to question her. Any problem with that?'

'None.'

'Mind if I sit shotgun?' M.C. asked. 'She may open up with me there.'

'Happy to have the company.'

'I've got a question,' the young agent said. 'Breakneck. What's that all about?'

M.C. looked at Smith in surprise. Apparently, the agent had kept aspects of the investigation on the q.t.

Smith looked annoyed. 'We think it's a code name for an assassin. He may be involved with this series of murders, either as a hired gun or on a personal vendetta. Read the report back at the bureau. I don't have time for a history lesson right now.'

The rookie agent flushed. M.C. felt bad for him. Smith, it seemed, didn't always play well with others.

'I'll watch from here,' Kitt said. 'You with me, Phelps?'

Moments later the four had split into pairs and entered the respective interview rooms. Zoe looked like she was going to pee her pants when she learned Smith was FBI.

And when the agent began to question her, she sobbed almost uncontrollably.

It was interesting for M.C. to watch Smith. He was really good. Emotionless. Razor-sharp instincts. Questions that left no wiggle room.

But the agent was also surprisingly gentle. In tune with how far he could push the girl, and how he could reel her back in. It demonstrated a keen understanding of the human psyche.

Agent Jonathan Smith, M.C. acknowledged, was more complex than she had originally given him credit for.

At the tap on the door, M.C. turned. Kitt motioned for her to come out into the hall. She excused herself and joined her partner. 'What's up?'

'Update, Francis called. The girl from this morning, name was Roxanne Baumgartner. She didn't drown. No water in her lungs. Looks like an OD. Tracks up and down her arms indicate habitual drug use. The upshot is, it doesn't look like she's one of ours.'

Kitt motioned to the closed door. 'Smith's good.'

'Very.' M.C. smiled. 'I'm back in there,' she said. 'Keep me posted.'

M.C. reentered the room. Zoe was sniffling and hiccuping, but seemed calmer.

Smith turned to M.C. 'Ms Petersen has informed me she wants a lawyer. Since she can't afford representation, I agreed we would arrange one for her.'

'I have to use the bathroom,' Zoe said.

'I'll call the public defender,' M.C. said, then looked at Zoe. 'And get a uniform to escort you to the bathroom. You want a Coke or anything?'

'I think I'm done here,' Smith said. 'For now anyway.'

Zoe nodded, expression lost. 'Thanks.'

'I'll round that Coke up,' Smith said. He crossed to the door, then stopped and looked back. 'Good-bye, Zoe. Good luck to you.'

As the door shut behind them, M.C. heard Zoe whimper.

63

Friday, January 30
5:00 P.M.

Kitt's desk phone jangled, startling her. 'Detective Lundgren.'

'Hello, beautiful.'

She smiled. 'Joe. How did you know I needed to hear your voice?'

'Because I needed to hear yours. Can I come up?'

'I'll meet you at the elevators.'

Moments later the elevator doors slid open and Joe stepped off. He held up a Subway bag. 'Eat fresh.'

'Perfect timing. I was just about to raid the VCB fridge for abandoned lunches.'

They walked toward the staff lunchroom. 'I brought your notebook with me,' he said. 'You left it behind this morning.'

'Which notebook?'

'With all the phone numbers. From Tommy Mariano's contact list.'

'Right. Thank you.'

They reached the empty lunchroom and sat at the first clean table they came to. He handed her a six-inch sub and a bag of chips. She didn't ask what variety he'd brought; it didn't matter. He knew what her favorites were, what she couldn't stomach and everything in between.

He had picked the chicken club for both of them. The man was a genius.

'I was playing with the numbers,' he said, tossing the tablet on the table. 'To see if I could figure them out.'

'Come up with anything?' she asked, taking a bite of her sub.

'Depends on what you call anything. Each string is nine numerals long and simply a variation of the other.'

'All the same, just scrambled.' She took another bite of the sandwich, then wiped her mouth with a paper napkin. 'What's your point?'

'No point. Just an observation. Since they're nine numbers long, they are not phone numbers.'

'Account numbers?'

'Maybe. But maybe not numbers at all.'

She looked puzzled and he smiled. 'Tommy was a kid, right? So he was super-tech literate.'

'Right.'

'Text messaging was no doubt a way of life.'

'No doubt. So what?'

'Have you ever sent a text message?'

'Never,' Kitt said.

'I have,' said M.C.

They both turned toward the doorway. M.C. smiled. 'Joe, it's good to see you.'

He returned the smile, stood and crossed to her. 'It's good to see you, too.' He kissed her cheek. 'How're you holding up?'

'Better now that I know I didn't totally decimate your and Kitt's relationship.'

His smile faded. 'Any problems we have were around way before you entered the picture.'

Kitt stepped in. 'Joe's been doing a little investigative work.'

He grinned. 'Business is slow.'

'And he likes a challenge.'

'Why I married you.'

'What kind of investigative work?' M.C. asked, crossing to the refrigerator and poking her head inside.

278

'On the numbers from Tommy's cell phone,' Kitt answered. 'The strings are all nine numerals long and are all a mix of the same numbers.'

M.C. came out of the fridge with a slice of leftover pizza. 'I think that was Schmidt's.'

'Oops,' M.C. said, then took a bite. 'Too late.' She grabbed a paper towel and sat at the table, taking the chair beside Joe's.

'Got your cell phones?' he asked. They both did. 'Open them up. Look at the numbers. For example, the two key represents the *a, b* and *c*.'

'Sure,' M.C. said. 'That's how you send a text message. What about it?'

'Look at the list.' He handed her a page of numbers. 'They all look different, but they're not.'

Kitt read them: *222557638, 678232552, 678552322.*

'Now, look at the combinations. For example, the two is an *a, b* or *c*. And there are three of them.'

'That's a whole lot of combinations.'

'Not as many as you'd think. Do the math.'

'No, thanks.' Kitt took a last bite of her sandwich. 'Maybe I'm wrong, but someone who's really good at math doesn't become a cop. Engineer, maybe. An accountant.'

'Yo, Lundgren? Riggio?'

That had come from Schmidt. They looked toward the doorway. 'Public defender's here. Looking for Peters – Hey, Riggio, that's my pizza.'

'Sorry, Schmidt,' she said around a mouthful. 'I owe you.'

'You bet your ass. A large Mama Riggio's. Delivered.'

'About the PD?' Kitt prodded.

'Looking for Petersen.'

'Interview room number two.'

'No, she's not. I checked. Door was open, room was empty.'

'Are you kidding me?'

'Nope.'

Kitt jumped to her feet. 'Shit.'

M.C. followed her, tossing the pizza crust into the trash. 'Where the hell'd she go?'

Kitt bent and kissed Joe. 'Sorry. I've got to run.'

'Mind if I chew on the numbers a bit more? I made a copy.'

'Chew away. I'll call later.'

She and M.C. hurried out. 'There's some mistake,' Kitt said. 'Just a screwup.'

'She's here somewhere,' M.C. agreed. 'Somebody needed that room, so they moved her.'

But she wasn't. The only screwup was someone leaving the interview room door unlocked.

Kitt flipped open her cell phone. 'What's Smith's number?'

She punched it in as M.C. rattled it off. 'You let her go,' Kitt said when the agent answered. 'You brought her a Coke and forgot to relock the door.'

'Excuse me?'

'Petersen's gone.'

'You lost Petersen?'

'Someone didn't lock the goddamn door. You know anything about that?'

'Don't put police department incompetence off on me. When I left the room, I called one of your guys over to lock it.' He sounded furious. 'Phelps was with me.'

'Son of a bitch. Who was it?'

'Don't know. He was in uniform. Medium height. Thirtyish. Average-looking.'

'Could you identify him from a picture?'

'Absolutely.'

Kitt clicked off and reholstered. She looked at M.C. 'He said he asked one of our guys to lock it. Phelps was with him.

'You going to tell Sal? Or am I?'

64

Being the friend she was, M.C. had reminded Kitt that as case lead, Kitt had the privilege of sharing bad news. Sal had been supremely pissed off and sent them all scrambling.

An all-unit bulletin had been issued; she and Kitt had personally checked Zoe's apartment and favorite hangouts, all without luck. She had spoken with Sam, ordering him to call her if he heard from Zoe. The young woman had vanished. Again.

Now, all they could do was wait. And pray that when the phone rang, it wasn't bad news.

M.C. poured a cup of freshly brewed coffee and added nondairy creamer. Atrocious stuff – both the coffee and the creamer – but she needed the jolt. The night had all the markings of a really long one.

She carried the coffee back to her desk. When she'd called Sam about Zoe, he had asked if she'd had any luck deciphering the numbers from Tommy's phone. She'd filled him in. Maybe she should take a crack at Joe's number theory herself. She sat, took a sip of the coffee and gazed at the numbers.

Her desk phone jangled. 'Detective Riggio,' she answered.

'Detective, this is Officer James in Communications. There's an Erik Sundstrand here, asking to see you.'

281

Interesting. 'Send him up,' she said.

M.C. met him at the elevator. The typically *GQ* therapist looked bedraggled. He held a big manila envelope.

'This is a surprise,' she said.

'I had to talk to you.'

'Your lawyer wouldn't approve.'

'Tough shit.'

'Know up front, anything you say that incriminates you is on the record.'

'Put this on the record, then. I didn't have anything to do with Gina's death or your supposed ring of cyberthieves. And neither did Dan.'

Sudden tears choked her. She fought to keep her emotion from showing and motioned to the hallway ahead. 'Then you won't mind me recording our conversation?'

He hesitated a heartbeat, then shook his head. 'Bring it.'

'Great. Cup of coffee?'

'No, thanks.'

They made their way into the interview room. 'Let me make certain I'm all set up. Make yourself comfortable.'

M.C. stuck a blank tape in the recorder, then flipped open her cell and dialed Kitt. 'Where are you?'

'ID.'

'Guess who came to visit me?' She didn't wait for an answer. 'Sundstrand. Without his lawyer.'

'That's an unorthodox move.'

'No kidding. And he agreed to talk to me on tape. You want in?'

'Go ahead. Got the bullet that killed DeLuca, Jackson and I are playing with Tommy's numbers while the computer searches for a match.'

M.C. ended the call and returned to the interview room. Erik was pacing. 'I need you to sit,' she said, closing the door behind her.

He nodded tersely and took a seat. 'Ready?' she asked.

He nodded and began. 'First off, you can't possibly think I'm involved in this cybertheft thing.'

'What I do or don't believe is irrelevant. Evidence will either incriminate or clear you. Period.'

'You trust evidence before people, is that what you're saying?'

'Pretty much. I'm a cop.'

'Look, what's so ludicrous about this is, I don't care about money. I have lots of money. Lots of stuff money buys. I've spent much of my adult life giving the money away. Helping charitable organizations. Building things that help people.

'But the thing I'm the proudest of is Kids in Crisis. *Was* proudest of,' he corrected. 'Until today. If even a few kids who came to me for help were betrayed . . . I don't know how I'd live with that.'

'A pretty sentiment, Erik. I want to believe you. It'd be a great world if people really felt that way. But mostly they don't.'

'Dan felt the same way about the kids. It was one of the things we shared.'

'This isn't about Dan,' she said stiffly. 'It's about you. What's in the envelope?'

'Zoe Petersen's and Jenny Lindeman's files.'

'Why?'

'I can't stop thinking about what you said. That there might be other kids. That they could be in danger. That they could die. Is there some way to protect them?'

'Find them before the killer does.'

'Exactly. I've got a plan to help you do that.'

M.C. had to admit, she was intrigued. 'Okay. Let's have it.'

'If what you were saying about Gina is true and she was handpicking teens to be part of her ring—'

'She was.'

'She was being discreet. Careful not to alert me, one of the other therapists or a parent. She picked Jenny and Zoe because they fit the profile.'

'Of computer geek?'

He shook his head. 'Gina looked for weaknesses, not strengths. Being a computer geek means you're smart about

283

computers. That's not a weakness. But being addicted to the computer is.'

'Addicted to the computer? C'mon, Erik, don't screw with me.'

'It's a behavioral addiction, not a chemical one. Same as say, pathological gambling. Or sex addiction.'

At her skeptical expression, he said, 'How do you define an addiction?'

She thought a moment. 'Something you can't stop doing, even when you know you should.'

'That's definitely part of it. With a real addiction, the activity or substance becomes the most important thing in your life. It's a way of self-medicating – it either makes you feel high or numbs you out. Increasing amounts are needed to achieve the same feeling. Withdrawal symptoms appear when the substance or activity is unavailable. Because of the activity, the participant has increased conflict in his relationships.'

He paused, then went on. 'Use of the Net has exploded and the technology has become unbelievably sophisticated. Every year we're seeing more PIU in young people.'

'PIU?'

'Pathological Internet Use.'

'I had no idea.'

'A lot of parents don't either. They just know they're having a lot of conflict with their kids. Sometimes it's drastic. I saw a teenager who tried to kill his mother when she took his computer away. Another flew into rages when his parents attempted to limit his online gaming.'

'That's the behavior Jenny Lindeman's parents described to me. I figured she was an isolated case.'

'I wish. Not that all cases are so dramatic. Sometimes, the parents just know something's wrong.'

'And the teenager lands at your center?'

'Yes. Diagnostically speaking, a high percentage of those with PIU are afflicted with moderate to severe depression, low self-esteem and poor social skills as well.'

'And those are the weaknesses Gina looked for?'

'Yes.' He patted the manila envelope. 'Jenny and Zoe had all the markers. Jenny in the extreme, Zoe to a much lesser degree.'

'The time I've spent with Zoe, I don't see it. She seems social and well-adjusted enough.'

'She ever mention her family?'

'No.'

'Because they kicked her out of the house.' He slid her file out of the folder. 'Conflict at home. Troubles at school. Depression. Couldn't hold a job.'

M.C. sat back. 'Why the addiction lesson, Dr Sundstrand?'

'Because you thought there may be others. Using Zoe and Jenny's diagnoses, I started going through patient files, looking for kids with similar issues. I've got six names for you. So far.'

He handed her an envelope. She opened it, drew out the neatly typed sheet. Six names. Three female, three male. She scanned the list, then lifted her gaze to his. 'You said so far.'

'We see a lot of patients at Kids in Crisis. This is the tip of the iceberg.'

'What about federal privacy laws? Seems like what you're doing might be breaking them.'

'HIPAA?' He made a sound of disgust. 'Let's put it this way, I lose my license but save some kid's life? In my book that's a no-brainer.'

It could be some sort of trick. A lie to suck her into believing in him, his mission.

If so, it was a good one. Damn convincing.

'Can I go?' he asked.

'You came to me, remember?'

He smiled without humor and stood. She followed his lead. 'Thanks,' she said. 'I'm going to follow up on these names now.'

'I'm going back to KIC, and I'm not leaving until I've evaluated every patient's file.'

'Wait. My cousin Tommy . . . didn't fit this profile.'

'Like I said, often family doesn't really see what's going on.'

'That's not the case. He really didn't fit the profile.'

He drew his eyebrows together. 'Tell me about him. Conflict with his parents?'

'None.'

'Problems at school?'

'Never. Seemed very focused on his future. Already had a viable business started. For the most part, supported himself.'

'He a loner? Moody.'

'Social enough. Easygoing. Nice group of friends. Played baseball in high school. Dated, went to prom.' She lifted a shoulder. 'Honestly, the last person I'd ever expect to get involved with something like this.'

'If you are accurately describing your cousin, you're right; he didn't fit the profile.'

'But he was involved.'

'You're sure?'

She hesitated and he leaned toward her. 'Look, M.C., young people who believe they have everything going for them, who are confident of their place in the world and their futures, don't get involved in things like this. They don't.'

He had been helping a friend. Zoe? Someone else? If so, why the six bank accounts? Where'd all the money come from?

M.C. walked him to the elevator. The doors slid open; he stepped on. She stopped the door as it began to close. 'Erik?' He met her eyes. 'Why didn't you tell me about Dan and Gina?'

'It wasn't mine to tell, M.C. And after he was killed, there wasn't any point.'

He reached up and brushed his knuckles across her cheek, the contact brief and feather-light. 'His involvement with her was over long before he met you.'

The door started to close; she stopped it again. 'Wait. Zoe's missing. I'm worried about her. Considering her profile, where would she go?'

'Zoe would run to someone like her,' he answered. 'Someone involved in what she's involved in.'

65

The elevator doors slid shut. M.C. stood unmoving. Staring at them.

'Zoe would run to someone like her. Someone involved in what she's involved in.'

Sam, M.C. realized. It made perfect sense. Only Sam knew everything that was going on. About the crackers, the money, Breakneck. Sam had kept her confidence before; she would trust him to do it again.

Tommy hadn't fit the profile.

She recalled what Sundstrand had said. *'Young people who believe they have everything going for them, who are confident of their place in the world and their futures, don't get involved in things like this.'*

She pressed a hand to her stomach, the truth hitting her hard. Who had been closer to Tommy than anyone?

Sam.

Who would have had access to Tommy's computer? Who could have gotten ahold of his social security number, username and passwords?

Sam.

287

Who would Tommy have moved heaven and earth to help out of a scrape?

Sam.

And who fit the profile Erik Sundstrand had laid out for her? She shook her head, not wanting to believe what she was thinking.

Sam had had trouble in school, conflict with his mother and father. He was moody, suffered from a lack of self-confidence and poor self-esteem. He never stayed with a job, dropped college classes before completing them, had girlfriends, but no relationships. To Sam, focusing on the future meant thinking about what to have for dinner.

Sam was the one who had been involved with the crackers, she realized. Not Tommy. He had probably gotten involved through Zoe.

Zoe, of course. She hadn't been in love with Tommy. She was in love with Sam. So much in love, she had been lying for him. The two of them had choreographed everything they'd told her.

M.C. recalled Zoe's voice when she'd claimed to love Tommy, claimed everything she'd done had been for Tommy. She had said one brother's name, but had been thinking of the other. *Of course.*

Disappointment and betrayal tasted bitter on her tongue. It hurt. All of it. But mostly because Tommy was dead. Because he'd loved his brother so much.

Was Sam a killer? Was Zoe?

M.C. considered the way Tommy and the others had been killed. With precision. And cold-blooded calculation.

Where would Sam and Zoe have acquired such skill? The kind of skill that delivered near instantaneous death?

Sam would be on Breakneck's list.

'You actually have to push a button to call the elevator.'

M.C. glanced over her shoulder at Kitt. 'Hey.'

'Sundstrand's gone?'

'Just now.'

'What'd he have to say?'

288

'He profiled the kind of kid who'd get involved with something like DeLuca's ring of cyberthieves.'

And Tommy hadn't fit it. But Sam did.

'He gave me some names.' She held out the list. 'Clients of KIC who could be involved.'

Kitt frowned. 'Are you okay?'

'I need to call Sam.'

'Sam?' Kitt repeated. 'Why?'

'Erik believes Zoe would run to a friend. Someone in the know.'

'You think she's with Sam?'

'I think there's a good chance.' M.C. flipped open her cell and dialed him. The call went straight to voice mail. 'It's me,' she said. 'Call ASAP. It's urgent.'

She reholstered the device, mind racing, forcing herself to focus on Kitt. She should share her thoughts. But she couldn't say them aloud. Not yet.

She would find Sam first, talk to him.

'Computer hit on anything?'

'Nada. I think Smith was right, a professional's too smart to use the same weapon twice. Miller's finishing up an autopsy on DeLuca's phone. I thought I'd hang around, see if anything turns up there. What about you?'

'I'm going to look for Sam. I'll keep you posted.'

Sam was nowhere to be found. M.C. had made some calls, conscious of the time and not wanting to alarm anyone – particularly her aunt Catherine. She'd done a dozen drive-bys as well, looking for his Jeep. Friends. Family members. Places she knew he hung out.

She'd even stopped by her own place, on the chance he and Zoe had gone there.

Her cell jangled. It was Michael.

'Hey, little sister, hear you're beating the streets, looking for Sam.'

'Have you seen him?'

'Nope. Just wondering what's going on. Sam in some sort of trouble?'

She should have expected this call. Her family's communication network rivaled AT&T's. 'Aunt Catherine called Mama, and Mama called you.'

'Bingo.'

'This family is hopeless.'

'Hey, you're the one making mysterious calls at ten o'clock at night. What did you expect?'

'It's no big deal. I need to talk to him. His phone's off.'

'No big deal?' He lowered his voice. 'After what Aunt Catherine's been through? What the hell's going on?'

'I can't talk about it.'

'Is he in trouble?'

'Michael—'

'I need to worry, don't I?'

'It doesn't matter what I say, you'll worry anyway.'

'Nice dodge. But you make me sound like a little old lady.'

'You said it, I didn't.'

'I'll work the network. If I locate him, I'll call you back.'

She ended the call and tossed her phone onto the passenger seat. It went off before it hit the seat. She snatched it up. 'That was fast,' she said.

'M.C.?'

'Kitt? I thought you were Michael, calling me back.'

'Any luck finding Sam or Zoe?'

'None. How about there?'

'Struck gold. You might want to get your butt back here.'

'What's up?'

'I've sent a couple uniforms to Sundstrand's house to pick him up. Guess who DeLuca called twice the morning she was killed?'

'Dr Erik Sundstrand.'

'Blows his tidy little story to bits.'

'I'm on my way. And Sundstrand isn't at home. He's at Kids in Crisis.'

M.C. ended her call with Kitt and dialed Smith. 'We're bringing Sundstrand back in for questioning. He lied about not having spoken to DeLuca yesterday morning.'

'Mind if I sit in?'

'I'd be disappointed if you didn't. Bring Phelps along, just for fun.'

'Tear his rookie butt out from in front of the tube?' He sounded amused. 'I'd be delighted.'

66

Friday, January 30
9:50 P.M.

M.C. found Kitt in the viewing room, setting up for the interrogation. 'Sundstrand here yet?'

'Just arrived,' Kitt answered without looking at her. 'I set him up in number two. He's waiting on Kolb.'

'Smith and Phelps are sitting in. I figured a little bureau attention might scare the truth out of him.'

'I've got a question, Riggio.'

Something in her partner's tone rang alarm bells. 'Sure.'

'When are you going to start trusting me?'

'What do you mean?'

Kitt held up a videotape. 'Your interview of Sundstrand from earlier. I reviewed it, to be ready for this.'

'And?'

'And I'm not stupid. I know the conclusions you drew about Sam. But you didn't share them with me. Why is that, M.C.? Who are you protecting?'

M.C. couldn't deny that Kitt was right about the interview. 'I'm not protecting anyone. And it wasn't about not trusting you. I didn't trust myself. I thought if I spoke to Sam first—'

'You talk to me first. Always. *Especially* when you don't trust yourself.'

'I'm not interrupting anything, am I?'

They turned toward the doorway. Smith stood there, expression amused. Obviously, he had overheard some of their conversation.

'Not at all,' Kitt said. 'Happy to have you aboard.'

'Phelps on his way?' M.C. asked.

'He didn't pick up. I left a message. You have Sundstrand?'

'All set in interview room number two.'

The attorney arrived. He looked pissed. Before he could begin spewing a bunch of crap about his client's rights, Kitt said, 'We have proof your client lied about his reason for being at Ms DeLuca's home yesterday morning.'

'Proof? Or suspicion? I'm not in the mood for a fishing expedition, Detective.'

'Proof.'

Smith stepped in. 'Hello, Mr Kolb. Special Agent Jonathan Smith. FBI cybercrimes division.'

The attorney wore the expression of a man who had just bitten into something sour. He shook Smith's hand, then turned back to Kitt. 'Could I have a word with my client before we begin?'

'Of course.'

They escorted him to the interview room, unlocked the door and motioned him inside. After relocking the door, they stood at the window watching the two. Kolb pulled a chair up to Erik's.

The two spoke, heads close together, obviously aware they were being watched. Neither gestured or glanced toward the door. After a couple of minutes, they separated and the lawyer motioned that they were ready.

M.C., Kitt and Smith filed into the room. They took seats directly across from Erik and his attorney.

Kitt took the lead. She introduced Smith, though from Erik's expression she needn't have wasted the time – his lawyer had already dropped that bomb. M.C. had difficulty looking at Erik. She had bought all his pretty speeches about the teenagers and how they were more important to him than money or reputation.

293

Wanted to buy them, she corrected. Just like she wanted to buy that Dan was the man she had believed him to be.

Kitt held up a plastic evidence bag. Inside was Gina's cell phone. 'Do you know what this is, Dr Sundstrand?'

'It's a cell phone.'

'Do you know whose it is?'

He studied the bag a moment, then shifted his gaze back to Kitt. 'Not a clue.'

'Gina DeLuca's.'

To his credit, his expression didn't change.

'Do you know who she called the morning of her death?'

'I'm sure she had many friends. I could only guess.'

'You, Dr Sundstrand. Twice.'

He didn't respond and M.C. wondered what he was thinking. Surely he knew what this meant? He was a highly intelligent man, surely he understood he had no choice at this point but to come clean?

Kitt continued. 'That blows a very big hole in your story, Dr Sundstrand. Would you care to change that story? Why were you at Gina DeLuca's home yesterday morning?'

'May I have a minute with my lawyer, please?'

Kitt nodded and they filed toward the door. The lawyer stopped them before they exited. 'The tape, Detective?'

M.C. cut the switch, then joined Kitt and Smith in the hall. The agent was leaving Phelps another voice mail.

'What'd you think?' she asked Kitt.

'Cold SOB. Calculating. When he opens his mouth, he's 100 percent certain of what he wants to say and what its desired effect will be.'

'They're ready,' Smith said.

They reentered the room. M.C. switched on the video recorder.

'Dr Sundstrand,' Kitt began, 'are you prepared to change your story?'

'Gina did call me that morning,' Sundstrand began.

'Why'd you lie?'

'Because it looked bad.' He folded his hands on the table

in front of him. 'And because Gina had been blackmailing me.'

For a moment, the room went dead silent. Kitt broke it by clearing her throat. 'Over what, Dr Sundstrand?'

'I was going to fire her. I suspected improprieties with some of the teens. I had no idea the level of impropriety, not at all.'

'By that you mean?'

'The criminal hacking.' He let out a breath. 'I'd seen her out with a couple of the kids. She explained it away. She ran into them, they were talking, whatever.'

'You didn't buy it.'

'Not entirely. Then at the center, I caught her exchanging what seemed like knowing glances with some of the patients. As if they shared a secret of some sort. It made me uncomfortable. Very. I asked some questions and hired a PI.'

'Name?'

'Rod Alexander.'

'When was this?'

'Just a couple weeks ago. Three at the most.'

'Go on?'

'She caught wind of it. Claimed she was innocent, then threatened me with a very public, very ugly sexual harassment suit.'

'You believed she'd follow through with it?'

'Yes. I told you I'm not proud of our affair.' He shifted in his seat, looking uncomfortable for the first time. 'She kept a detailed record of every time we were together. Where we went. E-mail I sent. Made copies of all my phone messages.'

This sounded like the girl M.C. had known in high school.

'I'm a public figure. It would have been humiliating.'

'So you killed her.'

'No! God, no. We were working out terms. A settlement.'

'A rather nice word for hush money, don't you think?'

He looked stricken. 'No. I—'

295

'How much did she want to keep quiet?' Smith asked.

'A half a million dollars.'

With that and the amount in the Breakneck account, she would have been sitting pretty. 'Did you agree to pay her that amount?' M.C. asked.

'We were still negotiating. But yes, I was going to agree depending on her signed promise to get out of my life forever.'

'She was going to quit?'

'That was part of the agreement, yes.'

'Your lawyer will back up what you're saying?'

Kolb stepped in. 'The documents were being prepared.'

'Let's get back to yesterday morning.'

M.C.'s cell vibrated. She checked the display, recognized her brother Neil's number and reholstered the device. She would call him back later.

'I didn't call her that morning,' Sundstrand said.

'She contacted you?'

'Yes.'

M.C. jumped in. 'That morning, when I inquired about Matt Martin and Zoe Petersen, you said you called her.'

'I didn't.'

'You lied again.'

'I didn't trust her. Not after everything that had happened.'

Kitt cleared her throat. 'Tell us about her calls that morning.'

He subtly straightened. 'She said she had reconsidered our agreement. Now she wanted more. She wanted me to come over and talk about it.'

M.C. saw by his expression that he understood just how damning his words were. 'How'd you feel about that?' she asked.

'Pissed. Very.'

'So, you headed to her house.'

He shook his head. 'I knew that would be a bad idea. I called Rick, asked his advice. He told me to sit tight; he was on his way over. We'd talk to her together.'

Kitt glanced at the attorney. 'That's exactly the way it happened,' he agreed.

'Go on.'

'Before he arrived, she called for the second time. The price had just gone up again, she said. She was laughing.'

'That got to you,' Kitt said.

'Big time. I just lost it.'

The attorney put a warning hand on his arm; he ignored it.

'I headed over. She didn't answer the door. I figured it was just another one of her games.'

'She liked to play games?'

'Oh, yeah.' He flexed his fingers. 'I tried the door. It was unlocked. I called out, she didn't answer. I figured I'd find her in the bathtub or on the bed naked.'

'Part of the game?'

'Yes.'

'Would she expect you to make love to her?'

'She knew better. That was over. It gave her a perverse feeling of power, I think. Control.'

'What happened next?'

He visibly pulled himself together. 'I entered the house. Called her name. When she didn't answer, I went looking for her. Found her in the bedroom. Dead. I ran outside, puked in the bushes and called Detective Riggio.'

'Were you relieved she was dead?' Smith asked.

He turned to the agent. 'What kind of question is that?'

'A fair one. She had your balls in a vise, Dr Sundstrand. Not a comfortable position to be in. Especially for a man like you.'

He narrowed his eyes. 'Relief was not an emotion that even crossed my mind.'

'Yet, you admitted you were furious. So furious you ignored the advice of your lawyer and raced to her house.'

'I often ignore the advice of my attorneys.' He looked at M.C. 'I think Detective Riggio would back me up on that?'

The other three looked at her; she didn't blink. 'You expect something from me I can't deliver, Erik.'

Smith pressed. 'You went over intending to have a

confrontation with the woman. You were angry. Furious. You suspected she was playing a game with you. Your words. You took a gun with you—'

'That's quite enough, Agent Smith.'

He ignored the lawyer's warning. 'Maybe just to scare her a bit. Intimidate her.'

'No, absolutely no. I don't even own a gu—'

'She pushed your buttons anyway. Laughed at you. She knew she had you by the balls. You lost it. Again, your words. Then you popped her. In the heat of the moment—'

'Blinded by rage,' Kitt added. 'You didn't mean to—'

'No! I didn't kill her!'

Kolb slammed his tablet on the table. 'That's quite enough!'

The room went silent. In the quiet, came a tapping. A uniform at the interview room door. He motioned to Kitt.

'Excuse me,' she said, stood and exited the room.

A moment later she returned, expression set. 'We're going to take a break here. Mr Kolb, we're holding your client.'

'On what grounds?'

'Suspicion of murder.'

The three filed to the door. When they reached it, Smith stopped and looked back at Sundstrand. 'I do have one last question. Does the name Breakneck mean anything to you?'

Recognition crossed his features, but he shook his head. 'No.'

They exited the room, the door snapping shut behind them. Smith looked at M.C., then Kitt. 'He was lying. About Breakneck.'

'I want a search warrant tonight,' Kitt said. 'Home, business and vehicles. The minute a suspect claims he doesn't have a gun, I figure he's got at least one stashed someplace stupid.'

Kitt shifted her gaze to M.C. In it, M.C. saw regret. 'What?' she asked. 'That uniform, what—'

'Bad news. Zoe's been found. She's dead.'

M.C. took an involuntary step backward. *Her fault. She*

298

had promised to keep Zoe safe, instead she had gotten her killed.

'How?' Smith asked, tone grim.

'She was shot.'

'Shit. Where is she?'

'Parking lot beside Tommy's apartment.'

67

Saturday, January 31
12:30 A.M.

M.C. gazed at the crumpled heap that had been Zoe Petersen. The girl's bright pink jacket taunted her. The matching knit cap and gloves. The spray of brown hair, matted with blood and brain matter.

'Two shots,' Kitt said. 'Not one.'

'Looks like she attempted to shield her face with her hand.' Smith squatted beside the body. 'Check it out.'

The first bullet had penetrated her right hand.

M.C. swallowed past the lump in her throat. She had seen it coming. Maybe in that last second and had held up her hand – to ward off the bullet. Or to plead for her life.

M.C. cleared her throat, fighting the guilt that threatened to choke her. She had handled this all wrong. If not for her, Zoe might still be alive.

How had it happened? Why had she run here, to Tommy's apartment? Had she figured she could simply hide, that nobody would find her?

Had Breakneck been waiting?

Around her, the scene bustled with activity. Scene lights had been set up; ID had begun their work.

'Hey,' Kitt said softly, coming up beside her.

'We had her. This is our fault. We should have made certain the interview room was locked. *I* should have.'

'Things happen. She walked out of her own accord. You can't beat yourself up.'

'Tell that to her folks,' M.C. said, turning on her. 'Tell that to her friends. Shit!'

The last drew gazes. Kitt laid a hand on her arm. 'Get ahold of yourself, Riggio. Now.'

M.C. turned back to the body. 'I'll tell you what I'm going to get, the son of a bitch who did this. I'm going to stop him before he kills anyone else.'

'We'll do it together,' Kitt said.

'Right,' Smith agreed. 'Consider the bureau fully on board.'

Sal arrived. He didn't mince words. 'The witness who walked out?'

'Yes.'

M.C. knew what he was thinking. That he, the VCB and the entire department would be crucified over this lapse. That this screwup very well may have cost this young person's life and that if her family chose to, they could sue the department. Never mind that she was far from squeaky clean, or that she had gotten herself involved in the activities that had gotten her killed.

'I'm assigning White, Canataldi and Schmidt to assist. Lundgren, I expect you to bring them up to speed. Fast. I want this son of a bitch stopped.'

M.C. watched him walk away, then turned to Kitt. 'I'm sorr—'

Kitt held up a hand stopping her. 'I don't have time for that right now. Why'd Petersen come here?'

'Sundstrand said she'd run to other kids,' M.C. murmured. 'Ones in the network. If we can trust anything he said, there's a reason.'

'So, why here? Tommy's gone.'

'She felt safe?'

'She was meeting someone,' Smith offered. 'Maybe Breakneck.'

'I felt certain she was with Sam,' M.C. said.

'Maybe she was.'

That came from Smith. M.C. looked at him. 'What's that supposed to mean?'

'You know what it means. He's involved.'

Hearing it from Smith pissed her off. 'He could be. Or maybe he was simply trying to help her.'

'The way Tommy was helping a friend?'

The comment struck a nerve. Heat flew to her cheeks. 'I don't need your shit right now, Smith.'

M.C. strode off, working to get a grip on her emotions. To focus.

Smith was right. Sam *was* involved. He had lied to her. To Tommy. She lifted her gaze to the third floor, what had been Tommy's apartment, her gaze settling on the dark windows.

Aunt Catherine and Sam had begun emptying it. A difficult job. Painful. Not yet complete.

Sam. He had a key. Maybe Zoe had come with Sam, looking for something? Or to meet him? If so, where was he now?

Her phone. The call from Neil. Maybe Sam had surfaced there.

M.C. checked her voice mail. Neil's message was short and to the point: 'Sam was here. Call me.'

She did, though it was obscenely late. This was family; Neil expected her to call. If she didn't, he'd be pissed – and worried.

He answered with the first ring. 'M.C.,' he said.

'Sorry about the hour. Sam's there?'

'Was here. Acting very weird. Hyper. Nervous.'

'What'd he want?'

'To use my computer.'

Neil was the Riggio family alpha geek. He was the one they all turned to for tech support. Even so, Sam's request was strange.

'You let him?'

'Sure. He's family.'

'I hate to do this to you, but I need to take a look.'

'I'll be waiting. Don't ring the bell, Benjamin's a light sleeper.'

She holstered her phone and crossed to Kitt and Smith. The agent was on his phone. 'I've got to go,' she said.

'What's up?' Kitt asked.

'It's Sam. He's at my brother Neil's.'

'Bring him in,' Kitt said. 'I'll finish up here.'

M.C. nodded and started off. 'I'll be in touch.'

'Riggio,' Smith called, 'wait!'

M.C. stopped and turned back.

'I just got a call. Phelps is dead. Shot in the back of the head.'

68

Saturday, January 31
1:20 A.M.

They'd split up. Kitt had gone with Smith to the Phelps scene. M.C. had gone to 'collect' Sam. Of course, she hadn't been quite honest with her colleagues. Again.

She could only hope the difference between collecting Sam and picking up his trail proved inconsequential.

Neil's front porch light was on. She pulled into his driveway and he appeared at the door. He waved to her, then ducked back inside. It was too freaking cold to do anything else.

M.C. climbed out of her vehicle and hurried up the walk. He and Melody came to the door. She was in her pajamas; Neil was still dressed. He held a finger to his lips and motioned her to the kitchen. He closed the door behind them.

'You know where Sam is?' she asked.

'No. He showed up here asking if he could use my computer. He said his crashed. He was—'

'Wild-eyed,' Melody supplied. 'He made me uncomfortable.' She handed M.C. a mug of something warm and fragrant. Tea, M.C. realized and took a sip.

'When was this?'

'A couple hours ago.'

'More than that,' Melody said. 'Tenish.'

'How long was he here?'

'Twenty minutes. Thirty tops.'

'And he was on the computer the entire time?'

'Yes. And then he left.'

'Just walked out?'

'More like bolted.' Neil rocked back on his heels. 'I could tell he was really upset and I asked if he wanted to hang around.'

'Do you mind if I take a look at the computer he was using?'

'Not at all.'

M.C. set her tea on the counter and followed her brother to his home office.

He flipped on the overhead light. 'I'm sort of embarrassed to admit this, but after he left, I took a look myself. I figured he'd gone on the Net and since he was acting so weird, I thought I'd better investigate.'

A high school teacher, Neil lived being skeptical of teenage motives. Kind of like being a cop – without the gun. 'What sites did he visit?' she asked.

'See for yourself. Computer's still on.'

She slid into the chair behind the desk. 'Amcore Bank?' she said, experiencing a stirring of excitement.

'Four different banks, actually.' Neil came to stand behind her. 'Check the history.'

She did. Sure enough, he had visited four bank sites: Amcore, Alpine, Blackhawk and Rockford Bank and Trust.

He had been trying to get the money.

M.C. looked over her shoulder at Neil. 'Did he make a transaction of any sort?'

'Don't know that. The sites are protected. If you try to go back, it takes you to the main log-in page and asks for your username and password.'

Username and password. Keys to the kingdom.

She stared at the screen. Did Sam have the 500K? Had he been checking on it? Moving it?

Or had he been searching for it?

'There was one screen still up when I came in here. It said, "Password invalid. Try again."'

He didn't have the money, she realized. He'd been trying to get it.

Why now?

She stood. 'Don't delete this history just yet. If Sam comes around again, call me. Don't let him know you're doing it and don't tell him you talked to me.'

'M.C., what the hell's going on?'

'I'm not sure,' she said, grateful she could at least be that honest. 'Sam's in trouble and I'm trying to get him out of it.'

69

Phelps had been shot once in the back of the head. He'd been eating his dinner in front of the TV; he'd liked his steak rare. Kitt gazed at the plate, at the stained red potato and the congealed mess of animal flesh and human gore.

It would be a long time before she could eat a steak and baked potato again.

'He was a nice kid,' Smith said, turning his head away. 'What a waste.'

The small show of squeamishness surprised Kitt. 'I'm sorry,' she said.

The agent cleared his throat. 'Thanks.'

Phelps owned a sixty-inch Sony flat screen. Dumpy little apartment, impressive TV. Typical guy. Kitt moved her gaze over the system. Surround sound. Wall-mounted. All the components. Tuned to VH1. Sound muted.

Kitt looked blankly at the screen, at the music video.

'The Killers,' Smith said, as if reading her mind.

Kitt had never heard of them. It made her feel each of her fifty-one years.

Phelps had the remote in his right hand, a fork in his left. 'Why'd he mute the sound?' she asked.

'To hear someone talking to him?' Smith offered.

Kitt shook her head. 'Someone at the door. Back of the couch faces the door.'

'What kind of idiot agent leaves his door unlocked?'

Kitt nodded. 'Maybe they had a key?'

'Or knew where he kept a spare?'

'He knew whoever killed him. Well enough to keep his back to them as they entered his apartment. He didn't go for his gun, it's in its holster on the couch next to him. He went for the remote. Put down his steak knife, picked up the remote and muted the sound.'

'Son of a bitch,' Smith said. 'This is so out of control.'

'Agent Smith, take a look at this.'

Kitt nodded as the agent excused himself. Out of control. An apt description. One murder had ballooned into seven. Until Phelps, all the victims had been involved with the crackers – maybe even Dan. Phelps had been involved in the investigation.

As if Breakneck was cleaning up loose ends.

Loose ends. Kitt caught her breath and looked over at Smith. Phelps had seen the officer whom Smith asked to lock the interview room door. So had Smith.

Anyone who'd had access to his information was a loose end. That included M.C. Sam. And most probably her, too.

'Lookie, lookie, come to papa.'

Kitt blinked, focusing on the white-suited crime-scene tech. He held a chunk of wallboard in his gloved fingers. Embedded in the wallboard, a bullet. It had passed through Phelps's head and embedded in the wall across from him, missing the Sony by a hair.

'There's a happy find,' Kitt said.

'Yes, indeed. Stupid fuck should have dug it out of the wall, taken it with him. Some of the smart ones do that, if they've got the time.'

Kitt thought of what Smith had said of Breakneck. 'And some of the smart ones never use the same piece twice.'

'Right.' He smiled at her. 'John Collins.'

'Detective Kitt Lundgren, RPD.'

'RPD. Who brought you to this party?'

'I'm Smith's date.'

He chuckled. 'Wow, dating outside his species.'

Kitt knew he referred to the two branches of law enforcement and laughed. 'A .38 caliber?'

'It is indeed.'

'We had a shooting tonight. Not far from here. Hoping to recover the bullet from the victim. I'd like to compare the two. When do you think you'll have this one imaged and online?'

'For you, I'll put imaging it at the top of my list. But it'll still be midmorning. I'll call, let you know.'

'I appreciate it.'

'Lundgren, RPD. Right?'

'Right.' Her cell vibrated; she answered. 'Lundgren here.'

'Good news, Detective. We have the Sundstrand search warrant.'

70

Saturday, January 31
3:00 A.M.

Back at headquarters, Kitt found M.C. at her desk, staring blankly at the paperwork spread across the desktop. 'Where's Sam?' she asked.

M.C. didn't look up. 'I don't know.'

'I thought he was at your brother's house.'

'Was. Gone now.'

Kitt frowned. 'Are you playing a game with me, M.C.?'

Her partner lifted her gaze. 'I wish I was. Where's Smith?'

'Busy.'

'And Phelps?'

'One bullet to the back of his head. Poor bastard never saw it coming.'

'Breakneck.'

'There's a good chance. In my opinion anyway.' She looked away, then back. 'Has it occurred to you that Breakneck is taking care of loose ends? Until Phelps, the victims were all involved with the cyberthieves. Killing an agent takes it to a new level.'

'Sam's involved,' M.C. said softly. 'Big time.'

'I think so, too. But we don't know that for certain.'

M.C. went on as if Kitt hadn't spoken. 'He lied to me.

He's the friend Tommy told Smith about, the one he was trying to help. Because of him, his brother is dead. Maybe Dan, too.'

Kitt crossed to her friend and laid a hand on her shoulder. 'I'm sorry.'

M.C. pulled in a deep breath, as if to prepare herself for the worst. 'If he's—' Her throat closed on the words, and she tried again. 'If he's dead, how will I tell Aunt Catherine? How do I tell her both her boys are gone? How do I face her knowing . . . I didn't stop it from happening?'

'You're human, M.C. And this bastard we're chasing isn't.'

'That doesn't make it any easier. Not for her.'

Or for M.C., Kitt acknowledged. 'Maybe we have him. Maybe Sam's in hiding and we have Breakneck locked up.'

'Sundstrand?'

'The warrant came in. I've called Kolb and am assembling a team.'

'You go. I have to find Sam.'

Kitt thought about telling her there was nothing she could do. But there had to be. Someone like Riggio couldn't sit back and do nothing. It'd either kill her or make her crazy.

Instead, Kitt squeezed her shoulder, then dropped her hand. She glanced at the desktop and saw the strings of numbers Joe had been working on. M.C. had copied the numbers on a piece of paper, assigning letters to the numbers, like a big word scramble puzzle.

'You think solving that will lead you to Sam?' she asked.

'I think Sam needs this information. I think it's the key to the money.'

She frowned slightly. 'What was Sam doing at your brother's?'

'Trying to access bank accounts.'

'You think Breakneck wants his money?'

'Yes. Sam didn't have the password.'

Kitt didn't point out that Breakneck seemed more interested in eliminating anyone who had come into contact with the money than in the money itself. Nor did Kitt share her

311

theory that as part of the investigative team, they were targets, too.

'Keep me in the loop.'

M.C. nodded. 'You do the same.'

Kitt crossed to the doorway, then stopped and looked back at her partner. 'I'm really sorry, M.C. We'll make it all okay. Somehow. And we'll do it together.'

71

M.C. watched Kitt walk away. Okay? she thought. By whose standards? Certainly not her aunt Catherine's. Things would never be 100 percent okay for her, ever again.

She dropped her head into her hands. They were shaking. Hopelessness tugged at her. Where did she turn now?

She couldn't give up. She had to focus. Think it through. Try to put the pieces together in a new way.

Sam had been attempting to access bank accounts. One account that she knew of had denied him access. He'd needed the correct password.

Zoe said Tommy had taken the money. That she had gone to his apartment that morning to convince him to give it back. Smith's version of the story had Tommy calling the FBI, telling Smith about the crackers, the money and his friend's desire to get out.

If what M.C. had deduced from Sundstrand's profile was accurate, Tommy hadn't been involved with the crackers. Sam had. Sam was the friend Tommy had been trying to help.

Tommy hadn't taken the money. He'd somehow discovered what Sam was involved in, where the money was stashed

313

and moved it. Zoe had gone to Tommy to convince him to give it back to Sam.

Excited, M.C. got to her feet, began to pace. Tommy'd had the money; Sam wanted it but couldn't access it. Where could Tommy have hidden five hundred thousand dollars?

What had her cousin Carla said? That banks track daily transactions of ten thousand dollars and up. Because of his bookkeeping business, Tommy had probably known that. He would have split the money among a number of accounts. Perhaps transferring money several days in a row.

She shifted her gaze to the tablet on her desktop, to the rows of numbers from Tommy's cell phone contact list. Twenty-five numbers, all nine numerals long. Twenty-five accounts? Each containing a portion of Breakneck's money?

Not the accounts they had uncovered at the bank. These accounts hadn't surfaced in connection with Tommy's social security number.

M.C. drummed her fingers on the tablet, working to recall exactly how those numbers had been listed.

A name, first and last initial. Then the number.

Originally, Sam had those numbers. He'd given the complete list to her, she'd made a copy for Kitt. Where was hers now?

In the file with her case notes.

She dug the file out from under a stack on her desk, flipped it open and thumbed through until she found the list. First names, last initial, just as she'd remembered.

When creating a password, the experts advised something not too simple, but not so convoluted it couldn't be recalled. M.C. imagined Tommy would have tried to do the same when creating this code.

Her cell phone vibrated. M.C. checked the display, but didn't recognize the number. 'Riggio.'

'Detective M.C. Riggio?'

'Yes, how can I help you?'

'I'm so glad I caught you. Or should I say, your cousin Sam is so glad I did.'

A chill moved over her. Her palms went damp. 'Did you just say—'

'I did. I should introduce myself. I'm Breakneck. You've been looking for me.'

Dear Jesus, Breakneck had Sam.

'I've caught you by surprise.' He sounded pleased. 'Sam's a lovely young man. For a thief. And a liar.'

M.C. fought to keep focused. She didn't recognize the voice. It had a slightly mechanical edge, as if it was being changed by a voice-altering device.

'We're getting on quite well, unfortunately he was unable to get me what I wanted.'

'The money.'

'Yes. In fact, poor Zoe's life depended on it, and he couldn't produce. I have more faith in you.'

Her stomach dropped. 'What do you mean?' she asked, though she had a pretty good idea what.

'Sam's clock is ticking. I want my money. I want you to find it and bring it to me. Or Sam-boy dies. Just like Zoe died.'

M.C. scrambled to come up with a convincing argument. Some sort of stall. 'I don't know where the money is. I don't even have a clue where to look.'

Breakneck went on as if she hadn't spoken. 'Tell anyone about this call and Sam dies.'

'I've already—'

'Anyone,' Breakneck repeated. 'Involve your partner, and she dies, too.'

He meant it. Everyone and anyone who had touched his information was a target.

'I hear everything and see everything, so don't try to get over on me. It won't work.'

'You'll kill him anyway. And me. It's what you do.'

'It *is* what I do. But I give you my word, bring me my money and I'll let both you and Sam go.'

'And your word should mean something to me?'

'Don't fuck with me, Riggio. You won't like what happens.'

'How do I know Sam's even alive?'

'You'll just have to trust me.'

'Forget it, then. I'd sooner trust a snake.'

315

'You can't win, Riggio. You have until eight thirty, when the banks open.'

She looked at her watch. *Five hours.*

'I want to hear his voice. Otherwise, I do nothing.'

For a long moment Breakneck was silent, then he murmured something she couldn't understand. A moment later, a voice came over the phone.

'M.C., I'm sorry! For everything. So, so sorr—'

'That's all you get, Riggio.'

'You're using a voice-altering device. How can I tell if that's really—'

'Deal with it.'

'Wait! I need more time. I don't know where the money is.'

'Figure it out. Your cousin's worth it, isn't he?'

'One more hou—'

'The money really doesn't mean that much to me. Getting it back is more about proving a point.'

'You're not going to get away with this.'

'That sounded a bit movie-of-the-week desperate, even for the RPD. And actually, I will get away with it. The best, the strongest and smartest, always do.'

'You're overconfident.'

'Sundstrand's going to fry. Poor bastard.'

'You son of a bitch. What'd you do?'

Breakneck laughed again. 'Don't worry too much. Rich guys like him have resources. They don't need to be smart.'

'What did you do? Plant a gun? Something else?'

'Don't worry your pretty little head over it. You have other things to think about.'

'Son of a bi—'

'You're repeating yourself.'

She was. Shit.

'The real beauty of this is, you can't tell anyone about Sundstrand, unless you care more about his predicament than Sam's life. And even if you did, I know cops. They live and die by the evidence and wouldn't believe you anyway. Until the banks open,' he repeated. 'I'll be in touch.'

72

Saturday, January 31
3:35 A.M.

Breakneck ended the call and for long, precious moments, M.C. stood unmoving, heart pounding and thoughts racing, phone pressed to her ear. Twin emotions of fury and fear warred inside her.

She had just under five hours. Where did she start?

Erik. She had to tell him. He had to know – just in case she didn't make it out of this. M.C. folded the list of names and numbers, stuck it in her pocket and headed for her car.

Until late 2007, City Jail had been conveniently located on the third floor of the PSB. Then it had moved to the new Winnebago County Justice Center, two blocks down.

Two blocks that tonight seemed like a hundred miles. By the time she had parked, signed in and made her way to the interview room, she had burned twenty precious minutes.

Sundstrand's arraignment was scheduled for the morning. Because of his wealth and political connections, the presiding judge would most probably grant bail. But even that wealth, and the legal expertise it could buy, hadn't been able to get him out of a night in jail.

The guard led Erik into the room. He didn't look thrilled

to see her. 'Pound on the door when you're finished,' the guard said and closed and locked it behind him.

'Hello, Erik,' she said. 'How are you?'

'About as well as can be expected.'

He looked like a fish out of water. Even with a day's growth of beard, no sleep and having just spent no doubt the most stressful night of his life, he exuded an aura that shouted, 'Don't belong here. Big mistake. Get me out.'

'What I have to say won't make you feel any better.'

He grimaced. 'Then don't say anything.'

Her mother's voice filled her head: *'Mary Catherine, if you can't say something nice, say nothing at all.'* Lovely sentiment. Unfortunately, sometimes ugly couldn't be avoided.

'The judge granted the search warrant,' M.C. said. 'Kitt and a team are there now. Your lawyer's with them.'

'You're not going to find anything. Because I didn't do anything.'

'I believe you.'

That took him by surprise. 'You do?'

'Yeah. But I can't get you out of here. Not yet.'

'Suddenly, you "believe" me? What makes you so certain now that I'm not this killer you're looking for?'

She held his gaze. 'Because I talked to him fifteen minutes ago. He's not behind bars. Not yet, anyway.'

'I've got to admit, I didn't expect that.'

'I'm trying to save my cousin Sam's life.'

'He was one of Gina's crackers?'

'Yes. His brother Tommy was killed by mistake. The killer knows that now.'

'I'm sorry, M.C.'

He sounded as if he genuinely meant it. Big of him, considering she was one of the people who put him behind bars. 'You recognized the name Breakneck. Where from?'

'Gina. I found it written on a notepad at KIC. I asked her about it. She said it was nothing. A password on one of her accounts.'

Invalid password. Try again. Could it be so simple?

'I've got some bad news.' She leaned forward. 'The search

318

warrant, they are going to find something. Maybe more than one thing.'

He looked as if she had hit him. 'How do you . . . you mean the cops planted—'

'No, not the cops. The killer. He told me.'

She saw him struggle to process what she was telling him. 'But why? What have I done to him?'

'Nothing. Basically, using you is convenient. Your arrest will be a diversion. He'll have taken care of his business by the time the smoke clears. If it does. And he'll be long gone, tracks covered.'

'Why are you telling me this?'

'Just in case.'

'In case what?'

'I'm not around tomorrow to tell anyone else.'

'You're not saying you might be—' He didn't finish the thought, but it hung ominously between them.

Tomorrow she could be dead.

'I've got to go, I'm on the clock.'

'Wait. I have to tell you something. No, scratch that. I want to tell you.' He paused. 'The first time I met you, I decided Dan was the luckiest guy in the world.'

M.C. didn't know what to say. She opened her mouth, then shut it again.

'That's it. I felt like a traitor, sort of, for feeling that way. And I never would have said anything but now, with all this . . . what the hell.'

'Thank you.' She cleared her throat, took a step back. 'Good luck, Erik. I hope to see you around sometime.'

M.C. decided Neil's would strategically be her next, best move. Breakneck indicated that Sam hadn't been able to get the money, even though Zoe's life had been at stake.

She made her way up her brother's slippery front steps. It'd begun to snow a couple of hours ago and instead of letting up, was falling faster and heavier. The roads were a mess, and had forced her to slow down, losing valuable time. At least she hadn't landed in a ditch.

When she reached the door, she stomped the snow off her boots, then rang the bell.

Melody answered the door. She wore her robe and looked bleary-eyed. 'M.C.?'

'Sorry to be here so early, Mel,' she said. 'It's really important.'

She yawned. 'Don't worry about it, Ben already got us up. Little stinker. C'mon in.' She stepped aside so M.C. could enter, then started for the kitchen. 'Have you heard? The weather service is calling this *the* blizzard of the winter and predicting it'll dump more than a foot of snow on the metro area.'

'Wonderful.'

M.C. unbuttoned her coat. The house smelled of brewing coffee. 'Neil up?'

'He should be down any minute. Want some coffee?'

'And here, I was prepared to beg.'

Benjamin caught sight of her, squealed and raced over. 'Auntie Crackers!'

She scooped him up into her arms and hugged him tightly. 'Ben-Ben!'

As he pressed his little face into her neck, she went cold with fear. Had she made a terrible mistake by coming here? Could she have put him, Neil and Melody in jeopardy?

He squirmed in her tight grip, and she set him down. 'I don't have any crackers this morning, buddy.' She rummaged in her coat pocket and came out with a half pack of Juicy Fruit. 'How about a piece of gum?'

His eyes lit up and Melody snatched it out of M.C.'s hand. 'Maybe when you're older. Auntie Crackers *is* crackers.'

Ben laughed and took off; Melody handed her a mug of coffee, then poured herself a cup. 'You haven't located Sam, have you?'

The sip of coffee caught in her throat, and M.C. forced it down. She lifted her gaze; it landed on the clock. *Three hours, ten minutes.* Her stomach dropped to her toes. 'Maybe you better tell Neil I'm here.'

'Consider me told,' her brother said, entering the kitchen. 'What's up?'

320

His concern was obvious and she hurried to reassure him. 'I don't have any real information. But I need to look at what we were talking about last night.'

He nodded. 'Let me get my coffee first.'

He filled a mug, then led her to his office. He fired up the computer, went online and pulled up the first of the pages Sam had visited.

M.C. sat down. 'Why don't you go have breakfast, Neil. I've got it now.'

'It's no problem. You might need my help.'

She looked over her shoulder at him. 'I don't think you should be here.'

He opened his mouth as if to comment, then shut it without speaking. 'Okay. I'll be in the kitchen if you need me.'

He left the office. She returned her attention to the screen. Sam had visited four banks the night before.

Amcore. Blackhawk. Alpine. Rockford Bank and Trust.

M.C. hoped to God he hadn't been guessing. She didn't have time to try every bank in town.

She called up Amcore first. A request to log in popped up. She typed B-r-e-a-k-n-e-c-k in the box. It accepted her log-in; a dialogue box asked for the password.

Username. Password.

Breakneck was the username; could it be the password as well? Heart beating heavily, she typed it in.

Invalid password. Access denied.

She sat back, deflated. The system would lock her out after another try or two. When it did, it would get the attention of the bank's smart software. She logged off the Amcore site.

Think Riggio, think.

Not too simple, not too convoluted. Something Tommy would be able to recall. Or have at his fingertips.

His phone. The contact list. Of course.

She retrieved the list. She accessed the Amcore site once more. She logged in. The site greeted her and asked for the password.

M.C. looked at the list. A first name and last initial. And the number.

This account's 'owner' was Carol. Sure enough, there was a Carol on Tommy's list. With shaking fingers, she typed in the corresponding number. She held her breath and hit submit.

And hit pay dirt.

The blood rushed to her head. There it was, account balance, record of activity. The ability to use or move the account's funds. As if it were hers. No wonder Zoe had gotten so excited. She – and the other crackers – lived by the finders keepers rule.

Easy, she thought. Way too easy.

Her elation was short-lived. The money wasn't there. Not anymore anyway.

In transactions she saw a deposit of $9,500. And a week later, the day before Tommy died, a debit for the same amount.

She wanted to cry in frustration. Who'd moved it? Tommy? Sam didn't have it. Neither did Breakneck.

How the hell did she find it in time to save Sam's life? M.C. checked her watch. *Two hours, fifty-seven minutes.*

Not a lot of time to check the other banks, the other accounts. One by one, M.C. accessed each one. And one by one, she uncovered the same thing she had with the first account: the money had been there, but was no longer.

Panic settled in the pit of her stomach. Now what?

Neil tapped on the office door, then stuck his head inside. 'How're you doing?'

'Not great.' M.C. quit the program and stood, hoping he couldn't see how upset she was.

'Anything I can do to help?'

She thought of Breakneck's threat to kill anyone she involved in this. She met his gaze. 'Yeah, there is something you can do. If anything happens to me and Sam, you don't know anything about this.'

He forced a choked-sounding laugh. 'Mary Catherine, that's not funny.'

'I'm not trying to be. Delete this Internet history. Now. Sam was never here and neither was I.'

322

73

Saturday, January 31
6:25 A.M.

The man who had claimed to not even own a gun had one tucked into a pair of Cole Haans in his closet.

Considering Sundstrand's wealth, it wasn't a great piece of hardware. A serviceable .38 caliber pistol. Judging by the smell of gunpowder and the dirty barrel, it had recently been fired.

They'd found some other interesting gadgets. Knives. Sniper rifle. Maps. Most damning of all, Zoe Petersen's name jotted on a piece of paper by the phone.

Kitt handed Rick Kolb the list. He scanned it, paling slightly. 'Yeah,' she said, 'your client's in deep shit.'

Kolb was a business attorney. With this turn of events, Kitt hadn't a doubt Sundstrand would be contacting a top criminal defense attorney. He could afford it. And he would need it.

Kitt picked her way to her vehicle, cursing the weather. If they got the predicted amount of snow, the whole frickin' city would come to a white standstill. Inside her car, windshield wipers doing their best against the onslaught, she dialed M.C. 'Haven't heard from you,' she said when she got her voice mail. 'That must mean no luck on your end. We struck gold. Heading back to HQ now.'

Kitt glanced at her dash clock: *6:45*. She was dirty, hungry and exhausted. A shower, meal and smile from Joe would take her a long way toward making her right.

He was up, dressed and making breakfast.

She came up behind him and circled his waist with her arms. 'Hi,' she said, resting her cheek against his back.

He turned in her arms. 'Hi to you.' He smiled. 'Nice surprise.'

'Thanks.' She made a sound of distress. 'I'm getting you wet.'

'You're worth it.'

She kissed him, stepped away and slipped out of her coat. 'It's getting nasty out there.'

'Maybe you should stay? You look beat.'

'I am. Rough night. An all-nighter, actually.'

'Hungry?'

'Are you kidding?' She motioned to the back of the house. 'Mind if I shower and change clothes?'

'Are you kidding?' he said, mimicking her words of a moment ago. He bent, kissed her, then shooed her toward the bathroom.

Kitt showered quickly, though she would have loved to linger. She wasn't sure what called more strongly to her – Joe's cooking or her duty to the job.

This morning she was leaning toward the food.

She reentered the kitchen in just under fifteen minutes. He smiled at her. 'Now you look more like Kitt Lundgren.'

'I feel more like her, too.' She sat at the table. 'I'm getting too old for this.'

'How's the investigation going?'

'Good, I'm glad to say. Big breakthrough last night. I think we got him.'

'Congratulations.'

Kitt sensed he wanted to ask if she still meant to quit when she closed the case. But, knowing Joe as she did, she knew he didn't want to push. So the unspoken question hung in the air between them.

Kitt decided to leave it there. She was too tired to do anything else.

'Pancakes okay?'

'Carb bombs? Perfect.'

He laughed and slid a plate with two flapjacks and two sausages in front of her. He made himself a plate and sat across from her.

'Sam stopped by last night,' he said, taking a bite of food.

Her own forkful stopped halfway to her mouth. 'What did you say?'

'Sam stopped by.'

'M.C.'s cousin Sam?'

'Yeah. Why the look?'

'What did he want?'

'The numbers I was helping you with. He said M.C. had sent him to get them.'

The numbers M.C. had been working on. The ones she felt certain Sam needed. That they would lead to the money.

Kitt laid down her fork.

Sam had lied to Joe. Or M.C. had lied to her.

'What's wrong?'

'What time was this?'

He thought a moment. 'Nine o'clock, give or take. He seemed a little . . . jittery.'

'He say anything else?'

'Nothing much. I asked how he was doing. Told him how sorry I was about Tommy. He looked pretty broken up.'

'How far did you get with those numbers?'

'I came up with eleven words. I'm not saying there couldn't be more, but that's what I came up with.'

'You have the list?'

She saw by his expression that he didn't. 'I gave it to Sam,' he said. 'I'm sorry if I did the wrong thing.'

'Do you remember any of them?'

'Sure. Black ford. Cake maker. Fake banks. Naked bark. My personal favorite, beer block. Oh, yeah, and break—'

'Neck,' she finished for him.

'Yeah. How'd you—?'

'I've got to go, Joe.'

'You hardly ate.'

She glanced down at the plate, stomach growling. She snatched up the sausages, wrapping them in her napkin. 'Sorry to do this to you.'

She went around the table and kissed him. 'If Sam happens to come around again, I don't think he will but if he does, try to keep him here. And call me.'

She kissed him again. 'I love you.'

'Wait. You never said what's wrong.'

She hadn't and she shouldn't. She did anyway. 'Sam's missing. At least we think he is.'

Saturday, January 31
6:59 A.M.

Kitt arrived back at the PSB. Instead of going up to Violent
Crimes, she headed for the Identification Bureau. ID was
empty save for Jackson. 'Another early bird,' she said.

'No family, no girlfriend, just this stinkin' job. A sad case,
I am. What's your excuse?'

'Psycho maniac running the streets, offing people. Sal
breathing down my neck. Partner on the verge of a meltdown. Same old shit.'

He laughed. 'What brings you down here?'

'A couple things. I need a test fire on the weapon we
confiscated during the Sundstrand search.'

'There's always room for gel-o,' he said, grinning at his
own play on the Jell-O brand tag line and the gel blocks
they used for ballistic test fires.

'Next, we need to compare a couple bullets. The one
from the Petersen homicide and the one from Phelps
tonight.'

'Phelps wasn't ours.'

'But the nice FBI tech promised me he'd get an image
online first thing. Name was Collins.'

'Nice and FBI don't go together, Lundgren.'

327

She thought of Smith. 'Learn some tolerance, Jackson. Some of them aren't the enemy.'

'Yeah, right.'

She headed to the door, stopping when she reached it.

'Call me on my cell the moment you have either.'

75

Saturday, January 31
7:35 A.M.

M.C. sat at her desk. *Fifty-five minutes.* Where did she go from here? Somehow she didn't think Breakneck would be satisfied with 'I found the money – but it's gone now.'

'Have you been outside?' Kitt said as she entered the cubicle. 'What a mess.' She tossed her coat over the top of the partition.

'You get my message?' Kitt flopped into the chair in front of M.C.'s desk. 'About the Sundstrand search?'

'You turned up something damn compelling?'

'Bet your ass. How'd you know?'

Breakneck called and told me all about it.

Sorry to be the one to bear the bad news, your 'compelling' evidence is shit.

'Call me psychic,' she said instead.

'Among other things, we found a .38 caliber pistol, recently fired. Jackson's test firing now. We're waiting for ballistics on the Phelps bullet to compare to the one taken from Petersen.' Kitt leaned forward. 'I've got this gut feeling that Sundstrand's the one and that he screwed up by using the same weapon for both crimes, then not disposing of it.'

'It all makes perfect sense,' M.C. muttered. 'Ties up nice and neat.'

Kitt chuckled. 'When this all comes together, I'm going to enjoy telling Smith he was wrong. Not very big of me, huh?'

M.C. glanced at her watch, feeling herself beginning to sweat. 'What do you mean?'

'A professional never uses the same weapon twice. Breakneck's too smart for that. That's what he told me. Thought running ballistics was a waste of time.'

'You're almost giddy.'

'You should be, too. We got him.'

Forty-six minutes. 'Seems to me you're jumping the gun.'

'It's all coming together. I feel it.'

'Certain you're not just tasting your freedom?'

Kitt frowned and looked at her. 'What's with you?'

Tell her. Everything. They could do this as a team.

She opened her mouth to do just that, then shut it, Breakneck's warning filling her head. If she involved Kitt, Breakneck would kill her. She couldn't take that chance.

'I'm fried,' she said instead. 'Worried about Sam. That's all.'

'I saw Joe this morning, He said Sam came by last night. To get the other copy of the list of numbers. He told Joe you'd sent him.'

'I sent him?' she said. 'That didn't happen. Did Joe—'

'Hand over the list? Yeah. And get this, M.C. Joe figured out the code. The numbers spell Breakneck.'

'I know,' she murmured, thoughts on Sam. How had he known Joe had the numbers?

'You did? How?'

'Deduced it. From something Sundstrand said.'

Username. Password. Where had Tommy moved the money?

'You talked to Sundstrand?'

Someplace where it would fly under the radar. Avoid detection by the antimoney-laundering software.

'Yeah.'

'When?'

M.C.'s cell phone vibrated. She saw from the display that it was her aunt. She answered. 'Aunt Bella,' she said. 'Is everything okay?'

'I've got a problem with the business.'

M.C. frowned. 'The cookie business?'

'Yes. I need your help.'

'What's wrong?'

'It's the books. Tommy always did that for me. And now I don't know what to do. My account is all wrong.'

M.C. looked at her watch. 'Aunt Bella, I'm not the right person to ask about anything financial. Call Carla. She'll know just what to do.'

'I did. But she told me to call you.'

'Carla told you to call me? That doesn't make any sense.'

'That's what she said.'

'Exactly what problem are you having with your account?'

'I opened my statement this morning, and it says I have too much money in it. I tried going online, the way Tommy taught me, but it wouldn't let me.'

M.C. glanced over at Kitt. The other woman was checking her voice mail. 'Could you log on?'

'Yes. But it said my password was incorrect.'

'Did you try again?'

'Three times! And still, it told me no.'

Computers had become such a big part of people's lives, they sometimes referred to them as having human characteristics. 'I'll try to take care of this for you, Aunt Bella. What's your username?'

'Bellalicious.'

That's the word she and Michael had coined to describe Bella's cookies when they were kids.

'I've had some big orders,' she said, sounding rattled. 'But none for nine thousand and five hundred dollars.'

'How much did you say?'

Her aunt repeated the number and a moment later, M.C. ended the call. Of course, she thought, mind racing. Tommy's clients. Existing accounts he already had access to. Accounts that money regularly moved in and out of. Zoe had been killed at Tommy's. Maybe that was why Zoe had gone back there, to get into Tommy's client files.

But they weren't there. The night of his murder, she'd brought them in, looked them over, then sent them to ID. They would then assign them to a forensic accountant. She hadn't followed up. She hoped to God they were still down in ID.

Heart pounding, she looked at the clock. Her time was slipping away.

'What's wrong?' Kitt asked.

She got to her feet. 'I've got to go.'

'Where?'

'There's something I've got to do.'

'Are you losing your mind?'

Forty-one minutes.

'Maybe. Yeah, I am. Definitely.'

'Tell me what's going on. Your aunt Bella's call, it had to do with the case, didn't it?'

'She needed my help with something. That's all. She's family.'

Kitt caught her arm as she moved to pass her. 'Tell me, M.C. Trust me. I'm your partner.'

'Involve your partner, and she dies, too.'

'Were my partner,' M.C. corrected. 'You're out of here, remember? And if Sundstrand's our guy, you're that much closer.'

M.C. saw that her words hit their mark. Angry color flooded Kitt's cheeks.

'We're still partners now,' Kitt said evenly. 'Until this case is put to bed.'

Thirty-nine minutes.

'Partners means commitment. You used to know that.'

Kitt dropped her hand. 'Whatever. Do your thing, blow your career. As you say, I'm out of here.'

M.C. walked away, wishing she'd had another choice.

76

Saturday, January 31
7:53 A.M.

As M.C. entered the ID Bureau, Jackson looked out from behind his computer screen. 'Hey, Riggio. You here for the test fire?'

'Sounds like fun, but I have to pass. I'm looking for the Mariano files you were sending to the forensic accountant. By any chance, are they still here?'

'They are. Our guy's been backlogged.'

She worked not to show how relieved she was. 'Great. Point me in the right direction and I'll—'

'I'll get them.' He stood, stretched, then grinned at her. 'Sorry, I've been sitting too long.'

A moment later he returned, carrying the cardboard file box. 'Where do you want 'em?'

'You have a computer I can use?'

'Use mine. I'm heading down to the firing range anyway. What's up?'

She forced a casual tone. 'Still chasing down my cousin's killer.'

'I hear you're close to an arrest.'

Either that or getting whacked. 'It looks that way.'

'Great.' He logged off the system and cleared a place on his desk for her.

M.C. thanked him and he exited the room. She logged on to the system, then thumbed through the box of files, stopping on the one for Bella's Biscotti. She removed it from the box and flipped it open. Bella banked with Carla's employer, City Bank. No surprise there.

She accessed the site, logged in with her aunt's username. *Now, the moment of truth.* She held her breath and typed in B-r-e-a-k-n-e-c-k.

The account opened. And there it was – $9,500. Deposited two days before Tommy died.

M.C. recalled what Carla had told her. Banks used smart software to track suspicious bank activity – transactions more than the $10,000 mark.

Tommy'd had twenty-five active accounts at his fingertips. A couple of them, like Mama Riggio's, that a lot of money moved through. He'd probably thought the funds would only be in the accounts a day or two and once he and Sam were under the protection of the FBI, everything would be all right. No harm, no foul.

She deduced by her aunt Bella's account that Tommy had kept his clients' original log-in names, but changed all the passwords to the same one: Breakneck. No doubt he'd planned to reinstate the originals as soon as the feds were on board.

He'd died before that happened.

She checked her watch, a sick sensation in the pit of her stomach. *Nineteen minutes.*

She needed to test her theory. She opened her cell, dialed her brother Max. He answered, still half asleep. 'Max, this is going to sound weird, but I just need you to trust me. Can you do that?'

'Sure, M.C. If you promise to hang up so I can go back to sleep.'

'What's your Mama Riggio's online banking log-in name?'

That woke him up. 'What the hell, M.C.? I can't give you that.'

'It has to do with the investigation. I'm a cop and I'm family, if you can't trust me, who can you trust?'

'I think you've lost your frickin' mind.'

That was the second time today it had been suggested. If it happened a third, she might opt for a psychiatric evaluation. But she didn't have time for that right now. 'I'll explain everything later, Max. I promise.'

He groaned. 'I'll give you the log-in but not the password.'

It wouldn't work anyway. 'Fair enough.'

'It's 3pizzaguys. With the number three, not spelled.'

God, she loved her family, she thought as she hung up. A moment later, she opened the Mama Riggio's file; her brothers also banked at City Bank. She cruised through the log-in page, then the password page. The account opened.

Three large transactions two days before Tommy's death. One for $8,000, one for $7,500 and one for $9,200. The next day he made three similar deposits. She dug the contacts list out of her coat pocket and noted the amounts.

Her cell phone vibrated. She answered, sounding as breathless as she felt.

'Time's up. Do you have what I asked for?'

'According to my watch I have four minutes.'

'Too bad, we're going by my watch. I repeat, do you have what I asked for?'

Lie, Riggio. And be convincing.

'Yes, usernames and passwords. Money divided between twenty-five accounts.'

'You don't disappoint.'

'Go to hell.'

'What's interesting to me,' he said, sounding amused, 'is that saying that really means something to you. Good, God-fearing Mary Catherine.'

She did believe in a final justice, meted out by the Father. With the evil and injustice she saw day in and out, that belief comforted and strengthened her.

'There's nothing beyond this dying planet,' Breakneck spat. 'We come from dust and to dust we return.'

'Why don't we get together and debate the subject? Just you and me?'

'And Sam. Wouldn't want to forget cousin Sam. The one

335

who got you into this mess. The one who got his brother killed. And your fiancé. Isn't that right, Sam?'

She heard a moan. Sam was there, she realized. By the phone. And he was still alive. 'What now?'

'Bring me the usernames and passwords. I'll take it from there.'

'I guess someone as brilliant as you knows a way to outwit the bank's filtering systems.'

'Breakneck doesn't make mistakes. You do. You're hapless and blind, fumbling around looking for answers when they're right in front of you the whole time.'

'Somebody's got a big ego. Sure you can live up to the legend? The one in your own mind?'

'You have a large family, Detective Riggio. You should be more mindful of that.'

She went cold. 'Leave my family out of this.'

'Don't you have a little nephew? What's his name—'

She felt ill. 'Just tell me wha—'

'Ben. That's right. Benjamin. He's an adorable child.'

Fear took her breath. 'If you touch so much as one hair on his—'

'It's Saturday. I'm sure he's looking forward to playing outside. In the snow.'

'—or any one of their heads, I swear to God, I'll—'

'Does Melody watch him every moment, I wonder? Or does she busy herself inside, peeking out every few moments to see that he's okay?'

'—kill you. I swear to God, I'll hunt you down and cut out your heart.'

'Those are very long moments. Anything could happen.'

Not Ben. Dear God, not Ben. A sob rose in her throat, she fought it back.

'Meet me at your place,' he said. 'Bring the necessary information. You're on the clock.'

'Wait! How long . . . the snow—'

'You're already late.'

And then the line went dead.

77

M.C. breathed deeply, fighting the fear that threatened to immobilize her. An empty threat, she told herself. Made in anger. Breakneck wanted total control – over the situation, his adversary. When he'd felt himself losing it, he'd used the most powerful weapon in his arsenal.

Her family. The fear he would hurt them.

She fisted her fingers. Arrogant bastard. All-knowing son of a bitch.

M.C. stopped on the thought, recalling what Kitt had quoted Smith as saying.

'A professional never uses the same weapon twice.'

It'd been at Gina's. Smith had said Breakneck was too smart to make that mistake. Almost the same thing Breakneck had said about himself just moments ago.

M.C. caught her breath. Her thoughts raced. *'You're hapless and blind, fumbling around looking for answers when they're right in front of you the whole time.'*

In front of her the whole time.

'Phelps was with me.'

And now, Phelps was dead. Her thoughts tumbled forward.

337

'Then it's not about the money. His anonymity is every-thing to him. He lives – or dies – by it.'

Breakneck hadn't been waiting for Zoe. He had been *meeting* her.

Of course.

Breakneck had been able to get close to his victims because they trusted him. He was someone they looked up to. Someone they felt safe with.

Special Agent Jonathan Smith was Breakneck.

That's how Smith had known so much about Breakneck and what motivated a professional killer. It's how Breakneck had managed to always stay a step ahead. It's how the killer had gotten to Zoe – Smith had made a deal with her.

M.C. worked to recall the moment she had reentered the interview room. Zoe had been calmer. Smith had been finished. Had claimed Zoe requested a public defender.

Smith had taken those moments M.C. had been out of the interview room to make a deal with Zoe. She could almost hear him: 'Tell me everything you know, give me names, and I'll make certain this goes away.'

Smith had made certain the door was unlocked. There had been no uniformed officer asked to relock it.

M.C. narrowed her eyes, remembering. They had all taken Smith's word for it that Phelps had been with him, that he had heard him ask the officer to take care of the door. M.C. hadn't double-checked with him. No one had.

A rookie. Brought in for effect. He'd been clearly out of the loop. Smith had used him. He had used *her.*

Could what she was thinking be true? M.C. brought the heels of her hands to her eyes. Smith was a federal agent. M.C. needed sleep. A real meal. To see Sam's face and know he was safe.

The tape of Smith interviewing Zoe. Heart pounding, M.C. headed to the evidence room. She greeted the officer stationed there, requested the tape and signed for it.

Minutes later, she plugged it into the viewing room's machine.

Nothing. It was blank.

Smith hadn't even turned the machine on. There was no record of him questioning Zoe.

Smith hadn't worried about it being uncovered. Sure, the tape being blank might have raised questions later – if they'd needed it for review or trial. But the snafu could have been explained away to human error. And as he had with the unlocked door, Smith would cry RPD incompetence.

M.C. snatched the interview tape from the machine and hurried to her desk. As she neared Kitt's cubicle, her steps slowed. A part of her prayed her friend was there. She imagined telling her everything and the two of them working together to save Sam and beat Smith.

M.C. reached the cubicle and saw it was empty.

For the best, she told herself. Absolutely. Involving Kitt could have gotten her killed. It could have endangered Neil, Melody and Ben.

A bloody image filled her head and feeling ill, she pressed a hand to her stomach. She would die a hundred times over before she'd allow that to happen. Her choice was clear.

Her gaze landed on her partner's desk. M.C. wished she had time to write a note for Kitt, one that expressed how important their friendship had been to her, how important Kitt's loyalty had been. One that told her how much she regretted not having been as good, as loyal, a friend in return.

She didn't have much hope of getting out of this alive, M.C. acknowledged. She would do her best to save Sam, though the truth was, he could already be dead.

M.C. looked at the tape clutched in her hand. Kitt would know what to do with it.

She entered the cubicle and set the tape on the desk. From a pad, she grabbed a yellow Post-it and jotted: *Interesting viewing. M.C.*

A lump in her throat, she whispered, 'Good-bye,' and headed to meet Breakneck.

78

Kitt stepped on the elevator, heading back up to the VCB. She'd just left Jackson. They'd hit pay dirt. The ballistic signatures of the bullets recovered from Petersen and Phelps matched. The shots had both been fired from the same gun: the .38 caliber pistol found during the Sundstrand search.

Nice and neat. Kitt smiled. Take that, Special Agent Know-it-all Smith.

Her thoughts turned to M.C. and her smile faded. She had been prepared to talk to Sal, have him confine M.C. to the desk until this thing closed or went completely cold. *If* the ballistics hadn't panned out.

With the killer behind bars, she didn't see what harm M.C. could do – to herself, the department or the investigation. Let her search for Sam. Kitt prayed she found him unharmed.

Nan stopped her on her way past the desk. 'Detective Lundgren, lockup called. Erik Sundstrand is asking to speak with you.'

'Send White or Schmidt.'

'Tried that. They say he'll only speak to you.'

She frowned. M.C. had mentioned talking to him. What was he up to?

340

She would love to blow this off, but suspects had been known to make deals or fork over confessions after a night in the slammer. They had also been known to tell stories that later incriminated them at trial.

With what she knew now, it might be fun to have a little one-on-one with Dr Erik Sundstrand.

'Let them know I'm on my way over now. And look, tell Sal we have compelling evidence against Sundstrand. I'll give him a full report when I get back.'

Fifteen minutes later she faced Sundstrand across the interview room table. 'You wanted to see me, Dr Sundstrand?'

'Yes. It's about M.C.'

'That's a surprise opening, but I'm willing to play. She was here earlier.'

'She came to see me.'

'You're certain that's the way it went down? You didn't insist on speaking to her, the same as you did me?'

'She came to me,' he said evenly. 'Unprompted.'

'Why, Dr Sundstrand?'

'She said the killer had contacted her. Breakneck, she called him.'

Kitt narrowed her eyes on the man. 'We completed the search of your home. Did you know that?'

He nodded. 'And?'

'We found a gun, among other things.'

'I don't own a gun.'

She ignored that. 'The gun, it turns out, was used in two murders last night. Zoe Petersen's and FBI agent Austin Phelps.'

'Zoe's dead.' He brought his hands to his face, a convincing picture of despair. 'How could I not have known this was going on?'

'What's that, Dr Sundstrand?'

He ignored the question. 'She told me it would go this way,' he said bitterly.

'Who told you that?'

'M.C. The killer told her he'd framed me.'

'I see where this is going now.'

'No, you don't.'

'We searched your place, found incriminating evidence and now you create this story in an attempt to explain it away.'

'The real killer's using me as a diversion,' he went on. 'Handing the police a killer. Giving himself a chance to cover his tracks.'

'I don't have time for this.' She stood and crossed to the door, rapping on it to get the guard's attention. 'Good luck to you, Dr Sunstr—'

'M.C. said she wanted me to know now, because she was afraid she'd be dead tomorrow.'

Kitt stopped, a chill moving over her.

'I thought if I told you, you could make certain that didn't happen. That's all I wanted.'

She looked over her shoulder at him. 'Did she say anything else?'

'She asked where I'd heard the name Breakneck before.'

'And?'

'I told her. I heard it from Gina. She said it was a password to one of her accounts.'

As Kitt made her way out of the jail, she told herself she shouldn't believe him. He was a suspected murderer. A man with everything to lose. But in this case, what would he gain by lying? A simple conversation with M.C. would verify his claim – or not.

M.C. had been acting so strangely. Secretive. Combative. Not herself at all.

Kitt's thoughts raced. If Sundstrand had been telling the truth and Breakneck had contacted M.C., it would explain her behavior.

But why call M.C.? She answered her own question – because he wanted something.

The money, of course. That's why M.C. had been so focused on the list of numbers. She'd been trying to decipher the code, looking for the money. For Breakneck.

He would have threatened her – by threatening people she cared about. Sam. Her other family members. Her partner.

342

M.C. had purposely made Kitt angry. So she would stay away.

And Kitt had fallen for it. How could she have been so blind?

Again, she answered the question herself. She was exhausted. Her nerves raw. Distrustful of M.C. because of her recent actions.

She reached her cubicle. What did she tell Sal now? He would be thrilled with the ballistics evidence, would resist believing it had been manufactured.

Her gaze landed on a videotape on her desk, a bright yellow Post-it stuck to it. She crossed to the desk, ripped off the Post-it note.

Interesting viewing. M.C.

She checked the tape's label: Petersen interview, 01/30/09.

M.C. had checked it out of the evidence room. Why? And why had she found it interesting viewing? Only one way to find out, she thought, snatching it up.

Her desk phone jangled, stopping her at her cubicle door. 'Detective Lundgren,' she answered.

'Kitt, this is M.C.'s brother, Neil. You know where M.C. is?'

'I don't. Did you try her cell phone?'

'She didn't answer. I was worried and just wanted to check in with her.'

'You want to talk to me about something?'

He sounded troubled. 'It's probably nothing. But coming on the heels of all this craziness with Sam—'

'What craziness?'

He went silent.

'Neil, I'm M.C.'s partner, if there's anything going on, I need to know about it.'

'It's just that, she asked me—' He bit the thought back. 'Sam was here last night, he used my computer.'

'Go on.'

'M.C. came by after, then again this morning. And she said something that's really been bothering me.'

'What was it?'

'If anything happened to her and Sam, to forget she'd been here. To tell no one.'

Kitt went cold. That was two times M.C. warned someone she may not be around much longer. 'You did the right thing, Neil. I'll take care of this, don't worry.'

'Wait. There's something else. An FBI agent came by.'

'Smith?'

'Yes, that's right. Looking for M.C. He seemed pretty concerned.'

'What did you tell him?'

'Nothing. That I hadn't seen her, just like she told me to say. Then, while he was here, he got a call from M.C. I only heard the agent's part of the conversation . . . but he was trying to calm M.C. down. Sam was with M.C. and . . . I heard Smith say he would meet them. And for M.C. to hold tight.'

'Where was he meeting them, Neil?'

'I don't know.'

Shit! Kitt thanked him, hung up and dialed Smith. She got his message service. 'Smith, it's Lundgren. Are you with M.C.? Call me.'

She ended the call, stood and began to pace. Where was Smith meeting M.C. and Sam? It could be anywhere.

M.C.'s house. It was the logical choice. And if she was wrong, she would have lost nothing.

She grabbed her coat and started for the door. When she reached it, she stopped and looked back at the tape. It would just have to wait.

79

When M.C. had exited the parking garage, a white night-mare greeted her. Traffic creeping on the slick roads, snarled by accidents. An eighteen-wheeler in the ditch.

She'd been on the road nearly an hour and still hadn't come up with a real plan. Breakneck had slightly leveled the playing field by choosing M.C.'s house as their meeting point. She knew every nook and cranny, every squeaky floorboard. If she could make it to her kitchen, she kept a loaded revolver in a basket on top of the refrigerator.

Smith was nothing if not calculating. He had chosen to meet at M.C.'s house for a specific reason. One that could be as simple as logistics, or as complex as forecasting a crime scene analysis.

M.C. navigated the messy roads calmly, thoughts on what lay ahead of her.

There was a chance Smith would shoot as M.C. entered her home. But she didn't think so. Smith wanted the money. To get it, he needed the information M.C. had.

Supposedly had.

She would cross that bridge when she came to it.

M.C. reached her neighborhood, turned down her street.

Children were out, building snowmen and forts. Their laughter floated on the air and she found herself smiling at the sound.

She believed her own death today was a real possibility, yet she felt no panic. Her palms were dry, her heartbeat steady. She was ready. To face Smith. And beat him.

Or to die.

M.C. turned into her drive. Her garage door was open; Sam's Jeep sat inside. No sign of Smith's Camry. M.C. stopped, shut off the engine. She checked her Glock, made certain she had a full magazine. After chambering a bullet, she reholstered the piece.

M.C. climbed out of the SUV. Her neighbor across the street stopped shoveling his drive long enough to wipe his brow and call a greeting to her. She responded with a wave and started up the walk.

She reached the door; removed her weapon. If her neighbor was watching, it would appear she had paused to find her key.

The door was unlocked. She eased it open. Gun out, she took a step inside. Pausing to listen.

Silence greeted her. M.C. made her way forward, swinging left, then right. 'Sam,' she called softly. 'It's M.C., Sam. Where are you?'

She checked the front hall coat closet, then made her way through the living room, then dining room and into the kitchen.

The room looked just as she had left it. Half-full coffeepot, sweetener packets and used spoon on the counter beside it. Empty cereal box beside the sink. The trash was full, she remembered. She hadn't had the time to take it out.

The room was just as she left it – except for the laptop computer, sitting open on the table. By the glowing power light, she saw that it was on.

Her mouth went dry. She stared at the device. Once she woke the computer up, whatever move Smith was making would be in play.

After searching the rest of the house, M.C. returned to

the kitchen and the sleeping laptop. She tapped the touch pad and the machine sprang to life. An image filled the screen. A cry sprang to her lips. Sam. Bound to a chair, mouth duct-taped. He sat slumped, head hanging.

Not a static image, she realized. A Web cam, transmitting in real time. Which meant Smith could be anywhere. In the house or across town. Watching her. Watching them both. Judging her reactions. Getting off on being in total control of the situation.

Not total control. She wouldn't allow Smith to control her emotions, M.C. decided. She wouldn't give the prick the satisfaction of seeing her squirm.

M.C. felt herself begin to sweat under her coat. She unbuttoned it and slid into the chair in front of the monitor. There were some things even the great Smith didn't know. The biggest being that he had been outed.

M.C. looked directly at the Web cam and smiled in challenge. *Let the games begin.*

She returned her attention to Sam. He stirred, then lifted his head, looked into the camera. Her breath caught. He was beat up. Black and blue. Eyes swollen and bloodied. He'd either fought the agent or Smith had battered him for effect.

Breathing deeply through her nose to steady herself, M.C. studied the image. He was trembling. No, she realized. Shivering, violently. He wore blue jeans, sneakers and coat, though it was unbuttoned. No hat or gloves.

Where was he? In some sort of outbuilding or shed, she realized. Plywood floor. Uninsulated walls. One source of artificial light.

No heat, she guessed. He was protected from the wind and the wet, but not the temperature. Bound, he couldn't move around to try to keep himself warm.

How long before hypothermia set in? It might have already. If so, what stage? The shivering was actually a good sign, she remembered. The third and final stage of hypothermia was marked by the cessation of shivering – and then death.

He had been there for hours. Since Zoe was killed.

Sudden, debilitating fear swept over her. Her heart began to race, her palms grew damp. She thought of Smith watching and fought to control the emotion – with limited success. She had to find him. She had to do somethi—

Her cell phone vibrated. M.C. didn't have to check the display to know who it was. 'You bastard,' she answered.

'Isn't technology amazing? Poor Sam, he looks cold, doesn't he?'

Smith was still using the voice changer. Which meant he still thought his secret was safe. 'Where is he? How long's he been like that?'

'Let's not get ahead of ourselves, everything in due time.'

Smith was watching, she reminded herself. Getting off on this. 'What do you want?' she asked.

'He's suffering from hypothermia already. Who knows how much longer he'll last? Maybe only a couple hours. So if you had any ideas of taking me out, I'd rethink them.'

'I only care about my cousin's life. Not about taking you out, or the investigation, or your precious money. They all mean squat to me.'

'I'm not certain he's worth it, Mary Catherine. He got you into this. Got his brother killed. His girlfriend killed. Your fiancé. He's a thief. What's to care about?'

'He's family. I wouldn't expect you to understand that.'

'And why's that?'

M.C. realized her slip. 'I'm not interested in verbal sparring. Just tell me what you want.'

'My information. There's a document on the computer desktop titled My Stuff. Input it there. I suggest acting quickly.'

The line went dead. M.C. snapped the phone shut. Where was Smith? He could be anywhere, even with Sam. Not far – he'd want to collect the computer after M.C. finished inputting the information. He could have established remote access, but M.C. figured he wanted the information *and* the computer.

M.C. took the information from her bag. The moment of truth. Or rather, partial truth. She opened the document. She topped the list with the Bella's Biscotti and the Mama Riggio's

348

accounts. The only two accounts where Smith would actually be able to access the money.

If Smith didn't kill her, her brothers might.

For the rest, she simply made up usernames. She wondered how long it would take Smith to realize what M.C. had done – and how he would respond when he did.

M.C. finished the list and looked expectantly at the Web cam. Sure enough, her cell phone went off.

'Go to your bedroom window,' Smith said.

M.C. did. 'Two yards over kitty-corner. The butt-ugly blue house.'

M.C. knew that house. The owners had just moved out; it'd been for sale for several months.

It had a shed in the backyard. She could just see it.

Her heart leapt. That was it, Sam's prison. M.C. waited for the big bang, the other shoe dropping in the form of an unpleasant surprise.

'I believe thank you is in order.'

'Excuse me?'

'Go get him.'

'Just like that?'

'I gave you my word I wouldn't kill you.'

'It's not that I'm ungrateful, but—'

'You're right, there is a caveat. Go back to the kitchen. Now.'

M.C. did as he asked. 'Good. Lay your cell phone and Glock on the table. So I can see them.'

M.C. hesitated.

'I'm giving you a gift. But I'm not stupid. I need time. If you have a phone, the first thing you'll do is call in reinforcements.'

'And the gun?'

'So you won't manage to find me and shoot me.'

It could be a trap. Or a trick. Probably was. M.C. glanced toward her refrigerator, the basket above it, the gun nestled inside. She needed to get her hands on that piece.

'Fair enough,' she said. She took her gun from the holster and laid it on the table in front of the laptop.

'Farther forward, please. That's good. Now I have a perfect view of it and the doorway. And, M.C., one final thing. If you get the urge to borrow a phone or ask a neighbor to call 911, picture Sam dead. I'm close enough to pop him, one step out of line and I will. I expect to see you walk through that door five seconds after you lay your phone next to your gun. If you don't, consider Sam dead.'

80

Saturday, January 31
10:05 A.M.

M.C. stepped out in the bright cold air. She shut the door firmly behind her. Now for the tricky part – retrieving the pistol from the basket above the fridge.

The laptop computer had been positioned so the camera pointed away from the rear of her kitchen – which included the door to the backyard and the refrigerator. She would circle around the house, enter through the rear door, retrieve the weapon, then make her way to Sam.

M.C. took quick stock of the area. Kids playing. A few neighbors shoveling out. One using a snowblower. She studied each parked car. None sat idling, tailpipe sending telltale exhaust to the sky. No vans or vehicles with darkened windows.

Was Smith watching? He could be. He could have anticipated something like this and set up a camera at the back door. Or here, to see her entrance and exit.

But she didn't think so. And she had no choice but to take the chance.

M.C. picked her way down the slippery walk to the driveway. Her gaze landed on Sam's Jeep, parked in the garage. Her steps faltered. The Jeep would have been the perfect choice for an observation point, close enough to see M.C. come and go, then grab the computer when the time came.

Heart pounding, she moved cautiously toward the vehicle. What did she plan to do if Smith was in the Jeep? She was unarmed. M.C. scanned the ground, looking for something she could use as a weapon. Her gaze landed on a piece of yard art her brother Michael had given her as a joke last Christmas – a frog prince. Literally, an extremely ugly frog wearing a crown. Michael had teased her about having to kiss a lot of frogs before she found her Prince Charming.

She hated that ugly frog. There would be a sort of karmic justice in busting it over Smith's head. She snatched it up and closed the distance between her and the Jeep.

And found it empty.

Saved to croak another day, she thought, and set the frog on the hood of the vehicle. Aware of time ticking past, she hurried to the back of the house. She unlocked the rear door and slipped inside. The computer had not been touched.

She tiptoed across to the fridge, reached for the basket, praying Smith hadn't done a sweep of the place and confiscated it.

He hadn't. M.C. curved her fingers around the grip, a small measure of calm settling over her. She tucked it into the waistband of her pants at the small of her back, hidden by her hip-length coat and bulky sweater.

Time to play.

Within minutes, she was in the Explorer, backing cautiously down the drive. Even so, the vehicle slid into the street, earning the blare of a horn.

She eased on the gas and her wheels spun in an attempt to gain traction. They grabbed hold and she inched forward.

Heart thundering, she glanced at the dash clock. Minutes mattered to Sam. How many would it take for her to reach him? How many more did he have?

How to care for a hypothermia victim had been part of her academy training. She'd never had to use it and racked her brain to recall what to do. Get the victim warm. Cover his head

352

and neck to preserve heat. Rubbing extremities to warm them could cause tissue damage; jarring movements could cause the victim's heart to stop.

She kept a blanket and flashlight in her backseat; she reached around to get them, taking her eyes from the road. In that moment, a truck skidded through the four-way stop.

He hit her broadside sending her into a 360-degree spin. M.C. fought to right the SUV but couldn't and flew across the road, landing in the ditch. At impact, her airbag deployed, slamming her back against the seat, knocking the wind out of her.

M.C. heard shouts, the scream of a horn. Her face and chest hurt from the impact of the air bag. She wiggled her fingers and toes, turned her head from side to side, moved her arms and legs. Nothing was broken.

Sam. She had to get to Sam.

With shaky hands, she freed herself from her safety belt, popped the door open and stumbled out, falling onto her hands and knees in the snow, dragging herself back to her feet.

She saw several people running her way. She motioned them off. 'Check the other driver,' she shouted, holding up her shield. 'I'm a cop!'

One of them was on her cell phone, no doubt calling 911. With the roads the way they were and the number of accidents, it would be a while before assistance arrived. If it did at all.

She could see the blue house now, just ahead. M.C. collected the blanket and flashlight and started forward. She realized she was limping. She tasted blood and brought a hand to her face. She had a cut above her eye.

M.C. pushed harder. Nearly there. She was nearly there. She imagined the people at the accident scene, watching her walk away, probably wondering if she was crazy. She wondered herself.

She reached the house. The backyard was enclosed by a six-foot wooden privacy fence. The gate was padlocked. Another of Smith's moves, meant to slow her down. To stretch her already frayed emotions to the snapping point.

She went to the front door, which was locked. With the flashlight she broke the sidelight glass, reached inside and unlocked the door. With a quick glance behind her, she slipped inside. It was blessedly warm. Completely quiet. Her wet boots made a creaking sound as she crossed the old linoleum kitchen floor.

A door at the back of the kitchen led to the big backyard. Tracks, she saw. Lots of them, leading to and from the shed. Some fresher than others. Smith had made the trip many times.

M.C. exited the kitchen, thinking of her gun. Reassured by its weight against her spine. It felt wrong not to have it out and ready, but her instinct was telling her not to tip her hand just yet.

Using the existing tracks to conserve energy, she made her way to the shed.

Almost there, Sam. Hold on.

The shed had a single door with a hasp and unlatched padlock. She hesitated outside the door. If Smith was in there, who'd hung the padlock on the hasp? Could the agent really be giving her and Sam a chance to escape?

M.C. took a deep breath, removed the padlock and eased open the door. She blinked, adjusting to the sudden change in light from snow-bright to murky. For a split second she wondered if it had all been a lie and Sam wasn't here. She snapped on the flashlight, the beam landed on him. He lifted his head, eyes wide with terror.

'It's me,' she said. 'I've come to get you.'

He shook his head, gaze going past her. In that moment came a sound from behind her, the softest exhalation of breath. *Smith.*

M.C. swung around, hand going to the small of her back. Blinding pain exploded in her head. She dropped to her knees, fighting to stay conscious. She heard the second blow coming, the *whoosh* of the object arcing through the air.

And then, she heard nothing at all.

81

M.C. came to with a throbbing headache. Not only did her skull ache, but her teeth and jaw, shoulders and neck. She cracked open her eyes and it all came crashing back: Sam, Smith, the sound of an object whizzing toward her.

She tried to move her arms and legs but found she couldn't. Her ankles were bound with duct tape, as were her wrists. She lay on the shed's floor, she realized, the plywood cold and rough under her cheek.

Where was Sam?

She craned her neck, trying to see in the dim light.

'I'm here,' he whispered, voice thick, words slightly slurred. 'Are you okay?'

He was coherent – a very good sign. She shifted so she could see him without wrenching her neck. 'Yeah. How about you?'

'I'm cold.'

'I know, buddy. I've got to get you out of here.'

'You thin' he's coming back?'

'My bet is, yes. He went to collect his gear.'

'You foun' the mon'y?'

'Yeah, Sam, I did.'

355

'Sorry, M.C. So . . . sorry.'

'We'll talk about that later, right now, I have a little surprise for Agent Smith, but I need your help.'

With her hands bound in front of her, she needed Sam to get her gun. It was still there. She felt it nestled reassuringly against her skin. Her plan was to have it pointed at the door when Smith returned – and she would take him out.

Using her feet to push and her elbows to pull, she dragged herself toward him. The movement was agony. Her neck, head and shoulders screamed protest. It felt as if her arms were being wrenched from their sockets.

As cold as she was, she started to sweat.

She glanced at Sam, saw his head was down. 'Sam,' she said sharply, 'stay with me. Come on, I need your help.'

His head jerked upright. 'Owl t'y.'

'Talk to me, Sam.'

'Y' shouldn't have come f' me. I don't d'serve your help . . . First Dan an' Tom'y, now you . . .'

His guttural sob broke her heart. 'I tell you what, Sam. Let me get us out of here, then you can beg my forgiveness.'

His head dipped, then bobbed upright – as if he was having a hard time staying awake.

Grunting with exertion, she doubled her efforts. 'Look, Smith's going to check I gave him accurate information, then he's coming back for us. Depending how deep he goes, he may be mighty pissed off when he gets here. You with me, Sam?'

He nodded and though his mouth moved, no sound came out.

M.C. came within reach of his chair, grabbed one of its legs and pulled herself closer, careful not to upend it.

She was out of breath, sweating and light-headed. But she couldn't rest. She didn't know how long she'd been out or how long before Smith returned.

'Sam? You awake?'

'Wide 'wake.'

That sounded like something he used to say when he was Ben's age. In different circumstances she would have laughed, teased him about it. 'Good. I'm going to try to get to my knees, then turn around. I've got a gun under my coat, at the small of my back. I need you to get it for me.'

'Roger that.'

She smiled grimly and drew her knees as tightly as she could to her chest. Then, using her elbows for leverage, she rolled onto her knees and dragged herself up. White-hot pain shot through her shoulder; she clenched her teeth against it and rocking from knee to knee, turned around so her back faced him.

'Try to get the gun, Sam. Hurry.'

He was bound tightly to the chair. She felt his fingers clawing at the fabric of her coat, then sweater, trying to burrow under. Her heart thundered, his breath came in shallow pants.

'I've got it,' he whispered, voice cracking.

'Hold on to it,' she said. 'I'm going to turn around—'

From outside came the sound of a key being fitted into the padlock, of the lock turning over.

Smith. The gun slipped from Sam's fingers, hitting the floor with a loud thud, skidding at least a foot.

There was no way Smith hadn't heard that.

The door began to open; light from outside streamed in. M.C. threw herself on the weapon, praying that when the time came, she would be able to get to it.

82

Smith stood silhouetted against the bright rectangle of light. He snapped on the flashlight and shone it in M.C.'s eyes.

'Hello, Smith,' M.C. said.

'You don't look surprised to see me.'

'I'm not. It seems a supergenius like Breakneck makes mistakes, after all.'

Smith laughed. 'Really? And what mistake would that have been?'

'Underestimating me.'

'Right now it doesn't look that way to me.'

'Looks can be deceiving.' An almost ridiculous statement, considering her predicament. But M.C. figured that besides the snub-nosed revolver digging into her side, all she had left was bravado.

'You've been busy, I see.' Smith motioned with his gun. 'Cozying up with your cousin. A lot of wasted effort.'

'I thought you said you'd let me and Sam just walk away?'

'I changed my mind. Okay, scratch that. I planned on killing you all along.'

'At least you're consistent.'

'What tipped you?' Smith asked.

358

'Your bloated ego. Remember your little speech about professionals like Breakneck not making mistakes? You said almost the same thing to Kitt. After I connected that piece, it was easy to put the rest of the puzzle together.'

'You still don't have all the pieces.'

M.C. smiled grimly. 'Maybe you don't either. We'll see.'

'Shame it had to end this way,' Smith said. 'I really liked you.'

'Sure you did, you psychopath.'

'Come on now, be a good sport.'

'Go to hell.'

He didn't respond to that, but said instead, 'You figured me out, bet you feel smart now.'

She felt a lot of things, but she couldn't say smart was among them. Not at this moment.

Smith turned the flashlight beam to Sam. 'He put up a fight, little shit. Unfortunately for him.'

'How's that going to look? The great and glorious Breakneck resorting to an old-fashioned ass-kicking?'

'You don't get it, there is no Breakneck.' Smith laughed, sounding delighted with himself. 'No Breakneck. Only me, an underpaid, underappreciated agent on the take.'

'That's not possible.'

'Of course it is. I made him up.'

'But the murders . . . the evidence . . .'

'The murders were real, true. All execution-style hits. The kind of killing only a trained professional can carry off.'

An agent was a trained professional. So was a cop. Different mind-set, that's all. 'You planted the seeds,' M.C. said, realization dawning.

'Yes. I told you everything you needed to know about Breakneck. About professional killers. Nice of your clever pathologist to reinforce my story. I should send him a plant.'

Smith paused, expression almost wistful. 'I created the legend of Breakneck years ago. I have to bring him out from time to time. He was my online log-in name.'

So Zoe and Sam had recognized it, further supporting the story.

'Funny how people are so happy to believe rumor or myth. Of course, the best lies contain a grain of truth.'

'And Breakneck's grain?'

'An old news story about a professional killer.'

'One of our guys had heard of Breakneck.'

'Like I said, he pops up from time to time. And the numbers in law enforcement who have heard of Breakneck are growing, they'll certainly grow after this go-round.'

M.C. searched her memory – it did, indeed, all come back to Smith. He was the one who'd told them about Breakneck. The one who laid the threads, wove the story, then led her and Kitt through it.

There was no 'evidence' of the involvement of a professional hitter. Yet M.C. had believed him. So had Kitt. And Sal.

'But why?' M.C. asked. 'So many deaths—'

'I wanted my money! It was the principle of it. It was mine. Mine,' he repeated. 'I popped somebody for it, and I wanted it back.'

'So, you are a hitter.'

'Just not near so romantic or mysterious a figure as the great Breakneck.'

No remorse, M.C. thought. Just a sort of arrogant pride.

'I'm sorry about killing your fiancé. He was a mistake. I thought it was Tommy in the car; I hadn't been able to get his computer but figured I could go back for it. It would look to all the world like a botched robbery, wrong place, wrong time thing. I didn't even realize I'd killed the wrong dude for a couple days.'

He shook his head, pitying M.C. 'It's hard to find real love. I know. I imagine it's harder to lose it.'

As if he could know anything about love. Loving someone meant you had to have a heart. She told him so.

He let out a bark of laughter. 'Sam here's the last. That's good news, isn't it?'

She didn't respond, but asked instead, 'How'd you find Martin?'

'Backtracked. When I realized my money had been jacked.

I never use free Wi-Fi, because of the risks. But mine was down and I had to confirm that money had been deposited in my account.'

'So you accessed your account online at the Rockford Bread Company.'

'Yes. And I remembered seeing a couple kids in a parked car. They had a laptop. Between the café's security tapes, my own recollections and the bureau's databases, I narrowed it down to Martin. He gave me the e-mail address marioman at Yahoo dot com, which belonged to your cousin Tommy. Or so I thought.'

'Okay, you wanted your money. The ring of crackers lifted it. I get all that. But why the ruse? Why use the legendary Breakneck?'

'To keep you looking elsewhere. And to intimidate you.'

'Intimidate—'

'Of course.' Smith smiled. 'Who would you be less likely to buck? Your average, everyday criminal? Or a professional killer, so smart, so deadly, he's eluded the authorities for years. You bought that he was unbeatable.'

She had, hook, line and sinker. It's why she'd opted not to share information with Kitt. She'd been too frightened for her friend's safety, and later for the safety of her family members.

'Just so you know,' he went on, stomping his feet, as if to warm up, 'you saved your partner's life by not involving her. You really did. And my bringing your adorable little nephew into it was genius. Icing on the cake.'

'You never intended to hurt him.'

'I'm not a complete monster.'

'And Phelps? You killed him because there was no FBI file on Breakneck?'

'Exactly. No great loss there, by the way. He wasn't that bright.'

M.C. bit back a defense of the young agent. 'You'd already decided to eliminate him when you used him in your story about the unlocked door.'

'Yes.'

'And when I left the interview room, you made a deal with Zoe?'

'Yes. I was going to help her. All she had to do was tell me everything.'

'She gave you Sam.'

It wasn't a question. Smith agreed anyway. 'She was so grateful. So . . . relieved. And DeLuca gave me Zoe. Of course, you had her safely hidden away. For a while, anyway.'

M.C. shivered, the cold seeping through her clothing. 'Why'd you kill Tommy? He's the one who called you. He was ready to hand you everything.'

'Not me. He was going to hand the FBI everything. I couldn't chance a slipup.'

Smith rubbed his arms. 'Funny, once I got his computer, I didn't think I needed him anymore. In the end, he was the only one I really needed.'

Smith glanced at Sam, expression disgusted. 'The friend Tommy was trying to help was actually his brother. A brother he remained completely loyal to.'

He trained the flashlight beam on Sam. 'How does that make you feel, you little punk?'

M.C. saw that Sam was crying.

Smith faced M.C. once more. 'You see, Detective, playing Breakneck is easy for me. He and I are very much alike – down to our motivations. Like Breakneck, I have to protect my identity. Anyone who could lead the proper authorities back to me has to be eliminated. Plus, we both want the money.'

'The big difference,' M.C. said, 'is Breakneck's a genius. And you're just a low-level agent in a cheap blue suit.'

'You sound so disappointed. I suppose it's kind of embarrassing, being taken out this way.' He grinned. 'But it'll be our little secret. Everyone will think the legendary Breakneck got you and Sam – a belief I will support 100 percent.

'Of course the killings will stop and the world will right itself. The RPD will close the case. The FBI will move on. Perhaps the name Breakneck will surface again in a few years, here or elsewhere, but again he'll get away.'

M.C.'s teeth began to chatter. 'It's all about greed, then. Is that it? Betraying your oath, taking lives, it's just about money?'

Smith shook his head. 'It's about survival. The law of the jungle, the strongest, most ruthless will survive. And money is strength. My parents were living proof of that. They gave their adult lives to the government, then were cast aside when their views were no longer politically correct.'

He glanced at his watch. 'I've got to go now, I've got a date with a half a million dollars.'

'What about us?'

'That's the bad news. I have it on good authority you're not going to make it. Shot with your own weapon. That's just sad, isn't it?'

'It'll blow the Sundstrand setup completely.'

'Big deal. He was a diversion, a way to keep your partner focused in another direction. Besides, I know how law enforcement works, nothing happens quickly.'

Kitt would know. She had the blank tape. She would fight for the truth.

Smith took aim at Sam. 'I'll put him out of his misery first, that's the humane thing, don't you think?'

M.C. shifted slightly, working to move the pistol within grasping range. 'How can you be certain I gave you all the correct information? What if I lied?'

'You're not the lying type, Mary Catherine. Besides, I checked a few, they worked like a charm.'

'Maybe you should have checked them all?'

Smith paused, then made a sound of disgust. 'You're grasping now.'

'Am I? Cover your ass. Padlock us in here. Go make sure I didn't trick you. Then come back and shoot us. Or let us freeze to death.'

'Remember all those old James Bond movies, where the superbad guy would plan some extravagant and outrageous demise for Bond? He would leave him to die, but James would escape, every time. I used to watch those and think, "Idiot, just shoot him." And that's what I intend to do – just shoot you.'

Smith leveled the gun on Sam. M.C. rolled sideways, got her hands around the pistol's grip, aimed and fired.

She was a second too late. Smith's shot rang out. M.C. heard a shout and an oath. Light flooded the room, followed by a third and fourth shot. The thud of a body hitting the floor.

Smith's body.

The third and fourth shots hadn't come from her gun, M.C. realized. She lifted her gaze. Her partner stood above her, grinning. 'Looks like I saved your ass again, partner.'

M.C. returned the grin, relief flooding her. 'Looks like. See, you can't quit.'

83

Controlled chaos had ensued. Kitt had brought White, Canataldi and a half-dozen uniforms. The small shed filled with the thud of boots and shouted orders.

'Call 911!'

'Two units on the way!'

'She's still alive.'

'Get a blanket on the kid!'

The scream of sirens had followed. The squawk of the two-way radios. Kitt cutting the duct tape and helping M.C. to her feet, all the while on a call with Sal, filling him in.

Now, by comparison, the hospital ER was eerily quiet. M.C. had insisted on walking out of the shed – no stretcher for her. She had refused the ambulance, but had known better than to buck being checked out by a physician.

And now, here she sat. Waiting. Worrying about Sam. Needing to be at the scene instead of cooling her heels here.

Kitt peeked around the curtain screen. 'Hey, partner. Want some company?'

M.C. waved her in, wincing at the movement. 'Where's Sam?'

'He was admitted.'

365

'I need to call Aunt Catherine and Ma—'

'Mama and Michael. Done. Also Melody and Neil.'

M.C. scowled. 'The doctor was going to "be with me directly" thirty minutes ago.'

'You've got somewhere you need to be?'

'Yes, damn it! Anywhere but h—' She bit the word back, tears stinging her eyes. 'You saved my life. You saved Sam's. Thank you.'

Kitt squeezed her hand. 'You're welcome.'

'I should have trusted you.'

'Yeah, you should have. But you did okay. You left me the tape.'

'I figured if it turned out bad for me, you'd know what to do with it.'

'I almost didn't look at it. We had our guy with a ballistics match. How much trouble could you get into?'

'A hell of a lot, apparently.'

'Apparently. I got all the way to the elevators and went back for the tape. Something, some instinct, told me to.'

They fell silent. M.C. thought of Tommy, of Sam. Of those final moments and what might have happened.

She thought of Dan. Of the future they'd almost had.

'How'd you find us?'

'A call from Neil got me headed to your house, then I saw your SUV in the ditch. I asked around, learned a crazy lady who claimed to be a cop climbed out of it and walked away carrying a blanket and a flashlight.'

'One of my finer moments.'

'First place we come to, the front glass is broken. We go inside, there are about a million tracks to the shed. You all but left a trail of bread crumbs.'

M.C. cleared her throat. 'What about Smith?'

'In surgery. I hope he lives to stand trial. All along, he was Breakneck. Unbelievable.'

'Actually, you don't know the unbelievable. It was all a lie. There is no Breakneck. He made him up.'

At Kitt's incredulous expression, M.C. shared what Smith had told her about the fictitious killer.

When she'd finished, Kitt shook her head. 'Don't feel bad, I fell for it, too. We all did.'

'Hello, Detectives, I'm Dr Daniels.' The woman, who looked to be about the same age as M.C., drew the curtain aside. The nurse who had been in earlier was with her. 'Nurse Johnson tells me you're anxious to be on your way.'

'What took you so long?' M.C. asked, glaring.

Grinning, Kitt stood. 'I'll leave you three alone to work this out.'

'You can stay.' The doctor smiled slightly. 'As feisty as she is, my guess is she's just fine.'

Kitt smiled. 'Not that I don't appreciate the offer, but as feisty as she is, I'd rather go.'

'Coward.'

She started for the door. 'I don't deny it.'

The doctor directed M.C. to stand. She winced as she put her weight on her feet. 'Damn, that hurts.'

'Could be worse,' Kitt said.

She could be dead. 'You got that right, partner. You got that right.'

84

Saturday, January 31
2:20 P.M.

M.C. tapped on Sam's hospital room door. 'Hey, buddy,' she said. 'How're you doing?'

He looked at her, expression stricken. Aunt Catherine sat by his side. She looked over her shoulder at M.C. and smiled. 'Mary Catherine, Sam was just asking about you.'

'And here I am.' She crossed to her aunt, bent and kissed her cheek. 'How is he?'

'The doctor says my Sam will be fine. He might have some nerve damage in his hands and feet and will likely be more susceptible to future colds and other respiratory ailments, but we can live with that.' She crossed herself. 'It could be a lot worse.'

He could be dead.

But he wasn't out of the woods yet.

'Could Sam and I have a few minutes alone?'

'Of course.' She stood, wiping tears from her cheeks. 'I need to call Bella to tell her we're coming home.'

She took a moment to fuss over her son, smoothing his blanket, making certain his pillow was just so, then straightened and turned to M.C. She kissed both her cheeks. 'Thank you, Mary Catherine. You saved his life. If I'd lost him . . .

I don't know if I could have . . . I don't know what I would have done.'

A moment later the door clicked shut and she and Sam were alone. M.C. sat in the chair her aunt Catherine had occupied just moments ago. She didn't speak, wanting to give him the opportunity to take the lead. He had more to say to her than she to him.

Sam gazed at her, tears making his eyes glassy. 'I'm so sorry, M.C. I didn't mean for any of this to happen. I've wished it was me who was dead every minute since Tommy—'

He choked on the words, and she covered his hand with one of hers. 'When Dan was shot, I didn't think it had anything to do with me or the money. But then Tommy . . . in his apartment like that . . . I knew. I didn't know what to do.'

'Did you even consider the truth?'

'I was' – he let out a broken-sounding breath – 'afraid. So was Zoe. Especially after Jenny. I knew this Breakneck wanted us.'

'And the money.'

He nodded. 'And I didn't have it, not anymore. Believe me, I would have given it back, a hundred times over.'

'Tommy never turned over on you, not even to the FBI.'

He hung his head.

'Why, Sam?' She leaned forward, heart aching to understand. 'Why'd you do it?'

'It seemed like easy money. Gina told us it was foolproof.'

Real foolproof – eight dead, lives ruined.

'Why'd you involve Tommy?'

'He had his own business account already. Good credit record, no history of trouble. I figured nobody'd bat an eyelash if he had a few accounts.'

Sam balled his hands into fists. 'A part of me was angry at Tommy. He was always so perfect. He never screwed up, never hurt anybody. And here I was, Sam, the screwup.'

M.C. recalled what Sundstrand had said about kids who get involved in this sort of thing, that it wasn't the ones who were certain of their futures and confident in their abilities.

It was kids like Sam. It broke her heart.

'How'd you create all those accounts under Tommy's social?'

'I installed keystroke logging software on Tommy's computer. To get his username and passwords. Social security number. Basically, the software picks up everything you keystroke in and transmits it.'

'He caught on to you,' M.C. said. 'How?'

'He found the money. The five hundred thousand.'

'And you made up that story about being in trouble and needing help. About not being able to get free of the crackers and planning to use that money as leverage.' He nodded, looking miserable. 'He was your brother. He trusted you.'

'If I could take it back I would. God, I wish I could!' Sam brought the heels of his hands to his eyes. After a moment, he dropped them; his eyes were red and wet. 'I want so bad to make this right. He was my best friend. I loved him. But I did . . . that. And now . . . it hurts almost more than I can bear.'

Tears rolled down his cheeks. 'I thought it was all going to be cool. He bought the story. Then I found out he'd changed all the account passwords. And called the FBI.'

'You sent Zoe to his apartment that morning to try to convince him to give you the money.'

'Yes.'

'It's not over, Sam. You know that, right?'

He nodded, throat working.

'You're going to have to accept responsibility for what you did. I've got superiors to answer to, a report to write. I can't cover this up. I won't. It's time to man-up, Sam.'

For a long moment he was silent, as if working to come to grips with what lay ahead. 'How will I face the family?' he whispered. 'What about Mom? She'll never forgive me.'

A part of her wished she could sweep it all under the carpet for him. Make it go away, try to protect him – if for no other reason than to shield Aunt Catherine from more pain.

She couldn't do it.

'You didn't kill Tommy, Smith did. You broke the law and lied to them and me. They'll forgive you. But it's not going to be easy.'

He took a moment, as if to digest her words. When he spoke, his voice shook. 'What's going to happen to me, M.C.? Am I going to . . . prison?'

'Maybe. I don't know for sure. The judge may be lenient. It's a first offense. You've clearly paid consequences for your actions. Because of you a renegade agent's been uncovered, and,' she added, looking him dead in the eye, 'you'll co-operate by handing over any information you can.'

Truth was, Smith had made himself the star of this story. How it had all come about was going to take a big back-seat – on every front. A blessing for Sam. For the family.

'What about Smith?' he asked as if reading her mind.

'He made it through surgery. If he lives, he'll stand trial.'

'Sweet.' He plucked at the blanket. 'What you said to Smith, M.C., about the money, about the information he wanted, was it true?'

'Which part?'

'All of it, I guess.'

'I did find it. Tommy moved it in pieces into his clients' accounts. And he changed all the account passwords.'

'To Breakneck.'

'Yeah. Aunt Bella tipped me off. She called me because her bank statement was off by almost ten grand. She tried to access her information online but couldn't.'

'Because he'd changed the passwords.'

'Yes. But not the log-in names. She gave me her log-in name so I could help her, then I wheedled Max out of Mama Riggio's.'

'You checked and the money was there.'

'But I ran out of time and didn't get any further. So I faked it, hoping Smith wouldn't take the time to check them all—'

'Just the first couple on the list.' A funny expression crossed his face.

'What?' she asked.

He shook his head. 'I want so bad to make this right,' he said. 'I want to do something good for a change.'

He let out a shuddering breath. 'M.C., there's something I have to tell you. About Dan.'

Her chest tightened. She covered his hand with hers, squeezed his fingers. 'No, you don't. I already know, Sam.'

He met her gaze, the expression in his fierce. 'He was—'

'Sam, really. I—'

'A good guy,' he went on. 'Gina hated him. Because he dumped her. He saw through her and moved on. Left KIC because of her.'

Her mouth went dry. Her heart beat so heavily she could hear it in her head. 'But Zoe said Dan helped recruit—'

'No. Never. Gina was a liar. I think she fantasized the two of them working in tandem like that, but he dumped her before she'd even had a chance to put out feelers.'

Tears flooded her eyes. M.C. blinked against them. She felt as if a heavy, dark cloud had just been lifted from her. Now, she could simply grieve Dan's loss. The loss of a good man who had loved her. And who she had loved back.

'Thank you for that, Sam. It means a lot.' She kissed his cheek, then stood. 'Crazy as it may seem right now, I believe in you.'

85

Thursday, February 5
10:10 A.M.

Sal had generously offered M.C. the week off. R and R, he'd said. A chance to decompress, and to heal physically and emotionally. When she'd tried to refuse the offer, it had become an order.

She'd been bored out of her mind.

But a bored mind was a creative mind, and she'd put hers to work. She had some amends to make.

'Hi, Nan,' M.C. said, entering the VCB office. 'Any messages?'

'You're still on leave.' Nan wagged a finger at her. 'Sal better not see you in here.'

'Not to worry, I warned him I was stopping by. Just dropping off something for my partner.'

M.C. tucked the manila envelope under her arm. 'She's in, right?'

'At her desk.'

As she strolled by the various detectives' cubicles, she was greeted with applause and a few calls of 'Way to go, Riggio!' Not only had her work led to a suspect being arrested and charged – the bad guy had turned out to be FBI. To some of the guys on the force, that was just shy of a dream come true.

M.C. found Kitt at her desk. 'Hi there, partner,' she said, stopping in the cubicle doorway. 'Did you miss me?'

Kitt smiled. 'You know me, I love trouble.'

'I'll take that as a yes.' She crossed to Kitt's desk and perched on the edge. 'Anything new around here?'

'Actually, yes. The five hundred K's gone. Transferred out. Sal was fit to be tied.'

M.C. sat forward. 'Transferred out? Of Tommy's client accounts?'

'Yup. But get this, the amounts in question were all deposited into charity accounts. Catholic Charities. The Mildred A. Berry Center. Food for the Poor and United Way, among others.'

She handed M.C. a typed list. M.C. scanned it, fighting a smile. Sam had made it right. He had taken the blood money and put it where it would be used for good.

She dropped the list onto the desk. The money had no legitimate owner, as such the department would have confiscated it. 'What does Sal want you to do?'

'Let's put it this way, he said taking food from the mouths of babes or from the hands of the Blessed Mother wasn't an option for him. And the chief "would just have to get over it."'

'Good choice. You look tired, Kitt.'

'Thanks. Unlike some of us, the boss didn't give me the week off.'

'Like you could use a vacation,' she went on.

Kitt cocked an eyebrow. 'Don't you have somewhere you need to be? Like a couch? Recuperating?'

'I brought you something.' M.C. tossed the manila envelope on her desk.

'What is it?'

'Open it and see.'

Kitt did and slid out a travel itinerary and two airplane boarding passes. She looked up at M.C. 'What is this?'

'Air tickets to Mexico. For you and Joe. Hotel's taken care of. You'll have to buy your own chimichangas. Sorry.'

Kitt looked at her, dumbfounded. 'But I don't . . . how?'

'It's from the Riggio family. I took up a collection.'

'I can't accept this. We can't accept—'

'You don't have a choice.' She leaned toward her. 'You saved my life, you saved Sam's. Because of you, Tommy, Dan and Gina's killer will be brought to justice.'

'I don't know what to say.'

M.C. grinned. 'Hold your thanks, there's a caveat.' Kitt waited. 'You're pretty much family now, so Mama's expecting you at Sunday dinner, the first Sunday you're back.'

Kitt's eyes filled with tears. 'Back. But when are we—'

'Today.'

'Today?' Her eyes widened. 'But Sal—'

'Is in on it.'

'I'm not packed.'

'Yeah you are. Of course, Joe might not have packed you anything but a bikini and lingerie. Guess you'll just have to deal with it.'

'But . . . but, I can't just—'

'I'd offer to help you get ready, but Erik and I are going in to the city. Bulls versus Celtics, tonight at the United Center Stadium.'

At Kitt's surprise, M.C. shrugged. 'Just friends. Besides, you know me. I'm a sucker for the promise of beer and a hot dog.'

Look out for the next thriller from Erica Spindler in 2010

BLOOD VINES

Thirty-something Alex Owens knows very little
about her childhood or who she really is, her only
family an absent, emotionally fragile mother. Alex has
always felt something was missing and spent most
of her adulthood in search of it, moving from
job to job, relationship to relationship.

But when an infant's remains are unearthed in
back-country California, Alex suddenly realises that she
has a connection to the case. As if opening Pandora's box,
long-lost memories start flooding in, leading her back to
California – and to dark and terrifying nightmares that
haunt her every waking moment.

The tight-knit community greets Alex with silence
and suspicion, but she presses on, determined to get
to the heart of a secret no one wants to see uncovered.
As more violent deaths and a series of deadly rituals
shock the small town, Alex is finally forced to
confront the terrible truth about a single night
that changed her family's lives forever . . .

Sphere Fiction
978-1-84744-230-7